THAT POOR MAN!

Joanna walked down the school steps toward the shrieking twins and their frazzled father with a welcoming smile.

The girls looked up at her and their screams stopped with such abruptness that the silence was deafening. Joanna smiled a little nervously, and was rewarded with two matching exuberant grins. She couldn't believe the instant turnaround.

"Mama!" they cried. "You came back!"

Joanna's mouth dropped open and the two girls hurled themselves into her arms, laughing and crying and calling her Mama. She couldn't do anything but cuddle them.

Their father looked shocked, his blue eyes wide in disbelief. "My God," he said. "You look just like her. The same dark hair, the same eyes, the same mouth."

Joanna swallowed hard as his intense gaze moved from her hair, to her eyes, to her lips. "Their—their mother?"

"Yes." His voice turned gruff. "She died a year ago."

Other Avon Contemporary Romances by
Barbara Freethy

DANIEL'S GIFT
RYAN'S RETURN

Barbara Freethy

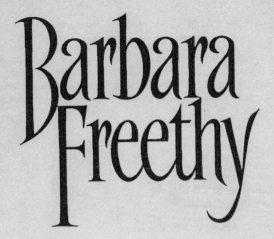

ASK MARIAH

AVON BOOKS  NEW YORK

AVON BOOKS
A division of
The Hearst Corporation
1350 Avenue of the Americas
New York, New York 10019

Copyright © 1997 by Barbara Freethy
Published by arrangement with the author
Inside cover author photo by Dave Dornlas
Visit our website at http://AvonBooks.com
Library of Congress Catalog Card Number: 96-95178
ISBN: 0-380-78532-3

First Avon Books Printing: May 1997

AVON TRADEMARK REG. U.S. PAT. OFF. AND IN OTHER COUNTRIES, MARCA REGISTRADA, HECHO EN U.S.A.

Printed in the U.S.A.

RA   10   9   8   7   6   5   4   3   2   1

To the Sweet Treats women's softball team—Janet Arata, Julia Bernier, Crystal Duke, Linda Fisher, Linda Hower, Tracey Hudelson, Kathy Leon, Carol Nowlin, Lorraine Simmons, Kari Smith, Sara Stenger, Karen Wagner, and Elizabeth Wolfe—for great stories and lots of laughs.

1

Michael Ashton beat the fire engines to his house by thirty seconds. Smoke poured from the kitchen window of the old Victorian as he jumped out of his car and ran up the walkway. His daughter's favorite teddy bear lay abandoned on the top step. Cups from a tea party were scattered across the welcome-home mat as if the participants had left in a big hurry, as if they had smelled smoke and run inside to see what was wrong.

Michael's heart raced as he reached for the door-knob. Locked! He fumbled with his keys, swearing, sweating each second of delay. His children were inside. He had to get to them. The keys slipped out of his grasp and fell to the ground. He stepped backward, crushing a tiny pink teacup.

To hell with the keys. Panicked, he slammed his body against the door, forcing it open.

All he could think of were Lily and Rose, his six-year-old identical twin daughters. If anything happened to them, he would never forgive himself. They were all he had left.

"Please, God, let them be all right," Michael whispered as he entered the house. Smoke drifted through the hall and dining room, darkening the white walls, covering the hardwood floors with dust. "Lily! Rose!" he shouted as he moved toward

1

the thickest area of smoke. "Where are you?"

The girls burst through the kitchen door, two whirling, smoky figures in blue jean overalls. Michael swept them into his arms, pressing their heads against his chest for one thankful second. "You're all right. You're all right," he muttered. "Let's get out of here." He ran toward the front door. Two firemen passed him on the steps.

"Anyone else inside?" one of them asked.

"Mrs. Polking, our nanny." Michael didn't stop moving until he reached the sidewalk. Then he set the girls down on the pavement and tried to catch his breath. Lily and Rose stared back at him.

They didn't appear to be hurt. Nor did they seem overly concerned about the fire. In fact, on closer inspection there was a light of excitement in Lily's dark eyes, and Rose looked guilty, so guilty that her gaze seemed fixed on the untied laces of her tennis shoes. At that, Michael's panic began to fade.

He squatted in front of them so he could look directly into their eyes. Their long brown hair was a mess. Lily's pigtails were almost completely out. Rose still had one rubber band clinging desperately to a couple of strands of hair, while the rest swung free past her shoulders. There were no bumps or bruises on their small faces, no scratches to mar their tender skin, no sign of blood. "Are you hurt?" He ran his hand down Rose's arms, then did the same to Lily.

Lily shook her head, then Rose. Neither one said a word. Not even now. Not even in the midst of a crisis would they speak to him. Michael sighed, feeling the tear in his heart grow bigger. Since their mother, Angela, had died almost a year ago, the girls had refused to speak to him. No one had been able to tell him why. Thousands of dollars of family therapy had not helped him get to the root of their problem.

The doctors said the children, for whatever reason, didn't trust him. They were supposed to trust him. He was their father, their protector. He would die for them, but he couldn't seem to convince them of that fact.

"This is not my fault," a woman said from behind him.

Michael straightened as their nanny, Eleanor Polking, came down the steps, assisted by one of the firemen. Eleanor was a short, robust woman in her late fifties who carried an extra forty pounds.

"What the hell happened?" he asked.

"The girls set the kitchen on fire. That's what happened," Eleanor said in obvious distress.

She tried to push her hair away from her eyes, but the sweat from her forehead glued it in place. There was a wild light in her eyes. She looked as if she wanted to run as far away from them as possible, if she could just figure out an escape route. Michael had seen that expression before, on the faces of the four nannies who had previously served time in his home.

He glanced at Lily, then at Rose. They wouldn't look him in the eye. Damn.

"We were just making pasta, Mrs. Polking," Lily said defiantly, directing her explanation to the nanny. "Like Mama used to make."

"For our tea party. We didn't mean to cause a fire—" Rose darted a quick look at her father. "We didn't know you had to put water in the pot. When the pot got all red and smelled funny, we threw it in the trash."

Michael groaned. "Let me see your hands. Did you burn them?"

Lily and Rose held out their hands. Their pudgy little fingers were covered with streaks of red and green paint, but thankfully there were no burns.

"We used a hot pad, Mrs. Polking," Lily said. "Just like you told us."

"Why were the girls alone in the kitchen?" Michael asked. "Don't I pay you to watch them?" He knew his anger was unreasonable and misplaced, but he had to yell at someone, dammit.

"I was in the bathroom, cleaning the paint off my dress." Eleanor turned around, revealing a circle of green paint on her ample bottom. "Do you want to know how this happened?" she demanded, her anger matching his.

Michael sighed. "Not really, no."

"The girls painted the chair in my bedroom green."

He scowled at Lily and Rose. "You've had a busy day, haven't you?"

"Too busy for me," Eleanor declared. "This is the last straw. I'm leaving just as soon as I get my suitcase packed."

"Yea—" Lily's spontaneous cheer ended with Michael's glare. "I mean, that's too bad. Come on, Rose, let's look at the fire engine."

"You can't just leave, Mrs. Polking." Michael ran a hand through his hair in frustration. "You agreed to stay the summer. I know the girls are difficult, but they just need a little extra attention."

"That's not all they need."

Michael ignored her comment. "I'm in the middle of a bid for a very big job. At least give me a week or two to make other arrangements."

"I'm sorry, Mr. Ashton," Eleanor said, not sounding a bit sorry. "I think the girls have made it clear that they want you."

"I can't work full-time and take care of the girls. I'm only one person."

Mrs. Polking softened just a bit. "I understand. That's why I took the liberty of making you a list of summer school programs. You'll find it on the credenza in the dining room."

"When did you decide to do that?"

"This morning, after the girls glued my shoes to the floor. Perhaps they'll do better in a more structured environment." Eleanor checked her watch. "It's not yet five. If you hurry you may be able to find one for Monday. Good luck," she said, turning away.

Good luck? Since when had he ever had good luck?

His wife was dead. His children wouldn't speak to him. The demands of his job as an architect, combined with the responsibilities of being a single father, made him feel as if he were running around in circles, chasing after his tail like a foolish dog.

He had never imagined that his life would end up like this. As he stared at the house, he was thankful it hadn't burned down. The house had belonged to his in-laws, the De Marcos, for almost 100 years, since they first emigrated from Italy in the late 1800s. More than a house, it was a symbol of tradition, of family, of responsibility, of loyalty, of everything that a man should be.

His father-in-law had told Michael he was worthy of this house, that he knew Michael would take care of his daughter, Angela. Michael had felt the burden of that generous gift every day of their marriage. The burden had doubled in weight after the birth of the twins, and tripled in weight upon Angela's death at the tender age of twenty-six.

He hadn't taken care of Angela as he had promised. But he still had the girls to raise. He still had a chance to give the De Marcos back some of the love and respect they had given him.

The sound of voices brought him back to reality. Michael looked up as the firemen left his house.

"The fire was limited to the stove and the trash

can," one of the men said. "You have damage to the ceiling and walls from the smoke. The floor around the trash can is pretty beat up, but that's about it. Otherwise you're okay." He paused. "I hope you'll have a long talk with your kids about fire safety in the kitchen and elsewhere."

"Oh, don't worry, I intend to have a very long talk with them—about a lot of things."

The fireman grinned. "They sure are cute kids. One of them called 911. Sounded calm as could be. Well, we're off."

"Thanks," Michael said.

"No problem. That's what we're here for."

As the fire engine left, Mrs. Polking returned to the house and Lily and Rose wandered back to Michael, obviously uneasy now that they were alone with him. Lily dug her hands into the pockets of her overalls and tried to look confident. Rose chewed on a piece of her hair, the way she always did when she was nervous. For a few moments Michael let them suffer in silence.

The more he looked at them, the more they reminded him of Angela. They were their mother's daughters, all right, same dark brown hair, same big brown eyes, same stubborn chin, same impetuous, spoiled nature.

Oh, they were cute all right, and dangerous, especially Lily. The older twin by two minutes, Lily was the leader of the two girls. She was rambunctious, loud, and often clumsy, but she would defend her little sister to the death.

Rose was his sensitive, emotional child, quiet and introspective. She tried to do what was right more often than Lily, but loyalty to her sister always came before anything else.

Looking at them now, Michael wondered which one of them would crack first—which one would finally break down and talk to him.

Sometimes he thought Lily would be the one, because once in a while she impulsively started to say something, then stopped. Other times he thought Rose might provide the breakthrough, with her guilty, apologetic smiles. Neither one spoke to him now.

"We have to talk about Mrs. Polking." Of course, he'd be talking and they'd be listening, but he couldn't let their behavior go unnoticed. "You know you're not supposed to touch the stove."

No answer. No explanation.

"Maybe if you tell me why you did it, I could understand." Michael tried to be patient.

Lily made some motions with her hand, mimicking eating.

"If you were hungry you should have asked Mrs. Polking to fix you something."

Lily shrugged. Rose smiled apologetically. They were getting nowhere fast.

"What you did was dangerous. This isn't like gluing Mrs. Polking's shoes to the floor, although I'm not happy about that either. You could have been hurt. Mrs. Polking could have been hurt. I know you wouldn't have wanted that."

Rose sniffed as she shook her head.

Lily put her arm around her sister to give her courage.

"Can you tell me what all the trouble is about? Why are you giving the baby-sitters such a hard time?"

No answer.

Lily whispered in Rose's ear, loud enough so Michael could hear her. "I have to go to the bathroom. Do you want to come with me?"

"Yes."

"Wait a second; we're not done."

Lily pointed to her pants, Rose too.

"Fine, go to the bathroom, but this isn't over."

With that the girls disappeared into the house.

Michael knew the bathroom plea was an excuse to get away from him. Maybe it was for the best. He needed time to think. He needed a cold beer. Hell, he needed a new life.

"I think he's mad," Rose said, opening the bedroom door so she could peer into the hallway. She listened for angry footsteps, but heard only silence.

"Is he coming?" Lily asked.

"No."

"Good." Lily let out a sigh of relief.

Rose closed the door and sat down on one of the twin beds. She pulled her legs underneath her and rested her chin in her hands. "Maybe we shouldn't have tried to cook the pasta."

"We didn't know it was going to catch on fire."

"And we shouldn't have painted the chair," Rose added, knowing they'd been really bad.

"We had to, or else Mrs. Polking wouldn't have left."

"He's just going to get someone else to watch us."

"Not if Mama comes back."

"I don't think she is coming back. It's been so long."

"Yes, she is. She promised. Maybe we should look for her," Lily said. "Like hide-and-seek."

"We don't know where to look."

"We could go down by the boats, where Mama took us that day. Maybe she's there."

Rose shook her head, feeling her stomach turn over at the thought. She hadn't liked their trip to see the boats. She didn't even want to think about it. "Daddy says Mama is in heaven. Besides, we can't cross the street by ourselves, and we don't even know where the boats are."

"I bet I could find them," Lily said confidently.

"We're not going. Mama said she'd come back. We just have to wait for her."

Lily's eyes sparkled with a new idea. "Maybe Mariah can help us."

Mariah. Rose watched as Lily took the crystal ball off the dresser and set it on the bed between them. They'd gotten it a week ago for their sixth birthday, a present from their grandmother, Sophia. Inside the glazed blue glass were the head and shoulders of a beautiful lady with long blond hair, a glittery face, and a bright pink wizard's hat.

Sophia had found the wizard in an antiques shop. She told them it had belonged to a little girl who swore it could make magic—but only for people who believed in it.

Lily rubbed her hand over the top of the ball. A spark of light surprised them.

"What was that?" Rose asked, her eyes widening with alarm. She felt butterflies in her stomach, the kind that came whenever a new nanny arrived.

"I don't know. It didn't do that when I touched it yesterday."

"Well, ask the question."

Lily rubbed her hand over the ball again, drawing another flash of light. "Mariah, we want to find our mother. Do you know where she is? Do you know where we should go to look for her?"

The lady's mouth began to move. Lily looked over at Rose in awe. "Did you see that?" she whispered.

Rose swallowed hard. She felt scared, but she wanted to hear the answer.

Mariah's voice came across, sounding as lovely as a melody. "For children who believe in me, a school is just the place to be."

"What?" Lily demanded.

"Go to school?" Rose repeated. She didn't want to

go to school. It was summer, and they'd already done kindergarten.

"I'm going to ask her again. I don't think she heard me right." No matter how many times Lily asked the question, the crystal ball remained dark and Mariah remained silent. "Maybe the batteries are dead." Lily turned the ball over in her hand.

"Where do the batteries go?" Rose asked.

"I don't know. I can't find anything."

"Maybe we should ask Daddy."

Lily rolled her eyes. "I don't think so."

"I didn't mean out loud," Rose said, although it was getting more difficult not to talk to Daddy, especially when he was being nice or when he kissed her good night. But they'd promised their mother they could keep a secret, that they wouldn't speak to their dad again until she came home. Rose couldn't give up now. If she did, Mama might never come back.

"We'll try Mariah later," Lily said. "Maybe she needs to rest."

Michael stared at his waterlogged, smoke-filled kitchen in disgust. The cookbooks on the counter had been doused with water. The edges of the yellow-trimmed curtains that his mother-in-law had hung for them just after they moved into the house were charred around the edges. There were puddles on the floor with ashes floating like little boats in a murky river. What a mess. Just like his life.

He wished he had a magic wand that he could wave and everything be all right again. "Abracadabra," he said, waving his hand in the air. Nothing happened—no big surprise. He didn't know why he kept hoping for a miracle. He'd said enough unanswered prayers to know that magic and miracles did not exist.

Michael took off his suit coat and tossed it over

the chair at the breakfast room table. He loosened the knot in his tie and rolled up the sleeves to his elbows. Wading through a couple of inches of dirty water, he made his way to the refrigerator and opened the door. The inside was dark. Apparently the firemen had turned off the electricity, but the beers were still cold. Thank God!

He pulled out a can and opened it. One draught went a long way toward easing some of his frustration. As he took another sip he walked into the dining room, eager to get away from the kitchen disaster. That's when he saw the list of summer schools Mrs. Polking had left on the credenza. He reached for the paper, but his foot caught on the carpet and he stumbled, spilling beer all over everything.

"Damn. Damn. Damn." Michael shook the beer off the top of the paper, but the ink smeared and only one of the school names remained legible. "Happy Hollow School—summer school programs, kindergarten through second grade," he read aloud.

Why not, he decided. The school was in North Beach, just a mile away. Maybe he could convince the twins' grandmother to take the girls after school until he could find another baby-sitter.

Of course, he didn't have much credit left with the family. The girls had terrorized their aunt, uncle, and grandparents long before they'd started in on the nannies. And he hated to ask Sophia to baby-sit. She usually spent her afternoons at De Marco's, helping her husband, Vincent, and her son, Frank, run the family restaurant.

A school was the best answer, at least until he could find another nanny. With any luck the teachers at Happy Hollow would be tough enough to take anything his girls could dish out.

2

"You've got to be strong, you've got to be bold, you've got to be . . ."

"I've got to be stupid," Joanna Wingate muttered, adding her own lyrics to the music that blasted through the aerobics class at the San Francisco Health Club. Sweat dripped down her neck and between her shoulder blades as she tried to keep up with the class.

Joanna glared at the mirror, not just at the sight of herself in navy blue bicycle shorts and an oversize T-shirt, but at the image of her sixty-two-year-old mother beside her. Caroline Wingate, decked out in a hot pink leotard and tights, was kicking her thin legs almost as high as their instructor, a twenty-something blond goddess in purple spandex named Crystal.

Sandwiched in between their sleek figures, Joanna felt like a clumsy elephant. Although she wasn't fat by anyone's standards, she knew she was definitely not a lean, mean fighting machine. She was a twenty-nine-year-old teaching assistant at Stanford University working on her PhD in American history—and she was tired.

She had spent nine months supporting her father during a futile struggle with lung cancer that he'd lost two months earlier. She'd given up her apartment, her job, and her boyfriend—actually, he'd given her up—to help her mother take care of her father. She'd lost just about everything in her life during the past year except the extra ten pounds she'd gained sitting by her father's bedside.

Her mother, of course, had not gained an ounce. Caroline's stress had led to days of wanting nothing more than a bowl of soup and a cup of tea. Her mother found comfort in classical music and long walks on the treadmill. Joanna found comfort in chocolate-covered strawberries—make that chocolate-covered anything.

"Let's go now, ladies. Follow me." Crystal pranced around the room, leading something akin to a conga line. Joanna reluctantly joined in behind her mother, who didn't even appear to be sweating.

But then Caroline Wingate never perspired. A petite ash blonde, with a hairstyle that never went limp, Caroline was the exact opposite of her daughter. Joanna had long, curly brown hair that drifted past her shoulders and always looked a bit wild, a generous bosom, and a smattering of freckles across the bridge of her nose.

As the conga line neared the doorway, Joanna dashed out and collapsed against the wall outside, rubbing the sweat off her forehead with the back of her hand. A minute later she was joined by her long-time friend, Nora Garvey, a plump redhead who was working off the lingering weight of her second pregnancy.

"Are you okay?" Nora asked.

"I need oxygen." Joanna bent over, placing her hands on her knees.

Nora laughed and patted Joanna on the back. "Shall I call 911?"

"Just shoot me and put me out of my misery."

"You've got to be strong, you've got to be tough," Nora teased.

"I've got to be crazy for letting my mother talk me into this."

Nora leaned against the wall. "Your mother is amazing. She doesn't look a day over forty. She's in great shape."

"Tell me about it." Joanna walked over to the water fountain and took a drink. Then she stepped aside so Nora could take a turn.

The fitness club, which was popular with the downtown San Francisco work crowd, was filling up, although Friday nights tended to be slower than the rest of the week. Most people probably had dates, Joanna thought with disgust. She picked up a complimentary towel and wiped the sweat off her face.

She was not only out of shape, she was also out of sorts. Bored, restless, frustrated were only a few of the words that came to mind whenever someone asked her how she felt. Of course, she didn't express those words aloud. She simply said she was fine and kept her private anguish to herself, a trait she had learned early on from her mother. Caroline didn't confide in anyone, and to a certain extent Joanna didn't either. The only one who had even an inkling of the misery she had been in since her boyfriend dumped her and her father died was her good friend, Nora.

As Nora turned away from the drinking fountain, Joanna tossed her a towel. Nora missed, and the towel landed at the feet of an incredibly tall and muscular man. He picked up the towel and handed it back to Joanna as she stared at him in amazement.

Good Lord, the man's muscles were huge. His round, bulging pecs glistened with sweat or some kind of body oil. He wore a tight tank top and a pair of small shorts that emphasized his other bulges. He was the most incredible specimen of a male she had ever seen. Pure brawn.

Nora cleared her throat, and Joanna realized she was staring.

"Uh, thanks," Joanna said.

His eyes drifted over her body. Joanna hadn't had a man look at her that way in quite some time. She wondered what she would do if he asked her out.

Nora would say go for it. A new man was just what she needed to take her mind off her problems. But this man was not her type. She dated intellects, thin men with glasses and faraway looks and hair that needed cutting and clothes that needed fitting.

This man didn't need clothes, period. Maybe she ought to expand her horizons.

"Why don't you give me a call?" he said.

Nora gave her a subtle thumbs-up sign.

"Maybe," Joanna prevaricated.

The man reached into a tiny pocket in the back of his shorts and pulled out a card. "I could whip you into shape in no time," he said with a smile as he continued down the hall with an arrogant swagger.

Joanna looked at the card. "Hawk Cunningham, personal trainer. I guess he didn't want my body after all."

"He wanted your body all right."

"Yeah, as a before picture. Now I'm thoroughly depressed."

"Don't be. He probably would have spent far too much time in front of the mirror. And personally I've never liked a man who has bigger breasts than I do."

Joanna laughed. "I'm not sure what my type is anymore. I certainly didn't fit in with David and his intellectual cronies." Actually she didn't fit in with anyone.

In the past five years she'd dated a variety of men. One had been too short, the other too tall; one too studious, another too boring; one talked incessantly about biogenetics, and another had spent one very

long dinner hour describing the different types of
bacteria she was putting into her mouth with each
bite of food.

When she'd met David Richardson, a professor of
English literature at Stanford, she thought she'd hit
the jackpot. Unfortunately he'd turned out to be as
big a jerk as the rest of them.

"Of course you didn't fit in with David," Nora
said. "He was safe, just like the others. That's why
you went out with him. You knew exactly what you
would get. It was a no-risk situation."

"What do you want me to do—date an ax mur-
derer?"

"I want you to date an interesting, exciting man,
not some scrawny professor who cares more about
his research than his girlfriend, and thinks having a
good time is spending the evening at the library."

"I like the library," Joanna protested.

"You might like a few other things, too, if you
ever gave them a chance."

"Like what?"

"Like sex."

"Nora." Joanna looked over her shoulder to see if
anyone had overheard her loudmouthed friend, but
they were alone. "I've had sex. To be perfectly honest, I think it's the one thing that has been lied about
the most in history. I mean, really, the things some
people have written in their diaries would make
your hair curl. I just don't get it."

Nora laughed. "If you don't get it, then you really
haven't had sex."

"Oh, please, are you going to tell me you saw
fireworks, that the room spun around in dizzying
delight, and you thought you'd die from too much
passion?"

Nora smiled somewhat smugly. "I'm not going to
tell you anything, except this. If you find yourself

the right man, I guarantee all those things will happen."

"Yeah, and I believe in magic, too," Joanna said.

Actually she wanted to believe in love and magic. Unfortunately reality kept slapping her in the face. "I think it's time to go back into the torture chamber." She motioned toward the aerobics room.

"My muscles are burning."

"I think that's the point."

"Your mom seems to be doing well these days," Nora commented as they glanced into the aerobics class, where the group was dancing to a new beat. "At least on the outside."

"She likes to stay busy. It keeps her mind off the fact that my dad is gone."

"You're lucky to have a mother like her. She's always been your best friend, one of the girls. You wouldn't catch my mother in an aerobics class to save her life."

"Your mother is wonderful, always baking cookies and pies and decorating your house for every holiday," Joanna said wistfully. "My mother hasn't cooked a Christmas turkey in twenty years."

"I guess we always want what we don't have."

"I guess." As an only child Joanna hadn't wanted for much. She had been the focus of Caroline's life. They had done everything together. They had gone to the ballet, art museums, and the symphony. She had accompanied her parents on trips to Europe and the South Pacific. She'd been incredibly fortunate. The only thing she'd ever lacked was a little space for herself.

Since she'd given up her apartment, since her father had died, things had gotten worse. Caroline wanted to do everything with her. Joanna could barely go to the bathroom without her mother calling out and asking where she was and what she was doing.

On cue, Caroline appeared in the doorway. "Joanna, there you are," Caroline scolded, shaking her finger. "You need to cool down or your muscles will tighten up. Come walk with me."

"Too late. My muscles are on a coffee break," Joanna said, retreating against the wall. "I can't move until they come back."

"Really, Joanna." Caroline smiled at Nora. "I love your haircut. I'm thinking of doing something different with my hair, something more cool," she said with a self-conscious smile. "That is the right word, isn't it?"

Nora laughed. "You are the coolest, Mrs. Wingate. I got my haircut at Capelli down on Union Street."

"Mm-mm, I may have to try them." Caroline patted her hair, which she had worn in the same style for the past twenty years. "Do they do manicures? I'd love to get one. And a pedicure would be heaven. We'll call them on Monday. We can make a day of it," Caroline said, gaining enthusiasm. "What do you think, Joanna?"

Joanna smiled faintly. Caroline seemed to be on a quest to find something new to do each day. She never wanted to just be home.

"Joanna? Did you hear me?"

"I heard you."

"I have an idea," Nora said brightly, although she darted a somewhat worried look in Caroline's direction.

"What is it?" Joanna asked.

"One of the teachers at Happy Hollow School is having a difficult pregnancy, and her doctor wants her to go to bed for six weeks. The summer session starts Monday and, well, we're desperate for a first grade teacher."

Joanna looked at Nora in amazement. "You're not asking me?"

"Yes, I am. You love kids, Joanna. And you're an experienced teacher."

"For eighteen-year-olds, not six-year-olds."

Nora waved a hand. "Oh, there's hardly any difference. The lesson plans are done. You just have to follow the schedule."

Joanna didn't think for a second it would be that easy, but she had to admit to feeling tempted. She loved kids. Lately she'd found herself stopping at the park, drawn to the laughter of the children, the smiles of the young mothers bouncing babies on their hips while they chatted with their friends. She'd found herself wondering what it would be like to be married, to have children of her own, to be a wife and mother as well as a professor.

Since her father died, she'd begun to question all of her goals. She didn't seem to have a passion to do anything anymore. Her thesis on the structure of family throughout American history no longer interested her. She had several hundred pages and tons of photographs, but she just couldn't find the heart to finish it, especially since her own family had been shattered.

Could you have a family with only two people, with just a mother and a daughter? It didn't seem enough. Although some days it seemed too much. Like today.

"What do you say?" Nora asked. "It's only six weeks, and you'll love the summer program. We do a unit on gardening, and the children plant their own vegetable garden. We also cook. You love to cook."

"It does sound like fun."

"It will take up all your time," Caroline protested. "What about that trip to Hawaii we were planning and the line dancing class?"

Joanna looked from Nora to her mother. She didn't want to learn line dancing or go to Hawaii.

She also didn't want to hurt her mother's feelings. "You can do those things without me."

"It wouldn't be the same without you."

Joanna hesitated. Her mother was still grieving. Was it fair to leave her alone every day? But it had been two months, and she simply could not continue to spend every second with her mother. Joanna needed time for herself—a chance to figure out what she wanted to do with the rest of her life. One thing she'd learned from watching her father die was that life was far too short, and she'd already wasted too much of it.

"I'm sorry, maybe I shouldn't have brought this up," Nora said apologetically. "If you need to be at home with your mother, I understand."

Joanna glanced at her mother in her fashionable pink tights and thought Caroline could probably get along without her if she just gave it a try. "You have to understand, Mom," she said. "I feel restless. Maybe this job will help me figure things out."

"I don't understand. What about your research? Your PhD? You've worked so hard, and you're so close. How can you even consider taking a part-time job in an elementary school when you could be working on your thesis?"

"I can't do it right now," Joanna said in frustration. "My mind is blank. My goals are lost. Sometimes I don't know why I started all this in the first place." She rested her palms against the wall, taking pleasure in the feel of the cool plaster beneath her fingertips. "Do you remember that last day Dad felt well enough to sit up with us for a few hours? He told me he didn't regret anything he had done in his life, only the things he hadn't done, too afraid to take a risk or too busy to take the time. He told me not to make the same mistake. He told me to dream, to reach for the stars, to grab on to something and make it mine."

Her mother looked at her as if she'd lost her mind, but then Caroline was not a dreamer. She was a doer. She got up in the morning, looked at her calendar, and followed her schedule. At night she sat down and planned the next day. Her life was a series of little things, and they seemed to keep her happy, but Joanna wanted more.

"Joanna," her mother began. "It's only natural that you feel empty, but you'll get back in the swing of things."

"Mom, please," Joanna held up her hand. "At least let me think about it."

"Fine. I'm going to cool down." Caroline returned to the aerobics class, her shoulders stiff, her head erect.

"I guess this wasn't a good idea," Nora said with a sympathetic glance. "I didn't realize your mom had so many plans."

"My mother always has plans."

"They sound fun. Hawaii would be great."

"I've been to Hawaii. I'd rather spend time looking for an apartment."

"You're tired of the luxurious Bellarmine Towers?"

"I'm tired of living on the eighteenth floor. I want a garden and a deck. I want to look up at the trees and the sky instead of down at traffic jams."

"But you're so close to everything, the theater, great restaurants, shopping."

"I want dirt under my feet, land, trees, a view of something that isn't concrete. I want to walk out my front door and not look at an elevator panel." She shook her head, feeling her frustration boil to the surface.

"Then come and work at the school, Joanna. I can guarantee you a ground floor classroom, lots of sunshine, and plenty of dirt. It's only for six weeks. Just think, you can fill their little minds with history."

"I'll do it," Joanna said impulsively.

Nora smiled approvingly. "Good. You'll love the kids. First grade is an adorable age."

Bloodcurdling screams did not sound adorable, Joanna decided as she walked out of the teachers' lounge on Monday morning. The school was a long one-story building with the office in the center and two hallways leading to the classrooms in each wing.

Joanna spied Nora standing behind the reception desk, apparently oblivious to the racket.

"Is something wrong?" Joanna asked.

"What?" Nora looked up, her mind still focused on the papers in front of her. She was a veteran of eight years in the elementary school trenches and didn't exhibit any of the signs of nervousness that Joanna had experienced since she woke up that morning.

"The screaming," Joanna said as a fresh burst of wailing rang through the open front door.

"Oh. That's just a father trying to drop his kids off at school. Come see."

Joanna walked across the hall and looked out the front door.

Two identical twin girls were clinging to a tall dark-haired man. Their clothes were completely mismatched. One wore jeans, a T-shirt, and different colored socks; the other wore a long-sleeved dress that would have her sweating in the summer sunshine before noon. Their hair was falling out of rubber bands, made worse by the rapid shaking of their heads every time their father told them to go into the school.

"Looks like it was a tough morning," Joanna said.

Nora joined Joanna at the front door. "Oh, my. Where did he come from—the cover of *GQ*?"

"It looks like it." The man on the street wasn't just

attractive, he was gorgeous. Joanna blinked to make sure she wasn't hallucinating. Her first impression got better as she noted the details. He was taller than average, athletically built, with dark curly hair a shade too long for his fine Italian suit. His tie was a daring shade of red, another contradiction to the conservative gray of his coat and pants.

She knew this man would look good in a boardroom, surrounded by other power suits, but she doubted he could be more appealing than he was right now, with a crooked tie, a large wet spot on his jacket, and a doll poking out of his pocket. There was something about a man with his children that tugged at Joanna's heart.

"Those two are obviously running the show," Nora said.

"Maybe we should help."

"Let's give him a chance. It's still early. It's better in the long run to have the parents and children separate on their own." Nora nudged Joanna with her arm. "But you know all about that, don't you—Miss College Professor."

"We don't have to worry about separation anxiety with eighteen-year-olds." Joanna shook her head. "I must have been crazy to take this job. The director must have been crazy to hire me. I don't know how to teach little kids."

"It's not that hard. Besides, you're the most educated person I know."

"Educated in history, not six-year-olds." Joanna winced at a particularly shrill shriek. "They do eventually stop screaming, don't they?"

"If you're lucky. Relax. This job will be good for you. You said you were tired of your thesis, tired of spending all your time reading about dead people. This is real life, kiddo. If you can handle six-year-olds, you can handle anything."

"Right." Joanna moved closer to the door so she

could hear the conversation going on outside.

"We talked about this," the man said, squatting in front of the girls. "You have to go to school today because you made Mrs. Polking leave, and I don't have anyone to watch you."

The two girls crossed their arms at the exact same moment and tilted their chins in the air like warriors going into battle. One girl shook her head so hard, her ponytail fell out. She looked down at the rubber band on the sidewalk and began to cry.

"It's okay, Rose," the man said. "I'll fix it." He grabbed the rubber band and roughly pulled her hair into it. The little girl cried louder.

"I wonder where their mother is," Joanna said quietly.

"Probably at work or home sick. I've never seen them before. They must have just signed up. I think they're in your class though. I saw twins on the list. Their names are like flowers. Lily and Rose, I think."

"How sweet."

Nora laughed. "They look anything but sweet."

Joanna reluctantly had to agree as one of the girls took off running down the street.

"Come back here, Lily," the man said.

Lily stopped ten yards away from him and pointed in another direction.

"We're not going home," he said. "I told you, I have to go to work so I can make money to buy you clothes and toys and food. Okay? Now, listen, if you go to school, I'll buy you a big pizza at Grandpa's restaurant and we'll rent a movie tonight."

The girl standing next to him stopped crying. He turned to her in relief. "All right, Rose?"

Rose pointed toward home.

"How about a triple-fudge sundae after dinner?" the man tried again. "And we'll go to the zoo on Saturday. You love the zoo."

"He might end up giving them the house before

he's through," Nora said with a chuckle.

"You are bad," Joanna replied as the girl named Rose ran to join her sister. She felt sorry for their father. He looked like a nice guy who was completely at his wits' end. "It's strange," she said, watching him move from bribery to threats. "The girls haven't said anything to him. I wonder if they speak."

"They may not talk, but they can certainly scream." Nora winced as a loud, piercing shriek rang down the street.

Their father grabbed each girl by the hand and tried to drag them into the school. Joanna had seen enough. She walked down the steps with a welcoming smile.

The girls looked up at her and their screams stopped with such abruptness that the silence was deafening. Joanna smiled a little nervously, not sure what to do now that she was here. She was rewarded with two matching exuberant grins. She couldn't believe the instant turnaround.

"Mama!" they cried. "You came back."

Joanna's mouth dropped open as the two girls hurled themselves into her arms, laughing and crying and calling her Mama. She couldn't do anything but cuddle them. They wouldn't have settled for less.

Their father looked shocked. His light blue eyes widened in disbelief. "My God," he said. "You look just like her. The same dark hair, the same eyes, the same mouth."

Joanna swallowed hard as his intense gaze moved from her hair, to her eyes, to her lips. "Their—their mother?" she asked tentatively.

"Yes." His voice turned gruff. "She died a year ago."

Joanna's heart broke at the thought of these young girls being motherless. No wonder their father looked frazzled. No wonder the girls had difficulty separating from him. He was the only parent they had left. Still, she felt uncomfortable about her own position and decided it was time to clarify the situation.

"My name is Joanna," she said.

"No, Mama," one of the girls corrected her.

"I'm sorry. You must think we're crazy. It's just the resemblance." He waved a hand toward the girls. "Look at them. Don't you see yourself?"

Joanna licked her lips. Yes, there was a slight resemblance, but it was just in the coloring of their hair and eyes. She didn't really look like them. Although . . . A stray thought ran across her mind that if she did have children they would probably look something like these two.

"I guess we do look a bit alike," she conceded.

"More than a bit. My name is Michael Ashton," he added. "These are my daughters, Lily and Rose."

"It's nice to meet you." She extended her hand and an incredible feeling of warmth crept through her as Michael's fingers curled around her palm. "I'm Joanna Wingate."

"Wingate? That doesn't sound Italian."

"I'm not."

"Angela, my wife, she was Italian." He cleared his throat. "So, do you want the girls to call you Miss or—"

"It's Miss, but Joanna will be fine."

"Joanna," he repeated with another long, searching look. His gaze turned toward the girls. "I know she looks like Mommy, but she's not. She's . . . Are you their teacher?"

"Yes. First grade, right?"

"We already did kindergarten," Lily explained.

"That's good. I bet you learned a lot, too," Joanna said. "How would you like to be in my class this summer?"

Both girls beamed at her, their tear-streaked faces glistening like rainbows in the morning sun. Joanna took each one by the hand. "Tell me your names again."

"I'm Lily. And she's Rose. She's the youngest by two minutes," Lily added. "Sometimes people can't tell us apart. Especially when we dress the same."

"But you'll know who we are, because you're our mommy," Rose said with a quiet intensity that wiped the smile right off Joanna's face.

"I'm not your mother, Rose, but I'd like to be your friend. Do you think we could be friends?"

"How come you don't want to be our mother anymore?" Rose asked.

"She's your teacher," Michael said firmly. "Rose—"

"It's okay," Joanna interrupted as Rose began to sniff. The last thing she wanted to do was start another round of crying. She turned to Michael. "Why don't you go now? The girls and I will work this out."

"Are you sure?" Michael asked, but he was already backing toward his car, sensing freedom.

No, she wasn't sure. But she had a feeling she would have an easier time dealing with the girls alone than with him. "We'll be fine. Say good-bye to Daddy, girls."

Rose and Lily waved, but they offered no loving words of departure. Nor did they hug him or give him a kiss. Strange, Joanna thought. One minute they didn't want to leave him, and the next they seemed happy to turn their backs on him.

"Mariah was right," Lily said to Rose. "She told us to go to school, remember?"

Rose nodded in agreement.

"Who's Mariah?" Joanna asked as they walked into the school together.

"She's a lady in a crystal ball," Lily replied.

"Oh." That seemed to explain everything.

3

Michael was still thinking about Joanna Wingate when he parked his car in the subterranean garage beneath the Embarcadero Center in downtown San Francisco. The woman's resemblance to Angela was incredible. For a second he'd felt as if he'd seen a ghost.

Although he saw Angela in his daughters' faces, they were children. Lily and Rose reminded him of the Angela he'd met when he was a mere boy and she was just a child. But this woman, this Joanna Wingate, had to be close to Angela's age, which made the similarity startling.

Still shaking his head in bewilderment, he reached for his briefcase and the set of blueprints he had picked up at the printer. He took a minute to set the car alarm before he headed toward the elevators.

The upcoming ritual of work pleased him. He wanted to forget what he had just seen. He wanted to pretend that nothing was wrong. But as he boarded the elevator for the sixteenth floor, he knew something was definitely askew.

Who was Joanna Wingate? Why had she suddenly appeared in his life now—now that he had gotten used to Angela being gone, when he had begun to think that the girls would give up their crazy fantasy that Angela was coming back.

She had come back. Only her name was Joanna.

Michael stepped off the elevator and walked toward the double glass doors that led into the offices of Lawton, Hill and Cox, his home away from home for the past nine years. He had started out at the bottom of the heap in the prestigious architectural firm, working at a drafting table in a tiny cubicle with no windows.

He now had an office that overlooked the Bay Bridge. Instead of working on small parts of big jobs, he had become a project leader, overseeing five other architects and numerous support staff in the design and construction of high-rise office buildings.

As he stepped through the doors of his office, Michael breathed a sigh of relief. The thick burgundy carpeting that sank beneath his feet and the rich look of brass and glass felt right. He knew what to expect from his job, from his coworkers, and from his clients. His business life was predictable, and he was always in complete control.

"Michael, we need to talk," said Jackson Cox as he walked out of the conference room.

Jackson, one of the senior partners in the firm, was a short, balding man with a frenetic personality. He smoked cigarettes almost as fast as he talked, and his eyes darted constantly around the room as if he didn't want to miss the latest happening. Jackson was their marketing man, the one who went after the big jobs, the driving force behind Lawton, Hill and Cox's rise to the top.

"What's up?" Michael asked as Jackson kept pace with him down the long hallway.

"Gary Connaught just bought the Stratton Hotel. He wants to tear it down and build a fifty-story office building."

"The Stratton? That's a San Francisco landmark. It's been around forever."

"Exactly. It's old, crumbling, and the owners are

going bankrupt. Connaught snapped it up for a song. He wants you to design the new building." Jackson slapped him on the back. "He loved your work on the Van Houstra building, by the way."

Michael stared at Jackson for a long moment, flooded with conflicting thoughts. It was a hell of an opportunity; Jackson was right about that. But the Stratton? A lot of people would be upset to see that building go down in a pile of rubble. He had to admit to feeling somewhat bothered by the idea.

A long time ago he had dreamed about restoring old buildings, museums, cathedrals, libraries, civic centers. But Lawton, Hill and Cox rarely restored; they built new, they built high, they built bigger than anyone else. And they made a lot of money. Sometimes his conscience called him a sellout. Most of the time he ignored it. Today he couldn't.

"Are you sure Connaught has thought this thing through?" Michael asked. "The Stratton means something to the people of San Francisco. Nixon stayed there when he was president and—"

"Nixon is dead," Jackson interrupted.

"Mae West stayed there."

"She's dead, too."

"And Lucille Ball."

"Dead. All dead. The Stratton is past its prime. It's time to move on, and frankly I thought you'd be delighted to put your signature on a brand spanking new fifty-story tower. Do you want me to tell Connaught you're not interested?"

"No." Michael immediately shook his head. "Of course not."

Jackson laughed and slapped him on the back again. "Thank God. For a minute there I thought you were turning into some self-righteous restoration fanatic."

"Who me? Never." But his voice didn't sound as confident as his words.

Jackson's eyes narrowed. "You okay?"

"I'm fine."

"Good, because Connaught is important to us. We need one hundred percent from you, Michael. Hell, make that one hundred and fifty percent."

Great, which left him with minus fifty for the girls and the rest of the family.

"I've set up a meeting with Connaught for nine A.M. tomorrow morning," Jackson added. "See what you can dream up between now and then."

"Tomorrow? I'm still working on the Dutton project."

"Pass it down the line. I want you on this one. You're the best we have."

"I'll remember that come review time."

Jackson laughed. "I'm sure you will."

As Jackson left, Michael set his briefcase on his secretary's desk. Helen Reed, a slender blonde with hazel eyes and creamy skin, slammed down the phone.

Michael looked at her in surprise. Helen rarely had words with anyone. She was one of the friendliest, nicest people he'd ever met. In fact, sometimes she was too nice. Her biggest fault was letting other people take advantage of her. "Something wrong?"

"Tony is back in town."

Anthony De Marco, his best friend and former brother-in-law? The biggest troublemaker to come out of North Beach in the past fifteen years? Michael smiled at the thought. Not that he wasn't still pissed that Tony had taken off so soon after Angela's funeral.

Tony could have stuck around. He could have helped with the kids, with the rest of the family. But as usual Tony had bailed out.

Michael knew Tony had been devastated by his little sister's death, and he could hardly blame the guy for wanting to crawl away and lick his wounds.

He'd wanted to do much the same thing. But, of course, that was the difference between them. Tony cut and ran whenever problems came up. Michael usually had to stay and clean up the mess.

Helen handed him several pink slips. "When you call him back, you can tell him—" Her voice faltered.

"Tell him what?" Michael asked.

"That I'm engaged to be married. That I don't need grief from him."

"Why didn't you just tell him that?"

"Because he wouldn't let me get a word in. He just kept talking about how he's bought a boat, and he's come home, and I should wear something sexy when he comes to pick me up tonight." Helen shook her head, bitterness filling her eyes. "As if I've been sitting here on the edge of my seat, desperately waiting for his call."

Michael didn't think it would be prudent to mention she'd done exactly that for almost six months, until she'd gone to a reunion party of their old high school gang and fallen in love with Joey Scopazzi.

"I'm sure he'll stop bothering you once he finds out about you and Joey."

"I hope so." Helen cleared her throat as she changed the subject. "I understand Mrs. Polking quit."

"She didn't like wearing green paint."

Helen smiled. "Too bad. Green might have been an improvement."

"Tell that to my daughters, and you're fired. By the way, any messages from Happy Hollow School?"

"No."

"Good. I dropped the girls off there this morning. They must not have burned down the school yet."

"Shall I call another agency for after-school care?"

"Please. See if you can find someone with a sense

of humor, someone pretty and fun, young." Michael suddenly saw Joanna in his mind, her warm brown eyes, her soft skin, her gentle manner—her eerie resemblance to the woman he had sworn to love for all time. Maybe that's why he'd felt such a connection to her. It couldn't be anything else.

"I don't think Mary Poppins is available," Helen said. "Maybe you should think about getting someone for the girls on a long-term basis."

"I can't get a nanny to stay three weeks, Helen. One month would look long-term to me."

"I'm talking about dating again, meeting someone else. The girls could use a woman's influence."

"The only woman they want is their mother," Michael said, adding under his breath, "And they think they've found her."

"What did you say?"

"Nothing." Michael looked up as someone called his name from down the hall. "Speak of the devil," he said.

Tony De Marco strolled down the corridor, a big grin on his tanned face. Michael shook his head as he noted Tony's attire: faded blue jeans, a muscle man T-shirt, and a baseball cap. The guy never changed. While Michael grew older Tony seemed to stay the same, a happy-go-lucky, carefree guy.

He and Tony had met in sixth grade. They had been best friends ever since. When Michael's mother had decided to remarry for the third time and move to New York just three months before Michael's high school graduation, Michael had moved in with the De Marcos, so he could finish his senior year. The De Marcos had given him the stable family life he had always wanted. When he married Angela he and Tony had truly become brothers.

"Talking about me again?" Tony asked. "Hi, beautiful," he said to Helen. "Miss me?"

"Uh, Tony. Check out the finger," Michael said pointedly.

Tony's grin faded as he looked down at Helen's hand. "What's that?"

"An engagement ring. I'm marrying Joey Scopazzi in three weeks." Her words came out rough and edgy.

"You're what?" Tony asked in a shocked voice.

"I'm—I'm getting married."

"But—but why?"

"Because I—" She looked at Michael as if she couldn't remember why.

"Because you love Joey," Michael prompted.

"Right, because I love Joey."

"Joey Scopazzi? The kid who wore braces for eighteen years, whose glasses always slid off his face into his tapioca pudding? You're marrying him?"

"He doesn't wear braces or glasses anymore, and yes, I'm marrying him. I want a family and a house and kids, things you don't have any interest in." She stood up abruptly, clutching a batch of papers to her chest. "Excuse me, I have copies to make."

Tony shook his head in bewilderment as she walked down the hall. "Engaged. I can't believe it. She's been following me around since seventh grade. We've been dating on and off for twelve years. She's always been there for me."

"But you haven't always been there for her. She's an attractive woman—"

"Yeah, yeah, I know. Why the hell didn't you tell me?"

"Tell you? I got three postcards from you in the past year, none with a return address."

"I can't believe she got engaged that fast. She knew I was coming back. I told her I needed time to think after Angela died."

"Time to think? People take a couple of weeks to think, a month at the most. You've been gone almost a year." Michael opened the door to his office, and Tony followed him inside.

"So I had a lot to think about."

"Did you come to any conclusions?"

"As a matter of fact, I did." Tony smiled proudly. "I bought a boat, Michael. She's a beauty. Wait until you see her."

"The boat is here?"

"Yeah. The brother of a friend of mine has been sailing out of the San Juan Islands up north, but he needed some quick cash and decided to sell his boat."

"And you just happened to have some cash? What did you do—rob a bank?"

"I saved it."

Michael laughed. "No way."

"I did. Okay, I had a few good hands of poker, too."

"Did you cheat?"

"Does it matter?" Tony asked with a grin. "Anyway, I came home to pick up the boat, say hello to the family, and see if Helen wants to go back with me. She would love the Caribbean."

"Helen?" Michael sat down behind his desk. "My loyal secretary who never calls in sick, who never arrives late, and who dutifully calls her mother every day of the week? That's the woman you're thinking of asking to sail across the world with you?"

"She's great in bed."

"Oh, man. I'm going to pretend I didn't hear that."

Tony sprawled in the chair in front of Michael's desk. "Of course, I didn't know she was fooling around with Joey Scopazzi. Why did she have to pick him? Why couldn't she find someone who didn't grow up with us, who wasn't such a weasel?"

"Joey is a nice guy. He runs his father's dry cleaning business now. He's very responsible."

"Yeah, and he sounds like a barrel of laughs. So, what's new around here, besides Helen and Joey?"

Michael's mouth curved into a smile. Tony would love his next piece of news. "Frank and Linda are planning a surprise party for your parents' fortieth wedding annniversary on Saturday night."

"Oh, man." Tony propped his feet on the edge of Michael's desk. "Anniversary parties and weddings. My timing sucks."

"As always. Maybe that's why your old girlfriend is marrying someone else."

"She's not married yet."

"Why can't you just accept that Helen is with someone else, and be happy for her? Be her friend."

"I don't know how to be friends with a woman. If there's no sex involved, what's the point?"

For a moment Michael thought Tony was serious, then he saw the hint of a smile playing around Tony's mouth. "Yeah, right. You know, you don't need Helen, you need a woman who won't take crap from you. Helen is too nice for you."

"Then tell me where I can find myself a gorgeous bitch."

"Try any bar in the financial district after five." He paused. "So, what are you going to do with this boat?"

"Run charters. I finally get to be my own boss."

Michael laughed. "Don't kid yourself. You open your own business and you'll do nothing but cater to everyone else, to your clients, to your banker, to your crew. It's called being a grown-up."

"No, not that, please."

"Do you have a business plan?"

Tony made a face. "Unlike you, Michael, I don't plan out every move I'm going to make. Sometimes I just jump and then look down."

"That's a good way to break your neck." Michael

sat back in his chair. "Owning your own business is a risk."

"Yeah, well, if you took a risk once in awhile, you wouldn't be stuck building square boxes for business suits."

Michael frowned, once again reminded of how far he had strayed from his original goals, but he had made the right decisions. He had a family to support. Ideals were fine, but they didn't put food on the table.

"How are the girls?" Tony asked, changing the subject.

"They're the same. Happy most of the time, at least on the surface. God knows what's going on in their heads."

"Still not talking?"

"Not to me."

"What are you supposed to do about it?"

"I'm supposed to be patient, to wait until they feel comfortable enough to talk to me. By that time I'll probably be too old to hear them. Sometimes I just want to shake them until the words come out or they yell at me to stop. But I don't."

"Of course you don't. You love those kids." Tony leaned forward, resting his elbows on his knees. "What do the doctors say?"

"The doctors say that while the girls are happy to live with me, they don't want to talk to me. They don't trust me for some reason—which maybe some day they'll be able to tell me."

"Mama can't get anything out of them?" Tony asked.

"No. But Sophia has been distracted since Angela died."

"Angela was everything to her, the only daughter. She was one of a kind," Tony said.

Michael stared at him for a long moment.

"What did I say?" Tony asked.

"You're not going to believe this."

"What?"

"I saw a woman who looks just like Angela at the school where I took the girls this morning."

"No way."

"The girls even called her Mama. They threw themselves at her."

"What? She has dark hair?"

"And big brown eyes, and an oval face, and a soft, warm mouth, and . . ." Michael's voice drifted off as he realized just how much Joanna had affected him.

"Michael?" Tony snapped his fingers. "What the hell is wrong with you?"

"Nothing."

"This woman—she really got to you, didn't she?"

"You'd have to see her to believe it."

"So when can I see her?"

"I pick up the kids at three."

Tony checked his watch. "I'll be back."

4

"We waited so long for you to come back," Rose said as Joanna sat down with the twins at the art table. "Where were you?"

Joanna sighed, looking from Lily to Rose. She had tried to convince them for the past six hours that she was not their long-lost mother, but to no avail. It didn't matter that everyone called her Joanna. They seemed to think she was playing a game with them.

Wishing she had majored in child psychology instead of history, Joanna opened her purse and took out her wallet. "I want to show you a picture."

She handed Rose a photo taken of her family a year and a half earlier at Christmas, before her father had gotten sick. "That's my mother, her name is Caroline; and the man is my father. His name was Edward. He died a couple of months ago." Her voice softened. "I still miss him a lot. Just like you miss your mother. It's hard to say good-bye, isn't it?"

Rose and Lily stared at the photo, then at her.

"Where are Grandma Sophia and Grandpa Vincent?" Lily asked in confusion.

Joanna tried again. "I'm not your mother, Lily. These are my parents."

"We did something bad, didn't we, Mama?" Rose's chocolate brown eyes filled with tears. "I remember when you said we were driving you crazy, that you had to go away. You made us promise—"

"Rose, she wants to be sure we didn't break our promise," Lily interrupted.

Rose looked relieved. "Oh. It's okay, Mama, I haven't told Daddy anything. I told you I could keep a secret."

Secret? What secret? Joanna tucked her hair behind her ear as she realized the children still believed she was their mother. "Come on, girls. Look at the photo. Do I really look like your mother? Are our clothes the same? Our hair? Our teeth?"

Lily tilted her head as she stared into Joanna's face, then back at the photo. "Your hair is longer and curlier now."

Joanna let out a breath of relief. They were finally making progress. "What else?" She turned to Rose. "Can you see the difference, honey? Can you understand that I'm Joanna, that I'm not your mother?"

"If you want us to call you Joanna, it's okay," Rose replied. "It's a pretty name."

"We like it," Lily added.

"I give up," Joanna said with a helpless laugh.

"Are you mad at us?" Rose asked. "Please don't be mad."

Rose threw her arms around Joanna, burying her face in the curve of Joanna's neck. Her hair brushed against Joanna's skin, bringing with it the sweet scent of flowers. Joanna couldn't help but hug Rose back. The child felt so right in her arms, a perfect fit. Lily stepped up next to them, running her hand down the side of Joanna's hair, twirling her fingers in the long strands.

"I like your hair longer," Lily whispered. "I think Daddy likes it, too."

Daddy. Joanna's heart caught at the simple word, at the reminder of their father, Michael Ashton. She'd been thinking about him all morning, and it had to stop. She hadn't spent this much time thinking about David, and they'd gone out for six months.

But David had never looked so sexy, so endearing, so human. She could still see Michael in her mind, wrestling with the girls, his tie crooked, his hair ruffled, his eyes shocked at the sight of her.

"Mama—I mean Joanna," Lily said, "do you want us to clean up now?"

Joanna looked at the clock, suddenly realizing the bell had rung.

"Good idea." She stood up and helped the other children in her class prepare for departure. Her first day of teaching had gone well. Aside from putting several children to sleep during her recitation of Emily Dickinson, she'd done okay. And she had been surprised at how much she'd enjoyed it. She'd always felt awkward with the college kids, never feeling all that secure or confident in herself.

Here she was definitely in charge, and the kids were so loving, she couldn't help but connect with them. They hugged her before recess. They showed her their pictures and shared their excitement. They fought over who would get to sit in her lap during story time.

Joanna had never felt so loved, and even though she'd spent more time tying shoelaces than teaching numbers, she felt good about the day.

The twins helped her put the chairs on the tables as various children were picked up by their parents. Michael Ashton was the last to arrive, and he brought someone with him.

"Uncle Tony!" the girls said in unison, running over to the other man.

Uncle Tony had a shadowy beard, windblown hair, and a smile guaranteed to charm. Despite Tony's obvious good looks, Joanna still felt drawn to Michael. Maybe it was Michael's eyes, so blue, so light in contrast to his dark hair. Maybe it was his broad chest, his confident stance. Maybe she had been alone too long.

"Hi midgets," Tony said, receiving a smacking kiss from each of the girls. "I brought you candy."

Joanna smiled at the girls' pleasure. She turned to Michael to tell him about their day. Once again the intensity of his gaze caught her off guard. He seemed as shocked to see her now as he had been that morning.

"Mr. Ashton," she said slowly.

"Yes?" He sounded distracted.

"Are you all right?"

"No. No, I don't think so. All morning I told myself it was my imagination." He turned to his friend. "Tony. I want you to meet Miss—"

"Joanna," she said.

Tony stepped forward. His smile faded as he looked at her. Joanna put a hand to her temple, pressing hard against her threatening headache. She didn't think she could stand much more emotion. She'd used up all her energy and patience with the children.

"Wow." Tony took in a deep breath. "You weren't kidding, Michael. She looks just like Angie."

Joanna abruptly turned around. She was beginning to feel like a bug under a microscope. She walked over to her desk and began organizing her papers.

After a moment Michael joined her. "I didn't mean to make you feel uncomfortable."

"Well, you did," she said shortly, unwilling to admit that her discomfort had more to do with attraction than dislike.

"Joanna." Michael's voice came out low and husky, making her name sound like a caress.

She raised her head, and his gaze drifted across her face, as if he were memorizing each line. Comparing her to his wife, probably. There was far too much intimacy in his look for two strangers to share.

She cleared her throat. "Perhaps the girls should have another teacher. I'm not sure it's good for them to be with me every day." *I'm not sure it's good for me.*

Lily and Rose immediately disagreed with the plan. "No! No!" they cried, abandoning their uncle Tony for Joanna. They threw their arms around her waist, holding on with stubborn determination.

"Girls, it's okay," Joanna said, trying to ease their distress. "The other teachers are good."

"We want you," they chorused.

Michael put a hand on each of their heads, bringing him into even closer proximity to Joanna. His expression was clearly troubled as he looked into her eyes. "I don't think the girls will stay with another teacher. They seem so happy with you."

"But is this good for them?"

"They've had a lot of counseling since their mother died. Time seems to be the only answer. If they stay in school, I think they'll realize that you're not their mother, but if I take them away now, I'm afraid they'll think I'm taking them away from their mother."

"I can't look that much like her," Joanna said, wanting him to contradict her.

Michael exchanged a glance with Tony. "You could be her sister," he said, his gaze returning to her.

"My sister," Tony added. "God, this is weird."

Joanna thought so, too. Nothing in her experience had taught her how to deal with a situation like this. She took in a breath and let it out. But she would deal with it, as she'd dealt with everything else in her life in the past year. Her father's illness had given her strength, his legacy to her. She couldn't go back to being the dependent, cautious, wishy-washy woman she'd once been.

"All right, we'll let things stay like this for now," she said.

The girls cheered. Joanna smiled. It was nice to be loved. She just wished it could be for herself.

Sophia De Marco carefully ironed out the wrinkles in her husband's monogrammed handkerchief. When it was perfectly flat and creaseless, she folded it in neat squares and set it on the couch next to her. Then she picked up the embroidered linen cloth that had graced the top of Angela's dresser since her birth and set to ironing it with the same sense of purpose and determination. It didn't matter that Angela would never again see the cloth. It didn't matter that no one went into Angela's bedroom anymore.

Sophia couldn't stand to take the room apart, to put Angela's things away, to change the bedspread or the curtains. Angela hadn't lived in that bedroom since she was eighteen years old, but Sophia had kept it exactly the same so that her daughter would have a room to come home to, just in case.

Angela had never come home, and like so many things Sophia kept "just in case," Angela's bedroom went unused.

Picking up the starched linen cloth, Sophia climbed up the stairs from her sewing room on the first floor to Angela's bedroom on the second.

She carefully placed the cloth on the dresser and put the silver brush and mirror and Angela's favorite music box on top.

As she looked around the room, she was assaulted with a longing that grew stronger with each passing day, a desire to go back in time or at least to stop the clock from moving forward. She couldn't believe it had been twenty-seven years since she had brought Angela home from the hospital, since she had sat in the rocking chair by the window and sung lullabies to her baby, some in Italian, some in English, all filled with love and promises. How quickly the time had passed.

Sophia sat down in the rocker and ran her hands along the smooth wood. Her husband, Vincent, had built the rocking chair for her just before the birth of their oldest son, Frank. Every night, after a long day in the restaurant, Vincent would go down to the basement and work on the rocker, shining it, polishing it.

They had been so in love then, dreaming of the family they would have. Frank had come almost immediately, but it had taken another four years and one miscarriage in between before she'd given birth to Tony, then . . . She shook her head, not wanting to think about that time any more.

She preferred to remember the day Vincent had given her the rocking chair, the day she'd brought her firstborn son home from the hospital. There were so many memories in this chair, hours alone with her babies, in the dark of the night, when the world slept. That's when she had felt the closest to them. That's when she had cried.

A tear ran down her face as she rocked, thinking about her life, about how silent the house was now.

Frank, his wife Linda, and their four children lived a few blocks away. Frank had made a good marriage, and at thirty-seven he was ready to take over De Marco's when Vincent retired at the end of the year. Frank would continue their traditions. He would bring honor to the family, because he knew no other way to live.

Sophia had been in awe of Frank's principles since he was six years old, when Frank had decided that he would not be friends with anyone who lied, called him names, or didn't do their homework. Needless to say, Frank didn't have a lot of friends as a child. But he was a good man despite his rigid ways. And he adored his mother, held her up on a pedestal.

He didn't know her at all.

Tony, at thirty-three, was the complete opposite of Frank: emotional, unpredictable, sensitive, passionate. Tony took after her. Frank took after his father. Maybe that's why she worried more about Tony. Sophia knew how much trouble he could get himself into if he wasn't careful. And Tony was never careful.

Oh, how she missed him. He'd taken off after Angela died, sailing his way around the world, picking up odd jobs, dropping the occasional note home. She knew Vincent was disappointed in Tony, that her husband very much wanted his youngest son to come home and run De Marco's with Frank. Then Vincent could retire, knowing that his sons' futures were secure.

But Tony didn't want security. He wanted more than that. Sophia remembered feeling that way a very long time ago.

Now she could feel nothing but pain. As she glanced around Angela's bedroom, as she saw the remnants of her daughter's life, the posters of pop stars on the wall, the school yearbooks in the bookcase, the clothes in the closet, the pain filled her stomach like too much pasta. It got worse every day. She could barely eat anymore. Not even her favorite chianti eased the pressure rising within her. She felt that she might burst at any moment.

But she couldn't let the words out. She had to stay silent. She had to keep going for the sake of her family, for Vincent and Frank and Tony—for Michael and the girls, her other grandchildren, her daughter-in-law, her nieces and nephews. It had always been that way. No real time for her. No moment when she could cut loose, when she could scream at the injustice of life.

Not that it would matter. Angela was gone. Sophia pulled out the simple gold cross she wore around her neck and fingered the four points, silently asking again why God had taken her baby away. The answer was the same—because she had sinned. She, alone, knew the truth.

"I don't think you should tell Sophia about Joanna," Michael said as he parked the car in front of the De Marcos' house in North Beach. He glanced over his shoulder to see if the girls were paying attention, but they were tossing a doll back and forth in the backseat. "It might upset her."

Tony stared straight ahead for a moment, then turned to Michael with a troubled expression. "Do you feel like we just entered the Twilight Zone?"

"Oh, yeah. I've been feeling that way all day."

"Who is this woman? How could she look so much like Angela? It's crazy."

"Maybe she's a distant relative."

Tony drummed his fingers restlessly against his thigh. "Do you think it's good for the girls to be with her?"

"You saw how they reacted to the thought of leaving. It's not like she's Angela's twin. Her hair is much longer. And she doesn't dress the same. There's a resemblance, but I think after awhile they'll begin to see differences between Joanna and Angela." *We all will*, he added silently.

"I hope you're right. Because if you're not, I think your problem with the girls just got bigger." Tony turned to the girls. "Hey, midgets, shall we go surprise Grandma?" The girls eagerly agreed, and the four of them made their way into the house. The De Marco home was a two-story Victorian with hardwood floors and throw rugs in the entryway, living room, dining room, and hall. The stairs were carpeted in dark blue, with the walls painted a lighter shade of blue.

It was a warm, colorful house, filled with antiques and bric-a-brac that Sophia collected during her weekly trips to secondhand stores and flea markets. Like the De Marco restaurant a few blocks away, the family home invited guests. There were comfortable chairs and sofas to sit on, paintings from Italy, and Sophia's collection of music boxes from around the world.

"The place looks the same," Tony said. "Home sweet home."

"Can we get some cookies, Uncle Tony?" Lily asked.

"Michael?"

Lily and Rose looked at their father inquiringly, but didn't speak. Michael nodded agreeably. For a while he had tried denying them anything they wanted unless they asked for it with words, but that maneuver had turned out to be as big a failure as the rest. Now it seemed pointless to encourage a full-fledged temper tantrum over a few cookies.

Tony watched the interaction with a troubled eye. "I don't get it, man," he said as the girls ran into the kitchen.

"Neither do I."

"How do you stand it?"

"I just tell myself that some day it will end. Some day they'll look me straight in the eye and say, 'We love you.' And that will probably be the happiest day of my life." Michael cleared his throat. "Of course, then they'll probably start arguing with me over every little thing, and I'll wish they would just shut up."

Tony smiled. "Probably. And just wait until they start talking on the phone all the time."

Michael held up a hand. "I don't want to think about it. Raising the girls alone—sometimes, it

scares the hell out of me. I think it would be different
if they were boys. I know how boys think. But the
female mind is a complete mystery to me."

"Speaking of females, I wonder if Mama is home.
It's so quiet." Tony tilted his head to one side. "Certainly not like it used to be. Whenever I came home
from school, Mama would be in the kitchen cooking.
Usually one of her sisters, Aunt Carlotta or Aunt
Elena, would be here, and sometimes a couple of my
cousins. We never had to bring someone home from
school to play with, because there were always a few
extra kids hanging around here. Now there's no
one."

"Everyone grew up."

"Too bad, huh? We used to have some good times,
until you got all responsible on me." He slugged
Michael on the arm.

"I didn't have a choice. I had a wife to support,
kids." He sounded defensive, and he knew it, but
dammit, he'd worked his butt off for Angela and the
girls.

"You were good for Angie," Tony said. "I mean
that."

"Yeah, well, I don't think Angela would have
agreed with you. Anyway, it's all in the past." Or it
had been until today, until he'd come face-to-face
with a ghost. He tipped his head toward the stairs.
"Sophia is probably upstairs. Why don't you go see
her? I'll keep the girls occupied for a while."

"All right."

As Tony walked up the stairs, a thousand memories flooded his mind. He hadn't actually lived in
the house for a couple of years. But coming back
now, he felt like a kid again, and he hated that feeling. Maybe that's why he had stayed away, hoping
that somewhere in the world he'd find a place where
he felt like a grown-up.

His parents' bedroom was empty. Angela's door

was partly open. He hesitated, then knocked.

"Come in," Sophia said.

Tony pushed opened the door. "Hi, Mama."

Her face lit up like the morning sky after a winter storm. She held out her arms to him, and he went into her embrace as if he were ten years old again. She smelled like Chanel No. 5, with a lingering trace of garlic. She smelled like home.

"Tony. My darling Tony," Sophia whispered, cupping his face with her hands. "You've come back."

"How are you?" Tony asked.

"I'm fine."

"Are you really?" He searched her dark eyes for the truth, then looked away, not sure he wanted to find it. He wanted her to be the strong woman he remembered from his youth, not the shattered woman he'd seen at Angela's funeral.

"I—yes." Her voice turned brisk as if she'd seen his need and decided to fulfill it.

She stood up and tucked her black hair into place. That's when he noticed the new streaks of gray at her temples, the lines around her eyes, the paleness of her olive skin.

"You look tired, Mama," he said quietly.

She touched her hand to the side of his face with a loving smile. "Your father snores so loudly, who can sleep?"

He accepted her answer because he wanted to, because it was easy.

"You must be hungry. I'll fix you something to eat. And you'll stay in your old room, of course. You are staying, aren't you?"

"For a while. I bought a boat, Mama. She's gorgeous."

"A boat? Oh, my." Sophia put a hand to her heart.

"She needs a little work, of course, but wait until you see her."

"I'm sure it's a beautiful boat, Tony. But how long is a while?"

He shrugged. "I'm not sure yet. A week or two."

"That's all?"

"Yeah."

She nodded after a moment, understanding and sadness mixing in her eyes. "I wish you didn't feel such a need to run away. Not that I've ever been able to keep you here. You climbed out of your bedroom window so many times, I had to replace the frame." She paused. "Where will you go?"

"The Caribbean, most likely. Wherever the wind and the current take me. It's a big world out there, Mama, and I want to see all of it."

"I almost wish I could go with you," Sophia said. "Not that you'd want your old mother along for the ride."

"I'd be happy to take you for a sail, Mama. In fact, I'd like to."

Tony saw a light come into his mother's eyes, and he was suddenly struck with the notion that he didn't know this woman at all. Had she changed so much since he'd been gone? Or had he just never really looked at her before?

"I couldn't. I have so much to do here, ironing, cooking, shopping, running bingo down at the church, helping your father with the restaurant. My life is so full—so very full." Her voice broke, but she covered the sudden burst of emotion by clearing her throat. "I have some chicken. Would you like a sandwich before dinner?"

"I'm fine." Tony reached into his pocket and pulled out a small box. "I got this for you in Barbados."

"A present for me?" Sophia took the box with a pleased smile. Her smile broadened as she opened it. A small miniature glass music box lay inside.

"It plays Vivaldi," Tony said, pushing up the tiny

lid with his thumb to reveal a small velvet bed big enough to hold a ring but nothing else.

"It's beautiful. I will treasure it always." Sophia kissed him on the cheek. "I'm glad you're home. For as long as you choose to stay."

The sound of pounding feet and loud voices interrupted their conversation. Lily and Rose ran into the room.

"Grandma! Grandma!" they said in unison. "You'll never guess what happened."

"Lily, Rose," Michael shouted from the hallway. "I said, stop."

The girls ignored him, intent on sharing their news with Sophia.

"What's happened?" Sophia asked.

Lily took a deep breath. "Mama came back. She's not in heaven anymore."

5

Sophia put a hand to her heart. "What?"

"It's not what you think," Michael said immediately. Like the girls, there was a spark of hope in Sophia's eyes, a gleam of a miracle. He almost hated to disappoint her. "She just looks like Angela, that's all."

"I don't understand."

"I took the kids to a new school today, just a few blocks from here. Their teacher looks—"

"Like Angie," Tony finished.

Sophia's sharp eyes pinned Tony in place. "You saw her, too?"

"Yes. I couldn't believe my eyes. She was the spitting image of Angie. Same shaped face, same big brown eyes. Could have been her sister."

Sophie's mouth dropped open as if she was going to speak, but no words crossed her lips. The sound of her ragged, uneven breathing seemed to overwhelm the room.

"It's not that close a resemblance," Michael said, trying to defuse the situation.

"This girl—what's her name?" Sophia asked.

"Joanna."

"Joanna," she repeated. "What's her last name?" She grabbed Michael's arm, her tense fingers twisting the sleeve of his suit coat. "Her last name."

"Uh . . ." Michael tried to remember Joanna's last name, but it wouldn't come. "Winston, I think. Why?"

"Are you sure?"

"I think so. Does it matter?" For some reason it did matter, but Michael didn't know why. "Sophia?"

She let go of his sleeve and forced a brief smile. "It doesn't matter, I guess." She checked her watch. "Oh dear, it's almost four. I have so many things to do today. And I should get dinner going. We'll celebrate Tony's return. You'll all stay, yes?"

"Are you sure you're all right?"

She patted his arm. "I'm fine, Michael."

She did seem fine now. But then Sophia wasn't one to share her feelings. Michael wished he could talk to her about Joanna, about the strange resemblance, about his own bizarre feelings. But after her strong reaction he knew he couldn't say anything more.

Sophia turned to Rose and Lily. "Do you want to help me make the sauce for dinner?"

"Yes, Grandma," Rose said.

Lily nodded, then spoke. "Her name is Joanna Wingate, Grandma, not what Daddy said. I don't understand why Mama has a new name."

"She's not your mother. How many times do I have to tell you that?" Michael asked in frustration.

Lily sent him a hurt look and crept closer to her grandmother. Nothing was going right today, not the girls, not their school, not his job. "I'm sorry. I didn't mean to snap at you, honey." Michael's gaze drifted over to Sophia. She seemed frozen in place, in time.

"Wingate," she whispered.

"Do you know the Wingates?" Michael asked.

"No. No, of course not. How would I know this teacher?" She pulled herself together. "Are you going back to work, Michael?"

"If you don't mind watching the girls?"

"Not at all." Sophia turned toward her son. "Tony, are you staying?"

"I'll be back. I need to check on my boat." He paused. "I hope Papa doesn't still think I'm going to work in the restaurant."

"You know that's always been his dream."

"But it's not mine."

"That is between you and Vincent, a father and his son."

"You won't help me?"

"No."

"How come no one will help me?" Tony asked, looking from Sophia to Michael.

"I bet Mariah could help you, Uncle Tony," Lily said.

"Mariah? Who's that?"

"She's a really pretty lady," Rose explained. "And she makes magic."

"Sounds like just what I need," Tony said with a grin.

"Don't get too excited," Michael said. "Mariah lives in a crystal ball. Sophia found her in an antiques shop."

"Yes. As soon as I saw her, I felt a connection," Sophia said. "The ball was warm to my touch, even though it was covered with dust. The shopkeeper got it at an estate sale."

Michael smiled at Tony. Sophia's flea market and antiques store finds were legendary in the family, and there was always a story to go along with each purchase.

"It once belonged to two sisters," Sophia continued. "Apparently one of the sisters got lost in a snowstorm. The other sister asked Mariah to bring her home safely, and the next day she was rescued. The two sisters believed in Mariah's magical ability to bring families back together until the day they died."

"Mariah brought Mama back," Lily said.

Michael sighed. He hated to disillusion them, but he couldn't let them go on believing in magic, or that Joanna was their mother. "Mariah didn't do anything of the sort. She's just a toy."

Lily glared at him. He glared back.

Sophia put her arm around the girls. "Why don't you go back to work, Michael?"

"Good idea." At work he was surrounded by lines and symmetry, logic and reason—not wizards in crystal balls, children who wouldn't talk to him, or a woman who looked like a ghost.

Caroline shook the bottle of pale pink nail polish, unscrewed the top, and touched up her nails. While they dried she studied the brochures spread out on the kitchen table. She had picked up pamphlets for every imaginable dream vacation—the Bahamas, Hawaii, Mexico, Paris, London, even an adventure trip to Africa. There had to be something in this bunch that would tempt Joanna into giving up her crazy idea of working all summer.

They could have so much fun together, if Joanna would just go along with her plans. But lately her daughter balked at every suggestion. Since Edward had died, Joanna had gone from easygoing to tough and rebellious.

Caroline supposed it was only natural. Joanna had spent hours with her father before his death. She had held his hand through the terrible, debilitating attacks of pain. She had read to him, comforted him. She couldn't have made it through without drawing from some inner strength.

But now that strength was keeping them apart. And Caroline feared that Joanna had given so much to her father that there was nothing left for her mother. Caroline knew it was selfish to think that way, but she couldn't help it. She needed her daughter. She wasn't dying, but she was lonely and afraid of what the future held for her. She didn't have a husband anymore. No one to go on trips with, to take to parties, to dine with before a movie. She couldn't do those things by herself. It would be too uncomfortable. Everyone would stare at her, wonder why she was alone.

Caroline sat back in her chair, feeling completely useless and unwanted. What on earth was she going to do with the rest of her life? All she ever wanted to be was a wife and a mother. She had spent her days taking care of Edward and Joanna. Now her husband was gone, her daughter was pulling away from her, and she was left with nothing but an empty apartment and a long, endless summer ahead of her.

Maybe she could take up a hobby. But she didn't like to cook. She killed plants even when she was trying to take care of them, which was why Joanna's room was the only one in the apartment filled with live greenery. The rest of the rooms boasted silk flowers. Gardening was out, and she couldn't sew worth a damn. She wasn't sure she even remembered how to thread the sewing machine—if she could find it, that is.

Maybe music, she thought. The piano in the living room begged to be used. But what good was learning to play the piano when there was no one to play it for? What good was staying in shape, doing her makeup, painting her nails when there was no one to see her?

Frustration and helplessness rose within her like an unstoppable tidal wave. She had to think of something to do, something to look forward to, or she wouldn't be able to get through the day or the week or the month.

As the feeling of panic increased, Caroline got up. She filled the teakettle with water and set it on the burner to heat. A cup of tea would help, she decided. Edward had always made fun of her constant desire for tea. He'd preferred scotch and water, and a nice long puff on a cigar. She'd always hated the smell of his cigars. Now she longed for the scent, wishing she could find just a hint of it in the air, but there was nothing.

The front door slammed, and she felt immediately better.

"Mom, I'm home," Joanna called.

"I'm in the kitchen," Caroline said. At least for the next few hours, she'd have some company. She wouldn't have to think. She wouldn't have to remember what she couldn't have anymore.

Joanna pushed open the kitchen door with a weary smile. "Hi."

"How was your day, honey?"

"Tiring, but fun." She set a pile of children's books down on the counter. "I stopped by the library. I think I need to get up to speed on six-year-old literature. I've completely forgotten whatever Beatrix Potter stories I used to know."

"Jemima Puddleduck was your favorite," Caroline said. "You always loved the idea of building a warm, cozy nest somewhere."

Joanna raised an eyebrow. "How on earth do you remember that?"

"I remember everything. I loved reading to you. It wasn't nearly as much fun when you grew up and started reading to yourself."

Joanna smiled to herself. Every step of independence from kindergarten to wearing makeup had been met with resistance. Caroline had tried to keep her a child as long as possible, but eventually she'd grown up. "What did you do today?" she asked.

"I got some brochures from the travel agency."

Caroline walked over to the table and picked up a couple of pamphlets. "I think we should go on a trip, Joanna. It will be wonderful, just the two of us. We'll blow those cobwebs right out of your mind."

"Mother—"

"We could go to London. Remember how much you loved the scones?"

"Mom—"

"What?" Caroline asked with resignation.

"I have a job, remember?"

"I'm sure they can find someone else."

"That's not the point."

"We only have the summer before you go back to Stanford. I don't want to waste it. Just look at these pictures and tell me you wouldn't love to get away from here."

Joanna sat down at the table and flipped through the brochures. A week ago she probably would have gone along with her mother's plans, but that was before she'd started this job, before she'd met Michael and Lily and Rose, before she'd starting feeling like a whole person again. She set the pamphlets on the table.

"I can't go, Mom."

Caroline frowned. "I think a trip would be fun. And we'd be away from here—from all the memories."

"You can go without me."

"Not alone. No, I couldn't," Caroline said immediately. "I wouldn't know what to do. I hate eating alone in a restaurant, and I never know how much to tip the waiter or the bellboy. Your father . . ." Her voice softened. "He always did those things."

"What about one of your friends?" Joanna asked, but she already knew the answer. She was her mother's best friend; she always had been. Caroline had acquaintances, women she worked with on fundraisers and charity events, the wives of the other

men in Edward's office, a few of the neighbors, but
no one close enough to go on a trip with, no one else
who was a widow, no one else who was alone.

For the first time Joanna wondered what had happened to the women Caroline had grown up with.
Surely she had had friends in high school and college, yet she kept in touch with no one. In fact, the
only people who had come to Edward's funeral had
been friends of his or theirs. None were solely hers.

If Joanna didn't take a trip with her mother, Caroline simply wouldn't go. Joanna refused to feel
guilty.

"I'm sorry, but I want to stay here and do this job.
I like it," Joanna said.

"Are you sure?"

"Yes. It felt good to be with kids, to hear their
laughter, to see their joy, to listen to their silly stories. I haven't had this much fun in ages." Joanna
paused. "The strangest thing happened, though. A
man brought his two girls into school this morning,
and they were screaming and carrying on, but as
soon as they saw me, they stopped. It was so odd.
Then they threw themselves at me and called me
Mama."

"They what?" Caroline asked in astonishment.

"Called me Mama."

"But why?"

"Apparently I look like their mother, who died
last year. Their father thought so, too. By the way,
do we have any Italian blood in our family?"

Caroline stared at her as if she'd gone mad. "Excuse me?"

"Italian blood. The girls are Italian. Their grandparents own De Marco's Restaurant in North Beach.
Have you ever eaten there?"

"No. Your father never cared much for Italian
food. Why would you think you're of Italian descent?"

"I've always wondered where my dark hair and eyes came from. You and Dad are so fair."

"Your grandmother, Theresa. She had brown hair."

"Light brown, dishwater blond really, not almost black like mine."

"I'm sure someone else in the family had dark hair," Caroline said, although she couldn't come up with any specific names.

"No one did, Mother. I've done our genealogy charts, remember?"

"But you didn't have pictures of everyone. Some genes are dormant for generations. Who knows why?" The teakettle whistled, and Caroline turned off the heat. "Would you like a cup?"

"No, thanks. I feel like something cold." Joanna stood up and retrieved a bottle of mineral water from the refrigerator. "After I get something to eat, I thought I'd start going through Dad's things in the den," she said, changing the subject.

"Why don't we go shopping after you eat? I could use some new shoes."

Joanna sighed. All she wanted to do was stay home and putter around the house, but her mother rarely allowed her that luxury. "You have a million shoes."

"But nothing new. I want something new. I would have gone earlier, but I thought you'd like to go with me."

"What I'd really like to do is start organizing the den. We need to send information to the insurance companies, and I know Dad's lawyer wanted a copy of something. Do you remember what that was?"

"Just a letter or something," Caroline said with a vague wave of her hand. "It can wait."

"It can't wait."

"Dammit, Joanna. The man's dead. What could possibly be urgent about the things in his den?" Her blunt words drew a long silence between them.

"Mom? What's wrong?" Joanna asked.

Caroline couldn't seem to meet her eyes. "I don't want you to go into the den."

"Why not?"

"Because the papers belong to your father and me." Caroline pulled a cup and saucer out of the cabinet. "I should take care of it. And I will."

"When?"

"When I'm ready."

"A lot of what's in there just needs to be tossed in the trash. Dad never threw anything away. I bet his collection of fishing magazines goes up to the ceiling."

"He loved those magazines. Everything in that room meant so much to him. It was his personal, private place, Joanna."

"I know, but it's not as if he had a stash of private love letters in there or anything."

"How would you know that?" Caroline asked sharply.

Joanna was taken aback by her mother's question. "I don't know that, but are you saying there's something in there you don't want me to see?"

"No, of course not."

"Do you think he was—"

"No."

"You don't know what I was going to say."

"Yes, I do, and he wasn't. But some things are private between a husband and a wife. You'll know what I mean when you get married."

Married. Joanna took a sip of her drink as she leaned back against the counter. In the past year, whenever she had thought of marriage, she had thought of David. Now his image had been replaced by that of another man—of Michael Ashton. It was ridiculous. She didn't even know him. But there was something about him, something so compelling that she couldn't stop thinking about him. And the twins were adorable, affectionate, spontaneous, loving, honest. They wanted her to be their mother.

In her mind she saw Michael, Lily, and Rose, standing in a circle, holding out their hands to her. But she couldn't complete the circle. She might look the same, but she wasn't Lily and Rose's mother, and she wasn't Michael's wife. That spot belonged to someone else. She needed to remember that.

Dinner at the De Marcos' was a noisy affair. Everyone talked at the same time. The loudness in the room grew higher as the level of wine got lower. Arguing about everything from politics to religion to meat prices was required, and anyone who couldn't finish a sentence in thirty seconds could count on being interrupted.

It hadn't taken Michael long to realize that he couldn't keep up with the De Marcos. Angela had usually finished most of his thoughts, even if she didn't know what he was thinking. She had simply assumed that he thought the same way she did. In the beginning he'd been too infatuated to contradict her. Her passion and zest for life had appealed to him. He'd thought her crazy antics would brighten his life. But her endless energy had been tiring, her penchant for trouble wearing, and after they'd had kids her irresponsibility had turned him off completely.

"I think you should add that pasta dish Sophia made the other night to the menu, Frank," Linda said. "The shrimp and fettucine was delicious. You'll have to give me the recipe, Sophia, although I doubt I could re-create it. You're such a great cook. . . ."

Michael smiled as Linda De Marco lavished praise on her mother-in-law. Linda had been married to the oldest De Marco son, Frank, for thirteen years. A slightly plump brunet with a penchant for wearing colorful long sweaters over dark leggings, Linda had a tendency to try too hard to fit in. When Linda found out Sophia collected music boxes, she began a collection of ceramic angels. When Sophia tried out a new recipe, Linda asked for it. Linda shopped at the same markets and dress shops. She went to the same dentist as her mother-in-law, and the same doctor.

Not that Michael could blame Linda for wanting to emulate her mother-in-law or to create the same happy family as the De Marcos'. He'd tried to do much the same thing himself. Only he'd failed. Linda, on the other hand, seemed to be successful. She had four beautiful children and Frank.

Michael looked over at his brother-in-law, who was eating his linguine with the same seriousness Frank brought to every task. Instead of twirling the strands of pasta around his fork, Frank cut them with a knife and fork. He wasn't one to slurp or spill. He had to control everything and everyone around him. And the burden of such a need seemed to be aging him prematurely. Not yet forty, Frank had thinning hair and streaks of gray. His clothes were a little too tight, his shirtsleeves a little too short, his style a little too conservative.

"Michael?" Linda said.

"What?" he asked, realizing she was waiting for him to reply to a question he didn't remember hearing.

Before she could answer, Frank jumped in. "We would have to charge more to cover the cost of shrimp. It would be cheaper to stick with chicken."

Frank was also obsessed with the bottom line. No matter what the topic of conversation, with Frank it always came down to money.

"Chicken is so dull," Linda said.

"Everything is dull to you lately," Frank snapped.

Michael studied them thoughtfully, suddenly noting the tension in their faces. He had a feeling they were talking about more than chicken.

Sophia cleared her throat. "That's a lovely idea, Linda. I'm sure Vincent will consider it. And I certainly appreciate the compliment."

"Personally I think you should just stick with spaghetti," Tony said.

Vincent shook his head. "No one wants good, hearty spaghetti anymore. Do you know when I first started cooking for my father . . ."

Michael paid scant attention to the rest of Vincent's statement. He'd heard it before. Vincent loved his stories, and they got better with each telling. The rest of the family listened with appropriate smiles and encouraging expressions, because Vincent was the heart of the De Marcos.

A tall man with a lean body and stark white hair that provided a vivid contrast to his black eyes and olive skin, Vincent commanded respect. Despite his jovial manner, his word was law. The only one who had ever been able to bend his will was Angela. Vincent had always had a soft spot for his baby girl.

A burst of laughter rang through the room. Michael smiled again. He loved the De Marcos. They'd treated him like a son since the first day Tony had brought him home from school. They'd given him the fantasy family he'd always longed for.

Tony nudged him as Vincent went on to another story. "Have you been dating anyone lately?"

"Dating?" Michael said the word as if he didn't understand it. Actually it did sound foreign, not only the word but the thought. He hadn't gone on a date in eight years, not since he'd fallen head over heels in love with Angela.

"You know, going out with a woman," Tony prodded.

"No." Michael took a sip of his wine, wishing Tony would change the subject.

"Why not?"

Michael lowered his voice. "I don't think your parents would be happy to see me dating someone else."

"I don't think they want to see you alone for the rest of your life. You're still young."

"I don't feel that young, and it's too soon."

"It's been a year."

"I'm busy."

"You're making excuses."

Michael shot Tony an irritated look. "I've got my hands full just getting my work done and taking care of the girls. The last thing I need is a relationship."

"What about sex?"

"Jesus." Michael cast a quick glance around the table, praying no one had heard Tony's question. Sophia and Vincent were arguing with Linda and Frank about a movie they'd watched on television the night before. "There's more to life than sex," he murmured.

"Not much more," Tony said with a grin. "You can't tell me you don't miss it. You can't tell me you don't think about it."

"Maybe once in awhile. But my life is complicated. I've got children—kids who won't talk to me. I can't throw a woman into the middle of this mess. And frankly I've got enough females in my life."

"You can never have too many women in your life." Tony sent him a thoughtful look. "You sure seemed interested in—"

Michael held up his hand. "Don't say it. Don't even think it."

"You're right. It would be strange. Like dating Angela's twin sister or something."

"Sister? Whose sister?" Linda asked, interrupting their conversation with a curious smile.

"Michael met a woman today," Tony said.

"Tony, I don't think—" Michael began.

"She looks so much like Angie, she could have been her sister," Tony finished.

Vincent's fork clattered against his plate. He looked as shocked by Tony's words as Sophia had been earlier.

"More linguini, Linda?" Sophia asked.

"Who is this woman?" Linda said, ignoring Sophia's question.

"She's a teacher at the school where the girls are going," Michael replied.

"Who wants coffee?" Sophia tried again to change the subject, but no one went with her.

"What a strange coincidence," Linda said. "Maybe she's a distant relative or something."

"Michael, do you want coffee?" Sophia's question took on a note of desperation.

"She could be a cousin," Tony suggested.

"Enough," Vincent said. "No more of this talk. It upsets your mother."

"I've been doing some genealogy charts," Linda said, "with Aunt Carlotta. Maybe something—"

"I said enough." Vincent stood up so abruptly, his chair fell over backward.

"I was just trying to be helpful," Linda said.

"Linda, be quiet," Frank admonished. "This is none of your business." He helped his father with his chair.

Linda sat back in her seat, her lips tightly pursed together. "I apologize."

"I'll get coffee," Sophia said, rising to her feet. As she and Vincent stood facing each other at opposite ends of the long table, Michael could feel the tension sizzling between them. He just didn't understand why they were so upset.

Finally Sophia left to go into the kitchen. Linda followed her, and Vincent and Frank returned to their seats. Vincent turned to Frank and immediately began discussing business, as if nothing strange had occurred.

Tony looked at Michael. "What the hell is going on?"

"With Frank and Linda, or your father and mother?"

"Everyone is so tense. I'd like to know why."

"I'm not sure I want to know why," Michael replied.

"It must bother them to know there's a woman walking around who looks like Angie, when she's no longer here."

"That's probably it," Michael said, but as he thought about Joanna, his uneasiness deepened.

"How do you stand it?" Linda asked in anger and frustration as she pulled cups and saucers out of the cabinet.

Sophia felt her daughter-in-law's emotions as if they were her own. She wanted to tell Linda she understood how difficult a man like Frank could be to live with. Hadn't she spent the past forty years with just such a man? But Linda was not her daughter, and it was not her place to speak of such things.

"How do you put up with such domineering arrogance?" Linda added. "Frank talks to me as if I have no brain, as if I didn't exist before I met him. I have ideas. I have opinions. I may not have a college degree like he does, but that doesn't make me stupid."

"Of course, it doesn't."

"That's the way he treats me. It gets worse every day, every year. I never—I never thought things would end up this way."

"What way?"

"We're so distant. How do you and Vincent do it? How do you stay in love after so many years?"

Sophia didn't know what to say. She could lie and

make it sound easy. Or she could tell the truth and scare Linda to death. "You take it one day at a time," she said finally. "Frank loves you. You have to focus on that when things get difficult."

Linda gave a heartfelt sigh. "That sounds a lot simpler than it is."

"I didn't say it would be easy."

"He has such high standards. I never measure up. Frank wants me to be just like you. I couldn't even try to fill your shoes."

"You shouldn't," Sophia said, though she knew Linda did try. "You're not me. And Frank is not his father. You live in a different time. Marriage is more equal now. Men and women are partners."

"Not in my house. Frank thinks he's God."

"Do you still love him, Linda?"

Linda slowly nodded. "Yes. I love him when he's reading the kids a story. I love him when he acts protective if I'm driving home alone at night. And I love him when he loves me."

As Sophia filled the coffee maker she wished she could offer Linda some words of advice. She should probably be talking to Frank, telling him to take care of his wife before he lost her. But Frank wouldn't listen to her. He'd tell her she was wrong, that Linda was crazy in love with him, that their marriage was perfect. Frank, like his father before him, only saw what he wanted to see.

"Haven't you ever wanted to just say, 'No, Vincent. I'm going to do this. I'm making my own decision'?" Linda asked.

"I've wanted to," Sophia admitted as the truth weighed heavily on her heart. "But Vincent usually makes the right decision."

"Always, every time?"

Sophia knew Linda wasn't arguing against Vincent but against Frank, the man who wouldn't let her work, who rarely gave credit to her opinions, who molded himself after his father. Sophia felt she had to defend her son. She was his mother, after all.

"Frank is a good man," Sophia said. "Perhaps if you keep talking to him, you will be able to make him understand how you feel."

"I'm not sure I have that many years on this earth. And Frank is hardly ever home. The restaurant takes up so much of his time. Sometimes I think I talk more to Stanley Baker down at the grocery store than I do to Frank."

Stanley? Sophia's worry deepened as she looked into her daughter-in-law's troubled eyes. She heard the yearning in Linda's voice. She understood the temptation of a man who listened, who touched, who cared.

"Talk to Frank," Sophia said sharply. "And start shopping at Lucky's."

Linda stiffened. "I didn't mean there was anything going on. I have four children, for goodness' sake. It's not like I would even consider—you know."

The problem was Sophia did know, only too well.

6

Just past seven the next morning, Michael entered his daughters' bedroom. The sun peeked through the lace curtains, lighting the porcelain faces of the dolls on the dresser and the colorful rainbow mural painted on the wall.

This was his favorite time of day, when he could simply stand and stare at his two little angels in their matching nightgowns under their matching pink bedspreads. They were both still asleep. Lily, as usual, had kicked her way free of the covers. Rose still huddled like a baby in a womb, her hands tucked under her chin, her knees drawn up to her waist, covers still tightly in place.

The love he felt for his children overwhelmed him sometimes. He felt almost guilty to admit that it was far greater than what he had felt for their mother. He just wished he could make them feel what he felt, give them what was in his heart and make them take it.

Lily stirred and blinked. Rose also began to awaken. Michael didn't say anything to speed the process. There was plenty of time for Cheerios and teeth brushing and the mad dash to get ready for work and school. This moment was his and theirs—together.

Rose's eyes focused on him, and she smiled as she

sat up. Rose always woke up in a good mood. She'd been that way since she was a baby. It was Lily he hated to wake up in mid-dream. When she used to talk to him, he'd get an earful of angry whining at being awakened. Now she seemed content to just glare at him. Maybe there was some benefit to silence, he thought as she directed a scowl in his direction.

"Time to get up and have some breakfast." He pulled the curtains open. "Looks like a great day out there."

Rose got out of bed and stood next to him at the window. He put his arm around her shoulders as they looked out at the quiet street. After a moment she slipped her arms around his waist and hugged him, her face barreling into his stomach.

He felt his muscles tense, and his mouth actually trembled. But he didn't say anything. To comment on the behavior usually provoked a withdrawal, and right now he needed this hug a hell of a lot more than she did.

"I'm hungry," Lily said, swinging her legs over the side of the bed. "What do you think we should have today, Rose? Waffles or cereal?"

"I'd like a waffle," Rose said, replying to Lily as she pulled away from Michael.

"One waffle coming up," Michael said.

"I think I'd rather have cereal, Rose," Lily said.

"And one bowl of cereal," Michael added, playing the game they played every morning. "Slippers and robes, please. It's chilly this morning." He paused, his attention drawn to the wizard on the night table. Mariah really was a beautiful creature, sculpted so carefully that she almost appeared to be real. Her smile looked knowing. In fact, she seemed to be laughing at him. "I wonder if Mariah could tell me how to get you both to talk to me," he mused.

Lily and Rose glanced at each other. Then Lily

spoke to Rose. "Grandma Sophia said Mariah probably only talks to little girls."

"Or to people who believe in magic," Rose added.

"That's convenient." He turned to Mariah with a
scowl. "I think you're a troublemaker." Mariah's
smile seemed to grow wider. Michael shook his
head. He needed coffee. For a second there he could
have sworn her lips moved.

An hour and a half later, Michael helped the girls
out of the car and watched them run into the school
building without a backward glance. They weren't
crying today or dawdling or pretending to be sick.
They were excited and anxious to see Joanna again.

Joanna. His stomach turned over; his heart quickened. He was tempted to follow them inside. He'd
thought of her all night. Or had he been thinking of
Angela? The two women blurred in his mind, leaving him confused, restless, and ridiculously needy.

Stupid. It was stupid. His dreams had probably
been a result of Tony's relentless questioning about
his sex life. He'd started thinking about how alone
he was, how empty the bed was, how long it had
been since he'd held a woman in his arms.

But Joanna Wingate was not Angela De Marco. He
couldn't let himself think for an instant that there
was any connection between the two women. Joanna
was not attracted to him. Although the way she'd
looked at him yesterday . . . No, that was just wish-
ful thinking—make that foolish thinking. The last
thing he needed was attraction, especially to this
woman.

That's why he wasn't going inside the school. He
was going to the office, where he would work hard
until he forgot about her. But as he turned away he
caught a glimpse of a woman standing in one of the
classroom windows. A woman with dark brown hair
and a lovely profile. He could see her slender figure

bend as if she was saying hello to some children, possibly his children.

Michael's breath caught in his throat as she straightened, as she turned toward the window. He couldn't move. Silently he willed her to turn around. At the same time he prayed that she wouldn't.

"I dreamed about you last night, Mama," Rose said shyly. "I dreamed you came home, that you told us a bedtime story, and lay down with us until we went to sleep."

"Oh, honey." Joanna tucked a strand of Rose's hair behind her ear. "You know it was just a dream."

"But it seemed so real. You even kissed my forehead. And you smelled so good."

"She wasn't really there, Rose," Lily interrupted. "Because I went into Daddy's room last night after he went to sleep, and he was all alone in his big bed." Lily looked up at Joanna. "Daddy never sleeps on your side, you know. He's waiting for you to come home."

Joanna caught her breath at the image of Michael Ashton alone, waiting for the woman he loved to come back to his bed. She took in a deep breath and let it out. So much for starting the day off on a better note. They were getting in deeper with each passing minute.

"Your dad didn't come in with you today?"

"He had to go to work. He said we should call you Joanna," Lily added.

"I think that's a good idea. You need to remember that even though I look like your mother, I'm not her. Right?"

"I guess we still can't talk to Daddy then," Rose said with a sigh.

"What do you mean?" Joanna asked.

Rose sent a questioning look in Lily's direction. Lily shook her head.

"Nothing."

Joanna debated pushing the issue, then decided against it. She did not need to get more involved in the Ashton family. She would just treat them like any other students.

"Why don't you two start coloring? We'll have circle time in a few minutes." Joanna glanced out the window. Michael Ashton stood on the sidewalk, staring at the school—at her. She wanted to look away, but couldn't. Even from this distance, she felt a pull in his direction. It was so strong, it was almost frightening.

Suddenly Michael turned and walked briskly to his car. He got in and sped down the street before she had a chance to move. She should have been glad he was gone, but a part of her wanted him to come back.

"I'm glad you're back," Vincent said to Tony as they walked through the main dining room of De Marco's restaurant. As Vincent stopped to confer with one of the waitresses, Tony took in a deep breath, assaulted by the familiar scents of garlic, onion, olive oil, rosemary, and basil. The aroma of warm focaccia bread just out of the oven, mixed with the tangy scent of tomato sauce, made him hungry, not just for the food but for the past, for the family he had missed this last year.

He walked farther into the center of the room. De Marco's had changed little over the years. It was still a first-class dining room with quality linens and crystal. The luxurious, intimate booths around the periphery of the room were lit by hand-painted lamps that graced the center of each table. The thick carpet, the photographs on the wall, the carefully placed vases, and the fresh flowers made one think of home, of romance, of tradition, of family.

That's what De Marco's was all about. The dining

room was filled every night with extended family, neighbors, and friends who dined regularly at the restaurant, rarely looking at the menu but simply asking Louis or Vincent to make one of their special dishes for them.

The restaurant still drew celebrities, not the types who wanted to be seen, but those who wanted good food, privacy, respect, and a sense of home. Tony had grown up working at the restaurant, bussing tables, helping in the kitchen, serving, hosting, tending bar; anything and everything that needed to be done, he had done it. Not willingly, not with his heart, but out of duty and lack of funds.

His father had instilled in him the idea that one day he would run De Marco's with Frank. Tony had let the idea float for years. After all, who was he to turn his back on a ready-made job? He even majored in restaurant management because it was easier to go along with the plan than fight it, especially when he didn't have any better ideas.

He'd spent years sailing all day and bartending all night. Damn, he'd wasted a lot of time. A decade of his life had slipped by before he'd even noticed. It had taken Angela's death to shake him out of his aimlessness, although he doubted anyone else in the family would realize that. They thought he'd simply run away.

Okay, so he had run away. But he had also worked hard the past year, running charters, bartending, even dealing blackjack on a floating casino. He'd banked his money instead of spending it, working two and three jobs so he could afford freedom. Finally, with a lot of hard work and a little luck at the poker table, he'd managed to buy his own boat. He didn't know quite what he was going to do with it, but it was a start.

Now he just had to convince his father that his self-imposed hiatus was going to continue forever, that he wasn't coming back, that he wouldn't ever be the De Marco in De Marco's.

Tony stepped behind the gold marble-topped bar and studied the myriad of bottles on the shelf. He needed a drink to get through the next few minutes. A little buzz to dull the shouting when it began, and he knew it would begin. Vincent had never been one to discuss things calmly and quietly.

He picked up a bottle of tequila and poured himself a shot. The liquid burned his throat in a deliciously familiar way. He poured himself another shot.

"Are you planning to pay for those?" a woman asked sharply.

He turned in surprise. De Marco's had always been a family-owned and operated business. Most of the waitresses were related to him in some form or fashion, but not this woman, with her red hair, snapping blue eyes, and pale, lightly freckled skin. Her voice had a lilt to it. Irish, he guessed.

"Who are you?" he asked.

"I might be asking you the same question. We're not open yet."

"This place is always open for me. I'm the owner."

"Are you now? And I suppose you'll be saying your name is Frank or Vincent next."

"Tony," he said with a grin. "Anthony Enrico De Marco, to be exact."

"Ah, the black sheep younger brother. I've heard about you." She set her tray on the bar.

"What have you heard?"

"That when the going gets tough, you get going."

Tony felt the words puncture his heart like steel-tipped darts sinking into a board. He raised the shot glass to his lips and drained it. "You must have been talking to my big brother."

"Is it true what he says?"

"Would you believe me if I said it wasn't?"

"Judging by the tequila you're swigging, probably not."

"And what might your name be?"

"Kathleen Shannon."

"And what possessed my father to let a little Irish breeze blow through this place?" he asked, allowing his gaze to travel down her body. She was dressed in a short black skirt with a white blouse and a black bow tie, the typical De Marco's uniform. But her body was far too curvy and her legs far too slender and sexy to fit the supposedly demure nature of her uniform.

"I suppose he thought I'd please the customers."

"And do you please the customers?" he asked, enjoying her sharp wit more than was prudent.

"Depends on how big a tip they'll be leaving."

"Ah, but you don't know that until it's too late."

"Oh, I can tell right away. Believe me, I know when to suck up." She tossed him a saucy smile.

"Then you should be sucking up to me. I'm the owner's son. I could be your boss one day."

She gave a full, generous laugh that lit up her entire face. "All the saints will be in hell before that happens."

"Why do you say that?"

"Some men are born to rule, some to follow, some to ponder, some to wander."

"What the hell does that mean?"

Kathleen laughed again and disappeared into the kitchen. What an irritatingly smug, arrogant woman. Gorgeous, too, not that it mattered. She was right about one thing; he was definitely not going to be her boss. Not that he could picture anyone being that woman's boss, least of all his brother Frank.

Vincent walked over to the bar, and Tony hastily slid the bottle of tequila back in its place.

"Tony, my son," Vincent said. "What do you think of the place?"

"It looks pretty much the same."

"We've been waiting for you to come back."

Tony's stomach knotted. He'd hoped the issue wouldn't come up right away, but his father wasted no time. He shouldn't have been surprised. De Marco's was always at the front of Vincent's mind.

"You shouldn't have waited for me," he said.

Vincent's dark eyes slanted in anger. "Why not?"

"I came home to visit, not to work. I've bought a boat. I'm planning to open my own charter business."

Vincent shook his head. "No, no. You want to sail on the weekends, fine, but this is your business. This is where you belong. I'm not getting any younger. I want you and Frank to run the restaurant when I retire."

"You're not going to retire for a long time," Tony argued.

"This will be my last Christmas."

Tony looked at him in surprise. "Is something wrong?"

"I'm tired." Vincent waved his hands. "The customers are getting younger. They want new dishes. They don't recognize the people in the photographs on the wall. They don't talk about us in the *Chronicle* anymore. We're losing business. You and Frank can bring it back. Frank, he has the smart head. But you, you have the smile. The ladies, they will come to see you. Louis' son, Rico, will keep them here with his cooking, and Frank will make sure they pay the bill. It is the perfect solution."

Yeah, if he wanted to run a restaurant—which he didn't. "I'm sorry, Papa, but I can't do this. I'm not cut out to be inside all day long. I hate that it's so dark in here. I like windows and wide, open spaces and the sound of the ocean and the birds as they dive into the water to search for dinner. I belong on the sea, not here in this restaurant."

Vincent's eyes filled with disappointment. "Those are the words of a young boy. You are a man now. I provided for you. I gave you a roof over your head, food in your stomach, clothes on your back, and you cannot do this for me? For your mother? For your brother? For the loving memory of your sister? We are a family. This is what the De Marcos do."

"Not this De Marco."

"You would desert your family? We, who have loved you? You would turn your back on us? Did I raise a coward then?"

Anger ripped through Tony's body. He damned his father for making him feel guilty and damned himself for letting it happen.

Fortunately their conversation was interrupted when Vincent's brother, Louis, stalked out of the kitchen screaming about the scrawny chicken in his hands. Suddenly Vincent and Louis were arguing about the cost of meat as they had done every day of their lives. Frank came into the middle of it, then his cousin Rico. They all shouted at the same time, each one determined to make his point.

Tony slowly backed away. He couldn't do this. He couldn't work in this restaurant and argue about chicken wings for the rest of his life. He couldn't spend his days in a room with no windows. He couldn't cook worth a damn, and he hated to budget. The only remotely good thing about the restaurant was the free booze.

He shouldn't have come home. They didn't understand him. They never had. Not even Michael really knew how restless he was.

Tony moved toward the kitchen door, sensing freedom. The door opened behind him, and a voice spoke in his ear. "The back alley is clear if you're looking for a way out," Kathleen Shannon said.

He scowled at her knowing grin. "Who says I'm planning to leave?"

"Your eyes. You have the look of a desperate man who's seeing the prison doors slamming shut one by one, until there's no possible chance for escape. I've seen that look before."

Tony wanted to question her cryptic answer, but out of the corner of his eye, he saw Frank turn in his direction. Like a coward he fled through the back door into the alley, past the trash cans, and down the sidewalk until he hit the street, until he saw the bay in the distance, the marina, the flags on the boats, the Golden Gate Bridge—freedom. He'd escaped. And damn that Kathleen Shannon for reading him so right. Nobody knew his private thoughts, and that's the way he liked it.

Caroline Wingate took a deep breath and opened the door to the den, her husband's private sanctuary. She could still see him sitting in the leather chair behind the desk, chatting on the phone as he smoked one of his favorite Cuban cigars, or asleep on the couch with a fishing magazine resting against his chest, gently snoring.

"Oh, Edward," she whispered, placing a hand to her heart. "Why did you have to die first?"

Because Edward had done everything first. He had taken the lead in every decision they'd made. A warm, spontaneous man who loved life with every breath, he had overwhelmed her at their first meeting. She had been working as a secretary at a law firm. Her boss and Edward were partners in a land deal. Edward had begun to stop by once or twice a week to drop off papers.

Quiet and shy by nature, she had never imagined that a man so full of vim and vigor could be interested in her. She didn't have much confidence in herself or in her looks. She'd barely dated in high school. In college she'd buried herself in books rather than face lonely Saturday nights.

After graduation her friends had spent time planning their upcoming weddings. She, on the other hand, had looked for a job. When she met Edward at age twenty-six, she had yet to receive even one declaration of love, much less a proposal.

But somehow, mysteriously, Edward Wingate saw something in her that he liked. He proposed to her one month after they met, and she accepted, thrilled beyond belief to finally be moving into the next stage of her life.

It was 1961, and women were supposed to be wives and mothers. It was the ultimate goal in life. Oh sure, there were a few career women, but none that she knew. When Edward proposed, Caroline realized that she would no longer have to sit at the lunch table with her friends, listening to their tales about husbands and children without having anything to share. She would finally be a real woman.

Although the marriage started off right, the babies she longed for didn't come. Six years of trying elicited nothing. When she turned thirty-two, she began to panic. The doctors told her to relax. She read what few books there were on infertility, but no one seemed to have any answers. She researched the best possible time of the month to conceive, and insisted that she and Edward have sex at just that time, regardless of whether she felt like it or not. Having a baby became her quest.

The world outside ceased to exist. There was a war going on in Vietnam, and hippies, flower children, and drugs. But all Caroline cared about was the baby that she didn't yet have. She felt like a failure and withdrew from all her friends, refusing invitations to parties so she wouldn't have to explain why she and Edward didn't have children.

Sometimes she blamed herself for their problem. Sometimes she blamed Edward. The silences grew longer, the space in the middle of the bed colder.

It was the worst time of their marriage. But finally a miracle happened, and Joanna came along. Joanna pulled them back together with the force of her smile and the power of her love. Their family was finally complete. After that she and Edward never talked about the early days, both content to enjoy the daughter they finally had.

The three of them had been inseparable over the years. Until two months ago. Until Edward had died.

Now she only had Joanna.

Joanna, who wanted to go through her father's papers.

Caroline couldn't allow her daughter to do that. She took another deep breath as she looked at the papers in front of her, not sure where to begin. Edward had done everything for her, paid the bills, invested their money, repaired the cars, repainted the house, and remodeled the kitchen. He'd made all the decisions, and she'd never questioned his wisdom.

When something didn't look quite right, she had simply turned away. Now she was afraid to look away, afraid that if she didn't face this particular task head-on, Joanna would, and God only knew what she'd find out.

Caroline had loved Edward with all her heart, and he had loved her; she was sure of that. But there were secrets between them. She was sure of that, too.

7

"Can I tell you a secret, Joanna?" Rose asked in a hushed voice as the rest of the class worked on an art project.

Joanna sat back in her desk chair. On a logical level she didn't particularly like secrets. They always gave the recipient something to worry about, something to protect. But on an emotional level, having grown up as an only child with no siblings, she was unable to resist the temptation to listen. "Okay," she said.

"It's about Daddy."

Uh-oh. Warning bells rang in her mind. "What about him?"

"One day I almost broke my promise to you. I almost talked to him. He was saying good night and giving me a hug, and . . ." Rose's eyes filled with anguish. "And he said he just wanted to hear me say 'I love you' out loud. And I wanted to say 'I love you.' I started to, but then I remembered my promise. Is that why it took you so long to come back? Did you hear me say, 'I'? Did you think I'd forgotten?"

"Oh, Rose." Joanna didn't know where to begin to untangle the story she had just heard. "I'm not sure I understand everything you just said, but let's try to remember one thing. I'm not your mother, and you didn't make me a promise. Okay?"

Rose nodded, but she didn't look convinced.

"Now, why can't you talk to your dad?"

"Because she can't," Lily said, interrupting them. She shot Rose a dark look. "You weren't supposed to tell."

"But if she's Mama, she already knows."

"She wants to make sure you can keep the secret," Lily insisted. "It's a test, like when we went to the store and Mama said if we were good she'd buy us ice cream."

"Lily, I'm not testing you." Joanna looked from one to the other, wishing she could somehow make them understand she was not their mother. "Why don't you tell me what you promised your mother and why? Maybe then I can help you."

"If you're not our mother, we can't tell you," Rose said with a sigh.

"Just like we couldn't tell the doctors, who gave us jelly beans," Lily added.

"Or Grandma Sophia or Uncle Tony."

"Or Uncle Frank or Aunt Linda," Lily continued.

"Mama told us we couldn't talk to Daddy until she came back, that we had to keep this secret, and if you're not her, then she's not back yet."

Joanna sighed. In just two days of teaching at the elementary school level, she had already learned that six-year-olds were incredibly literal. "Girls, I know it's difficult to accept, but your mother isn't coming back. She's in heaven now. She'll always be with you, but only in your hearts."

"That's what the doctors told us," Lily said matter-of-factly.

"And Daddy, and Grandma Sophia—"

"Grandpa Vincent and Aunt Linda."

"Then don't you think you should believe them?" Joanna said, interrupting the litany of family names.

Rose looked at Lily. "Can I tell her?"

Lily shook her head.

"Mama said people might think she wasn't coming back," Rose said defiantly.

"Rose, you promised."

"Not that. I didn't promise that."

While the girls argued, Joanna stood up and began to put away the art supplies. She couldn't help wondering exactly how their mother had died. Was there some possibility that Angela wasn't dead? But how could that be? None of it made sense, not their cryptic promise or their mother's strange words. Of course, the fact that Joanna resembled this woman didn't make sense either. She'd never looked like anyone in her life, not even her own parents.

To think that her own face was so similar to this woman's that her children were confused was mind-boggling. Joanna wondered if Michael Ashton still had photos of his wife. A shiver ran down her spine as she wondered if she had the guts to ask.

Forty minutes later Michael arrived, once again adorably weary. His tie hung loose around his collar, his shirtsleeves were rolled up to his forearms, and a smudge of dirt streaked across one cheek. Joanna reminded herself to stay cool. Michael Ashton was a parent. She was a teacher. There was no other relationship between them, and there never would be. In the fall she'd go back to Stanford, and Happy Hollow School would be just a memory.

"Good afternoon," she said.

"Joanna." His warm, husky voice and inviting smile took away her calm.

"The girls had a good day," she said hurriedly, feeling a desperate need to launch into conversation, anything to distract him from looking at her the way he was looking at her, with intensity, with curiosity, with . . . "Lily, Rose, why don't you show your father your artwork? They painted animals today," she added as the girls retrieved their pictures.

"Great. I trust the paint went only on the paper," he said with a knowing smile.

She reluctantly smiled back. "Actually Rose's white tennis shoes are now pink. I'm sorry. I didn't catch it until it was too late. I scrubbed them with water, and we got most of the paint off, but not all of it. But it could have been worse. They started off bright red."

"It could have been a lot worse. Your shoes could be bright red."

"The girls aren't that bad. They're just exuberant and creative."

He laughed. "I think I love you, Miss Wingate."

Joanna felt her cheeks grow warm. He was joking, of course, but his words still brought them closer than she cared to be. She was relieved when Lily and Rose handed their pictures to their father.

While they were doing that, Joanna rearranged the books in the reading corner, hoping that keeping her hands occupied would also distract her thoughts. It didn't work. Maybe because the room was so silent.

She couldn't help glancing at the girls and their father. Rose and Lily held out their work, but didn't say a word to Michael, despite his encouraging responses. They smiled at him and looked pleased, but no sounds came out of their mouths. When Michael looked at her she saw a gleam of hopelessness in his eyes, and her heart went out to him.

"Why don't you tell your dad about your day?" Joanna said to Rose. "I'm sure he'd like to hear what else you did."

Rose looked unsure. Her gaze traveled to Lily, who once again shook her head.

"It's okay, Joanna. I'm used to it," Michael said.

"How could you be?"

"I don't have a choice."

"Do you want us to wash the paintbrushes before we go, Joanna?" Rose asked.

She hesitated. She should probably send them on their way, but she couldn't let Michael go without finding out more about their situation. "If your father doesn't mind waiting a few minutes," she said.

"No, in fact, I'd like to talk to you."

"What did you want to talk to me about?" Joanna asked as the girls ran into the back room to wash the brushes.

Michael walked over to her. She didn't mean to take a step back, but she did. He seemed to take up so much space. She was aware of everything about him, his bright blue eyes, his musky cologne, the deep timber in his voice. He was all male. That was it, she realized suddenly. David had been an intellectual, pale and thin with glasses and a faraway look in his eyes. Michael was rugged, athletic, alive. Just looking at him made her blood race.

"Did the girls tell you that they don't speak to me?" he asked.

"Yes."

"Did they say why?"

Joanna heard the desperation in his voice and wished she could give him a better answer. "No. Rose wanted to, but Lily stopped her."

"Lily always stops her. Damn." His fists clenched at his side, then slowly unclenched. "Someday they're going to come clean. I just have to be patient. God, I hate that word."

Joanna smiled as Michael paced restlessly across the alphabet rug. Judging by the way he always seemed to be rushing, she didn't think patience was his strong suit.

"They did tell me something else," she said.

"What?"

"They said their mother told them people might say she wasn't coming back, but that they shouldn't believe it. Do you know what they meant?"

"Hell, no. I didn't understand most of what An-

gela said those last few months. In fact, we had a
fight the day she died. She wanted to go to a party
with friends. I wanted her to stay home and take
care of the girls because I had to work. She wanted
to find yet another baby-sitter. I had begun to think
I was working overtime simply to pay for an endless
parade of teenagers who ran up my phone bill and
cleaned out my refrigerator." He shook his head in
disgust. "Anyway, I left the house in a fury, and I
have no idea what Angela said to the girls or what
they think happened between us. They've never told
anyone."

"Part of some promise they made to their
mother," Joanna said. "I got that much."

"You're doing better than most of us."

"Mr. Ashton . . ."

"Call me Michael."

"Michael." His name sounded so intimate on her
lips, she almost regretted using it. Despite her best
intentions they seemed to be moving from Mr. Ashton and Miss Wingate to Michael and Joanna.

"Yes?" he prodded.

Joanna hesitated. She might as well get as much
information as she could. Maybe then she would be
able to help them. "If you don't mind my asking—
how did your wife die?"

"Angela fell off a boat. There was a party going
on, a lot of drinking." The monotone of his voice
slid into anger. "Heavy drinking. Irresponsible
drinking." He paused, obviously fighting his bitterness. "The seas were rough that night. If they'd
stayed in the bay, they might have been all right,
but they headed out to the ocean to get away from
the crowds. The waves were so big, they came over
the side of the boat. People scrambled to grab on to
things. Somehow in the midst of the panic, Angela
fell overboard."

"My God," she whispered.

"They never found her body."

"No." She put a hand to her mouth in horror.

"None of us had a chance to say good-bye."

"Maybe that's why the twins—"

"Even if we had found her body, I wouldn't have let the kids see her like that."

Joanna impulsively touched his arm, wishing she could say something to ease his pain. "I am so sorry."

He stiffened for a moment, then relaxed. "So am I. It was such a waste. And it didn't—it didn't have to happen. I should have been able to prevent it."

"It sounds like an accident."

Joanna dropped her hand from his arm, suddenly realizing how close they were. She took a step back. Michael dug his hands into his pockets.

After a moment Joanna voiced the question she knew she had to ask, especially after Rose's earlier comment. "Are you sure she's—"

"Yeah, I'm sure." The expression in his eyes turned bleak. "Two people saw her fall into the water. Angela wasn't wearing a life jacket. The Coast Guard circled the area for hours. They sent in divers." Michael glanced over his shoulder to see if the girls had returned, but they were still in the back. "She was pretty wasted. She had a weakness for alcohol, among other things, and she wasn't a particularly strong swimmer, especially not in rough water."

"It must have been horrible for you and the girls."

"It was."

"Your wife couldn't have been very old."

"Twenty-six."

Joanna's heart caught. "Younger than me," she murmured. "I can't imagine what you must have gone through. No wonder the girls are so confused." She looked him straight in the eye. "Do I really look like her, Michael?"

"Yes."

She saw the confusion again in his eyes and the lingering traces of sadness that lurked behind his smile. "It's difficult to believe." Joanna paused, feeling like a moth drawn to a flame but unable to resist its allure. She felt drawn not only to Michael and the girls, but to this mysterious Angela who was haunting her life. She needed to put a stop to it. Unfortunately she had a feeling she was going to have to fly close to the flame to do that.

"If you could have seen her . . ." Michael began.

"I want to."

"You do?" Michael looked surprised.

"Is that a problem?"

"No. Of course not. I have lots of pictures of Angela. When—when did you want to see them?"

She could have said next week, next month, next year. Instead she said, "Now."

"Now?" he echoed. "Right now?"

Joanna nodded, suddenly determined to put an end to this ridiculous coincidence. She would see Angela's photograph and point out their differences. There was no way she could look exactly like another person. It was impossible. Once that was done she could go back to treating Michael and the girls like any other family in the school.

"All right. Maybe that's a good idea." Michael turned as the girls walked toward the front of the room, carrying coffee cans filled with clean paintbrushes. "Joanna is coming home—" he said, only to be cut off by the girls' exuberant cries.

"Just to see a picture of your mother," Joanna warned.

"Do you want to see our room, too?" Lily asked as she set the paintbrushes down on the table.

"Okay."

"Do you want to see the backyard?" Rose asked, clapping her hands in delight.

"All right."

"And the treehouse Daddy built for us last year?"

"Yes," Joanna said with a helpless smile, feeling herself wading into quicksand. "I want to see it all." And God help her, she did.

"When I said I wanted to see everything, I didn't mean your father's bedroom," Joanna said as Lily and Rose threw open the door to Michael's room.

Michael put a hand on the small of her back, a polite touch that should not have sent a tingle down her spine. But it did. She was attracted to him. Joanna just hoped to heaven he couldn't see it in her eyes or hear it in her voice. She still remembered the first time she'd told David she loved him, and his less-than-enthusiastic reaction. Now she kept her feelings to herself. It was easier that way, safer.

"I have a photograph of Angela in my bedroom," Michael said. "It's the girls' favorite picture. I think that's why they want you to see it first."

"Oh." He had a picture of his wife in his bedroom. Of course. He probably went to bed thinking of Angela, dreaming about her, wishing she hadn't died.

"This is where you and Daddy used to sleep," Rose said, interrupting her thoughts.

Joanna grew hot at the thought of Michael and herself in the king-size bed with the down comforter and the fluffy pillows. But this was not where she and Michael slept. This was where he had slept with his wife, with Angela.

For a moment Joanna couldn't move. Stepping across the threshold seemed suddenly terrifying. She didn't want to see Angela's picture anymore. She wanted to go home, back to her apartment, to school, to the library, where she could transport herself to another time as far away from Michael Ashton and his adorable children as possible.

But Michael was pushing her forward, urging her

into the room. There was no turning back.

Out of the corner of her eye she saw the portrait hanging on the wall across from the bed. She didn't look at it just yet. Instead she concentrated on the room itself, drawing courage from the normalcy of the decor. She wanted something to combat the eerie feeling, the sense of uneasiness that threatened to overwhelm her.

The room was a poignant mix of male and female. The floral curtains were soft and feminine. The exercise bike in the corner was stainless steel. The old Italian lace doilies on the dresser softened the dark, masculine cherry wood. The bright rainbow-colored pillows eased the hard lines of the antique lounger. There were knickknacks on every available shelf, music boxes and hand-blown glass figures mixed with basketball trophies and an autographed baseball.

Everywhere she turned she saw the contrasts, the hard edges, the soft curves. Man and woman. Michael and his wife. She swallowed hard.

"It's there," Michael said quietly.

Joanna slowly turned to face the picture and felt as if she were looking into a mirror. Her heart stopped.

Angela Ashton had dark brown wavy hair. It was shorter than Joanna's, but Angela had parted it on the same side. Joanna stared at the face, wanting to see the differences, but all she saw was a pair of brown eyes that matched her own, the same full mouth, the same straight nose.

"Oh my God." Joanna felt faint, hot, dizzy. The impossible had suddenly become possible. "She looks just like me," she whispered. "How could this have happened?"

Michael didn't answer, his gaze still fixed on the portrait.

"She could be my sister," Joanna added as she

took another look at the photograph. Angela was smiling, but as Joanna stared into Angela's eyes, it seemed as if the other woman was trying to tell her something—like "Get the hell out of my bedroom" and "Stay away from my husband and children."

For a moment Joanna thought Angela might have spoken the words aloud, so clearly had they rung through her head. "I have to go," she said in panic. "I have to get out of here." She ran from the room, hearing the girls call after her in surprise, hearing Michael tell them to go to their room.

Michael caught up with her at the front door. He slammed his hand against the wood as she tried to open it. "Wait."

"No, let me go. Please, let me go." In truth, she was asking him to do much more than move away from the door.

"I can't let you go." His husky voice told her he understood exactly what she was thinking, what she was feeling.

"This is wrong. I'm not her. I'm not your wife. I'm not the girls' mother. I can't stay here."

"Joanna, calm down." He put his hands on her shoulders to steady her. "No one is forcing you to stay. I just don't want you to drive home while you're so—upset."

Upset? She was terrified—scared to death of a photograph of a woman who'd been dead for a year. How could she tell Michael that? He would think she was losing her mind.

"Oh, God. I'm going crazy." She put a hand to her forehead.

"You're not crazy. Although I admit to being shaken up when I saw you yesterday morning."

She turned to face him. "I don't understand. I know they say everyone has a twin, but I never believed it."

"Maybe you're a distant cousin."

"There is no Italian blood in our family. My ancestors came from Germany and France, Norway and Sweden."

"Maybe it goes back a few generations. Maybe somewhere along the line the blood got mixed."

"I did our genealogy chart. I know where everyone came from. I know what most of them looked like. No one had hair or eyes as dark as mine." Joanna drew in a shaky breath. "I look more like your wife than I look like my parents."

"You do?"

"Yes."

As they stared at each other, a hundred silent questions raced between them. Joanna couldn't keep up with them. Nothing made sense. Her mind leapt from the realistic to the implausible. Maybe her mother had had another daughter and given her away. No, that didn't make sense, because her mother had always said she wanted more children.

Maybe Joanna had been switched at birth with another baby, one who had blond hair and looked more like Edward and Caroline Wingate than she did. Maybe she was really Italian, a distant relation of the De Marcos.

Maybe it was all just an incredible coincidence.

But she didn't believe in coincidences.

"There are differences between you," Michael said. "If you look closely enough."

And damn if he wasn't looking closely, Joanna thought as his face hovered just inches above hers.

"What differences?" she asked with desperation, trying to grab on to anything that made sense.

"Your voice. It's softer. And your build." He put his hand on top of Joanna's head and drew an imaginary line over to himself. She came up to his lips, to his mouth. He could have kissed her forehead if she'd taken a step forward. "Angela was shorter. She only came up to my shoulders. She was wiry and thin, not much flesh on her frame."

As Michael's gaze ran down Joanna's slender body, her full breasts, her long legs, she felt as if he were undressing her, comparing them both in his mind. She couldn't help feeling she would come up short. Her mother was gorgeous and thin. Models were gorgeous and thin. To her, beauty had a somewhat bony look, not her look, definitely not her look.

"What else?" she asked, trying to distract his gaze. It only made him look at her again.

He tipped his head to one side as he considered her question. "Your skin. Angela had dark skin, and her teeth were a little crooked in front."

"Braces. And I never go in the sun. I always worry about skin cancer." She gave a self-deprecating laugh. "I tend to read too much."

"There are two more differences between you. Angela never worried about anything, and her reading didn't extend beyond *Cosmo*." He shook his head at the memories. "She was one of a kind—at least I thought so until yesterday."

"Michael, I—"

"Joanna?" Lily said, interrupting their conversation.

Joanna turned as Lily and Rose came down the stairs, their expressions wary and uncertain.

"Are you okay?" Rose asked, worry etched across her small face.

Joanna took a deep breath. At least they had called her by her own name. Her panic began to subside. "I'm okay."

"Are you really?" Michael asked.

"I think so." Her heart slowed to a steady beat and she could almost think again. "It was just such a shock. No wonder you all thought I was your mother."

Lily and Rose exchanged a long glance.

"But I'm not," Joanna said forcefully.

The girls nodded, but they didn't actually say yes.

Joanna turned to Michael. "They don't believe me, do they?"

"You're asking me what they think?" He threw up his hands. "I have no idea what goes through their heads. Now do you want to see more pictures?"

Look into Angela's face again? Joanna immediately shook her head. "No, I've seen enough."

"You haven't. You just saw Angela's face." Michael took her hand and pulled her into the living room, where there were photos on the mantel of Angela and the girls at various stages of their lives. "Look at these. This is the woman we lived with."

Reluctantly Joanna studied each photo. After a moment she had to admit she could see the differences between them, especially when she saw Angela's build, when she made note of all the details Michael had brought forth earlier.

Besides the physical differences, Angela dressed in bright colors, in tight blue jeans and black leather pants, in bare midriff tops and tight short-shorts. Joanna preferred silky dresses and floral skirts; comfortable, loose-fitting jeans; and one-piece bathing suits.

"See," Michael said. "Not exactly twins."

"Angela has a great smile, and it doesn't really look like mine." Joanna felt a tremendous sense of relief at that realization.

"No, it doesn't."

"I should go," Joanna said, but she didn't move. A moment ago she had wanted to run. Now she felt curiously reluctant to leave.

"Don't you want to stay for a while?" Lily asked, nudging Rose into action.

"Yes, please stay," Rose said.

"Girls, Joanna probably has things to do." Michael checked his watch. "Besides that, I need to drop you off at Grandma's. I have to finish something at work."

"I don't want to go to Grandma's, Rose. Do you?" Lily turned to her sister.

"No, I want to stay here."

"Daddy never lets us do what we want to do."

"I know."

They folded their arms across their chests and glared at their father.

Michael smiled at Joanna. "Ah—another mutiny. If we were on a boat, the girls would have had me walk the plank by now."

Joanna couldn't help but respond to his grin. "So, Captain, what are you going to do with them?"

"Well, I have several options. I could throw them into the dungeon and make them eat broccoli for every meal, or I could—tickle them," he said as he tackled the girls and tickled them until their frowns turned to smiles and their giggles filled the room like a delightful melody.

Joanna watched them with a sense of yearning. There were no words spoken, but there was love. She could see it in the way they played, the way they touched, the way they looked at their father. And why wouldn't they love him? As far as she could tell, he was great, a strong man, a protective and loving father.

"Now go upstairs and get whatever you want to take to Grandma's," Michael said. "But no paint. No Play-Doh and no motorized cars that will crash into any of Grandma's furniture," he added as they scrambled up the stairs.

"You're great with them," Joanna said.

Michael tucked his dress shirt back into his slacks and fixed his tie. "I'm not great. If I was, they'd be talking to me."

"You're too hard on yourself."

"Yeah, maybe."

"I better go and let you get back to work."

"I don't mean to rush you."

"No, you're not. I should check on my mother anyway. My father died a few months ago, and she's having a difficult time adjusting to being in the house alone."

"I'm sorry. I guess we've both lost someone . . ." His voice drifted away and Joanna silently filled in the words *we loved*.

"Michael, would you mind if I took a photo with me to show my mother? I can't help feeling there has to be some logical explanation for my resemblance to your wife."

"Help yourself."

She picked one of the least outrageous poses, wanting her mother to compare the two women rather than the two outfits. "Thanks."

"I'll walk you out."

"I don't want to keep you from your work." She paused. "What do you do?"

"I'm an architect."

"Really?" Joanna asked with interest. As a historian she'd studied a fair amount of architectural history. "Homes or buildings?"

"For the past ten years I've specialized in high-rise office buildings. Skyscrapers."

"Oh." She couldn't help the disappointment in her voice.

"Something wrong with that?" he drawled.

"No, I'm sure the businessmen and women of San Francisco love you."

His eyes narrowed. "As a matter of fact they do. I've just been offered a chance to design a new fifty-story building downtown to replace the Stratton Hotel."

"The Stratton? You're going to tear down the Stratton?" Joanna had celebrated her sixteenth birthday at the Stratton. Her mother had taken her to afternoon tea at the Stratton. It wasn't just a hotel, it was a piece of San Francisco history as well as her own personal history. She couldn't stand the thought of it being gone. Every time she turned around, she seemed to be losing something else. "I can't believe you're going to tear down the Stratton."

Michael shrugged. "It's old."

"So what? You could restore it."

"It's not my call. I don't own the property."

"But you're part of the process," she argued, suddenly incensed that this man who had seemed so perfect was nothing more than a materialistic, greedy businessman who cared nothing for history or tradition. "It's people like you who are destroying our cities."

"It's people like me who bring new beauty to blighted areas."

"So it's out with the old, in with the new. Maybe if you're lucky, when you're old and sick someone will take you out and shoot you instead of trying to nurse you back to health."

"It's not the same thing." He put his hands on his hips and scowled at her.

"It's exactly the same thing."

"What's it to you?"

"I'm a historian. I believe in preserving our heritage, the traditions of our past."

"I thought you were a first grade teacher."

"Only this summer. In the fall I'll finish up my PhD in American history."

He stared at her for a long moment. "I didn't think anybody majored in history any more, much less got a PhD. There's no money in it."

"I'm not in it for the money."

"So you're independently wealthy?"

"I have enough to live on."

He tugged at his tie. "It's easier to have ideals

when you don't need money. But I've got two kids and a mortgage. We all have to make choices. And right now tearing down the Stratton is the least of my worries." He paused. "You know, you really are nothing like Angela."

This time it sounded like a criticism. "Well, if she thought like you do, thank God for that," Joanna snapped. She spun on her heel and stalked to the front door. She hated the fact that Michael got there ahead of her, that he opened it for her like a gentleman, when she really wanted to think of him as a louse.

8

Rose looked out the window, watching her father follow Joanna out to her car. "Joanna is leaving," she said with a sigh. "I wish she'd stayed longer."

Lily crept up on the bed next to her, and they both rested their elbows on the ledge, their chins in their hands. "She's so pretty. Just like Mama."

"You don't think she is Mama, do you?" Rose asked.

"I don't know. I like her long hair."

"Me, too."

"We have to make her stay," Lily said decisively.

"How?"

"Maybe you should pretend to be sick."

"Me? Why don't you do it?"

"Because everyone knows you get sick more than me."

"I do not," Rose said, even though she knew she did. Lily never even got colds.

"Let's ask Mariah what to do," Lily said. She slid off the bed and walked to the desk. She rubbed her hand over the glass ball. The light flashed, the globe sparkled, and Mariah smiled at them. "How can we make Joanna stay with us?" Lily asked.

"Don't be a fool. Don't leave your toys at school."

"Huh?" Rose asked. "What does she mean?"

Lily frowned. Then her eyes lit up. "Peter Panda

102

Bear. You can't find him. You must have left him at
school."

"No, I didn't. I brought him home in my backpack."

"If you left him at school, we would have to go
back and look for him with Daddy—and with
Joanna," Lily said proudly. "Because everyone
knows you can't go to sleep without Peter Panda
Bear."

Rose jumped to her feet, catching on. "Okay. I'll
do it."

"You have to cry really loud." Lily studied her
with a critical eye. "And sniff a lot. Remember, don't
talk to Daddy. Just talk to Joanna."

Joanna unlocked her car door, her hand still shaking from her exchange with Michael. He stood on
the sidewalk watching her, which made her even
more self-conscious. She didn't know why she was
so angry, really. He wasn't single-handedly destroying the city. It was just that he had disappointed her.
She wanted to like him. Or maybe she wanted to
dislike him. Maybe that's why she'd jumped down
his throat. Actually she didn't know what the heck
she wanted.

"I'll bring the picture back tomorrow," she said.

"You can keep it."

"I don't want to keep it."

"Joanna—"

"What?"

He dug his hands in his pockets. "Nothing."

She didn't like the way things were ending between them. But perhaps it was better this way.
"Well, good-bye."

"Good-bye."

Before she could get in the car, the twins came
running out the front door. Lily was yelling something and Rose was crying. Joanna came around the

car, disturbed by Rose's obvious distress.

"What's wrong?" Michael asked. He opened up his arms to Rose, but she ran past him and hurled herself into Joanna's embrace.

"Honey," Joanna said in surprise, "are you all right?"

She looked over the top of Rose's head into Michael's anguished glance. His arms were still outstretched, and she saw the rejection in his eyes, the pain of abandonment. Slowly his hands dropped to his sides as Lily skirted around him, too. Joanna's anger with him faded at the look of disappointment in his face.

"She forgot Peter Panda Bear," Lily said breathlessly to Joanna. "She left him at school."

Rose cried louder at the end of Lily's sentence.

"Oh, dear." Joanna patted Rose on the back. "What should we do?"

"Will the school still be open?" Michael asked.

Joanna checked her watch. It was almost four-thirty. She hadn't realized how long she'd been at Michael's. The other teachers would probably be gone. The summer staff didn't stay past the last bell. "I don't think so," she said.

Rose cried louder.

"It's okay, Rosebud." Michael patted Rose's head with a loving hand, but he looked at Joanna with desperation in his eyes. "She can't sleep without Peter Panda Bear," he whispered. "He's her security blanket."

And Rose needed security after the death of her mother, Joanna realized, her heart going out to the little girl.

"Can we go to school and look for her?" Lily asked.

"Joanna?" Michael asked.

"Yes, of course. Oh, but you were on your way to work. Do you want me to take the girls?"

Rose stopped crying. "I think Daddy should come," she said to Joanna. "Because—"

"Because what, Rosebud?" Michael asked eagerly.

Rose hesitated, then she took his hand and pulled him over to the car. She didn't finish her sentence, but she made it clear she wanted him to come along.

"I guess you're stuck with me for a while longer," he said to Joanna with a crooked smile.

"I guess." God, he was a hard man to dislike. He might tear down old, cherished buildings, but he was willing to put his little girl's bear ahead of his job. Why couldn't he just be black or white, good or bad, instead of a confusing mix of likable arrogance? Not that she'd ever thought those words went together—until now.

"I don't see your panda bear anywhere," Joanna said as Michael and the girls searched the classroom. "Do you remember if you took him out of your cubby during story time?"

Rose stared at her wide-eyed. "I don't remember."

Joanna patted her on the shoulder as Rose's eyes started to well up once again. "It's okay. We'll find him."

She walked to the back of the room, where Michael was restacking the shelves with building blocks and puzzles.

"He's not here," Michael said. "We've looked everywhere."

"I know."

She watched as Rose sat down in the beanbag chair on the floor, covering her eyes with her hands. Lily went over to her and patted her on the head.

Michael sighed as he studied their drooping figures. "Sometimes I think my life is cursed."

"The bear has to be somewhere."

"But where? We've looked in every corner, every desk. I don't see it." He paused. "I know how she feels, too. I used to have a stuffed pig when I was little. His name was Herman."

Joanna bit back a smile. "A stuffed pig?"

Michael grinned. "Yeah. Herman went everywhere with me, and I do mean everywhere. My father took off when I was four, and my mother moved about eighteen times in the next ten years. The only thing that always went with me was Herman."

"Do you still have him?"

He rolled his eyes. "I'm thirty-three years old."

"You didn't answer my question."

A tiny smile curved his mouth. "He might be around somewhere."

"You mean you didn't throw him out when he got old and dirty and lost some of his stuffing?"

He shook his finger at her. "You know, you're like a little terrier dog, your teeth clenched around the corner of a sock, trying to pull it away from its owner even though the sock doesn't belong to you."

"Maybe the owner isn't taking care of his sock."

"Maybe the owner thinks a new sock will be better than a chewed-up old one."

"Joanna?" Lily's voice interrupted them. "Did you lose your sock?"

Michael laughed, then covered it up with a cough.

"No, honey. I didn't lose my sock," Joanna said.

"Oh. Well, I don't think Peter Panda Bear is here," Lily said.

"I'm afraid I don't either."

"Did you take it in the yard, Rosebud?" Michael asked.

Rose shook her head, her bottom lip trembling. Michael went over to her and pulled her into his arms, pressing her head against his chest. "It's okay, sweetie. We'll get you a new bear. It will be okay. You'll see."

Rose shook her head and cried louder. Lily sighed

as she looked at Joanna with eyes as wise as an old lady's. "It wouldn't be the same, you know—a new bear."

"I know," Joanna said, reading far more into Lily's words than the little girl had intended. Michael couldn't replace Rose's bear with a new one. He couldn't design a building that would be as good as the Stratton, and she certainly couldn't take the place of Rose and Lily's mother.

Not that she wanted to, she reminded herself hastily. She wanted her own family, her own love, a man whose eyes lit up solely for her, children who came from her womb, her heart. The ties of blood and flesh were the basis for family. Any other relationship was just a pale imitation of the real thing, and she wanted the real thing, what her parents and grandparents had had.

"We might as well go," Michael said. "It's obvious the bear isn't here."

"I'm sorry," Joanna said.

"It's not your fault."

"I know, but I wish I could help."

Rose slid out of her father's arms and ran to Lily. She whispered something in her sister's ear. After a brief conference Lily stepped back, looking at Joanna.

"Rose thinks some ice cream would make her feel better."

"Ice cream," Joanna echoed. "Really?"

"We always get ice cream when we feel sad."

"Yeah, and we've had a lot of ice cream this year," Michael said. "What do you say, Joanna?"

"It's almost dinnertime."

"Do you have plans?"

"Well, no." Except that she shouldn't even consider spending any more time with them. She was getting too involved, breaking all the rules of a par-

ent-teacher-student relationship. "I thought you had
to work."

"It's not going anywhere. Besides, I'd just be worrying about Rose if I took her to Sophia's now. I
probably wouldn't get much done anyway. There's
an ice cream parlor a couple of blocks away."

"It would make Rose feel better if you went with
us, Joanna." Lily pointed to her sister, who was still
sniffing and wiping her eyes.

"Of course I'll come, if it will make Rose feel better." It was the least Joanna could do, not to mention
the fact that having an ice cream with Michael and
the girls sounded a lot more appealing than going
home to her mother's quiet apartment.

"I think we were had," Michael said a half hour
later as Rose and Lily slipped out of their chairs and
ran to check out a video game in the corner of the
ice cream parlor.

"What do you mean?" Joanna asked, spooning de-
cadent praline pecan ice cream into her mouth. She
should have ordered nonfat vanilla yogurt, as she
did whenever she went out with her mother. In fact,
she'd had every intention of doing just that, until
Michael had ordered a triple scoop of double chocolate fudge and the girls had gotten matching pink
peppermint confections. She had a feeling this trio
could be bad for her diet—among other things.

"I think Peter Panda Bear is residing comfortably
at home," Michael said.

"They made it up?" Joanna raised an eyebrow in
surprise. "Why would they do that?"

"Because I'm their father, and they think you're
their mother, or they'd like you to be." His blue eyes
darkened as he looked into her face.

She swallowed hard, wishing the idea didn't
sound so attractive. "Oh."

"You're lucky it's not Christmas. They'd probably hang mistletoe above our heads."

Lucky? Joanna couldn't help but look at his mouth, at the lips that would close over hers if a mistletoe kiss was required. Abruptly she set down her spoon.

Michael leaned forward, staring at her lips, too. She saw the same unanswered question in his eyes, the same unspeakable, unreasonable desire.

Instead of lowering his head, he touched her lips with one finger. She drew in a quick, sharp breath. Would he really kiss her here in the ice cream parlor, in front of his children?

His finger ran along her lip, then he held it up, exposing a dot of ice cream. He put his finger into his mouth, licking it off, in the most sexually intimate gesture Joanna had seen in a long time. She sat back so abruptly that she knocked her purse and keys onto the floor.

"Joanna."

"It's okay. I can get it."

Michael reached under the table for her keys and set them in front of her. "You feel it, too, don't you?"

"I don't feel anything except extreme embarrassment."

"There's something between us."

"There is something, Michael. Your wife. I'm not her. I can't help you recapture any long-lost love."

"Is that what you think is happening?"

"What else could it be? You don't know me. I don't know you. And frankly I doubt we'd get along all that well."

"You're probably right about that."

"Of course I'm right. You're attracted to me because I look like her."

"That might be true." He paused, offering her a challenging look. "So what's your excuse?"

"I—I don't know what you mean."

"Why are you attracted to me? Do I look like an old boyfriend?"

"God, no. And I'm not attracted to you."

He studied her thoughtfully. "I wish I knew who the hell you were."

"You know who I am. I'm Joanna Wingate, a historian and a teacher. That's it."

"Somehow I think you're a lot more than that."

"Don't be silly. I am the least mysterious person I know."

He smiled. "That's funny. Because you are the most mysterious person I've ever met."

Caroline Wingate stared at the manila envelope she had tried desperately to forget. It had first appeared in her life almost twenty-nine years earlier, shortly after Joanna's birth. She had asked Edward about it, but he'd simply smiled and told her not to worry, the way he'd always done. In the crazy days of taking care of a newborn, she had forgotten about it.

As the years passed she'd seen him take it out now and then and slip an envelope inside, an envelope that always arrived at their house addressed to him with no return address, something else they'd never spoken about.

Part of her had hoped that he'd thrown away the letters, that the envelope didn't exist anymore. But Edward had never thrown anything away. Thank God, she hadn't let Joanna go through his things.

She would burn it, Caroline decided. Unopened. She had never felt a need to look through the contents before, and she certainly didn't now.

With a strength and a sense of purpose she hadn't felt in months, she opened the desk drawers one after the other, searching for the gold engraved lighter that Edward had used to light his cigars.

She found it in the bottom drawer. His initials

caught at her heart. "Oh, Edward. I did love you,"
she said softly, wrapping her fingers around the cool
metal. "I know you'll understand why I have to do
this."

Still Caroline hesitated. Would he understand?
Would Joanna understand? Would the letters be important someday? It didn't matter what they said.
She would do anything to protect her family. Joanna
was all she had left.

Her parents had died years ago. Her older brother,
ten years her senior, had moved to Alaska as a
twenty-year-old, and aside from an occasional postcard, she rarely heard from him. She couldn't
remember the last time they'd spoken. When she'd
written to him about Edward's death, he hadn't replied. Perhaps he was dead, too.

An overwhelming depression filled her at the
thought. Every time she turned around, she was confronted with mortality. Several of Edward's friends
and business associates had died in the last year,
reminding her of her own age, her own tenuous hold
on life. But she didn't feel old at sixty-two. Sometimes she still felt as foolish and uncertain as she had
at twenty—like today, like this moment.

She took a deep breath as she stared at the manila
envelope. What good could come of it now? Certainly no good for her. And no good for Joanna. Getting rid of it was the right thing to do. She flicked
the lighter on and watched the flame erupt.

Before she could put the flame to the envelope,
the front door slammed and Joanna's voice rang
through the apartment. Caroline dropped the lighter
on the desktop and shoved the manila envelope to
one side as Joanna opened the door to the den.

"Mom." Joanna stopped abruptly at the sight of
her mother sitting in Edward's chair. "Goodness. I
didn't really expect to see you in here. You're going
through Dad's things?"

"Yes. Slowly."

"Are you all right?"

"Of course. They're just things, papers and books and old bills. You were right. I should have done this a long time ago. I don't know why I didn't."

"It was too soon." Joanna paused, acutely aware of the photograph clutched in her hand. She'd driven home with it on the seat next to her. At every stoplight she'd taken another look, wanting to believe that somehow the photograph would have changed and she would no longer look like a woman she'd never met.

Caroline stood up and walked around the desk. "Are you hungry, Joanna? Do you want to go out for dinner?"

"No. I'm not hungry. I want to show you something."

"What is it?"

Joanna handed the photograph to Caroline.

"It's a picture of you?"

"What do you think?"

"I—I've never seen you wear that outfit before, and your hair is different, and you seem . . ." Caroline looked at Joanna, her eyes troubled. "It's not you at all. The nose isn't the same, or the teeth, and the skin is much darker. Who is this girl?"

"Angela Ashton. The mother of the children I told you about yesterday."

"Really?" Caroline's hand trembled. The photograph slipped out of her fingers and fell to the ground.

Joanna sent her mother a thoughtful look, then retrieved the photograph from the floor. "It's amazing, isn't it? We could be sisters."

"You're not."

"No. But it's strange to think that Angela grew up in San Francisco just on the other side of town, and we never ran into each other."

"How do you know so much about her?" Caroline asked.

"Michael told me."

"Michael?"

"Her husband. His children are students in my class. Remember?"

"Yes, of course." Caroline's fingers splayed across her heart as if she were in pain.

"Are you all right, Mom?"

"Tell me more about this girl."

"Angela was only a few years younger than me," Joanna said. "Her maiden name was De Marco. As I was driving home I thought about those times when people I didn't remember came up and said, 'Hi, how are you?' and I felt silly for not remembering them. Maybe I never knew them. Maybe they thought I was Angela. Maybe some people thought Angela was me. It's so odd."

"Didn't you say she died last year?" Caroline leaned against the edge of the desk, bracing her hands on either side of her.

"Yes, she died in a boating accident. She left behind two adorable twin girls, Lily and Rose. They're only six years old. And Michael is in his early thirties. It's so sad." Joanna paused, knowing her mother valued family above all else. "I feel so lucky to have had Dad for as long as we did."

Tears filled Caroline's eyes. "Yes, we were lucky."

"I'm sorry, I didn't mean to make you cry."

"We were very, very lucky," Caroline repeated in a whisper. "I used to tell myself that almost every day. At least in the beginning. Then sometimes I'd forget, and days would go by and I wouldn't tell Edward I loved him, and I'd forget to tell you. Now Edward's gone."

"But he knew. He always knew."

"And you?"

"Of course," Joanna said with a reassuring smile.

"I know you love me, and I love you." Silence fell between them as they each pursued their own thoughts.

Finally, Joanna spoke. "How do you think this came to be—this resemblance between me and another woman? Just bizarre coincidence?"

"What else could it be?" Caroline walked around the desk and sat down in Edward's chair. She'd never sat there before, not as far as Joanna could remember. It had always been her father's chair. If her mother used the room at all, which was rare, she sat on the couch. Now Caroline seemed to need the support of the large mahogany desk.

"Maybe somewhere in the family tree somebody's baby got switched, or maybe someone gave up their child for adoption," Joanna suggested.

"Don't be ridiculous. That kind of thing only happens in movies. Besides, you charted the family tree years ago."

"I know I did. Someone must have lied. There has to be an explanation."

"It's a coincidence, just as you said," Caroline replied, her voice stronger now, as if she had summed up the situation and dismissed it as being of no importance. Caroline often did that with topics that she didn't want to discuss. Joanna usually gave in and dropped the subject, but she couldn't this time.

"You always said you wanted more children. Why didn't you ever have any?" Joanna asked.

Her mother avoided her gaze. "It wasn't meant to be."

"So you tried?"

"Yes, we tried."

"But you never got pregnant again after me?"

"What are you suggesting?"

"Nothing." Joanna knew she should quit. Her mother was getting annoyed. But a need to make logical sense out of the situation drove her on. "Was my hair always this dark?"

"You had a full head of hair even as an infant."

"What about my eyes—were they always brown?"

"Yes. Why? Do you think you suddenly changed after a few hours?"

"No, but—" Joanna perched on the edge of the desk. "Didn't you ever wonder how you had such a dark child when you and Dad are both so blond?"

"Why would I wonder?" Her mother's voice rang through the room, sharp and clear. "We knew you were our child. There was no mistake."

Joanna hesitated to ask the next question, but she knew she had to. "Are you sure there was no mistake? Are you sure you came home with the right baby?"

"How can you ask me that? Do you think we would let our child go to someone else?"

"No. It's just that—"

"It's just nothing—nothing but a coincidence," Caroline said firmly. "Everyone in the world has a double. You just found yours. But she's dead. You're never going to meet her or talk to her or know what she was like. Forget about it, Joanna."

Joanna didn't understand the coldness in her mother's voice, the cavalier way she spoke of the other woman's death. Her mother had always been a compassionate woman, but not now, not today, not about this.

"Yes, she is dead, but she left behind two darling children who seem to think I'm her."

"You're not."

"I know that," Joanna cried in frustration. "But it would be easier if I could explain why I look so much like their mother."

"You can't. There are some things that can't be explained. You have to accept it, and so do they."

"I'm not sure they can. Hell, I'm not sure *I* can."

"Don't swear, Joanna."

"I don't understand why you don't care about these children."

"I'm empty, Joanna. The only person I care about is you. I don't see any advantage to you developing a relationship with these children or with their father. You're not their mother. You're not his wife."

"I feel as if they need me."

"They don't need you. They need *her*."

Caroline's words hit her in the face like a splash of cold water. Joanna wanted to argue, but how could she? Her mother was absolutely right. She hated when that happened.

Caroline picked up some papers from the desk and looked through them, ending the discussion.

"Do you want some help in here?" Joanna asked.

"No. I'll do it."

"Are you sure? Most of this stuff looks pretty old. It's probably just junk." Joanna reached for a manila envelope that had been pushed to the side of the desk.

Caroline's hand came down on top of hers. "I said I'd do it."

Joanna stared into her mother's eyes and saw determination, anger, and something that looked like fear. "What's wrong?"

"Nothing. Why don't you relax? You worked hard all day. I'm sure you could use a break." Caroline patted Joanna's hand where it rested on top of the manila envelope.

Her words were casual, but Joanna had a feeling that if she dared to pick up the envelope, her mother might rip it out of her hand.

"You're hiding something, aren't you?"

"No. These are your father's things. I'm his wife. They don't concern you. I'd like to be alone, Joanna."

It was the first time in years Joanna had heard Caroline request to be alone. "Fine, I'll get dinner started." She walked to the door and paused, still disturbed by her mother's behavior. "I thought we were so close, Mother. I didn't think we had any secrets from each other."

"We don't."

"You're a terrible liar," Joanna said as she left the room.

Alone in the den, Caroline took several deep, steadying breaths. She wasn't a bad liar. She was a very good one, and she'd had years of practice.

She placed a piece of newspaper on top of the desk, picked up the lighter, and ignited the flame. Holding it to the edge of the envelope, she let it burn. As the ashes fell onto the newspaper, their heat was put out by the teardrops that streamed down her face, landing on the newspaper like blots on a ledger. She had to do this. She had to protect what was hers.

When there was nothing left but a pile of black dust, she set the lighter down on the desk with a shaky hand. She stared at the ashes for a long time. They reminded her of Edward's ashes, of the urn they had buried just two short months ago.

Finally she picked up the newspaper and dumped everything in the garbage. Then she reached for the telephone and dialed the number for Grant Sullivan, her former employer and Edward's long-time friend and attorney. She had to know if there was anything else that needed to be burned.

9

Joanna glanced at the clock. It was past midnight, and she was no closer to sleep now than she had been two hours earlier when she had crept into bed. She kept thinking about Angela, about Michael, about the girls, wondering where she fit in, how she fit in.

Her mother had brushed aside her concern, telling her to forget about it, but she couldn't forget. Something niggled at the back of her mind. After a moment she slipped out of bed and turned on the light.

Her room was a happy, messy mix of her childhood, adolescence, and adult years. The desk and dresser were white with gold trim, as seen in so many little girls' bedrooms. Her old aquarium sat empty on top of the bookshelf, reminding her that the only pet she'd ever been allowed to have was a goldfish named Harry, whose death she'd mourned with great passion.

She smiled to herself at the memories. Her bedroom was the only room in the apartment that boasted live plants, two hanging ferns and a ficus tree in the corner that was ridiculously large for a bedroom. But if she put it in the living room, her mother would probably kill it with too much watering and too much attention.

Her bedroom was also the only room in the apartment that wasn't spotlessly clean, because she liked clutter. She liked things, mementos, reminders of her past. She still had her first corsage from the junior prom, her graduation tassels, the Popsicle stick bridge she'd made in second grade. Like her father, she hated to throw anything away.

Her father. That reminded her. She walked over to the bookcase and pulled out one of her scrapbooks. Her father had always taken lots of pictures— of her first steps, her first food fight, her first swing, every dance recital, every winter concert, cheerleading tryouts, high school graduation.

There were so many memories in the pages that unfolded before her. Seeing her father so alive, so vibrant, reminded her of his death. She would never see him again, never hear his big barrel laugh, never crinkle up her nose at the smell of his cigar. Her eyes blurred with tears as she thought about the future ahead. He would never walk her down the aisle and never hold her baby in his arms. She would live so many years without him.

Oh, how she wished she could talk to him right now. Ask him how she could look so much like a stranger. Find out what he had hidden in his den that her mother didn't want her to see.

With a sigh she closed the scrapbook. She didn't know what she had hoped to find, but there was nothing there, no clues. There certainly hadn't been any sign of a pregnancy before or after her. Her mother had always been as thin as a rake.

Her mind stopped. Her heart quickened. Pregnancy photos. There were none.

The three words screamed at her again. There were none—no photos of her mother pregnant, not with another child and not with her.

Her pulse began to race as her mind dealt with the unthinkable.

"Calm down," she whispered aloud. Those photos

were probably in another album. Her mother kept scrapbooks in the den with photos of her family and her early days with Edward. They had to be there. She opened the door and glanced down the hall at her mother's bedroom. The door was shut, but that didn't mean Caroline was asleep. Lately she tended to sleep in the family room on the sofa, or the easy chair in the living room, anywhere to get away from her memories.

A quick glance in the living room and family room revealed nothing, so Joanna quietly opened the door to the den. After her mother's strong reaction earlier, she almost felt like an intruder, a thief in the night. But she wasn't here to steal anything, except perhaps some peace of mind.

She checked the bookshelves first. They were crammed with fishing magazines and books about real estate and brokering. Finally she spied two large, red bound books in the corner. Standing on tiptoe, she pulled them off the shelf and sat on the sofa.

The first book was a pictorial of Caroline's childhood, her older brother, her parents, none of whom Joanna could remember except in this way, as photos in a scrapbook.

The next book began with Edward and Caroline on their honeymoon in Hawaii. She smiled at how young and in love they looked, so adoring toward each other, her father with his arm around her mother's shoulders, her mother practically blooming in his arms.

The photograph reassured her that everything was right in her world. The camera didn't lie. Her parents had loved each other, just as they had loved her. There were no hidden secrets. It was simply her imagination. But as the pages turned, she began to notice blank spots, and fewer photos in between holiday occasions. The book ended with a picture of herself in a baby gown.

There were no pictures of her mother pregnant. No photos of them leaving for the hospital. Nothing.

Joanna tried desperately to remember the stories they had told. Surely they had talked about her mother's pregnancy, the labor and delivery. Hadn't they? She shook her head, feeling incredibly tired.

This was pointless. What was she thinking anyway? She was the daughter of Edward and Caroline Wingate, and it was just a crazy coincidence that she happened to look like Angela Ashton.

She closed the book and set it back on the shelf. As she walked by the desk, the lingering scent of smoke filled her senses, almost as if her father were standing in the room with her, smoking his cigar. But it didn't really smell like his cigars; it smelled like the lingering trace of a fire in the fireplace. But the fireplace was stone cold. She glanced over at the desk and saw a layer of thin black dust.

She cast a quick glance toward the door. It was closed. With a feeling of incredible dread, she walked over to the desk and ran her finger through the dust. Then she pulled the wastebasket out from under the desk. Inside was a pile of newspapers and black ashes. Her mother had burned something.

Joanna looked for the manila envelope she'd seen earlier. It was gone from the desk.

Joanna sank down in the chair, staring at the ashes. What on earth was her mother hiding?

The next morning Caroline strolled into the offices of Grant Sullivan, attorney at law, her handbag clutched in front of her like a shield. In terse tones she gave her name to the receptionist. She didn't want to be here, but she had no choice. Since she had seen the photo of Angela Ashton, she had been struck with terror, the same terror she'd felt when

Edward had been diagnosed with cancer and she
knew it would only be a matter of months before
she lost him. She could not lose Joanna—not now.

"He's just finishing a phone call, Mrs. Wingate,"
the receptionist said. "Would you like some coffee
while you wait?"

"No, thank you."

Caroline sat down on the white leather couch. As
she looked around the plush offices, she was struck
by how far Grant Sullivan had come. She had
worked as his receptionist thirty-six years earlier. In
those days he'd offered her a typewriter and a
scratched desk. Now his reception area was filled
with plush chairs, glass tables, ornate vases, and silk
flowers.

Grant had certainly done well for himself. Although she'd socialized with him over the years,
only he and Edward had conducted actual business,
so she hadn't really been aware of his success. Now
Caroline felt a burst of renewed confidence. Grant
was a smart man. He would know what to do.

"He'll see you now," the receptionist said.

Caroline stood up and walked into the inner office. Grant stepped out from around his large desk.
He was a rather short man, not many inches taller
than herself, with golden blond hair, the color of
which surely came out of a bottle; sparkling green
eyes; and a deep tan.

"Caroline, it's good to see you."

"Thanks for letting me barge in on you like this."

"I'm always available for you. Have a seat."

Caroline sat down in the chair in front of his desk,
nervous about what she should say. She didn't know
how much Grant knew. What if he didn't know anything? What if by telling him, she was jeopardizing
the very secret she wanted to protect?

"How have you been?" Grant asked, resuming his

seat. "I didn't get to talk to you much after the service. The house was so crowded."

"Edward had a lot of friends. It was nice to see so many people there."

"He was a great guy, right down to the end. I've never seen such courage. He had a lot of heart."

"Yes." Caroline hesitated. She hadn't come here to reminisce about a man they had both loved. She had come here for answers, and she wouldn't leave without them.

"How's Joanna?" Grant asked, distracting her again.

"Keeping busy. She's teaching first grade this summer."

"No kidding? I thought she was Ivy League all the way."

"It's just to fill in the time, take her mind off things. She'll go back to Stanford in the fall." Caroline wondered how long they would have to exchange pleasantries before she could tell him why she was here.

"I still can't believe Edward is gone. So fast," Grant added. "We were the same age, you know. And he was always in such great shape, except for the cigars, of course."

"He couldn't give those up."

Grant smiled encouragingly at Caroline. "What can I do for you? Do you have questions about the trust, the will, investments?" He sat back in his chair and waited for her answer.

"No. You explained all that to me after he died." She glanced over at his locked filing cabinets, wondering if the information she feared was there, wondering if he would give it to her.

"Caroline? What's wrong?"

She met his concerned eyes. "I wondered if Edward ever spoke to you about—about an arrangement that he made many years ago involving Joanna."

Grant's smile faded. "Why do you ask?"

"Because Joanna recently met someone. Apparently she looks like this man's wife. I saw a photograph, and the woman could have been Joanna's sister. I mean, if Joanna had a sister, which of course she doesn't."

Grant picked up a pen on his desk and twirled it between his fingers. He was silent for a long moment, then he looked at her through somber eyes. "Do you know the name of this woman?"

"I believe her name was Angela Ashton. But that would be her married name. I think Joanna said her maiden name was De Marco."

"De Marco. I see. Has Joanna met this Angela?"

"No. Angela is dead."

"Really?" He looked somewhat relieved.

"Yes, she died a year ago."

"If she's dead then it doesn't matter that Joanna looks like her, does it?"

Caroline scooted to the edge of her seat. "She's dead, but she has children, and a husband, and presumably a mother and a father."

Grant's expression wavered slightly. "That's true. What does Joanna think?"

"She has a lot of questions and a vivid imagination. You know how she is, Grant. She's a digger. She loves to sink her teeth into a good mystery and dig, dig, dig until she finds out what really happened. That's why she's such a good historian. She never accepts anything at face value." Caroline paused. "She asked me if we gave up a child after her. Apparently this woman is or was a couple of years younger than her."

"I'm sure you told her that was ridiculous."

"Of course, but she's worrying about it, Grant. I don't know what to do. Edward would have known.

But he's not here," she said with a growing sense of panic. "What I want to know—what I need to know—is if she starts digging, is she going to find out anything?"

Grant tossed the pen down on the desk. "For your sake, Caroline, I hope not."

"You know, don't you?" Caroline said pointedly.

Grant sat back in his chair and folded his arms across his chest. "Edward asked me for advice. He didn't take it."

"What was your advice?" Caroline changed her mind as soon as she asked the question. "Never mind, I don't want to know. I need your help, Grant. I need you to help me protect Edward's secret. You will, won't you?"

"Edward was my best friend."

"Is that a yes?"

"What exactly are you asking me to do, Caroline?"

"I want to know if there is anything in writing."

"I believe everything was in Edward's possession. I have no idea what he did with it."

Caroline let out a breath of relief. It must have all been in the manila envelope, and that was gone now. "That's okay then. I've taken care of that. I wasn't sure if you had any copies."

"No. Quite frankly, I didn't want any."

"Good. I won't take up any more of your time then. Thank you, Grant. I appreciate your help."

She reached out to shake his hand. Grant took her hand, but didn't let it go. His eyes became intensely serious. "There were always two sides to this secret, Caroline. You may be able to control one, but I'm not so sure about the other."

"But there are privacy laws."

"They don't always work. It depends on how badly someone wants to invade your privacy, how much they want what you have. And the way Edward did things—well, let's just say that the law is not on your side."

"I won't let anyone take Joanna away from me. Never."

"The decision may not be yours to make."

"Who else would make it?" Caroline asked, prepared to scoff at his suggestion.

"Joanna."

Her confidence fled with that one word. Joanna. Her daughter who loved history, who had always wanted to know who her ancestors were, where they came from, what they did for a living. Joanna. Somehow or other Caroline had to get Joanna away from the Ashtons.

"Today we're going to talk about who we are," Joanna said to the children, who were sitting at their tables, tired from recess, full from lunch, and for the moment blessedly quiet. "On the piece of paper in front of you, I want you to draw me a picture of your family."

Jeremy Tyler raised his hand. "Do I have to draw my sister? I hate her."

The kids laughed. Joanna sent him a scolding look. "She's part of your family, so you have to include her."

"Oh, man."

"You can also include your grandparents if you want," Joanna added. "And tonight I want you to go home and ask your parents where your ancestors came from."

Billy Dutton interrupted. "You mean like if they were from Mars? Because I think my brother is an alien."

"Your brother is not an alien, and your family is not from Mars." Joanna tried to hide a smile. She loved these kids with their crazy ideas and their wide-open minds, so eager to learn about everything in their world, even if it meant aliens descending from a distant planet. "Tomorrow, when you come into school, we'll look at the globe and figure out where all of our ancestors came from. We might find out that some of us were related hundreds of years ago."

As she said the words Joanna couldn't help looking at Rose and Lily. They stared straight back at her, as if they still believed she was their mother. Maybe she was something to them, something distant and in the past, a fifth cousin. At least then it would make sense.

"Okay, start on your pictures," she said. "We only have a few minutes before the bell rings."

Nora Garvey stopped in the doorway, motioning to Joanna to come over.

"What's up?" Joanna asked.

"I can't make aerobics tonight. My mother-in-law is in the hospital."

"I hope it's not serious."

"She had a minor heart attack, but I think she'll be all right."

"Thank goodness."

"By the way, your mother called earlier. I took a message."

"Thank you."

"Is she okay with this job?"

"Not really. But she's distracted with something else at the moment." Joanna glanced over at the children, who were involved in their pictures. She stepped into the hall, just outside the door, so they couldn't be overheard. "My mother started going through my dad's things, and she practically jumped out of her skin when I tried to help."

"Why?"

"I have no idea, but she did not want me to look in one of the envelopes on the desk. And get this—

last night I found no envelope, only ashes in the wastebasket."

Nora's eyes widened. "How strange. What do you think was in the envelope?"

"Beats me. I never considered the fact that there might be a side to my parents' marriage that I didn't know about."

"You think your father was having an affair?"

"Maybe. What else would be so personal that she would hide it from me? We've always been close."

Nora shrugged. "Heck if I know. By the way, how are the Ashton twins doing? Still calling you Mama?"

"Yes, and that's another thing. Not only do I find out that my father had some big secret, I also discover that all these years I had a double living on the other side of town." Joanna paused at the sudden look in Nora's eyes. "What?"

"Maybe they're connected, Joanna."

"In what possible way?"

"Maybe your father wasn't your real father. Maybe your mother had an affair—with an Italian guy."

An affair? Joanna hadn't considered that angle. Could her father have been someone other than Edward Wingate? The thought hurt deeply. Surely he wouldn't have lied to her all these years. They had spent so much time talking in the last few weeks of his life. He would have said something if there was anything to be said.

"Joanna, the kids are starting to wander," Nora said.

"I better get back."

"What do you have them working on?"

"Family pictures."

Nora raised an eyebrow. "Am I spotting a theme here?"

"I think children should understand where they

come from, their roots." Joanna smiled at Nora's skeptical expression. "Okay, I'm a little obsessed at the moment with family ties."

"Joanna, even if your mother or father turned out to be someone different, you'd still be you."

As Nora walked away Joanna thought about her words. *You'd still be you.* But would she? Or would she become someone else?

Michael glanced at his watch. Damn. He better move if he wanted to pick up the girls on time.

Helen buzzed him on the intercom. He reached for the receiver. "Yes?"

"Sophia is on line one. Are you still incommunicado?"

"Only to Gary Connaught."

Helen laughed. "Jackson has been wearing down the carpet out here. He's expecting you to emerge with complete schematic drawings."

Michael groaned. "Thanks for the warning." He punched the button on the phone. "Hi, Sophia."

"Michael, hello." She sounded a bit nervous.

"Is something wrong?"

"No. No." She added a laugh, but it didn't sound quite sincere. "I was just thinking about how hard you're working and how difficult it must be taking off at three o'clock to get the girls, when I'm really not that busy. I thought maybe I could pick them up for you."

"Sure. That would be great." Then he remembered. "Uh, Sophia. Maybe that's not a good idea."

There was silence on her end of the phone. Then Sophia spoke. "I'll be fine."

"You haven't seen her."

"I want to."

So that was the reason behind her unexpected offer. Michael hesitated. "I do have some work to finish."

"Then I'll pick up the girls and we'll spend the afternoon together. We'll have dinner at the restaurant. They can help Vincent and Louis in the kitchen. Just come whenever; it doesn't matter how late. I can even take the girls home and put them to bed if you have something else to do."

"Thanks, Sophia. You're incredibly generous, as always."

"Don't work too hard, Michael. I worry about you, you know."

He did know. She worried about him more than his own mother. "I appreciate the concern, Sophia, but I'm fine."

"You're trying to do too much. I want to help you more."

"Well, picking up the girls is a big help."

Michael hung up the phone with mixed feelings. Although he appreciated Sophia's offer he wasn't sure he wanted Sophia to meet Joanna. Maybe he should take the kids out of that school after all and try to forget he'd ever met Joanna. What was the point in getting to know her, in seeing her every day? She wasn't Angela. She wasn't the girls' mother, and she never would be.

Angie would have hated seeing Joanna. She'd always prided herself on being unique, different from other women. She'd dressed to stand out from the crowd, not to be part of it. She wouldn't have liked knowing she had a double.

He still had a difficult time believing it was all just a coincidence. But what more could it be?

"Michael?" Helen opened the door to his office, holding a bouquet of red and white roses mixed with baby's breath. "I wanted to thank you for the flowers. They're lovely."

He sent her a blank look. "I'm glad you like them, but I didn't send them."

Her smile faded. "I called Joey, and he didn't send them. I just assumed."

"Looks like you have a secret admirer."

Helen stared down at the flowers. Then she walked over to the wastebasket by Michael's desk and dumped them in the can.

"You don't like roses?" Michael asked.

"I don't like Tony."

"Tony? Why would you think they're from him?"

"Because he doesn't take no for an answer. He's a spoiled, immature guy who thinks he should get whatever he wants. But he can't get me anymore. Not with roses or chocolates or anything." Although her words were bursting with confidence, they ended on a sobbing note, and suddenly Helen sank into the chair in front of Michael's desk and began to cry.

Michael stared at her in bewilderment. He seemed to be surrounded by crazy females these days. He didn't think he would understand women if he lived to be 100. "Uh, Helen." He pulled a tissue out of his desk drawer and tossed it across the desk. "Here."

Helen wiped her eyes. "I'm sorry." She sniffed. "I just don't need this right now."

"Need what?"

"Tony. I wish he hadn't come back."

"I'm sure he won't stay long." Michael wanted to comfort her, but his words had the opposite effect.

"I'm sure he won't," she replied with bitterness and anger. "God forbid he should stay in one city with one woman."

"That's just Tony, Helen. You can't change him into somebody else, no matter how hard you try."

"I know that. But I've loved him for so long, since the seventh grade."

"Really?" Michael was a bit surprised. Although Helen and Tony had dated off and on for years, they'd never seemed passionately in love, more

friends than anything. But he knew they'd been lov-
ers, and in the months before Tony left, they'd spent
lots of time together. Still, he'd never been able to
see them together forever. Of course, he'd never
been able to see Tony with anyone on a long-term
basis. Commitment was not something Tony did
well.

"When Tony left I thought I would die, it hurt so
bad," Helen continued. "We'd gotten so close. I
thought he was on the verge of proposing, not leaving."

"I know it hurt, but you found someone else, Helen. Someone who can give you what you need."

"Yes, and Joey is a great guy. He's solid and loving and he wants a family just like I do, and a house
and a dog and the whole thing. But—"

"But?"

"He's not Tony," she said in anguish. "What if I'm
making a mistake? What if I'm marrying the wrong
guy just so I can be married?"

Michael didn't know what to say. Hadn't he done
the same thing by marrying Angela when she was
barely out of high school, when he was still in his
twenties and didn't know a damn thing about life?
But he had wanted a family. He had wanted what
Sophia and Vincent De Marco had, a loving relationship, a commitment, children. He had wanted
forever. He'd gotten eight years and a hell of a lot
of pain along the way.

As Michael studied Helen's face—the torment in
her eyes, the streaks of tears across her cheeks—he
wondered if she *was* making a mistake. If Tony
could affect her like this, how much did she love
Joey?

"You think I'm terrible, don't you?" Helen said.

"I don't think you're terrible. I think you're confused."

"I want to do the right thing."

"You will."

"I wish I had your confidence. And I wish to hell I wasn't attracted to the absolutely wrong person in the world for me."

Michael nodded. He felt exactly the same way.

10

Sophia paused in front of the sign that read Happy Hollow School. In a few moments she would go inside. She wished her sister Elena had come with her, but Elena had told her to forget what she had heard. That nothing good could come from seeing this woman. They were all happy now, Elena and her husband, Charles, Sophia and Vincent. What was the point? The bad years were behind them. Never to be remembered.

But there *was* a point. And Sophia knew exactly what it was. She just didn't know if she had the right to make that point. She certainly wasn't the only person involved.

The longer she hesitated, the more doubts flooded her mind. Maybe Elena and Vincent were right. It was none of her business. This woman, who looked like Angela, was nothing to her. Still, Sophia wanted to see her.

She was consumed with curiosity. She wanted to know what the woman looked like, hear her voice, watch her mannerisms. She wanted to know if there was any possibility De Marco blood ran through her veins.

There was so much at stake. Marriage. Family. Reputation. Honor. The foundation of their lives. They weren't young anymore, none of them, not

Vincent or her sister Elena or herself. They couldn't start over.

Just being here was a risk.

Part of her wanted to run away, but another part of her knew she had to go forward. How could she not see this woman who looked so much like Angela? How could she turn away?

The answer was simple. She couldn't.

"Joanna, you have a phone call in the lounge," Nora said. "My class is gone, so I can watch your last few stragglers."

"All right. It's just the twins."

"Aren't you going to say hello to Daddy?" Rose asked.

"I have a phone call, honey," Joanna said, secretly relieved that she might actually miss seeing Michael. She'd thought about him all night and all day. In fact, she couldn't get him out of her mind, and it wasn't healthy. She needed some answers, something to put an end to the mystery. That's why she had made a few calls during her lunch break. She hoped one of them was calling back.

"Are you mad at Daddy again, Mama? Are you going to go see that other man with the black mustache?" Rose pressed on, her brown eyes filled with worry. "I don't like him. He has scary eyes. Please don't go there again."

Joanna glanced at Nora, who sent her a compassionate look.

"Rose, honey, I'm not your mother. I'm Joanna, and I'm just going into the teachers' lounge to take a phone call."

"Why don't you two show me what you did today?" Nora said, drawing their attention away from Joanna.

Joanna hurriedly left the room before any more protests could form. In the lounge she sat down on the couch, slipped off her hoop earring, and picked up the phone.

"Hello," she said.

"Joanna Wingate?"

"Yes."

"This is Pamela Cogswell. I believe you called me earlier."

"Yes, I did," Joanna said. "You might not remember me, but I'm hoping you remember my mother."

"Of course I do, dear. Goodness, Caroline and Edward lived next door to us for eight years. That was before you were born, of course, and before they moved to San Francisco. How are your parents?"

"My mother is fine. My father passed away a few months ago."

"Oh, I'm sorry. I guess we all lost touch, didn't we? How can I help you, Joanna?"

Joanna hesitated, knowing she was about to take a step that she might never be able to retrace. Her mother wouldn't forgive her for calling Pamela, regardless of the answer. Family matters were always private with Caroline. She never allowed herself to be exposed in any way. But Joanna knew she couldn't simply pretend that Angela De Marco had never existed, not with the twins sitting in her classroom each morning, not with Michael's image taking up permanent residence in her mind.

"Joanna?" Pamela repeated.

"Yes, I was wondering if you remember when my mother first became pregnant with me."

There was a long silence on the other end of the phone. "What an odd question," Pamela said. "Why on earth would you ask me that?"

Joanna couldn't possibly give her the real reason. "I'm redoing our family albums, putting all the photos in order, and for some reason I can't find any photos of when my mother was pregnant. Since she said the two of you were very close, I was hoping that perhaps you might have one from a party or something." Joanna held her breath, knowing it was a lame excuse at best.

"No, I don't think so," Pamela said, her voice chilly. "Frankly I didn't see your mother all that much in the few months before she and Edward moved to San Francisco. I didn't even know they were thinking of moving. It came as quite a surprise. And they took off so suddenly. The For Sale sign went up one day, and the next day they were gone."

"Really?"

"Yes. Your mother was unhappy for a long time, I think. We all had children and she didn't. We tended to talk about our kids, their schools, their sports programs. We didn't mean to leave your mother out, but sometimes I think she felt that way. Those were different times, you know. Women didn't have as many options as they do now."

"No, I don't suppose they did," Joanna murmured, Pamela's words only reinforced the uneasy feeling in her stomach. *Her mother had felt left out. She'd been trying to have a baby. She'd been feeling desperate.*

"Anyway, a few months after your parents moved," Pamela continued, "I got a baby announcement, so I guess everything worked out in the end. We exchanged Christmas cards for a while, but neither your mother nor I were ever particularly good correspondents."

"So you never actually saw my mother pregnant?"

"No, but she was always so thin. She was probably months along before she showed."

"Probably."

"She must have been pregnant before she left. I think you were born just three or four months after they moved. I'm sorry I couldn't help you, Joanna. Say hello to your mother for me, won't you?"

"Of course," Joanna replied. As she hung up the phone, she knew she had absolutely no intention of telling Caroline anything about this phone call.

It didn't make sense. Her mother said she had moved to the city just a few weeks before Joanna was born. She had to have been pregnant when she lived next door to Pamela Cogswell.

Unless Caroline had never been pregnant. Unless she'd gotten her baby some other way.

Goose bumps ran down Joanna's arms. Her pretty, petite blond mother was turning into a stranger in her mind. And her father with his jovial smile, his twinkling eyes, his tender words. Had it all been a lie? A farce? Was she really their child? And if Caroline wasn't her mother, who was?

Sophia dawdled as long as she could, but the redheaded teacher named Nora seemed eager to usher her out the door. "I was hoping to meet their teacher," Sophia said.

"Joanna's on the phone," Nora replied. "I don't know how long she'll be."

"Could I wait?"

"Maybe you could speak to her tomorrow—or the next day." Nora glanced at her watch. "I need to close up the school."

"Can we go to the park?" Lily tugged on Sophia's sleeve.

"In a minute, dear."

Sophia darted another look toward the doorway, desperate to prolong her visit. She had summoned up the courage to see Joanna now, not tomorrow, not the next day—but today. She didn't know if she would have the guts to come back. Second thoughts already crowded her mind.

"Why do you want to talk to Joanna?" Lily asked. She leaned forward and lowered her voice. "Do you think she's Mama, too?"

Sophia stepped back, startled by the question. "No, of course not. I just wanted to meet your teacher, that's all."

"Why don't you come back tomorrow?" Nora said decisively, moving them toward the door.

Sophia walked as slowly as she could, but eventually they reached the front door, then the walkway, then the sidewalk. She stopped to take one last look at the school. No sign of Joanna Wingate. Maybe it was meant to be this way.

Joanna met up with Nora at the door to the teachers' lounge.

"Don't move," Nora said sharply. Then, contradicting her own request, she took Joanna by the hand and led her over to the window. Slitting the venetian blinds with two fingers, she tipped her head toward the window. "Look."

"Why?"

"Just look."

Joanna stepped up to the window. She saw Lily and Rose holding hands with an older woman. The woman had short black hair and was somewhat plump. Before Joanna could catch a glimpse of her face, the woman turned and walked away from the school.

"Who was that?" Joanna asked, surprised that Michael hadn't picked up the girls.

"Sophia De Marco, their grandmother." Nora lowered her voice. "She wanted to see you."

"She did?" Joanna felt a shiver run down her spine. She shook it off. "I guess that's only natural. I showed you that picture of her daughter."

Nora stared at her without saying a word.

"You're making me nervous," Joanna said.

"I didn't like the way she looked."

"How did she look?"

"Like—like you," Nora said. "She looked like you."

Joanna swallowed hard. "It's just the dark hair. People think I'm Italian all the time. My mom and I just laugh it off. Some people think I'm Hispanic and they speak Spanish to me. It's no big deal."

"Are you done?"

Joanna hugged her arms close to her body. "I'd like to be done."

"You've got to talk to your mother, Joanna."

"I have. She thinks it's a coincidence."

"What do *you* think?"

Joanna moved away from the window. "I don't know. They say everyone has a double. I think Oprah did a show on nonrelated doubles once. It happens. A fluke of genetics. I'm just a freak, but hey, we always knew that, right?" Joanna's attempt at humor failed to dislodge the worry lines around Nora's eyes.

"Your mother has always been so possessive of you," Nora said slowly. "She rarely let you out of her sight. Even in college she used to call you a couple of times a week and come down on the weekends. It was always fun to have her around, but now that I think about it, it was a bit odd."

Joanna held up a hand. "Please, Nora. Don't speculate. Believe me, I'm doing enough of that on my own."

"What if something really strange happened?"

"Like what?"

"Like you were kidnapped. You might have been one of those kids who was stolen as a baby."

Joanna's hand shook as she tucked her hair behind her ear. "Don't be ridiculous. You know my mother. Can you imagine her doing such a thing?"

Nora didn't answer.

"Neither can I," Joanna finished, but they both knew she was lying. "I have to get out of here."

"Are you going home?"

"I don't know. I need to talk to someone who can tell me something, someone who can make sense of this absurd situation. Maybe I should talk to the twins' father again. Find out more about the De Marcos."

Nora walked her to the door. "The girls told me about your trip to their house and the ice cream parlor. Are you sure talking to Mr. Ashton is a good idea? You're getting pretty involved with this man and his family."

"I'm not sure about anything anymore," Joanna said as she left the room. Her life had once been so calm, so peaceful, so boring. Now she felt continually uneasy, as if every second of each day brought her closer to the edge of a precipice, and she was terribly afraid that if she fell in, she wouldn't ever get out. Unless someone threw her a lifeline—someone like Michael.

Michael set down his drafting pencil. His sketch of the Connaught Office Building still didn't impress him. The lines were too bland. There was nothing exciting about it. It certainly wasn't special enough to replace the Stratton Hotel.

Impulsively he picked up the paper and crumpled it into a ball. "With two seconds on the clock," he said, mimicking a sports announcer, "he goes for the three pointer. At the buzzer he shoots and scores."

Michael tossed the paper ball through the small plastic hoop he had placed over the trash can. If nothing else, his shooting skills were getting better.

He sat back in his chair and tried to get inspired, but instead of lines and angles, he thought about Joanna, about her passionate plea to restore the Stratton. Of course, he could never convince Gary Connaught to do that. He wouldn't even try. Jackson

Cox would probably fire him if he even mentioned the word "restoration."

Michael rested his hands behind his head, staring at the ceiling. He needed a vision, something to spark his imagination. Who was he kidding? There was nothing to get excited about. He was designing a rectangle, a very expensive checkerboard of squares that would reach into the sky, blocking out sunlight and turning the street below into a dark and windy tunnel.

But he was not destroying the city. Contrary to what Joanna thought, there could be beauty in modern buildings, buildings that would withstand earthquakes, that could house offices, condos, and restaurants all within one structure. Each generation demanded its own monuments. Who was she to criticize Gary Connaught's choice of an office building?

A historian, that's who she was. He smiled to himself. Joanna might look like Angela, but she certainly didn't think like her. Angela had thrown food out before the expiration date just to make sure she didn't have anything old in the refrigerator. She had watched the fashion trends like a hawk, never wanting to be left behind the newest fad.

He'd been drawn to Angela's zest for life. She had always lived in the "now," not the past or the future but the very second at hand. She'd resisted his attempts to plan for the future, to draw up a will, to buy life insurance.

Sometimes late at night, when he was alone in the bed they had shared, Michael wondered what Angela had thought during those last few seconds of her life. Had she whispered "I love you" to him or the twins? Had she prayed to be rescued? Had she simply thought that this was just another adventure that she would live to tell about? Or had she known that the end had come?

Of course, he would never know the answers to

those questions or to the other questions he had, such as why Angela had gone to the party when she'd promised to stay home, how she'd come to be on the boat in the first place, and who the dark-haired man with the thick mustache had been who wept uncontrollably at her funeral when the empty urn was lowered into the ground.

Michael had never tried to find out the man's identity. He hadn't wanted to know what their relationship had been. He wanted to remember Angela as a faithful, loving wife—even if it wasn't true.

The intercom buzzed. "Iris Sandbury is on line one," Helen said. "I wouldn't have disturbed you, but she's at a pay phone."

"Thanks." Michael picked up the phone. "Iris? How are you?"

"I'm wonderful. Michael, I think I've discovered a gold mine."

Michael smiled at the enthusiasm in her voice. Iris Sandbury was in her mid-fifties, the wife of Michael's former boss, Greg Sandbury. Greg had brought Michael into the firm, mentored him through the early years, and taught him more about structure and design than anyone he had ever met.

Since Greg's death, Iris, who came from money, amused herself by buying and selling houses. Although Michael had explained to her on numerous occasions that he didn't design houses, she loved to ask his advice, swearing that Greg always told her Michael was the best.

"What have you discovered this time?" he asked.

"The house where Ruby Mae Whitcomb, San Francisco's most infamous madam, lived out the last fifty years of her life. And it's going to be listed next Tuesday."

"Ruby Mae Whitcomb?" Michael tried to place the name.

"Yes. Surely you've heard the legends. She made

a living running a very profitable whorehouse in the twenties. She supposedly died in a fire. At least that's what everyone thought, but I just found out that she has been living in seclusion in an isolated house in the Seacliff area."

"Seacliff," Michael echoed. The neighborhood of Seacliff, located on the northwestern edge of San Francisco, overlooked China Beach, aptly named for the Chinese smugglers who had landed there in the mid-1800s. The homes were large and expensive, many isolated by thick trees as they perched on the edge of the cliffs.

"Apparently Ruby Mae died a few weeks ago, and a very distant relative inherited the property," Iris continued.

"And that distant relative now wants to sell."

"Yes. And I want to buy it."

"You haven't even seen it," he said, amused by her impulsiveness.

"I saw a bit of it from the street. The house and the property look terribly neglected, but the land is valuable and the location absolutely superb. I want to jump on it as soon as I can."

"But—" Michael prodded, knowing she hadn't just called to share her good news.

"But I'm leaving for Mexico in thirty minutes. I'm at the airport now. Could you look at it for me, tell me if you think I would be able to preserve the house or if I need to raze it and build something from scratch?"

"Sure, I can get out there in the next day or two."

"You have to go in an hour," Iris said. "The relative is leaving on a business trip. He's willing to give you a key if you can get out there before he leaves."

"Iris, I'm busy." Michael looked at his plans for the Connaught office building, which were going nowhere fast.

"Oh, please, Michael. Gregory always valued your opinion. I know you won't steer me wrong."

Michael sighed as she pushed his guilt buttons. He'd always been a sucker for hard luck stories and lonesome voices. "All right, I'll go. Tell me how to get there." He jotted down the directions.

"Thanks, Michael. I really appreciate this."

"Have a good trip." Michael hung up the phone and reached for his coat. The intercom buzzed again. "Yes?"

"Michael, there's someone here to see you," Helen said, her voice somewhat hushed.

"Do you want me to guess?"

"She says her name is Joanna Wingate. For a moment there I thought I was seeing a ghost. What's going on?"

Joanna. His stomach muscles clenched. His heart sped up. Joanna. He took a deep breath. "Send her in."

"Aren't you going to tell me what's going on?"

"No."

"Fine," Helen said with a sigh.

Michael slipped on his coat as Joanna entered the office.

She looked beautiful; soft curves in a rose-colored short sweater worn over a long floral skirt. Her curly dark hair drifted past her shoulders, framing her big, dark eyes. Her lips glistened with a soft hue of pink. No bright red lipstick for her, no long painted fingernails with drops of glitter at the ends, no black leather or tight jeans.

With a shake of his head, he told himself to stop comparing Joanna and Angela.

"Michael," Joanna said tentatively, "I hope I'm not interrupting, but I need to talk to you."

"The girls—"

"They're fine. Their grandmother picked them up."

"So you met Sophia?"

"No, I didn't. I was on the phone when she came."
Joanna paused. "My friend, Nora, one of the other
teachers, told me that Mrs. De Marco waited, that
she wanted to speak to me about something. Do you
know what she wanted to talk about?"

"I have no idea."

"I thought she might have said something to
you."

"I suspect she wanted to see what you look like.
I told her about the resemblance."

Joanna licked her lips. "Something's wrong, Michael. I don't know what it is, but I can feel it in my
heart. I need to find out more about the De Marcos.
Maybe one of Sophia's sisters or a cousin or somebody . . ." Her voice drifted away, as if she hated
even to think of the possibility, much less voice it.
She lifted her head and looked directly into his eyes.
"Whatever happened in the past, I need to know."

Michael watched the emotions play across her
face, the uncertainty in her eyes, the fear, the determination. There was a certain strength in the grace-
ful tilt of her chin, the set of her shoulders. He had
never met a woman who could look so feminine and
so tough at the same time.

If she really had been Angela, he would have
stepped forward immediately and taken her in his
arms. He would have soothed her fears with mean-
ingless words of assurance. But he sensed that
Joanna didn't want empty gestures. She wanted real
answers, and so did he.

"I made some calls earlier today to some old
neighbors," Joanna continued. "My parents lived in
San Rafael before they moved to the city."

"And . . ."

"They never saw my mother pregnant," Joanna
said in a rush. "I went through the photo albums
last night because I couldn't sleep, and there were

no pictures of my mother pregnant. Nothing. My parents took photos of everything, Michael. Every breath I took. They were almost fanatical about recording each moment of my life. But the earliest photo they have of me is one taken in my bassinet at home, the day after my birth."

"Maybe your mother didn't want any pictures taken of her while she was pregnant," Michael suggested, although his stomach clenched in uneasiness.

"That's possible. The neighbor said she assumed I had been born several months after they moved to the city, but my mother always told me I was born just a few weeks after they moved. Surely she couldn't have hidden nine months of pregnancy."

He heard the doubt in her voice, the unspoken question. Michael silently made the jump in his own mind. But he had to hear the words from her to make sure they were thinking the same thing.

"What if my parents weren't really my parents?" Joanna asked finally.

Damn. They were thinking the same thing. "Are you saying you were adopted?"

"Or taken." Joanna slapped a hand to her mouth. "Oh, God, I can't believe I said that out loud."

"It's okay. It's just me."

Joanna looked at him with anguish in her eyes. "Just you, yes. But you're in the middle of this. In some ways you're the enemy, but I don't have anyone else to talk to. My mother simply says that I'm her natural-born child and anything else is nonsense. Yet she can't explain why I look more like the De Marcos than the Wingates."

Michael leaned against his desk as Joanna paced restlessly in front of him. What if she was right? What if she was related to the De Marcos? That could mean trouble for his family, for his in-laws, for the girls, for Tony and Frank, and God knows

who else. How could he be part of anything that
might hurt them?

If there was a De Marco secret to be kept,
shouldn't he be keeping it? Hadn't Sophia and Vincent adopted him to all intents and purposes, showering him with the love and affection he had never
gotten from his own parents? He owed them his
unquestioning loyalty, his love, his trust. He didn't
owe Joanna anything. She was a stranger to him.

An irresistibly attractive stranger, he silently
amended as she turned and looked into his eyes. She
was Angela, and yet she was more, a woman instead
of a girl, strong instead of weak, thoughtful instead
of impetuous. *And he wanted her.*

He wanted to kiss her, to drag his hands through
her hair, to watch the natural flush of her cheeks
turn red with passion. He took a deep breath and let
it out.

This was ridiculous. He needed to find a blonde
or a redhead, someone with green eyes or blue eyes
or red-rimmed eyes, he thought frantically. Someone
who wouldn't confuse him, who wouldn't torture
him like this.

"You want me to leave, don't you?" Joanna asked.

That was another thing. She seemed to have the
ability to read his thoughts. Angela had never come
close to guessing what he was thinking. "Hell, yes,
I want you to leave. You're turning my life upside
down."

She flinched but held her head up. "Then I'll go."

"No. I want you to stay, too." He ran a hand
through his hair. "Actually I don't know what I
want." He instinctively reached for the wedding
band on his finger, the one he had twisted and
turned on so many occasions, when he and Angela
had fought, when they'd made up, when he'd
waited to find out if she was dead or alive. But the
wedding ring was now tucked away in a box in his

dresser. His marriage was over, and his wife was gone.

Joanna had nothing to do with Angela or with that part of his life. He needed to keep the two of them separate. He glanced down at his watch, suddenly realizing the time.

"Damn. I'm supposed to be across town in twenty minutes."

"I'm sorry. I'll go."

For a moment Michael considered letting her go, but he didn't want to leave things like this—so strange and awkward between them. "Why don't you come with me?" he said impulsively.

"Come with you?" she echoed in surprise. "Where are you going?"

"To check out a house for a friend. She's thinking of buying it, and wants to know if the house should be torn down or remodeled."

Joanna stared at him, a slow smile turning up her lips. "You didn't just tell her to tear it down?"

"Not sight unseen, no, but it may be my recommendation in the end." Michael picked up his keys. "By the way, the owner of the house was supposedly an infamous madam of the twenties, Ruby Mae Whitcomb."

Joanna's eyes widened with excitement. "Ruby Mae Whitcomb? That's impossible. She died in a fire at her whorehouse."

"Maybe not." He laughed. "You look like a kid in a candy store."

"If Ruby Mae didn't die, there could be all kinds of stories in that house."

"Does that mean you're coming with me?"

"Just try and stop me."

He'd like to stop her, Michael thought as he followed her out of his office. He'd like to stop her from driving him crazy, from invading his thoughts, from being so damn sexy and appealing. Instead of stopping her he was pushing her forward. At this rate she'd probably end up in his arms before the day was through.

11

"I wish you could have met Joanna, Grandma," Lily said as she climbed onto the swing at the playground. "She's so pretty. And so nice."

"That's because she's Mama." Rose took the swing next to her sister.

Sophia gave each swing a push. She didn't know quite what to say to the girls about Joanna's resemblance to their mother. Maybe for the moment it was best just to distract them. She gave Lily's swing another push.

Lily liked to go as high as she could, pointing her tiny feet toward the tips of the trees in the distance.

"Are you ready to touch the stars, Lily?" Sophia asked.

"Yes. I want you to push me so high I can grab a star and bring it back down to you."

Sophia smiled at the familiar game. "Oh, good. I could use a few more stars."

"Where do you put them all, Grandma?" Rose asked, content to swing at a slower, more conservative pace.

"I put them back in the sky every night just before I go to bed, and I make a wish."

"What do you wish for?"

Sophia gave each swing another push as she considered the question. "Different things. Sometimes I

151

wish for a bright sunny day. Sometimes I wish for a big fat hug and a kiss from one of my grandchildren. Sometimes I just wish for another day as good as the last."

"Do you ever wish that Mama would come back?" Rose asked.

"Yes, I wish that all the time." Sophia felt a tug on her heart as she remembered the little girl she had once pushed on these very swings. Angela had liked to swing high like Lily, but she'd never swung for very long, always impatient to move on to the next activity.

At first Sophia had been against Angela's marriage to Michael. Then she'd realized that Michael was good for her daughter. He was stable and loving and responsible. She'd relied on Michael to bring Tony home in good shape from whatever party they went to, and it was easy to let Michael take care of Angela, too.

Easy but probably not fair. She and Vincent should have talked Michael and Angela into waiting. Although she doubted they could have changed Angela's mind. Her daughter's stubborn streak surpassed her father's.

For all her flaws, Angela had been her baby girl, and what a girl—full of joy, with a zest for life that kept them all going. Angela loved everyone, and everyone loved her—especially her children.

Angela had treated Lily and Rose like her little sisters instead of her daughters, spoiling them with treats, dressing them up in fancy clothes, helping them paint their bedroom wall with watercolors. It had been left to Michael to do the dirty work, to discipline the girls, to make sure they ate the right food and went to bed at a decent hour. Sophia had tried talking to Angela on more than one occasion, but her daughter wouldn't listen.

"Grandma," Lily said, "you got your wish. Because I think Joanna is Mama. She's just a little different."

"I think so, too," Rose said. "Mariah told us we would find Mama at school, and we did."

"Mariah is magic," Lily said. "You believe in her, don't you, Grandma?"

Believe in Mariah, a wizard in a crystal ball that she'd found in an antiques shop? Sophia smiled to herself. "I'll tell you a little secret. When I bought Mariah I took her home and rubbed my hands over her head and made a wish."

"What did you wish for?" Rose asked.

"I wished that my little girl would find her way home."

"And she did," Lily said with excitement. "Mama came back."

"I just don't understand why we have to call her Joanna," Rose said.

Sophia heard the wistful tone in Rose's voice. She understood the longing that never went away. The girls wanted their mother back so badly, they were willing to accept her as another person with another name.

Maybe she was doing the same thing, wanting to bring Angela back as Joanna. Vincent thought so. Elena did, too. Sophia knew there was much more to it than that.

The sound of Italian opera greeted Sophia and the girls as they opened the kitchen door of De Marco's restaurant.

Louis De Marco was rolling out dough for pizza at one end of the kitchen, while Vincent chopped up onions and other vegetables for the salads and pasta toppings. Louis sang along with Pavarotti, his voice blessed with enthusiasm but not talent.

Before Sophia could say hello, Vincent slammed the pizza dough down on the table and turned toward his brother. *"Mio Dio!* Have we not heard enough of your voice?"

Rose and Lily giggled as the two men argued, half in Italian, half in English. Sophia smiled to herself. Louis and Vincent had spent forty years together in this kitchen, cooking and arguing, arguing and cooking. They had prepared each dish with passion and a sense of tradition, but their time was passing.

Louis' son, Rico, had just graduated from the San Francisco Culinary Institute and was beginning to take over more of the cooking responsibilities. Frank now handled the accounting and ordered the food. In the next year Vincent and Louis would both retire. Sophia couldn't imagine this kitchen without them. She also couldn't imagine Vincent in her house twenty-four hours a day.

Time was moving on. So many things were changing. People coming in and out of her life, children growing up, children dying. As she glanced down at Lily and Rose, she thanked God for their presence. They kept Angela's memory alive with their crazy schemes and loving ways.

Vincent looked up and saw them standing in the doorway. *"Buona sera.* Come to Grandpapa," he said, opening his arms wide.

The girls ran into his embrace and took turns kissing him on each cheek. Sophia loved watching Vincent with the children. He was gentle and soft with them, loving, tender. Emotions that she rarely saw in him anymore.

With her he had always been somewhat stern, reserved, taking his role as husband and provider seriously. Too seriously, she had often thought. She had wanted a teasing, playful lover, an equal companion, but they had never been equal, and rarely playful.

But how could she complain of a husband who worked hard, who was generous with his money, who took care of his children and his family? She couldn't. She should be counting her blessings instead of wishing on stars.

"You have been good, yes?" Vincent said to the girls, raising one eyebrow.

Rose giggled. "Yes. We only had one time-out today, and it wasn't our fault."

"Not your fault?"

"No, it wasn't," Lily said. "Billy Dutton pushed me, and I had to push him back."

"Why did you not just walk away?"

"Because he was bad. He pushed me."

"How hard?"

"Very hard."

Vincent nodded with understanding. "Then perhaps it is good. You showed this boy he cannot mess around with a De Marco."

"Oh, Vincent. Lily shouldn't be pushing other children, and her last name is Ashton," Sophia said.

"She is a De Marco. Aren't you?" He tickled Lily until she said yes. Vincent laughed. "You are hungry, no?"

"I'm starving," Lily said. "Can I have some garlic bread?"

"With your spaghetti, *mia cara*. Here, this will keep your stomachs busy for the next few minutes." He handed them each a slice of pepperoni.

"Can we fold napkins again?" Rose asked.

"Of course. Your cousin Marlena is in the dining room. She'll help you."

As the girls ran out of the room, Vincent turned to Sophia. "Where is Michael?"

"At work." Sophia set her purse down on the counter and picked up the sponge to wipe off the remnants of a head of lettuce. "He works too hard, you know. What with taking care of the girls and all, I worry about him. Remember how much he used to love to sail with Tony or read those mystery

novels? And basketball, he was so talented. I don't
think he does anything for himself any more. He just
works and tries to keep up with the girls."

"Sophia."

She heard the censure in his voice. "What?"

"You picked up the girls?"

"Yes." Sophia waited for the flood of angry
words, the recriminations, the scolding, but none
came. When she turned her head she saw that Vincent had a knife in his hand and was chopping fast
and furiously, taking out his anger on a pile of
freshly washed mushrooms that scattered across the
cutting board with each slice of the knife.

Sophia set down her sponge and walked over to
him. "Stop it. You'll hurt yourself."

"Hurt myself?" He paused, turning the knife in
his hand until the blade pointed toward his heart.
"Why don't you just stab me now and be done with
it, instead of killing me slowly?"

"Don't be so dramatic," Sophia said, although she
was disturbed by the intensity of his words. "I'm not
doing anything to hurt you." She glanced over her
shoulder at Louis. He stared back at them with bla-
tant curiosity. "Would you mind leaving us alone
for a few minutes?" she asked.

Louis opened his mouth to argue, then nodded.
"*Si*. Five minutes only. We have food to prepare."

When they were alone Sophia said, "I wanted to
see her."

"Did you?"

"No. She wasn't there."

The muscles in his face relaxed. "Good. I told you
to forget her. Did you talk to Elena?"

"Yes. She said the same thing."

"Then let it be."

"I can't. Since the girls told me about her, I haven't
been able to think of anything else."

"Why?"

"You know why."

"You made me a promise, Sophia."

Sophia felt a rush of guilt at his words. Yes, she had made promises. Many promises. She had promised her dying mother to watch out for her little sisters, Elena and Carlotta, to take care of them, to protect them. She had promised her husband to love and to cherish him, to honor and to obey. But what had seemed so easy at twenty and thirty had become so difficult in the later years of her life.

Carlotta had been no problem, marrying a lawyer when she was nineteen. Her three children were all grown now, with children of their own. Elena had been a different story. Elena had grown up with a mind of her own, with no thought to the worries of her older sister, constantly making a mockery of Sophia's attempt to keep her promise.

And Vincent—Sophia had spent forty years with the man. She had lived with him longer than she had lived with her parents. She had slept in his bed longer than she had slept alone. She had cared for him when he was sick, as he had cared for her.

She had loved him, and she had hated him, too.

The words came to her mind before she could silence them, but she knew it was true. Vincent knew it, too. But they didn't speak of such things. Not of the love or of the hate. No one who knew them would suspect a thing. Together they had taught each other to lie.

"We can't replace Angela with this woman." Vincent stared down at the scattered slices of mushrooms. "She was our daughter. This other woman is not part of our family."

"Sometimes you can be so cruel."

"I'm being loyal to our daughter. Have you forgotten what loyalty is all about?"

"Loyalty?" Her anger turned to fury. "Have you forgotten just how loyal I can be?" She suddenly

wanted to hit him, shake him, scream at him, pum-
mel his chest with her fists, until the tension was
released, until the pain was gone, until she couldn't
feel anything anymore.

Vincent set the knife down. He walked over to her
and took her hands in his. There was still anger in
his eyes, but also love and worry. "This isn't good
for you. You must leave it alone."

"How do you know what's good for me?"

He looked at her in amazement. "Because I love
you, Sophia. I've always loved you. Through everything."

"Oh, Vincent, I can't forget what we did. You and
me and Elena—"

He put a finger to her lips. "Sh-sh."

She closed her eyes, wishing she had the courage
to speak out. Vincent drew her into his arms and
stroked her hair. For a moment she let him comfort
her.

"It will be all right, Sophia."

They were the same words he had spoken before.
But it would never be all right. Never.

Joanna had never imagined that she would be sitting in Michael Ashton's car, driving across town to
look at a house. She had told herself the night before
that she would not get involved with him. But here
she sat, letting the breeze blow through her hair as
Michael punched the buttons on the radio.

He was probably a killer with the television remote control, too, she thought with a smile. His fingers moved faster than her mind. She could barely
ascertain whether the station was rock, country, or
pop before Michael moved on to the next, finally
settling for a sports update.

It was early summer, and baseball was the talk of
the town. The San Francisco Giants were primed for
a good season, and as Joanna listened to the an-

nouncer talk about the team's chances for the upcoming year, she realized how much she had missed
while her father was ill, the whimsical things of life
such as baseball in the summer, ice cream cones, and
sitting on a blanket at the beach watching the
fireworks go off on the Fourth of July.

As a perpetual student and a teacher, summer had
always been summer, vacation time, big books to
read on sandy beaches, the smell of sunscreen, cold
lemonade sliding down a parched throat.

Last summer her father had just been diagnosed
with cancer. In the weeks that followed she'd spent
her days in hospital corridors and doctors' waiting
rooms, looking at X rays and trying to make sense
of medical reports with words that boasted more letters than the entire alphabet.

There hadn't been time for the lazy days of summer last year, or for the falling leaves of autumn, or
the chill of winter, and definitely not for the bounty
of spring. It would have seemed more fitting for her
father to die in the cold, rainy days of a dark winter
than to simply slip away on what might have been
the prettiest day of the year.

Joanna had cried against the beauty of that day,
appalled that flowers could still bloom, that kids
could graduate from school, that her friends could
make plans to travel, that they could talk about what
they were doing over the summer.

How could the rest of the world care so little?

Because he had been just one man.

A special man. Her father. And as the memories
filled her mind, she questioned how she could even
doubt that her father had been her father. He had
loved her. He had taken care of her. He had been
her adviser, her court jester, her tennis partner—her
friend.

It couldn't have all been a lie.

Michael's hand on her knee startled her out of her

thoughts, and like a spark igniting a fire she felt instant awareness. Another problem, she thought with a sigh.

"Are you all right?" Michael asked. "You're quiet."

"I do my best thinking in the car."

"What are you thinking about?"

"Throwing myself out the door when you stop at the next light."

He flipped the automatic locks. "No can do. You're trapped."

"I'm sure I can open it from my side."

"Nope, this is a childproof car. I'm the only one who can let you out." He grinned. "I kind of like this. There is actually one thing in my life I can control."

"Meaning you can't control the rest of it?"

"In case you haven't noticed, Lily and Rose both have a bossy streak. At work I have the illusion of control. I even manage several people, but every one of my ideas still has to be approved by someone else."

Joanna turned in her seat so she could face him. "When did you decide to become an architect?"

"In the seventh grade. We built a replica of city hall out of building blocks." He smiled at her. "I didn't like the way the other kids built it. I kept wanting to add floors and roofs and decks and arched doorways. It was supposed to be a team project, but the other kids got so disgusted with my ripping things down that I basically wound up doing it by myself."

"Obviously you were good at it."

"I think the teacher gave me a C. Said my design was interesting but not functional. She couldn't figure out how the people who worked in the back of the building could actually get to their offices without climbing through a window."

"Everybody's a critic," she teased.

"Tell me about it. Okay, my turn. Why history, Joanna?"

"Because I like old things. I like learning about the past. Actually I started out wanting to be a teacher, but growing up in my family as an only child, it didn't seem enough."

"Enough what?"

"Prestige, money, glory."

He sent her a curious look. "You don't strike me as the kind of person who wants those things."

"I don't, but my mother and father did. It wasn't that they were that ambitious themselves, but they wanted a lot for me. There was no one else in the family to distract them. Believe me, I longed for siblings."

"I have two half brothers," Michael said. "Both younger. My parents split up when I was four. I barely remember my father. My mother remarried when I was nine and had Connor. You would have thought the sun rose and set in that kid's face. She loved him to death. That marriage lasted until I was fourteen. She met someone else when I was seventeen and got pregnant with Brian. Once again she was in baby heaven."

Joanna was struck by the loneliness in his voice. "How do you and your brothers get along?"

"Like strangers. My mom and Brian came out for Angela's funeral. Brian is sixteen now. I've missed most of his life. I don't even know him. Connor is in the army. He sends me cards once in awhile. That's it."

"Sounds kind of sad."

"Nah. The De Marcos took care of me."

The De Marcos. They were back to them. No wonder Michael was so attached to his in-laws. They seemed to care more about him than his own family did.

As Michael reached for the buttons on the radio, she stopped his hand. "I like this station."

"You do? Are you sure?"

"Michael, we've heard every station beaming down a signal from here to Mars."

"If you stick to one channel, you might miss something."

"Or I might actually get to hear an entire song. Wow, what a novel idea."

He grinned as he put his hand back on the steering wheel. "All right. But no singing. I hate people who sing along to songs on the radio."

"Like you've never done it," she teased.

"Only when I'm alone."

"Funny how many things we do when we're alone that we would never admit to."

He pulled up to a stoplight. "That sounds interesting. Do you want to share?"

"Not a chance."

"Mm-mm, I'm getting all kinds of ideas here. Like maybe you strip down to your underwear and dance around the house like Madonna."

Joanna put a hand to her chest. "Me? Do I remind you of Madonna? Because if so, I think you might need glasses. I'm a historian. I read a lot. I like libraries and I adore museums. I'm a regular material girl," she finished with a smile.

"There's another side to you, I'll bet, one you keep locked away because it isn't appropriate for your job or your friends or your family."

She laughed nervously. He saw too much, way too much. "Don't be silly. I am who I am."

"Are you? Maybe we'll have to find out."

Joanna straightened in her seat as the atmosphere in the car went from light and breezy to personal. She didn't know why she had chosen to reveal so much to this man. She'd never told anyone about her parents' expectations. No one else would have understood. Her world had been limited until now, filled only with people who shared the same goals, the same ambitions. It was time to spread her wings. To look beyond the obvious. To see what else the world had to offer.

"Joanna—"

She didn't let him finish, suddenly nervous of what he would say. "The light has changed," she said.

"Too bad. Things were just getting interesting."

"*Too* interesting for me."

"Nothing can be too interesting."

"It can if it's dangerous. I've never been one to live dangerously."

He flashed her a smile as he proceeded into traffic. "Believe it or not, neither have I, but since I met you I suddenly have the urge."

"Well, control it, because nothing is going to happen between you and me. It can't, for obvious reasons."

"I know. It would be a huge mistake."

"Absolutely."

"I agree."

"So do I."

"Then why are you arguing with me?" Michael asked.

Because she hadn't wanted him to give up so easily. "Joanna, can you read the street sign?" Michael asked, changing the subject.

"El Camino del Mar."

"That's the one we want." He turned to the right. "Now we have to look for number one seventeen."

Joanna scanned the houses as they drove slowly along the winding street that would eventually lead them to the sea. The houses were large and set apart from their neighbors. Unlike most of San Francisco, there were shrubs and trees surrounding the homes, a suburban feel on the edge of a crowded city.

"It's hard to believe Ruby Mae Whitcomb could have lived here for fifty years and nobody knew," she mused.

"It's a secluded community. Not much in the way of neighborhood block parties."

"I wouldn't know about that. I grew up in a high-rise building. I always wanted a real house, something like these."

"Expensive taste."

"I don't think many people grow up dreaming about living in an apartment. I'm sure you didn't."

"No, I wanted a house with gables, turrets, towers, and dungeons. Something with secret passageways and hidden staircases, and bookcases that turned into revolving doors."

She raised an eyebrow in disbelief. "I thought you were the ultimate modern man."

"Not when I was eleven. I loved the Hardy Boys mysteries. I thought they were cool."

"The Hardy Boys?" She started to laugh, suddenly filled with joy at the absurdity of his answer. As a historian she liked to think people were influenced by powerful, important figures in history, past presidents, knights in shining armor, five-star generals. But not Michael. No, he'd been in awe of the Hardy Boys.

"What's wrong with the Hardy Boys? They had a great life. Every day was an adventure."

"I don't understand you," she said with a laugh. "You're a contradiction in terms."

"Me? You're a PhD candidate who spent yesterday afternoon making straw hats for ducks."

"You've got me there."

"Didn't you have any kind of a fantasy when you were growing up? Besides being an elementary school teacher?"

"I did think about becoming a ballet dancer. They were all thin, gorgeous, and bitchy. I wanted to dance on the stage in the spotlight with hundreds of men vying for the touch of my hand on their brow. But I'm as clumsy as an elephant, as inflexible as a stick, and I like to eat."

"You are gorgeous," he said gallantly.

"Yeah, and bitchy, too. Especially when I'm hungry."

"That's okay." Michael opened the glove compartment. "I'm prepared for hungry, cranky females."

Joanna laughed at the assortment of crackers, chips, raisins, and cookies. "You *are* prepared."

"A regular Boy Scout."

"Were you?"

"No. I never had a dad to take me to those things. My first stepdad tried, but he was a salesman and traveled a lot. We moved every year for a while."

"Does your mother live close by?" she asked.

"No, she and my second stepdad moved to New York when I was a senior in high school. I decided enough was enough, and I didn't go with them. I moved in with the De Marcos, and the rest is history, as they say."

"You married their daughter."

He flashed her a wry smile. "It seemed like the right thing to do at the time."

"What about now?"

"The biggest mistake of my life to date."

"To date?"

"There's still time, especially with you around."

Joanna looked away from his compelling gaze. She knew exactly what he meant. Only, she had a feeling she might be the one making the mistake.

12

Michael pulled the car over to the side of the street. "I think that's it—number one seventeen." He tipped his head toward a pair of wrought iron gates. "Let's check it out." He was more than ready to get out of the intimate confines of the car, because the more he learned about Joanna Wingate, the more he liked her, and he wasn't sure liking her was good for anyone.

Joanna opened her door and stepped onto the sidewalk. "Wow, the walls are so high, I can't even see the house."

"The owner is supposed to meet us with a key." He pushed on one of the gates, and it reluctantly opened with a great deal of squeaking and groaning.

"Doesn't sound like Ruby Mae got too many visitors," Joanna said, following Michael into the yard.

"Apparently she liked her privacy."

As they walked toward the house, a man came down the driveway. He looked to be in his midforties, and his expensive suit and silk tie spoke well of his success.

"Michael Ashton?" he asked.

"Yes. I'm here to pick up the key for Mrs. Sandbury."

"Of course. I'm Jeremy Gladstone. I'm the owner of this house, such as it is."

"Nice to meet you. This is a friend of mine, Joanna Wingate," Michael said as he shook hands with Jeremy.

"Are you really related to Ruby Mae Whitcomb?" Joanna asked, unable to contain her excitement at meeting a descendant of one of the city's most infamous women.

"I'm not sure," Jeremy replied with an apologetic shrug. "This house was owned by a woman named Rebecca Margaret Whitcomb. I do believe that might be the same woman you're referring to."

"Whitcomb? Yes." Joanna nodded. "Ruby Mae was her stage name."

"I don't know anything about her, I'm afraid. And there's no one left who does. My grandmother Elsa was apparently her illegitimate daughter. Rebecca Margaret or Ruby Mae, as you call her, apparently gave her up for adoption when she was an infant."

"Adoption?" Joanna echoed, exchanging a quick look with Michael.

Michael couldn't help but be struck by the word as well. He'd rarely thought much about adoption. He didn't know anyone who was adopted, and no one in his circle of friends or family had ever adopted a child. But now twice in one day—the word seemed to be haunting him.

Could Joanna have been adopted? He mentally ran through the list of De Marcos who would be the right age to have a daughter of Joanna's age. He only came up with three. Carlotta, Sophia's younger sister by two years; Elena, Sophia's younger sister by five years; and Sophia herself. But Sophia had three children. Carlotta had three and Elena had two. None seemed likely candidates to have given up a baby. Although Elena had lived a somewhat wild life before her marriage.

"Did Ruby Mae ever contact your grandmother?"

Joanna asked as Jeremy led them up the driveway toward the house.

"I believe she did once. My grandmother didn't want anything to do with the woman who'd abandoned her."

"But Ruby Mae was a legend," Joanna said.

"Not in grandmother's mind. She was just the woman who'd given her away. I guess she never got past that. Anyway, this Ruby Mae kept stacks of paper. Her house is filled to the rafters with things." Jeremy wrinkled his nose. "I can't even imagine what's in there."

"Maybe a gold mine of historical information," Joanna said. "Just think. She might have letters from some of the men who frequented her house of ill repute. Oh, the stories she could have told. . . ."

Michael smiled. He loved the way Joanna's eyes fired with enthusiasm, the passion in her voice. She looked as if she'd just been given the keys to a treasure chest that had been buried for hundreds of years.

He stopped abruptly as the house came into view. While Joanna had been excited by the prospect of what was inside the house, Michael was absolutely captivated by the house itself. The Victorian stood three stories tall with a mansard roof and a grand stairway in the front. The design was late 1800s, and the original craftsmanship took his breath away. There were small half-moon windows along the third story. Garlands and scrolls decorated the facade. It was a house of history, of beauty—of neglect. The dangerously weak roof, the chipped paint, the broken shingles, the cracked windows, made him sick to his stomach. How could anyone have let this house go?

"Not much to look at, is it?" Jeremy Gladstone said. "When I first came through the neighborhood, I thought I might have inherited a mansion, but

this . . ." He shook his head. "I think the best thing
is to level it and start all over."

"No!" Joanna shouted. "No," she said more quietly at Jeremy's look of astonishment. "The house is
part of history, especially if the owner was Ruby
Mae Whitcomb. It might even be considered a historical landmark."

"I don't know about that," Jeremy replied. "And
frankly, I'm from St. Louis. All I want to do is sell
this house and take whatever I can get for it and go
home." He handed Michael the keys. "Here you go.
I'll be back on Monday. I'm hoping to put the house
on the market next Tuesday. In fact, if you know of
anyone else who might be interested, you can have
them call Conrad Davenport, my real estate broker.
Here's his card. I promised Mrs. Sandbury an early
look, but when I get back I'll be eager to find a
buyer."

"Mr. Gladstone," Joanna said, "would it be all
right if we looked through some of the papers inside? Just to see if there's anything of historical
value?"

"Rummage to your heart's content, Ms. Wingate.
I'd be happy to turn over anything and everything
to the historical society. In fact, it would make cleaning out the house a lot easier."

Joanna moved next to Michael as Jeremy Gladstone got into his car and drove away. "I can't believe that man wants to sell this house. Can you?"

"It needs a lot of work."

She frowned at him.

"What did I say?" he asked.

"You don't agree that this house should be torn
down, do you?"

"I haven't looked closely enough to determine
that," Michael said, deliberately baiting her.

"Oh, come on. It's an architect's dream."

"It may be unsafe to live in."

"So you can make it safe with the right remodeling design," she argued.

"I bet you never throw anything away, do you?" Michael asked as he walked up the steps to the front door. "You're probably one of those people who has the first dollar she ever made and every certificate she won in school."

"And what if I do? Keeping things that are important to you isn't a crime. Someday future generations will be fascinated by the way we lived. But how will they know how we lived if we don't preserve things, if we send everything to the garbage dump or burn it until nothing is left but ashes?" She gasped at the end of her sentence, at the significance of what she had just said.

"What's wrong?" Michael asked, surprised at her change of mood.

"Ashes. My mother burned something last night, something she didn't want me to see."

"What are you talking about?"

"She burned something. It was an envelope. When I showed her the photo of Angela, she was in my father's den, going through his things. He was the kind of man who kept everything, too. I asked if I could help, and I reached for an envelope on the desk. She practically slapped my hand away. Later, when I went into the den, the envelope was gone, and there were ashes in the wastebasket."

Michael listened with growing disquiet, once again reminded that her identity could put him in a difficult position. It wasn't just her resemblance to Angela. It was the suggestion of a blood tie, a relationship that had been kept secret for thirty years, that bothered him.

"I should just go home and confront my mother," Joanna said. "But I'm scared. I'm afraid she'll lie, and I'm afraid she'll tell me the truth. Maybe I don't want to know what she burned. Maybe it's better if I don't."

"That doesn't sound like a historian to me."

"I'm also a woman and a daughter, and God knows what else."

Michael didn't think past the anguish in her eyes, the fear in her voice, the trembling of her lips. He pulled her into his arms and pressed her head against his chest. It felt right to hold her. He knew exactly how she was feeling, because he was scared, too.

He'd always wanted a good mystery to solve. Now he had one, and he wished he didn't.

Tony had barely set foot in De Marco's when he saw Kathleen Shannon, the pretty, sharp-tongued Irish lass he couldn't seem to forget. She was serving dinner to a party of four businessman, but the men appeared to be more focused on the undone buttons of her blouse than their arriving meals.

Tony scowled, not sure why he felt so damn irritated. His bad mood got worse when he saw Helen and Joey sitting in one of the dark booths against the wall. Helen was laughing at something Joey said. Joey Scopazzi, Tony thought with disgust. The guy had never been able to tell a joke. If he didn't forget the punch line, he usually screwed it up. In fact, Joey Scopazzi had been one of the biggest screwups at Our Lady of Angels Elementary School. And now Joey Scopazzi, of all people, was marrying Helen Reed. Tony would never understand women, not in a million years.

He turned his attention back to Kathleen.

When she saw him she quickly turned her head toward the kitchen, then back again, as if she were looking for someone else. She set down the plates and walked over to him. For some reason his stomach clenched and he felt expectant. For what, he had no idea. This woman never seemed to do what she was supposed to do.

Without a word Kathleen took his hand and led him across the room.

"Where are we going?" he muttered.

She ignored him.

What the hell? Wherever they were going had to be better than this room, where Joey and Helen were acting like people in love. He waved to Lily and Rose, who were having dinner with Sophia and Vincent and a couple of the cousins. Sophia's eyes narrowed when she saw him with Kathleen. Fortunately Vincent didn't notice him at all.

Kathleen left the main dining room and went into the hall that led toward the telephones, the rest rooms, and the two private dining rooms that De Marco's offered for special parties.

He liked the feel of her hand in his. He liked the scent of her perfume. She smelled like Ireland. Her reddish gold hair had been swept up off her face and knotted with a gold band at the top of her head, revealing the slender curve of her neck, the fineness of her bones, the tiny earlobes, the long, dangly earrings. He'd always been a sucker for long, sexy earrings.

In fact, there wasn't much about Kathleen Shannon that he didn't like, except maybe her personality. But that didn't matter. If she wanted to take him into the back room and fool around, who was he to say no? Helen certainly wouldn't care.

Kathleen stopped in front of the door leading into the larger of the two private dining rooms. Tony knew the rooms were empty, because they rarely used them during the week, and if there had been a party, the doors would have been open and extra waiters on duty.

He put his hands on her shoulders and smiled at

her. "How long until you have to pick up your next table?"

"Five minutes," she said with a wicked grin. "Is that enough time for you? Or is it too long?"

"I guess you'll just have to find out." He lowered his head to kiss her, but she slipped away with a laugh.

"In your dreams," Kathleen said, opening the door. "He's all yours."

She pushed Tony into the room. Great, he'd been expecting secret sex in a back room, and all he got was Frank and Linda. As Kathleen left he could swear he heard her laughing. One of these days he would turn the tables on her.

"Oh, good, you're here," Linda said. "I asked Kathleen to keep an eye out for you."

The door closed behind him. "What's up?"

"We need to talk to you about the party, but quickly, because Vincent and Sophia will be done with dinner soon and we don't want them to see us here together."

"You're always here together."

"Not hiding in the back room," Linda said logically.

"That's true." He stopped, suddenly struck by something. "Linda, are you wearing the same dress as my mother? I could have sworn I just saw her in the dining room . . ."

"No, this one is navy. Hers is black," Linda said, smoothing down the short-sleeved, Empire-waisted cotton dress. "Do you like it?"

He'd liked it on his mother. It made Linda look as old and matronly as Sophia. He didn't understand why she insisted on molding herself after a woman so many years her senior.

"Tony?" Linda looked at him somewhat anxiously.

"It's—it's . . ." He shrugged.

"You don't like it."

"It's fine, but you have a good figure, Linda. You ought to show it off."

Linda blushed. "You think so?"

"Yeah. Don't you think Linda ought to wear something sleek and sexy, Frank?"

His brother didn't respond, his attention focused solely on the adding machine in front of him. He punched the keys with a ruthless, determined speed that would absolutely crunch the numbers to the point where he wanted them.

"Frank bought me this dress," Linda said after a moment. "He thinks Sophia dresses with class and I should, too. Anyway, we're planning to hold a private dinner in here for the family on Saturday night beginning at seven. At nine o'clock we'll spill into the main dining room for a big party with all of their friends. Marlena is going to take fake reservations for anything after seven-thirty just to make sure we can clear the dining room of strangers. And we've booked this room in the name of another party so Vincent won't question the additional waiters."

"How are you going to prevent Vincent from wondering why all his friends are sneaking into the back room?"

"Aunt Elena and Uncle Charles are taking Sophia and Vincent out to dinner somewhere else. Frank is going to call them just before they leave and say there's a big problem at the restaurant and ask them to stop by on their way."

"Not that they'll believe I can't deal with any problem that comes up," Frank grumbled. "I don't like this idea at all. It makes me look like a stupid kid who can't handle his job."

"Oh, stop thinking about your ego. It's a party," Linda snapped.

Tony raised an eyebrow in surprise, although he was pleased to see Linda stand up for herself.

"Sounds like you've got everything covered," he said.

"Almost everything," Frank replied. "This party will cost money. We can't ask Papa to absorb the cost through the restaurant. So, little brother, time to ante up." Frank smiled for the first time since Tony had come home. "Unless you're short of cash—again." He laughed.

Linda frowned at her husband. "Frank, you promised to be nice to Tony."

Promised to be nice. That would be the day, Tony thought. He and Frank hadn't agreed on anything in their entire lives. The four-year age difference between them had always given Frank far too much power, and he'd used it. But Frank didn't put himself in situations where he couldn't control the outcome. Just like this party.

"Why don't you have the party somewhere else?" Tony asked. "Someplace they don't see every day."

"I thought about that, too," Linda said with a sigh in Frank's direction.

Frank shook his head, and Tony realized with pleasure that his brother had lost more of his hair. In fact, he was looking pretty damn middle-aged. For some reason that made Tony feel better. Maybe because Frank didn't seem to have everything anymore.

"This is where Papa would want the party," Frank said simply. "Here with his friends and his family. He doesn't like to eat anywhere else. He only agreed to try a new place on their anniversary because Elena insisted on it. You know how he hates change." Frank twirled a pencil between his fingers. "Or maybe you don't, since you're never here."

"Sophia likes to try other restaurants," Linda pointed out. "It seems a shame that Vincent always gets his way."

Frank scowled at her. "We've been through this

before. The party is in three days. You want to change everything now?"

"No, of course not." Linda sat back in her chair with a defeated look.

"Then why bring it up?"

"Because Tony made a good point."

"Tony? He doesn't know what he's talking about."

Tony didn't have to defend himself, because Linda did it for him.

"You know, you're not the only one who knows how to give a party," she said.

"I give all our parties."

"Only because you won't let me."

"I let you—remember Janine's third birthday party when the clown came drunk and popped all the kids' balloons?"

"That was out of my control," she yelled back.

Tony stared at them in amazement. Linda and Frank had been together forever. They'd started dating in high school, had gone together all through college, and married in their early twenties. They had four kids, for God's sake. He'd always assumed they were happy. De Marco marriages lasted a lifetime. Sophia and Vincent at forty years were just the next in a long line of couples to make it to that milestone.

He wondered if Frank and Linda were going to make it until next Christmas.

Linda stood up. "Fine. If you don't want my opinion, then I'll leave. You and Tony can make all the decisions."

"Hey, wait a second, this is your party," Tony said. There was no way he was going to get stuck with taking care of this surprise party. He had other things to do, like convince Helen to sail away with him next week.

"This is a De Marco family party, as Frank pointed

out," Linda said. "You two are the blood De Marcos. I'm just an in-law, isn't that right, Frank?"

Frank tossed his pencil down on the table. "You want to go home, go home. You can get rid of that fool baby-sitter and save us ten dollars."

"I don't feel like going home. I think I'll go to the bar and have a drink." Her eyes glittered with anger. "On second thought, I think I'll go down the street to Finnegan's Bar and have an Irish whiskey."

"You're not going into a bar by yourself. You're a married woman."

"I'm thirty-seven years old, Frank. I may be married, but I'm not dead, and I'm tired of living my life in two places, my house and this damn restaurant. Tony's right—this dress makes me look like a frumpy old housewife." She stalked out of the room.

"Come back here!" Frank roared. She ignored him, and the door slammed behind her.

"Trouble in paradise?" Tony said with a smile.

Frank picked up the adding machine and threw it at Tony's head. Tony ducked, and it smashed against the wall. It was the first time he'd ever seen Frank lose control. It was also the first time he'd ever seen Linda walk out on her husband. This upcoming party might prove to be more interesting than he'd thought.

"Joanna?" Michael called as he walked through the crowded, junk-filled rooms of Ruby Mae's house. He'd spent the past fifteen minutes checking out the structure itself, looking for cracks in the foundation and problems with the framing and the roof. He'd found plenty. It was an old house.

Despite its age, Michael felt a tingle of excitement as he looked around. The ceilings were high, the doorways and windows curved, and the wide, winding staircase perfect for making a dramatic descent. The hardwood floors could be restored to their former glory, and he believed the crystal chandelier in the dining room would probably glitter once again with the right care.

It was a great house, but although he appreciated its charm, he wasn't sure Iris Sandbury would. She liked master bedroom suites, Jacuzzi bathtubs, and large walk-in closets, architectural designs unheard-of in the late 1800s. And the small kitchen would have to be completely redone to meet her gourmet cooking standards. It would take a tremendous amount of time and money to turn this antique structure into a modern mansion. Iris might prefer to tear it down and start over. Certainly the land, with its proximity to the sea, was very valuable.

"Joanna," he called again as he mounted the stairs. He wondered where she'd disappeared to. They'd parted awhile back as she set off to discover the true identity of the house's owner.

Identity seemed to be at the front of everything he came across these days. But it was easier to worry about Ruby Mae's identity than to think about Joanna's—if, in fact, she wasn't whom she claimed to be.

"I'm upstairs," Joanna called. "In the attic."

When he reached the top of the stairs, he saw an open door at the end of the hall, with more stairs leading up to the attic. As he walked down the hall, he glanced into each room. There were four bed-rooms. Two of them were empty. The third had a single bed and some boxes. The fourth, obviously the master bedroom, smelled of medicine and mil-dew. A wheelchair was folded up in one corner and the bed was a mess of tangled covers.

He wondered if Ruby Mae had died at home. If she had been alone or if someone had been with her at the end. The sight of the room bothered Michael, reminding him again of the transience of life. It had taken him months to get rid of Angela's clothes, to rid the bedroom and bathroom of her scents. For a while, every time he had turned a corner, he'd expected to trip over her.

"Michael, where are you?" Joanna called out again.

"I'm coming," he said, eager to get away from Ruby Mae's bedroom.

Joanna met him on the steps to the attic. "You won't believe what's up here."

He smiled. There was a streak of dust across her cheek, and she had pulled her hair up in a ponytail, securing it haphazardly with a rubber band. She looked hot, dusty, and excited. He found the combination irresistibly appealing. "What did you find?"

"Lots of things." She tossed him a black felt cowboy hat. "Try that on for size."

He put on the hat as he climbed the stairs. In the middle of the room a single light bulb hung on a wire. With beams of sunshine spilling in through the cracked window, the attic had in a soft glow that seemed to transport them back in time.

"How do I look?" he asked, tilting the hat to one side.

"Very dangerous, cowboy."

"And . . ."

"Sexy. Is that what you were looking for?" she asked with a grin.

"As a matter of fact, yes."

He tossed her the hat. She caught it and set it on the ground, then held up a ruby red spangled dress that was cut low in the front and back.

"How do you think I would look in this?" she asked.

"Very expensive."

Joanna hugged the dress to her. "You know, Ruby Mae was only sixteen years old when she started dancing at Barney's Saloon. I wonder how she felt looking down on all those men who wanted her

more than they wanted their next beer. I wonder if
she loved any of them, or if any of them loved her,"
she said with a sigh.

"I'm sure they all loved her for a while."

She made a face and tossed the dress at him. "I
wasn't talking about sex."

Michael caught it before it hit the floor. "This was
made for sex, Joanna. Ruby Mae was a prostitute.
She ran a whorehouse. Her whole life was about
sex."

"She was a woman living in a rough western
town. Did you know her mother died when she was
eight years old? She didn't have any female influ-
ences. She used to sit on her father's lap when he
played poker."

"Where did you learn all that?"

Joanna waved her hand toward a box on the floor.
"Journals. There are dozens of them. She wrote
everything down. I've just begun to look through
them. This is a gold mine, Michael. I hope Mr. Gladstone is willing to turn her journals over to the historical society. It could change the history of San
Francisco as we know it."

"One tainted woman change the city's history?"
Michael asked with a skeptical tilt to his head.
"Aren't you romanticizing Ruby Mae?"

"Just because she lived what some considered to
be a sinful life doesn't make her existence any less
important," Joanna replied. "And don't forget, a
man died in the fire that destroyed her whorehouse.
Wouldn't you like to know if he was murdered or
if he set the fire and couldn't get out in time? Aren't
you the one who wanted to be a boy detective?"

"That's when I was a boy. What else is up here?"
Michael asked.

"I don't know. I didn't get past the journals and
the trunks of costumes. I'd love to keep going
through it. Do you think I can come back?"

"Sure. We have the key until Mr. Gladstone returns."

Joanna sat down on top of an old steamer trunk. "How does the house look to you in terms of remodeling?"

"Like a very expensive job."

"Michael, you wouldn't recommend that your client tear this place down, would you?"

"I don't know. It's not my decision. Iris just wants an opinion."

"And what is your opinion?"

"That it would be a shame to lose a house with so much historic charm," Michael said slowly.

Her smile blossomed. "I knew it. I knew you couldn't be that tough and cynical and modern, not a man who loves adventure stories." She got up from the trunk and hugged him.

She meant it to be a brief and friendly hug. He knew that. But once she was in his arms, he couldn't let her go. She was glorious, passionate; and when she looked at him he saw desire in her eyes. Want, need, everything he felt. He had to kiss her. He had to taste her lips.

Her mouth opened shyly under his, as if she wasn't quite certain of where they were going. But as his lips moved against hers, as he fit his arms around her and pulled her closer against his chest, he felt the last of her resistance slide away.

He deepened the kiss, pushing past her lips, letting his tongue tease the corners of her mouth until he could slip inside. It was the most incredible first kiss he had ever experienced. Their bodies seemed to mold together instinctively. She felt perfect for him.

Until she pulled away, until the desire in her eyes turned to worry. "Do you know who you're kissing?" she asked.

He felt as if she'd kicked him in the gut. "What the hell kind of question is that?"

"A logical one, I think."

"I know who you are." But did he? Hadn't there been one second when he'd thought how good it felt to be kissing Angela again—or was it that it just felt right to be kissing a woman again? Did it really matter that she looked like his dead wife? Or would any woman bring back those memories?

He didn't know anyone his age who had lost a husband or a wife. He didn't know how long it took to move on. He didn't know if it was possible to completely forget someone who had shared his life for more than eight years, and he'd known Angela even longer than that, since she was a girl and he was a boy.

He let go of Joanna. The only thing he knew for sure was that kissing her was a bad idea. Too damned confusing. And the last thing he needed in his life was more confusion. He just wished it hadn't felt so good.

"Michael, I know there's an attraction between us. Maybe we should just get it out in the open."

"I thought we did."

"Okay. I guess we did," Joanna said, wariness filling her eyes. "But we can't do anything about it, not with the kids and the way I look and your family and friends. I don't want to go through life as someone's ghost."

"I don't blame you."

"We still don't know if there's a blood tie between Angela and me. What if I turn out to be a relative?"

Then the De Marco family would have a lot of explaining to do, Michael thought. "I can't believe anyone in the De Marco family would have given up a child—for any reason. It doesn't make sense to me. They're good, solid people. They go to Mass every Sunday, to confession three times a year. They donate to charity." He shrugged at the end of his sentence. "I don't see how it could have happened. Sophia and Vincent are celebrating forty years of marriage this coming Saturday night. Carlotta and Steven have been married thirty-seven years. Elena and Charles have been married for the last twenty. Do they sound like the kind of people who would give away a baby of their own?"

"What about the younger woman, Elena? I'm twenty-nine. She wouldn't have been married when I was born."

Michael tipped his head in acknowledgement. "I have to admit she seems the most likely candidate. Do you want me to talk to her for you?"

"Would you?"

"I'll see what I can do."

"I better go." She looked down at her watch. "Oh, dear, it's past seven-thirty. I lose all track of time when it stays light this late. My mother is probably climbing the walls. I told her I'd be home around five."

"Does she worry that much about you?"

"She worries about me every second of her life. She's been a wonderful mom, but to the point of obsession some times. Especially since my dad died. Now I'm her whole life instead of just an incredibly big part of it."

"Maybe she's obsessive for a reason."

Joanna frowned. "Like the De Marcos, Michael, my parents were the most conservative, respectable people I know. I can't believe they could have lied to me all these years. I also can't believe this is a coincidence."

"It might be more difficult to believe it's anything else."

13

Sophia tucked Rose into bed and kissed her on the forehead. Rose's skin felt warm from her recent bath. Her hair lay damp against her forehead, and Sophia tenderly brushed it to the side. Rose and Lily both looked so much like Angela when she was this age. Sometimes the joy of being with them was tempered with pain from the loss of her daughter, their mother.

"Grandma," Rose said, "do you think there's a heaven?"

"Yes. Don't you?" she asked in surprise, not sure where this conversation was leading or whether she wanted to go with it. It had been a long, emotional day. She didn't know how much more she could take or how much more calm she could fake.

Lily came over and sat on the end of Rose's bed. "Do you think Mama is in heaven?"

"Absolutely." Sophia pulled Lily against her breast. "I think she's dancing with the angels right this second. You know how much she liked to dance."

"I like to dance, too."

"Then we'll dance."

Sophia pulled Lily off the bed and spun her around. Rose climbed out of bed and joined hands with Sophia and her sister. The three of them danced

around in a circle until they fell down on the bed in
a pile of giggles and breathlessness.

"I may have to sleep right here," Sophia said. "I'm
exhausted."

"You can sleep with me," Rose offered.

"No, me," Lily said.

Actually, sleeping with either of the girls was
more tempting than going home and getting into
bed with her husband. He had been tense all evening, even berating the twins for spilling their spaghetti and talking with their mouths full. Sophia
didn't want to get into another argument with him
about Joanna, because she knew she couldn't possibly win.

"Grandma, are you sad?" Rose touched Sophia's
face with her tiny fingers.

Sophia's eyes filled with tears at the question. It
had been so long since anyone had asked her how
she felt, had looked into her eyes and her heart and
seen what was really there, not what she wanted
them to see.

"I'm a little sad. I miss your mother, too." She
paused, knowing that she had to accomplish one
very important thing tonight. "I don't believe Joanna
is your mother."

Lily and Rose both stared at her with solemn eyes.

"Joanna is just a lovely woman who happens to
look like your mother. That's all."

"Then Mama must still be coming back,
Grandma," Lily said. "She promised she would."

"Sometimes people can't keep their promises, no
matter how much they want to. I'm sure your
mother had every intention of coming back, but God
decided he needed her in heaven."

"I don't think I like God," Lily said.

"Lily, you mustn't say that," Rose whispered. "It's
a sin not to like God, isn't it, Grandma?"

How could she possibly explain why the good

Lord had taken their mother from them? She didn't
understand it herself. But she had to try.

"It's about faith," Sophia said. "Believing in something even if it doesn't make sense."

"Then Mama is still coming home," Lily said. "Because I have faith."

Sophia sighed. That wasn't the correlation she had
been hoping for. "It's late, girls. Time to turn off the
lights.

"Wait, we have to say good night to Mariah."
Rose sat up in bed. The wizard was on the nightstand between the beds, her beautiful smile encom-
passing them all.

"Okay, say good night," Sophia said with a laugh.
She loved the romantic tale of the wizard's ability to
bring families back together. She wanted to believe
it could happen. That's why she had made her own
wish.

Her wish. Sophia's heart lightened as she thought
of all that had happened since she'd bought Mariah.
Maybe the wizard had heard her wish. Maybe that's
why Joanna had come into their lives.

Rose rubbed her hand across the top of the ball.
"Good night, Mariah."

Lily did the same, but she drew her hand back
with a disappointed expression. "Mariah didn't say
good night back. She did last night."

"Maybe it's because Grandma is here," Rose said.
"Or maybe she's sleeping."

"Just like you should be," Sophia said. "Back into
bed now."

"I don't think Daddy believes in magic," Rose said
as she slid under the covers.

"Mama believed, but Daddy always said she was
silly for reading fortune cookies and playing the lot-
tery and reading her hor—horrerscope," Lily stuttered.

Sophia laughed. "That's horoscope." She sat down

on the edge of Lily's bed. "Do you want to hear a secret?"

Lily's eyes lit up. "Yes."

"When your daddy was a boy, about thirteen or fourteen, he went to the county fair and spent all his money feeding quarters into the fortune teller machine."

"What's a fortune teller machine?" Rose asked.

"It's kind of like Mariah. It's supposed to tell your fortune. You put in a quarter and it gives you back a card. Unfortunately your father didn't like the cards he was getting, so he kept playing until he got the fortune he wanted."

"Then he does believe in magic," Rose said hopefully.

"Either that or he believes in persistence." Sophia tucked the covers around Lily's body. "Maybe it's good to believe in both. Hard work and a little bit of magic. Yes, I think I like that combination."

"Daddy says you're really smart," Lily said.

"He's smart, too. Good night, girls. Sleep tight. Don't let the bedbugs bite."

Sophia turned off the light and paused at the doorway to take one last look at the twins.

"Grandma," Rose said.

"What, honey?"

"Even if Joanna isn't Mama—she could still marry Daddy, couldn't she?"

The innocent question hit Sophia like an electric shock, drawing goose bumps down her arms and the back of her spine. Michael and Joanna. She had never considered such a possibility.

A tiny flicker of hope lit within her, but she doused it with a dose of common sense. Joanna and Michael could never be together. Never.

Michael burst through the front door as Sophia reached the bottom stair. "Sophia, I'm sorry. The time got away from me. I apologize."

She patted him on the arm. "It's fine. We had dinner at the restaurant, and I put the girls to bed. I like being with them."

"They love being with you." He paused, noting the weary lines around Sophia's eyes, the dark shadows that implied she hadn't slept well the past couple of nights. "Are you all right?"

"Why wouldn't I be?"

"That's not an answer."

"I'm a little tired."

"Did you see Joanna today?" he asked, knowing that she hadn't, but wondering what Sophia would say.

Sophia looked away, a more telling response than a verbal answer. Why did Joanna's name create so much tension in her? Simply because he'd told her about the resemblance? Or was there more?

"No, I didn't see her. Another teacher had the girls."

"Would you like to meet her sometime?"

Her eyes filled with an emotion that looked a lot like panic. "Maybe. Why?"

"I could bring Joanna by the restaurant."

"No. Vincent doesn't want to be reminded of Angela."

"But it doesn't bother you?"

"It might, but I feel compelled to see her."

"Why?"

"I just do. You look tired, too, Michael. You're not eating right, are you? Shall I fix you something?"

"You don't have to take care of me. I'm a grown man."

"That doesn't mean you don't still need a mother." Her eyes darkened. "I think everyone needs a mother, no matter how old they are."

"You've been a great mother to me. I don't know

what I would have done if you hadn't taken me into your home, into your family."

She smiled at him. "You probably would have spent the spring climbing up the trellis to Tony's bedroom window, crawling inside, knocking over the lamp, and praying that no one would know you were there."

He looked at her in astonishment. "You knew."

"Of course, I knew."

"Why didn't you say anything?"

"You weren't happy at home. Your mother was remarrying. I knew things were difficult."

"You're incredible."

"No, I'm a mother."

She was certainly the best mother he'd ever known, a warm, loving, nurturing woman who gave everything to her children. As he looked into her sweet face, he knew she couldn't possibly have given up a baby for adoption.

"Michael," she said, her tone turning serious, "the girls are getting very attached to—to Joanna."

"I know. I'm concerned, but I don't know what to do." He took a deep breath. "Sophia, do you think there's any possibility Joanna could be related to the De Marco family?"

"Why—why do you ask that?" Her gaze darted nervously from his face to his chest, to his shoes, anywhere but his eyes.

"Because of her looks," he said as an uneasy feeling crept up his spine.

"I've often thought that Italians have a common look."

"Joanna isn't Italian."

Sophia snapped her fingers. "I almost forgot to tell you. Tony said he had a lunchtime basketball game set up at the YMCA, and he wants you to play. Twelve o'clock tomorrow." She picked up her purse from the hall table. "I better go. Vincent will be waiting." She stood on tiptoe and kissed him on the cheek. "Sleep well, Michael."

As the door closed behind her, Michael realized she hadn't answered his question. In fact, she'd gone out of her way to avoid a reply. There was no way in hell he would sleep well now. He didn't want to believe Sophia was hiding anything or that there were any skeletons in any closet in any De Marco family home. They were the perfect family in his mind, and damned if that wasn't one fantasy he wanted to hang on to.

Caroline breathed harder with each new step on the stair climbing machine. She'd already been on it for twenty-five minutes, and sweat was dripping down her forehead and the back of her neck. But she continued relentlessly toward the thirty-minute mark. It was a goal she set for herself each day, and she was determined to reach it. Because if she could do this, if she could stay focused on the pain in her legs and the sweat on her arms, then she wouldn't have to think about Edward or worry about Joanna.

She'd always loved to exercise, but it had become an obsession the day after Edward had been diagnosed with cancer. She told herself she did it to stay fit, to relieve stress. She really did it because she was scared, afraid of dying, of being a widow, of losing her daughter, and terrified that if she didn't do this one thing, she wouldn't do anything. She wouldn't get up. She wouldn't get dressed. She'd have no reason to ever take off her nightgown. So she kept going until the timer went off, then slowed her steps until the heat in her cheeks began to cool.

The front door slammed. Joanna was finally home.

Caroline got off the StairMaster and wiped her face and neck with a towel.

"Hi, Mom." Joanna walked into Caroline's bedroom and flopped down on the bed. "Sorry I'm late."

"I was getting worried. You said you'd be home around five." Caroline took a sip of water from the bottle she'd set on the dresser.

"The time got away from me. How was your workout? Did you make thirty minutes?"

"Of course."

"Of course," Joanna echoed with a smile. "You really are amazing, you know that?"

Caroline felt pleased at the pride she saw in Joanna's eyes. At least she could do one thing right. Although Joanna was probably just trying to distract her. Yes, that was it, she realized as Joanna's smile faded and her daughter picked at the bedspread with nervous fingers. "Okay, where were you?" Caroline asked bluntly.

"I was with Michael Ashton."

The Ashtons again. Joanna seemed to get more involved with their family each day. Caroline tried to stay calm. If she knew one thing about her daughter, it was that telling Joanna not to do something was like waving a red flag in front of a bull. She would want to hear at least five good reasons why she should stop seeing Michael Ashton, and Caroline wasn't sure she could come up with that many.

"Isn't it enough that you teach his children every day?" Caroline slung the towel around her neck. "Do you have to see the Ashtons after work, too?"

"I don't have to. I want to." Joanna looked her mother straight in the eye. "Why does it bother you so much?"

"I don't see that you have anything to gain by getting involved with this man and his children. You can't replace the woman they lost."

"I'm not trying to do that. And to be frank, I didn't go to see Michael because of Angela. I want to see him because of me. I have questions that need to be answered."

"I told you yesterday there is no mystery to unravel. Why won't you believe me?"

"Because I look like the De Marcos and I don't look like the Wingates. I don't understand why."

"Sometimes things just happen. What do you hope to find out, Joanna? Would you rather have a different set of parents? Would you rather belong to this other family?"

"No, of course not."

"It's a good thing your father isn't here. He'd be hurt."

"It's not a good thing that he's gone, Mother. And I'm not trying to hurt you. Why are you defensive? I get the feeling you have something to hide."

"Don't be silly. We've been best friends since the day you were born. What could I possibly have to hide?" But she couldn't look at Joanna when she said the words, so she took another sip from her water bottle.

"I don't know. What did you burn yesterday? And don't try to deny it, because I saw the ashes in the wastebasket."

Caroline struggled to stay calm. "I burned some papers, that's all. Old bills from twenty years ago. I thought it would cut down on the amount of trash."

"Oh, Mother, please."

Caroline sighed. She knew what she had to do. "Look, I can put all this questioning to rest. Come with me." She led Joanna into the den and walked to the filing cabinet. Opening the top drawer, she pulled out a single sheet of paper and handed it to Joanna.

Joanna reluctantly took the paper from her mother's hand. As she glanced down at the notary seal, the official emblem for the state of California, she realized her mother was giving her her birth certif-

icate. The paper stated that a baby girl had been
born on July 28, 1968, to Caroline and Edward Wingate.

Joanna knew she'd probably seen her birth certificate when she got her driver's license, but it had
never seemed so important until now.

She was the child of Caroline and Edward Wingate. The state of California said so in black and
white. There was no mistake. An overwhelming
sense of relief flooded through her. Thank God. Her
mother was right. It was all just a coincidence.

"Are you satisfied now?" Caroline asked.

Joanna handed back the certificate. "Yes."

"Good." Caroline slid the paper into the filing
cabinet, then shut the drawer. She tucked Joanna's
hair behind her head in a gesture of motherly love.
"You are my baby girl," she said, her eyes softening
with emotion. "I wanted you more than any woman
could want her child. I used to watch you when you
slept. Sometimes in the middle of the night I'd creep
into your room and put my ear down to your chest
just to make sure you were breathing. I couldn't
have stood it if anything happened to you. I know I
stuck close to you, but I was afraid of losing you."

Joanna felt a rush of tenderness at Caroline's
words. She knew her mother loved her. She'd always known that. How could any loyal daughter
complain of too much love?

"You are a great mom, even if you are too skinny,
too pretty, and way too blond to be my mother."

Caroline put a hand to her heart. "I absolutely
swear that I did not have an affair with the post-
man."

Joanna smiled. "Knowing Mr. O'Hurlihy, I believe
that."

"Let's sit down for a minute." Caroline took
Joanna's hand and led her over to the sofa. "You
know, Edward picked your name for you. He liked

Jo because it was tough and Anna because it was soft. And he wanted you to be both." She smiled at Joanna, her pale face beaming with maternal pride. "When I saw you for the first time, your eyes were wide open. I thought you looked like a wise old lady who probably knew more than I did about everything. I got so scared. My hands shook when I tried to change your diaper that first time. I was afraid I would hurt you or do something wrong."

"But you didn't."

"I made it through the diaper okay, but that feeling of fear never went away. I know I worry too much and nag too much and drive you crazy, but it's only because I love you so much I can't stand it. I want your life to be perfect."

"I know you do." Joanna hugged her mother. How could she have doubted her even for a second? This woman was not a monster. She was the woman who had bathed her, fed her, thrown her the best birthday parties in town. So they didn't look like each other, so what? It didn't mean a thing.

But after the hug, after the rationalizations, a part of her still questioned why there were no photos of her mother pregnant, why no one in San Rafael remembered seeing her mother pregnant, and why her mother had felt the need to burn something. But to voice those questions aloud would betray the love she had just seen and heard.

On Thursday morning Tony felt a bit foolish and a lot desperate as he stood in front of Helen's apartment building with a bag of bagels in one hand and two cups of coffee in the other. He remembered his mother telling him how Vincent used to come courting. Courting. An old-fashioned word, and he was supposed to be a sophisticated guy. What the hell was he doing here?

Trying to salvage the only good relationship he'd

ever had, he decided. He couldn't let Helen marry Joey, not without putting up a fight, although his conscience questioned whether he wanted Helen more now because she was taken. He'd always wanted what other people had. He'd always liked to win.

He just had to convince Helen that he was better than Joey Scopazzi. Not that he intended to offer marriage. No, after seeing Frank and Linda the night before, he had a pretty good idea of what marriage looked like fourteen years down the road. Of course, Sophia and Vincent were still madly in love after forty years. Maybe if it was the right woman—maybe forty years wouldn't seem like a life sentence. With a decisive jab Tony pushed the button over the mailbox.

Helen's voice came over the intercom, sleepy and breathless. "Yes."

"It's Tony."

"Go away."

"Helen, I need to talk to you."

"I don't want to talk to you."

It suddenly occurred to him that Helen might not be alone. Maybe Joey was still in her bed. His stomach turned over at the thought.

"Are you alone?" he asked.

There was a long, pregnant pause.

"Yes."

"Let me in. You're not afraid to talk to me, are you?"

"Of course not." She hit the buzzer, and he managed to juggle the coffee and the bagels long enough to get the front door open.

Her apartment door was closed when he reached her floor, and he had to knock again. Helen answered the door wearing a terry cloth robe, her blond hair tousled from sleep, her feet bare. He handed her the bagels. She took them reluctantly. He wanted to kiss her, but decided not to risk it just yet.

"Joey is picking me up in fifteen minutes. So make this quick," she said. "I still have to get dressed. You know, Joey takes me to work every morning."

"I thought he worked on the other side of town."

"He doesn't want me to take the bus. He worries about me."

Direct hit number one, Tony thought. "I brought you some bagels and coffee. I know how you like your shot of caffeine in the morning." He set the bag down on her dining room table in a small alcove off the kitchen.

"I don't drink caffeine anymore. Joey and I want to have a baby right away, and caffeine isn't good for me."

Strike two. "How about a bagel? You still eat, don't you?"

"Yes. But I'm not hungry. Why don't you just say what you have to say and go?"

Tony sat down at the table. Helen stood a few feet away, her arms crossed in front of her chest, her face resolute, as if she would absolutely not give him an inch. He had to find a way to disarm her. He knew only one way.

"I'm sorry. I was wrong."

Her jaw dropped open. "You were wrong? I never thought I'd hear those words come out of your mouth."

"I should have come back sooner. I should have written or called. I worked a lot the past few months, Helen. Every second I could. I sweated blood so I could raise enough money to buy something of my own. I finally made it. I bought a boat, a fifty-footer. It sleeps eight. Perfect for running small charters. I'm going to have my own home and my own business. I want you to share it with me. I always did."

She shook her head in confusion. "Why didn't you

ever tell me what you were doing? You never said a word."

"I wasn't sure I could do it," he said, knowing he'd feared all along that he couldn't. Raising that money had been the hardest thing he'd ever done, and he felt proud of his accomplishment.

Helen leaned against the back of the sofa. "It's too late, Tony. I'm with someone else."

Her words were hard, but her face had softened. Her eyes no longer burned with hate. Maybe he still had a small chance.

"Helen, I love you. You know I never say that unless I mean it."

"I know you always told me that."

"It's true." He stood up and walked over to her. He put his hands on her shoulders and gazed into her eyes. "Don't marry Joey."

"Joey loves me, too."

"What about you? How do you feel?"

"Angry, hurt, confused. You walked away from me, Tony. You blew me off. Oh, sure, you said you'd be back, but the weeks and the months went by and all I got were a few postcards. You never said anything about buying your own boat or starting your own business or even about coming back. What was I supposed to do?"

"You could have trusted me."

"Trust? You didn't trust me enough to share your plans."

"I didn't want to let you down if I came up short. I wanted to come back with something to offer you."

"Like what, Tony? What are you offering me besides coffee that I don't drink anymore?"

Tony rolled his neck to relieve the tension in his muscles. "I'm offering you a—a long-term relationship," he said finally.

"As in marriage and children, or as in let's hang out on my boat and have great sex?"

Tony smiled. "The last two sound the best to me."

"Thanks anyway, but I'll stick with Joey. He may not have a boat, but he can give me the rest, including the great sex."

Tony winced. Strike three, you're out. Wait, maybe he could foul that one off, make her change her mind.

Before she could say anything more, he kissed her. He ran his hands under her robe and pulled her body against his, making her remember just what she was giving up. Helen struggled in his arms, but he persisted until her lips softened, until she threw her arms around his neck and kissed him back, until they both came up for air.

"You still love me," he said confidently.

She shook her head, her eyes glittering with unshed tears. "That was a good-bye kiss, Tony. Now all that's left is good-bye."

"It didn't feel like good-bye."

"Maybe because you always leave first. Maybe you don't know what good-bye feels like, but I do know, and it feels like this."

He stood there, completely stunned. God, she was right. He couldn't remember the last time a woman had dumped him, if ever. He didn't like it, not one bit.

14

Michael dribbled the basketball down the court, weaving through the defenders until he saw the net. His movements were hampered by a very persistent guard. For a moment he could see nothing but the hairy armpits of the guy in front of him. He ducked to one side and took a shot, colliding with the other guy as he did so.

The referee's whistle blew as they both landed hard on the gymnasium floor.

"Foul. No basket," the referee said.

"What?" Michael shouted, scrambling to his feet. "If anything, he fouled me."

"You were charging."

"I was shooting."

Tony stepped between Michael and the referee. "Forget about it. Let's play."

Michael muttered under his breath as he scowled at the referee. Any fool should have been able to see the other guy elbow him on his way to the basket.

The game continued for several more minutes. Michael had another shot at a game-winning basket in the final thirty seconds, and took it, pleased when the buzzer rang at the exact moment the ball swished through the net.

"That was sweet," Tony said, giving him a high

five. "Reminded me of senior year in high school all over again."

Michael laughed as they shook hands with a couple of other players, then headed over to the bleachers to get their bags. "I sure didn't feel this winded when I was seventeen." He grabbed a towel out of his gym bag and wiped his face and arms. His heart was pounding, his blood racing. He hadn't felt this good in a long time. "I'm glad you came home," he said to Tony. "I needed a workout."

"You haven't shot hoops since I left?"

Michael shook his head. "No time. I'm too busy with work and the girls and everything else."

"Man, you used to love basketball." Tony shook his head in bewilderment. "In fact, you are the mellowest dude in the world except when it comes to hoops. Then you're a crazy man."

"I still love the game." Michael sat down on the bench. "It just isn't as important to me as it used to be."

Tony sat down next to him, and they watched the new game with interest. After a moment Tony turned his head to look at Michael. "Did you talk to Helen this morning?"

Michael shot him a dry smile. "I talk to her every morning. She's my secretary."

"Did she say anything about me?"

"Nope."

"Did she say anything about Joey?"

"Nope."

"Did she look even remotely upset when she first came into the office?"

"Nope."

"Is that all you have to say?" Tony demanded.

"Nope. Stay away from Helen. She is a wonderful woman who's getting married in three weeks."

Tony leaned forward, twisting his hands together

as he rested his elbows on his knees. "I can't stop thinking about her."

"Why? You didn't think about her for a year. She only got two postcards from you, one less than you sent me. Why the sudden interest?"

"Maybe I just realized how great she is."

"Maybe you just realized Joey Scopazzi is getting your former girlfriend, and you hate the thought of him winning. You've always been a poor loser."

"I have not. And by the way, I'm not the one who almost got called for a technical foul a few minutes ago."

Michael shrugged. "So I hate to lose, too. But only in basketball. I don't break up other people's relationships. You have to accept that Helen is with someone else. You blew it."

"Hey, thanks for the pep talk."

"I'm calling it like I see it."

"Fine. Are you going back to work?"

"Yeah."

"What about later? You want to have a drink? Go by Brannigan's and toss back some whiskey?"

"No. I'm going . . ." Michael stopped, not sure he wanted to tell Tony his plans.

"Going to . . ." Tony prodded.

"I have some things to do."

"What kind of things?"

"Just things." Michael focused his attention on the game, but Tony persisted.

"What are you hiding? Are you seeing someone? That's it, isn't it? You've got a hot date."

Michael sighed, knowing if he didn't stop it here, there was no telling where Tony would end up. "I don't have a date. I'm looking at a house."

"With . . ."

"With Joanna Wingate."

Tony's teasing smile vanished. "What the hell for?"

"Because she's a historian, and the house might have historical value."

"Bullshit. You're interested in her. Man, I can't believe you're attracted to that woman. Actually I *can* believe it, because she looks just like my sister."

"Nothing is going on," Michael said.

"Because of you or because of her?"

"Because of both of us. I'll admit to being attracted, but that's the end of it."

"Then why are you spending time with her?"

"I told you why."

"I don't believe it. You want her because she's the closest thing you can get to Angela."

"Actually that's only the reason I don't want her," Michael said with annoyance. "She reminds me of the biggest mistake of my life."

Tony shoved Michael. "Don't ever call Angie a mistake."

Michael shoved him back. "I can say anything I want. She was my wife."

"She was my sister," Tony said belligerently.

Michael let out an angry breath. "Yeah, and we both loved the hell out of her."

His words defused the anger between them. Tony looked away from Michael to the game that went on before them. "You did love her, didn't you?" Tony asked after a moment.

"You know I did." Michael wiped his face with the towel. "But we weren't happy. I don't know what happened."

"She was crazy about you."

"In the beginning, maybe. As time passed I was about as exciting as an old shoe." He paused. "In fact, I think Angela was having an affair."

Tony looked surprised. "Are you sure?"

"No." But once again Michael remembered the man at the funeral, the one who had cried for Angela.

"I can't believe Angela would cheat on you," Tony said. "She certainly wasn't raised that way. Sophia was the perfect role model of what a wife should be."

"Angela wasn't Sophia. And she didn't want to be."

"I know Angie complained about stuff. But I didn't take her seriously."

"Maybe you should have."

"Maybe. I still don't understand how you can contemplate a relationship with this other woman."

"Who said I was?"

"Come on. I know you, man. You don't waste time with people who don't interest you. You were the original one-date wonder. Every girl had something wrong with her. Too slow, too fast, too talkative, too quiet." He paused. "Angela wouldn't let you walk away, though. She chased you like crazy. Mama and Papa thought you were the one pursuing her, but it was Angela all the time. She followed you everywhere, even spied on some of your dates."

"Yeah, and when she got me she didn't want me anymore," Michael said with a self-deprecating smile. "I always told her what to do, looked out for her like her parents had done. She married me to get free of the family, only to find out I was as much of a De Marco as any of you."

"Maybe even more so." Tony sent Michael a pointed glance. "Which is exactly why you should stay away from Joanna Wingate. She could be trouble."

Michael knew Tony was right. But he couldn't stop seeing Joanna. Her intelligent, sharp wit; her passion for old-fashioned things; her loyalty to her parents; and her caring for his children were all traits that appealed to him, not to mention the fact that he wanted her bad. Just thinking about her made him get hard.

One kiss and she'd gotten under his skin. He wanted to kiss her again, to explore every inch of her body—what he wanted was everything. What he needed was a cold shower. Then he would think about getting a chaperon for the afternoon. Make that two chaperons.

"It looks like a castle." Lily's eyes widened in amazement as Joanna helped her out of Michael's car.

"You think so?" Joanna smiled at her obvious delight.

"It's beautiful," Rose agreed, holding Michael's hand as they walked toward Ruby Mae's house. "It's much taller than our house."

"But not as big as some of the buildings Daddy draws," Lily said importantly. "Did you know he built that big tower downtown, Joanna? You can't even see the top because it goes through the clouds."

"I didn't know that. Your father is pretty talented."

"Aw, shucks," Michael said with an endearing grin that melted Joanna's heart. Dressed in a T-shirt and blue jeans, Michael looked carefree and attractive, Joanna thought, a perfect blend of a man, athletic, intelligent, confident about his work, yet vulnerable where his girls were concerned. She liked him, probably too much.

She had to remind herself this wasn't personal. They were working on a project together, the way she'd worked with many men at the university. Only those men hadn't made her blood race and her skin tingle every time they looked at her.

She stuffed her hands into the pockets of her jeans. She had changed clothes after work, knowing there would be plenty of dust and grime involved in her search through Ruby Mae's papers. The jeans and T-shirt were comfortable, but they took away her defenses. It was easier to be cool and calm in her schoolteacher clothes, where she wore authority like a cloak. Now she was just a woman, and he was just a man. And as she met his gaze she knew this outing was a bad idea. They weren't keeping their distance; they were getting closer, and God only knew where they'd end up.

"Is the house haunted, Joanna?" Lily asked, walking up the front steps.

"I don't think so."

"What about that lady—Ruby Mae? Maybe she's a ghost," Lily added, determined to add spice to the story.

"There are no such thing as ghosts," Michael said.

Joanna raised an eyebrow. "How do you know?"

He looked at her in amazement. "You're not telling me you believe in ghosts?"

"Maybe. There are some events in history that are difficult to explain. Actually there are some events in my own life that are difficult to explain," she added with a wry smile.

"You've got me there."

Michael opened the front door, and as they stepped inside, Rose sneezed and Lily wrinkled her nose.

"It smells like Daddy's socks in here," Lily said.

"Hey, wait a minute," Michael protested. "They're not that bad."

Lily's eyes twinkled, but she didn't respond to her father. She just giggled and grabbed Rose's hand so they could start exploring.

"Be careful. Stay away from the back fence and don't even think about going down the cliffs to the beach. Oh, and don't break anything," Michael added. "This isn't our house."

"Does that mean it's okay to break things in your house?" Joanna asked as the girls scampered away. She loved watching Michael with the girls. He was great with them, never losing his patience or his cool.

He put his hands on his hips as he smiled at her. "It's not okay, but that doesn't stop them. You may not believe this, but I can't always control them."

"Really? I never would have guessed."

"How have they been at school, by the way?"

"Great. Oh, they're inquisitive, and Lily loves to do everything first, but they're wonderful children. They're very easy to love."

Michael put one hand against his ear as if he couldn't believe what he was hearing. "Are you sure you're talking about my children, the ones who have terrorized five different nanny supplying agencies?"

"Those nannies must have been wimps."

"No, they just weren't you. You've got the touch."

"I've just got the looks," Joanna said with a sigh. "By the way, I spoke to my mother last night, and she showed me my birth certificate. Her name and my father's name are listed on it. They are my parents. There's no doubt."

Michael sent her a thoughtful look.

"What? You don't believe me?"

"It's not that."

"Then what is it?"

"Sophia's sister Elena called me last night, and she asked a million questions about you. She said she was curious, but I thought it was strange. Elena was wild in her younger days. She actually married and divorced before hooking up with her present husband. Since she met Charles and had two children, she has been very content, but she certainly wasn't before that. Sophia always used to bail her out. They're very close. In fact, I've often felt shut out when they're together. They seem to have so many secrets."

Secrets? Joanna felt her uneasiness return. "Are

you suggesting that Elena could have given up a baby for adoption?"

"I don't know what I'm suggesting. Maybe I made more out of the conversation than was there. Although Elena and I are friendly, she doesn't call me at home to chat like she did last night. I think she wanted to know something specific; I'm just not sure what. Look, let's forget it. Where do you want to start? Upstairs, downstairs, the attic? Shall we split up or work together?"

His gaze traveled across her face and down her body. Joanna felt herself grow hot. She couldn't remember what he had just asked her. All she could focus on was the fact that he was standing a foot away from her, looking at her as if he wanted to do more than clean the attic.

"Joanna?"

He didn't continue with his question. And she didn't answer. She just leaned toward him, and he leaned toward her. Suddenly she was in his arms. His mouth touched her lips, and it felt as if she'd come home.

"You do that really well, you know," Michael muttered as he lifted his head.

"So do you."

"I missed you today."

"I missed you, too." She couldn't believe she was admitting that to him. But there was honesty in his eyes that demanded honesty in return. "I couldn't help it. I've only known you for three days, and I can't get you out of my head."

"It's hell, isn't it?"

She started as she heard Lily call out to Rose. "The girls." She clapped her hand over her mouth. "My God, I almost forgot about the girls. We can't do this. What would they think?"

Michael dropped his hands from her waist and stepped back. "You're right. I'm sorry."

"Maybe I should go home."

"No, don't. We'll keep our distance."

"That doesn't seem to be working." She looked over her shoulder to see if Rose and Lily were in sight, then turned back to him. "If the girls see you kissing me, they'll think I'm their mother again."

"You're right. I wasn't thinking. I'll check the basement. You can start in the attic. With any luck we won't even see each other for a few hours. That should cool things down."

Joanna sighed as he walked away. She didn't think anything would cool them down. Her attraction to Michael scared her to death. She had never believed in love at first sight until this moment.

Why did it have to be him? Why did it have to be now? Because this sure wasn't the right time or the right place. Not that there ever would be.

"Joanna!" Rose screamed.

Joanna turned sharply to see Rose run through the kitchen door. "What's wrong?"

"Lily fell down the cliff."

Joanna ran toward the back door. "Go get your dad. He's in the basement—down the hall to your left."

The backyard of Ruby Mae's house went straight back to the cliffs that overlooked the Pacific Ocean. There was a short picket fence edging the property, but any determined six-year-old could easily get over it.

Joanna climbed over the fence and carefully picked her way to the edge, hoping to catch a glimpse of Lily. As she did so she saw a path of crumbling cement stairs leading down the hillside. Before she could take a step toward them, Michael came up behind her, his eyes worried, his stance tense.

"Do you see her?"

"No."

"Lily! Lily!" he shouted, cupping his hands so the wind wouldn't take away his voice. "Where are you?" He turned to Joanna. "You try, just in case she won't answer me."

"Lily!" Joanna called, but there was still no reply.

"She went down the steps," Rose said, sliding her arms around Joanna's waist. "Then she screamed and I heard the rocks fall."

"I'm going after her," Michael said. "There's a cell phone in my car. Call 911."

"Joanna . . ." Lily's voice carried across the early evening breeze. "I'm stuck."

"Wait," Michael said, putting a hand on Joanna's arm. "She sounds pretty strong. Let me see if I can get to her first." He carefully picked his way down the first few cement steps, testing each one with his foot before putting all his weight on it.

Joanna held her breath, wondering if she shouldn't call 911 anyway. What if he fell? What if Lily was hurt?

"It's okay. I can see her," Michael called back. "And I think I can get her. Hang on, Lily, I'm coming."

A few minutes later Michael returned, carrying Lily in his arms. He set her down on the grass and tenderly stroked the traces of tears from her eyes. "Does it hurt anywhere, honey?"

Lily shook her head, sniffing back the last of her fear.

"Her foot was caught in the roots of a tree," Michael said to Joanna. "I thought she might have twisted it, but it doesn't feel swollen." He ran his hand down her slender ankle once again. "Are you sure it doesn't hurt?" he asked again.

Once again Lily replied to his question with a negative shake of her head.

Michael sighed as he stared at his daughter. "I told you not to go near that fence, didn't I? What

am I going to do with you? You scared me to death."
He paused. "But I am really glad you're okay."

Lily's bottom lip began to tremble, and Michael
put his arms around her. Rose knelt down next to
her father and put her hand on his arm. Joanna's
heart almost broke in two at the sight. The girls
might not talk to their father, but they truly loved
him, and he loved them. There hadn't been a moment's hesitation in his actions, not a doubt that he
might be risking his own life to climb down that
cliff.

"Joanna . . ." Lily said as she pulled away from
her father. "I'm sorry I went over the fence."

"I think you should apologize to your father,"
Joanna said sharply. "Not to me."

Lily licked her lips. "I can't," she whispered, her
face a picture of conflict. "Mama . . ."

"It's all right," Michael said. "I know you're sorry.
You're also in trouble, and as soon as I can think of
a fitting punishment, I'll let you know. Now, for the
rest of the evening you are confined to the house. If
you so much as set one foot out of the front or back
door, I'll take you home."

Lily and Rose nodded their agreement.

"Can you walk on that foot, honey?" he asked.

Lily cautiously stood up and took a few steps.

"All right then."

"I brought some coloring books and some cray-
ons. They're in the hall by my purse," Joanna said.
"Why don't you sit at the dining room table and
color for a while?"

As the girls left, Joanna turned to Michael. "Are
you okay?"

"I've probably added a few more gray hairs to my
collection, but other than that I'm fine. The girls are
only six. Do you think I'm going to make it through
their teenage years?"

"If anyone can, you can."

"Thanks for the vote of confidence."

He stood up. Joanna pulled a twig off his sleeve, feeling an incredible wave of affection toward this man.

"You're a great dad, you know."

"If I were a great dad, Lily never would have gone over that fence in the first place."

"You can't blame yourself. Lily has a mind of her own."

"I should have known better. A fence to Lily is like a beacon in the night. She simply can't resist seeing what's on the other side."

"Some day that curiosity will probably take her to the top of whatever field she chooses to go into."

"So you're saying it's a good thing."

"It could be."

"You're an optimist, aren't you?"

"I try."

"And you probably like to make people feel better."

"If I can."

"Then how about a kiss for the hero of the hour?" he asked with a grin.

"I thought we were keeping our distance."

"A simple kiss between friends. What could happen?"

What could happen? The question begged to be answered one hundred different ways, but Joanna could only make one reply. She put her hands on his shoulders and kissed his mouth in a way that made a mockery of the word "friends." In fact, this simple kiss made a mockery of every other kiss she'd ever given or received. There was more passion, more feeling, more love than ever before.

"How was that for a simple kiss?" she asked, pleased that he looked just as bemused as she felt.

"Not bad."

"I feel as if I've known you forever."

"Me, too."

"It's scary, isn't it?"

"Terrifying."

Joanna took a step back. "I guess I'll head up to the attic."

"I'll finish in the basement." He paused. "Joanna, I don't think you should kiss any of your other men friends that way."

"Why not?"

"They might get the wrong idea. They might think you want more than just a kiss."

"Of course, *you* didn't get the wrong idea."

"Me? No, of course not. I knew exactly what you wanted," he said with a gleam in his eye.

"You did?"

"Yes, but my children are coloring in the dining room."

"And if they weren't?"

"You wouldn't be standing up right now."

15

The rest of the evening sped by. Joanna sorted through the boxes in the attic, setting aside journals, newspaper clippings, and photos in one pile; old clothes and anything that fell into the category of "stuff" in another.

The upstairs bedrooms didn't warrant much more than a quick search, as three of them didn't appear to have been used in quite some time. Even Ruby Mae's bedroom was bereft of the attic's clutter of sentiment. It seemed as if she had locked the past away long before her actual death.

Lily and Rose had a grand time playing dress up, but by seven o'clock they were clamoring for dinner. Because Michael still seemed to be enthralled with studying the beams that supported the house, Joanna made a pizza and soda run and used his cell phone to call her mother and tell her she'd be late.

Caroline seemed resigned to spending yet another evening alone. Maybe if she spent enough time alone, she'd find someone else to do things with. After all, Joanna couldn't spend the next twenty years of her life entertaining her mother. But she still felt bad, which made her order extra cheese on the pizza. Guilt always made her hungry.

When Joanna returned to the house, Michael and the girls had lit candles and cleared off the kitchen table. As they picnicked on pizza, Joanna felt as if they were a family. It would be so easy to let herself forget Angela, even though she knew the other three could never forget.

"Tell me about your mother," Joanna said impulsively. "What was her favorite food?"

"Spaghetti," the twins chorused.

Joanna smiled at Michael. "I should have predicted that."

Michael didn't smile back. "Joanna, don't."

"I'm curious." She turned her attention to Lily. "What was your favorite game to play with your mother?"

"Dress up."

Rose agreed. "Sometimes Mama would let us wear her high heels and her jewelry, and we'd put on makeup and pretend we were going to a party."

"She trained them well," Michael said with disgust.

"Daddy didn't like it," Lily said to Joanna, obviously irritated with her father's comment. "Mama said we were the prettiest girls in the world."

"She was right." Maybe Joanna should end the discussion. Michael was growing more uncomfortable with each question, and the girls seemed to be taking sides against him. Somehow Angela had built a wall between the girls and their father. Her death had made the wall even bigger.

"Mama was fun," Rose said with a hint of sadness in her voice. "She laughed all the time—well, most of the time. Sometimes she cried." Rose darted a look at her father, then slid her chair closer to Joanna.

Michael suddenly stood up. "I'm going to take a few more measurements outside."

"It's dark."

"I'll take a flashlight."

"We can change the subject," she suggested.

"Why? I'm sure the girls would love to tell you about their mother and our fights and about how mean I was to Angela." He started to say more, then bit down on his lip, turned on his heel, and slammed out the back door.

"Daddy's mad," Lily observed. "Mama always made him mad."

Joanna stood up, torn between going after Michael and staying with the girls. Even if she went to him, she didn't know what she would say. None of this was any of her business.

"Let's go into the living room, girls," she said. "I cleaned up in there, so you two can lie on the couch, and I'll tell you a story while we wait for your father to finish."

"Okay."

Joanna carried two candles into the living room and set them down on the coffee table. Then she sat on the couch, the girls settling in on either side of her, resting their little heads against her arms. She loved the feel of their hair against her skin, the scent of their bubble gum shampoo right under her nose, the pressure of their soft, cuddly bodies against hers. For a moment she felt very much like a mother, and it touched her deeply.

She loved these girls. It had happened so fast. A look, a smile, a laugh, and her loneliness had fled. Lily and Rose had brought her back to life in four short days, reminding her of what it was like to love someone.

And their father . . . Michael reminded her of what it was like to want someone, to be so acutely aware of another's presence that the simplest glance, the briefest touch, the smallest smile, touched off a deep, compelling need to come together.

"Tell us again about when Ruby Mae first came to the city," Lily said, interrupting her thoughts. "I like the part where she dyes her hair blond."

"Okay, but don't get any ideas about dyeing your own hair."

Lily tilted her head so she could smile at Joanna. "Mama colored her hair once. She put a pink stripe right down the middle. Daddy yelled at her." Lily's smile disappeared at the memory.

They were right back where they'd been in the kitchen. Joanna knew she couldn't let the conversation go on without interjecting her own thoughts. "Sometimes people disagree. It doesn't mean they don't love each other," she said.

"I'm glad you and Daddy don't fight," Rose said. "I used to get scared when Mama locked herself in the bathroom. We could hear her crying, but she wouldn't come out. Once I tried to push some Kleenex under the door for her, but I don't think she saw it."

Rose's sadly matter-of-fact words tugged at Joanna's heart. She could see the girls standing by the door, scared that their mother was crying, not knowing what to do, how to help her. She found herself getting angry with Angela for not realizing how her behavior was affecting her children. And where had Michael been when his wife was in tears?

"Sometimes Daddy would ask her to come out. He'd say he was sorry and stuff, but she never came out until he left," Lily said, answering Joanna's silent question.

Joanna hugged the girls, wanting them to feel secure with her, not scared or worried, just safe. "Even though your mom and dad fought with each other, they also loved each other and they loved you. Sometimes you two argue over something you both want, but that doesn't change the fact that you're sisters and that you love each other."

"If Daddy loved Mommy, he wouldn't have made her go away," Lily said sadly.

"Are you sure he made her go away?" Joanna

sensed they were nearing the big promise that the girls had made.

"Mama said so," Rose replied. "She made us promise not to—"

"Rose, you almost told her."

Rose's lips trembled as she fought with herself. Her determination not to break her promise finally won out. "I'm sorry, Joanna, but I can't tell you."

"That's all right, honey. You just have to remember that sometimes secrets can hurt people."

"But no one is getting hurt," Lily said.

"Don't you think it hurts your father's feelings when you don't talk to him? He climbed down the cliff to save you from getting hurt, Lily. You couldn't even say thank you."

"I—I wanted to."

"Sometimes Daddy does look really sad," Rose said as Lily rubbed her eyes.

Joanna softened a bit at the look of remorse on Lily's face, but she couldn't let the little girl off the hook. Michael might be resigned to their behavior, but she wasn't. "I think your father deserves more from you than silence," she said. "He needs to know about the promise you made to your mother."

"But he's the one we can't tell, because if he knew then he'd get mad, and Mama could never come back. She said so," Lily replied.

"As long as Daddy doesn't know about the other man, she can still come back," Rose added, not realizing she'd given something away.

Another man? Had Angela been having an affair? Joanna remembered the girls telling her about a man with a mustache. Had they promised to keep the affair a secret? What mother would ask such a thing of her children, to involve two innocent little girls in her own deception?

Joanna disliked Angela more and more. Everything she'd heard about the woman pointed to An-

gela being spoiled, selfish, and immature. And it
annoyed the hell out of her that she had to look like
such a person.

Silently she counted to ten, knowing that the girls
adored their mother despite her shortcomings, and
it certainly wasn't up to Joanna to criticize, especially
a woman who was no longer around to defend herself. Whatever Angela's faults, she had certainly inspired a sense of loyalty in the twins. Angela must
have had something going for her. Maybe someday
Joanna would be able to figure out what that was.

"Do you want to hear about Ruby Mae now?" she
asked, playing with Lily's hair.

The girls nodded, obviously pleased by the change
in subject.

"Ruby Mae was born Rebecca Margaret Blakes-
dale, and she came to San Francisco in 1920, the beginning of a time in our history that was called the
Roaring Twenties."

"Were there lions then?" Lily asked.

Joanna laughed, forgetting how literal they were.
"No lions, but the people who lived then loved to
party. Ruby Mae was one of them. She was eight
years old when she came to San Francisco, the only
daughter of a widowed gold digger. Ruby Mae
loved music and she loved to dance."

Ten minutes later the girls fell fast asleep when
Joanna got to the part about how Ruby Mae had
decided to become a dancer in a saloon. It was a
good place to stop, since Joanna would have to do
some heavy editing of Ruby Mae's story to make it
acceptable for the girls.

She rested her head against the couch. She felt so
comfortable in this house, solid ground under her
feet, the yard outside, the waves of the ocean audible
through the open windows, the sound of crickets in
the garden. This wasn't just a house. It was a home,

or it could be with the right owners, with the right family in it.

Family. It was easier to think about Ruby Mae and her mysterious life than to consider the mystery going on in her own life. Although she had considerable imagination, Joanna had also inherited a sense of logic from her father, and deep down she knew she was missing some vital piece of information.

She thought about what Michael had said earlier, about Elena, Sophia's sister. Maybe she should talk to her. No. The woman would probably think she was crazy.

There were no secrets to be discovered, she told herself again. Her mind drifted back to Ruby Mae. Everyone in San Francisco thought Ruby Mae Whitcomb had died in a fire. But she hadn't.

Did anyone really know what went on in a family?

There was mystery surrounding Angela's death, too, and whatever the twins had promised their mother not to reveal. Yet Michael seemed as bewildered as anyone about what could have transpired in his own house, in his own marriage.

Of course, relationships were not always what they seemed on the surface. Joanna had learned that with David. She hadn't known him. He hadn't known her. They had showed each other their polite, social sides, not their souls.

She turned her head and saw Michael watching her from the doorway, bathed in the light of the burning candles. She couldn't see his eyes, or even his expression, but she could feel his presence as strongly as if she were touching him. It had been that way since the very beginning. She had finally found the missing part of herself.

But what had he found? A woman who looked like his wife. Was he seeing Angela even now as Joanna sat with his children tucked into her body,

as she held his daughters as if she were their
mother?

She wanted him to say something. Her body
tensed with each passing second of silence.

Finally he walked slowly into the room. He sat
down on the floor on the other side of the coffee
table, his gaze intent on her face.

"Do you want to go now?" Joanna asked.

"In a few minutes. Let them sleep."

"Michael—" she began, then stopped, because she
didn't know what to say.

"It's all right, Joanna. I still know who you are."
She drew in a quick breath as she met his perceptive
gaze.

"You must have seen the kids like this with your
wife a hundred times."

"It isn't the same."

As in better or worse? She didn't dare voice her
insecurity. She wasn't sure she could accept either
answer.

Michael's expression softened as he gazed at his
children. "Little angels," he said in a quiet voice. "So
sweet and innocent, and a whole world out there
waiting for them to be whatever they want to be. I
envy them that. I'd like nothing more than to start
over with a clean slate."

"I don't think any of us can do that. We are our
pasts."

"Now you sound like a historian." He paused.
"What else did you find out about Ruby Mae today?"

"Lots," she said with an enthusiastic smile. "Ruby
Mae had an ongoing affair with a very respectable
and very married city councilman. In fact, she got
pregnant. She wanted to keep the baby, but she
couldn't raise her in a whorehouse. She really loved
this guy for some reason that I can't quite fathom,
especially since he convinced her to give the baby

away." Joanna's voice faltered, trying not to think there was any connection between this story and her own life. "Anyway, that's what she did. Someone found out and tried to blackmail both her and the councilman. That someone died in the fire that burned down her house, which supposedly killed her."

"But didn't."

"No, it was a setup. Her lover bought her this house, and she lived the rest of her life in seclusion. He used to come to her whenever he could. She loved him to the end, until he died. It was so sad. She lost her baby and she never really had him, not totally." Joanna ended her story with a sniff.

"Don't tell me you cry at sappy movies."

She made a face. "I do. Those telephone commercials really get to me, too. The ones where everyone has been separated over the years and they finally reunite."

"You're something else." And she was, he realized. Any resemblance she'd had to Angela had disappeared in the hours they had spent together. Joanna was her own woman with her own faults, her own habits, her own style.

"I just don't understand how Ruby Mae could have given up her child for that man," Joanna said, drawing him back to the story. "How could she love a man more than her child?"

Michael glanced over at his own children, protectively wrapped in Joanna's arms. He couldn't have given them up for anything. They belonged to him. At one point, shortly after Angela's death, one of the therapists had suggested that the girls live with their grandparents for a while. The idea had horrified him. They were his family, his children. The only reason he could think of for giving them up would be to give them a better life. But he believed he could give them the best life possible, one with their father.

He met Joanna's gaze. "I don't know. Maybe Ruby Mae thought the child would be better off with someone else."

"Someone who wasn't her family? I don't understand that. Family is everything. My parents took such pride in our family, even though we were small, just the three of us. My father always told me to hold my head up high, because I was a Wingate. There was a lot of security in knowing who I was and taking pride in it." She paused. "Anyway. Have you spoken to your client yet? Do you think she'll want to restore this house?"

"She wasn't in. I left a message at her hotel."

"The girls really love this place," Joanna added. "Maybe *you* should buy it."

"Me?" He laughed. "I don't think so."

"Why not? It would be perfect for you and the girls."

"I couldn't afford a house like this, not on my own. Besides, we have a perfectly fine house, which by the way once belonged to the De Marcos."

"I didn't know that."

"Sophia and Vincent gave us the house. They always treated me like their son." Michael stared into the candlelight. "They stuck by me through everything. They came to my basketball games. Sophia took me to the hospital when I broke my arm. Vincent taught me how to cook. Tony and I were the best of friends. We used to talk about sailing around the world. Of course, Tony is actually still trying to accomplish that."

"Do you really want to sail around the world?"

"Some days more than anything." He smiled at her. "No, I could be happy with a small piece of the world. As long as I knew my family was happy, too." His eyes darkened as he looked at the girls. "I wish I could tear down this wall between us."

"They'll come around, Michael. They love you.

They're just confused. They want their mother back, and somehow you're in the way. When they're older they'll understand."

Her voice rang with conviction, and he wanted to believe her. "God, I hope so. I can live without a lot of things, but their silence—dammit, their silence is killing me. When Angela died I didn't just lose her, I lost them, too. I want them back," he said gruffly. "I want my kids back."

"Oh, Michael, come here," she said softly.

He didn't move, though he wanted to. "They don't want me. They want you." He watched the emotions play across her face in the candlelight. Joanna was a kind, caring, compassionate woman. Lily and Rose had seen that immediately. They weren't just drawn to Joanna because of her looks, but because she was giving them what their mother had not, the tender love, the quiet times, the gentle words.

"I'm not their mother," Joanna said.

"Maybe it doesn't matter. The De Marcos weren't my parents, but they loved me anyway. Sometimes we have to take love where we find it—if we're lucky enough to find it." He blew out the candles, shrouding the room in darkness, but he could still see her face in the moonlight that streamed through the windows.

"Is it all right for me to love Lily and Rose then?" Joanna asked, a longing in her voice that matched his own.

"Yes." *As long as it's all right for me to love you.* What was he thinking? He didn't love her. He couldn't love her.

16

Sophia opened the bottom drawer of her armoire and dug through the layers of underwear, bras, and slips until her fingers touched the soft velvet pouch. Only one other person knew about the pouch—her younger sister, Elena. Elena had refused to keep it at her house. In fact, she had wanted her to throw it away, but Sophia couldn't do that.

Slowly she pulled it out and loosened the white silk cords that held it together. Inside was a soft pile of tissue paper and several strands of brown hair, curled contentedly in their innocence. Baby's hair. She smiled, feeling the insistent push of tears behind her eyes, but she blinked them away.

Next to the curl was a tiny photograph of a baby girl. The baby's eyes were wide open, dark brown and inquisitive. Her tiny hands, still in fists, covered her ears as if she couldn't stand the noise of the real world. Or maybe she just couldn't stand hearing her mother say good-bye to her.

The front door slammed, and Sophia jumped. She couldn't let Vincent see what was in her hand. She tried to hide it as she heard the hurrying rush of steps on the stairs. She had barely touched the drawer when her bedroom door opened.

Elena came into the room, and Sophia breathed a sigh of relief. Elena was five years younger but six inches taller than Sophia. Her hair was a light shade of brown, her eyes the color of cinnamon. She dressed with style and a conservatism that pleased her banker husband and surprised the rest of her family, who remembered her fondly as a wild bare- foot girl who lived in shorts and tank top T-shirts.

"Oh, it's you," Sophia said with relief. "I thought you were Vincent."

"He's still at the restaurant. I came over to remind you that we're going out Saturday night, six o'clock sharp, and I absolutely refuse to take no for an an- swer. I know you said not to make a big deal, but your fortieth anniversary is a big deal, and I want to treat you both to dinner."

"It's not necessary."

"It is," Elena insisted. "You did so much for me, Sophia. All those years you took care of me, pro- tected me. The least I can do is buy you dinner for your anniversary."

Her anniversary. The date loomed in front of her, a reminder of all the time that had passed. Sophia didn't want to celebrate it at all. But how could she not? It was expected. She had always done what was expected of her.

Elena frowned when she didn't answer. "What's wrong?" Her gaze traveled down to the pouch in Sophia's hand. Her face paled. "What is that?"

Sophia stared back at her. "You know what it is."

"You still have it after all these years? I told you to throw it away. I never wanted you to take the picture in the first place."

"I know." Sophia could still remember that day, even though it had been thirty years. She had pushed it to the back of her mind, but now it seemed as clear as if it had been yesterday.

The baby had been brought to the room for only a few minutes. Sophia had taken the photo, and Elena had cut the hair. Then the nurse had taken the baby away to their murmured good-byes. She and Elena had cried. They had held each other, the experience bonding them for all time. Yet they had never talked about it again—not until tonight.

They were both older now, well past middle age, but in her heart and mind Sophia still felt thirty years old. She still felt scared, eager, worried, helpless, desperate, all the emotions she had felt that night. She knew Elena had felt those same emotions.

Elena sat down on the edge of the bed.

"Do you want to see the photo?" Sophia asked.

Elena shook her head. "No. Yes. I mean, no." She sighed at her indecision. "I'm afraid to look at it again."

"There's nothing to be afraid of." Sophia handed Elena the photo of the baby.

Elena let out a breath. "She's so beautiful. I'd forgotten how much hair she had, how big her eyes were, how her fingers curled into fists as if she were ready to fight the entire world." Elena bit down on her lip, obviously struggling for control as she handed the photo back to Sophia.

Sophia returned it to the pouch, then picked up the baby's hair between two fingers. "It's so soft, Elena, filled with innocence, love, and trust. We betrayed that trust."

"It's just hair. It doesn't stand for anything. Please, put it away." Elena stared at the carpet until Sophia returned the hair to the pouch. "Is it gone?" she asked.

"Yes, it's hidden away, so we can pretend it's not there." Sophia walked across the room and sat down on the window seat, still twirling the cords of the pouch between her fingers. "I never went to confession, you know. I never told the priest what we did."

"You couldn't. The priests knew us too well. If any one of us had said anything, it would have been disastrous for the family. Carlotta was recovering from that horrible car accident. Papa was drinking too much, and Vincent was working hard to keep the restaurant afloat after his father died. I was just getting my life together after the divorce. It was a difficult time. We did what was best for the baby."

"Do you really believe that? Do you believe that all of our problems were more important than that child's birthright?" Sophia shook her head, feeling the constricting band of guilt tighten around her heart. "I think we did what was best for us."

Elena crossed her arms as she stared at Sophia, worry written in every line of her face. Elena had always been able to escape guilt. Something within her simply shut down her conscience when difficult choices needed to be made. Sometimes Sophia wished she had that faculty.

"I spoke to Michael last night," Elena said. "He told me about Joanna Wingate. It can't be her."

Sophia uttered a short, bitter laugh. "Close your eyes to the truth, Elena, but please spare me your ignorance. You know it's her as well as I do."

"Okay, so it's her." Elena's foot tapped out a restless beat on the floor. "You have to let it alone."

"She has a right to know who her mother is."

"Her mother is the woman who raised her."

"But she's not the woman who gave birth to her," Sophia argued. "She's not the woman who carried her for nine months, who struggled to give her life. Have you forgotten how hard it was, Elena?"

"No. I could never forget that. In fact, it's haunted me for years—you, me, her." She paused, waiting until Sophia looked at her. "Michael asked me if I thought anyone in the family could have given up a baby for adoption."

"What did you say?"

"I said no."

"Did he believe you?"

"You know Michael. He can be persistent when

he wants to find out something. He told me this woman is very concerned about the similarity between Angela and herself, but that to her knowledge Caroline and Edward Wingate are her real parents."

Sophia didn't say anything.

Elena was silent for a long moment, too. "So that's good."

Sophia turned on her innocent comment like a vicious dog after a hummingbird. "It's good? That Joanna grew up without her real mother? That she doesn't know her history, who she is, where she came from? That's good?" Sophia was suddenly furious. She didn't understand how her husband and her sister could believe such a falsehood.

"She had a loving family. You keep forgetting that," Elena said.

"No, I'm not forgetting anything. That's the problem, Elena. Since this woman came into our lives, I can't stop remembering. I remember that that soap opera, 'General Hospital,' was playing on the television set in the lobby when we arrived at the hospital. I remember the rain beating against the windows. I remember the doctors and the nurses, the baby's first cry. And I remember how quiet the room was after they took her away."

Elena jumped to her feet, clapping her hands over her ears. "Stop it! We can't go back. It's too late."

"I can't stop it. I won't. Maybe it's not too late. Maybe this woman has come into our lives for a reason."

"You're twisting things around, Sophia. If you won't think of me or of Vincent, then think of her. Think of Joanna. Think of how much she has to lose. Maybe we did take away her birthright, but do you want to take away the rest of her life? Because that's exactly what's going to happen if you tell her the truth. Is that what you really want?"

*　　*　　*

Joanna was surprised to hear laughter and conversation when she returned home. It was past nine-thirty and her mother hadn't had company in—she couldn't remember how long.

She set her purse on the hall table and walked into the living room. Her father's good friend and attorney, Grant Sullivan, sat on the couch with a brandy snifter in his hand. Her mother sat on the opposite couch, dressed in a blue sundress. Her makeup was perfect, and there was a flush to her cheeks, as if she and Grant had been discussing something of an intimate nature. As if they had been flirting or something.

Joanna tried to dislodge the ridiculous thought from her mind until she saw Grant smile reassuringly at her mother. Something passed between them, something Joanna didn't understand.

She had never seen her mother in the company of another man. If Caroline wasn't with Edward, she was with Joanna. It felt odd to see her now, entertaining a man with a known history of womanizing.

Not that Joanna didn't like Grant. He'd always been like an uncle to her. But over the years she'd heard stories about this woman and that woman. She knew Grant had been married three times and was currently divorced.

Of course, it was probably an innocent visit between old friends, but Grant Sullivan had never been one to just drop by. He had to have a reason. She just hoped his reason wasn't her mother.

That sounded bad even in her own head. Why shouldn't her mother see other men? Caroline was still attractive. It just wasn't something Joanna had expected to happen this fast.

"How are you, Joanna?" Grant asked.

"I'm fine, and you?"

"Great. I thought I'd stop in and see how you and your mother were doing."

"Looks like we're doing pretty well," Joanna said pointedly to her mother as she sat down in an armchair.

"How was your evening?" Caroline asked. "You seemed rather vague on the phone about where you were."

"I took another look at that house I told you about, the one that belonged to Ruby Mae Whitcomb."

"Oh, that's right." Caroline glanced over at Grant. "I told Grant about your resemblance to that Ashton woman."

"You did?" Joanna asked, surprised. She would have thought that was the last thing Caroline would bring up.

"The world's a funny place," Grant said. "I knew another guy who met his double. He couldn't get over it. But there wasn't a speck of common blood between them."

"Really? I guess that's true in my case, too. Hard to believe, though."

Grant took a sip of his brandy. "As a lawyer I spend most of my day disbelieving my own eyes. Some of the people who walk through my door, some of their stories are completely bizarre." He smiled. "I guess it's that old saying about truth being stranger than fiction, huh?"

"Maybe." Joanna got to her feet. She felt set up. Grant and her mother weren't having some secret flirtation. The man was simply here to back up her mother's story, and his presence was doing exactly the opposite. "I think I'll go to bed."

"Don't go, Joanna. I'm sure Grant would love to hear about your teaching job."

"I'm tired, and frankly I don't like this whole thing."

Her mother's face tensed. "What are you talking about?"

"What are you really doing here, Mr. Sullivan?"

"I thought I might be able to answer some of your questions, Joanna. I've known your parents since the day they first met. We've been through a lot together."

Joanna nodded. That was true. She hadn't thought of Grant when she'd called Pamela Cogswell earlier in the week, but if anyone had a photo of her mother pregnant, it was probably Grant. "I suppose you must have seen my mother pregnant," Joanna said abruptly. "I think it's odd that there are no pictures of that time in her life."

"Joanna, what are you talking about?" Caroline asked.

"I looked through the photo albums. I couldn't find any pictures of you pregnant."

Caroline avoided her questioning gaze, concentrating instead on a piece of lint on her dress. "I thought I was so fat then. I didn't want your father to take any photos of me."

"Of course, she wasn't really fat," Grant jumped in. "She was lovely, blooming. Your father was, too. He used to get cravings right along with Caroline. For barbecued ribs, wasn't it?"

"That's right. And watermelon—I couldn't get enough. Luckily it was summer at the time."

"How long was your labor, Mom? Was it difficult? Did you go to the hospital in the morning or in the evening? And why haven't we ever talked about this before?"

Caroline looked stunned under Joanna's barrage of questions. "I—I don't know. I assumed we'd talk about it when you got married and were ready to have your own children."

"You're very convincing," Joanna said wearily.

Caroline looked hurt. "Joanna, I don't know what you want from me. I showed you your birth certificate. What else can I do? Tell me, and I'll do it."

"I wish Dad was here."

"Edward would have told you the same thing," Grant said. "Because if he had anything else he wanted you to know, he would have said something before he died."

Joanna wanted to believe that. She had talked to her father about so many things during those last few weeks. They had discussed life and death, their family, and what would happen when Caroline and Joanna were alone.

Her father had told her he wasn't worried about her, that he knew she could handle whatever happened in her life; but he worried about Caroline, her being alone, her desperate need to be a part of Joanna's life. Joanna had assured him that Caroline would always be in her life, that she loved her mother despite her possessiveness.

Her father had told her no matter how angry she got with her mother, she had to remember that Caroline always acted out of love for her. Joanna told him she understood, but now she wasn't sure that she did. Had her father been trying to tell her something?

Her temple began to throb as conflicting thoughts collided in her head. "I'm going to bed," she said. "I can't do this right now."

"Joanna, if you have any questions, you can ask me," Grant said. "I'll try to help."

"Who will you be helping, Mr. Sullivan? My mother or me? You were my father's best friend. If anyone would lie for him, it would be you."

A gleam of respect appeared in Grant's eyes. "You've grown into quite a woman, Joanna. Smart as can be. Your father had every reason to be proud of you. No matter what else you think, you must believe he loved you very much."

"And I love you, too," Caroline said.

"I believe in your love, but I'm not sure I believe

I'm your natural born daughter. I wish I didn't have doubts, but I do, and this charade didn't help your cause. If you weren't worried about something, you wouldn't have asked Mr. Sullivan to come here."

"It was my idea, Joanna," Grant said.

Joanna sighed. "Now I know you're capable of lying, Mr. Sullivan. Because this scene has my mother written all over it." As Joanna left the room she couldn't help pausing in the hallway, shamelessly eavesdropping.

"Grant, I told you," Caroline said.

"Sh-sh."

Then there was silence—as damning as any words Caroline could have uttered.

17

Sophia slipped carefully out of bed. She held her breath as Vincent turned. Then she walked to the closet and pulled out a dress, taking it into the bathroom so she wouldn't wake him.

It was just seven, and she was always an early riser, but this morning was different. This morning she had something important to do besides make eggs and toast and coffee for her family.

When Sophia finished dressing she made her way to the kitchen and pulled the phone book out of the desk drawer. She flipped the pages until she got to the one she wanted. Her finger slid down the column of Ws until she reached *Wingate, E.*

For a brief second she closed her eyes and prayed for strength and guidance. Then she picked up the phone and dialed the number. It rang several times before a woman answered.

"Hello," the woman said sleepily.

Sophia took a deep breath. "I'd like to speak to Edward Wingate."

There was a long silence. "Who is this?"

"I'd like to speak to Edward Wingate," Sophia repeated, twisting the cord between her fingers.

"And I asked who this is."

"Sophia De Marco."

A hiss of air came across the phone. Then the

voice returned, sharp and clear. "Edward Wingate is dead."

Dead? Sophia gripped the edge of the counter with her hands. Edward Wingate was dead. Her plan of action evaporated. She had known she couldn't go to the other woman, the other mother. But the father—she might have had a chance with him. Perhaps he would have listened to her plea to find some sort of compromising peace within the situation.

But Edward Wingate was dead.

"I want you to leave my daughter alone." The woman's voice jerked Sophia back to the present. "She's mine. She doesn't belong to you or to anyone else in your family. I don't know what you're trying to do to her or to me, but it stops here. Do you understand?"

How could she not? There was steel in the woman's voice. And maybe underneath it all a hint of fear, a touch of pain.

The woman didn't wait for Sophia to answer. She simply hung up. Sophia listened to the dial tone for almost a minute before she set down the receiver.

Edward Wingate was dead.

And Joanna Wingate didn't know that her life had been sewn from a fabric of lies—a fabric that was slowly unraveling, pulling apart, until there would be nothing left but worthless strings that didn't go anywhere.

Sophia knew she had two choices. She just didn't know which one to make.

She picked up the phone again and dialed the number for her sister Elena. "Meet me for coffee at Noel's," she said when Elena answered.

"Sophia, I'm not even awake yet."

"Edward Wingate is dead."

There was a pause. "How do you know that?"

"I just called him."

"I'll be there in ten minutes."

The De Marco house was similar to Michael's, the same structure, the same color paint, the same feel, Joanna thought as she sat in her car with the key still in the ignition. Her foot rested on the brake, the gear shift in drive. It was seven-thirty in the morning. Too early to drop in on anyone unannounced, but since she'd gone to bed the night before, she'd been filled with a desire to take action, to stop waiting to see what would happen next and charge ahead.

It had been surprisingly easy so far. The De Marcos' telephone number had been listed in the phone book along with their address. Now that she was here, she didn't know what to do. She could hardly walk up to the front door and ask Sophia De Marco if she was her mother or if she knew who was.

Joanna put the gear shift into park. She wanted to know the truth, but at the same time she didn't. What if Sophia or Elena had given her up for adoption? What if Caroline had lied or stolen her from the hospital, or made some kind of a deal with one of the two women?

Did she want to know any of it? Wouldn't it be easier to go on pretending?

She was a coward. An almost thirty-year-old coward. Her birthday was only a month away. At least she thought so. Maybe it wasn't even her real birthday.

Joanna pulled the key out of the ignition. She took another deep breath and opened the door, then shut it.

Her heart pounded. Sweat beaded on her forehead. Her hands shook so hard she had to clamp them together. She suddenly felt sick to her stomach, and she hadn't even made it out of the car yet.

She'd already lost her father. Was she ready to lose her mother, too?

"Where is your mother?" Vincent demanded, flinging open the door to Tony's bedroom.

Tony grimaced against the sound of his father's loud, booming voice. He slowly opened his eyes to see his father standing beside the bed, wearing a burgundy-colored bathrobe over a pair of cotton pajamas. His face was unshaven, his white hair sticking up in sleepy cowlicks.

"Your mother," Vincent repeated, his dark eyes worried. "She's not here."

"Maybe she went to the market."

"She went to the market yesterday."

"So she forgot something, and she went again. What's the big deal?" Tony muttered as he pulled himself into a sitting position. He rubbed his temple against the already pounding headache, probably the result of too many shots of tequila the night before.

"She didn't make coffee. She didn't leave a note," Vincent said.

"I'm sure she's fine."

"You—what do you know?" Vincent said scornfully, picking up the half-empty bottle from the dresser. "You're a bum. A drunk."

The words cut to the quick, leaving sharp, painful, scarring wounds. "You know, I don't need this shit," Tony said as he got out of bed and pulled on his blue jeans from the night before. "I'll sleep on my boat from now on."

"That's right. Run away. You always run away like a scared little boy, drowning your sorrows in a bottle of booze."

"I'm not running away. I'm leaving. And who the hell do you think taught me how to drink, Papa?"

"Don't swear at me."

"Why not? You're swearing at me."

"You're my son. I'm your father. You will show respect."

"As soon as you start showing me some respect." Tony lifted his chin in the air, staring back at his father with anger and determination. This showdown had been coming for a long time.

"What should I respect? You have no job, no wife, no money, no house."

"Those things are important to you, not to me. I have a boat. I have a dream."

"Dreams are for children. You are a man. When are you going to start acting like one?"

"You won't consider me a man until I come to work at De Marco's. That's not going to happen."

"Maybe it's for the best. You'd probably run it into the ground."

"Yeah, I probably would. You know, maybe Mama ran away, too. Maybe she got tired of your domineering ways and that's why she's not here cooking you breakfast and pouring you coffee." Tony meant the words to hurt. He just didn't expect to see his father crumple on the bed, his anger, arrogance, and passion fading from his eyes, from his stance, from his voice.

Vincent looked defeated, an old, tired warrior who simply couldn't keep up the fight. His hand shook as he reached for the bottle of tequila on the night table and put it to his lips, taking one long shot. His action surprised Tony even more. His father had always drunk red wine by the gallon, but not tequila and not at seven thirty in the morning.

"This isn't about me at all, is it?" Tony asked.

Vincent shook his head. "I love her, you know. All these years, I always loved her."

"I know that."

"I don't think Sophia does."

"Don't be silly," Tony said, but he could see his

father was being anything but silly. In fact, he was incredibly serious.

"Sophia could have married anyone. She was so pretty, so full of life when I met her. I had to marry her quickly, before anyone else had a chance. My friends were filled with jealousy that such a beautiful woman would pick me."

Tony sat down on the end of the bed. He didn't know what to say. He didn't understand his father in this mood.

"But I had to work hard during our marriage. I couldn't take time off. There were many places Sophia wanted to go. That's why she collects the music boxes, so she can bring the rest of the world to her. Sometimes Sophia . . ." Vincent shook his head and took another drink of the tequila.

"Sophia what?"

Before Vincent could answer, the doorbell rang. Vincent immediately stood up.

"Mama wouldn't ring the bell," Tony said, meeting his father's eyes.

"It's too early for visitors."

Vincent strode from the room. Tony pulled on a T-shirt and followed him down the stairs.

His father glanced through the lacy curtain that covered the window panel next to the front door.

"Who is it?" Tony asked.

His father froze for a second, then backed away from the door. "It's no one."

"It has to be someone."

"A salesman. He'll go away if we don't answer it."

"He'll go away if we answer it and tell him to go away," Tony said as he opened the door.

It wasn't a salesman. It was Joanna Wingate, dressed in beige slacks and a white sleeveless sweater. Her long hair was swept off her face with an ivory comb, emphasizing her big brown eyes. De

Marco eyes, Tony thought, feeling a shiver of uneasiness.

"I don't know if you remember me. . . ." Joanna said.

"How could I forget you?"

"Is your mother here?"

"No."

"She's not?" Joanna tried to look past him as if she didn't believe him.

"Don't you believe me?" he asked.

"It's early to be out."

"It is early. So why are you here?"

"I want to talk to your mother."

"Why?"

She hesitated. "I'd rather just discuss it with her. Do you know when she'll be back?"

"I don't even know where she is," Tony admitted, crossing his arms in front of him.

"Oh. I guess I'll catch up with her later."

"Look, I don't know why you're here, but maybe it would be better if you didn't come back." Tony dug his hands into the pockets of his jeans. "It's nothing personal," he added belatedly. "It's just—you know—your looks."

"I think that makes it very personal," she said quietly. "I need to know who I am, Mr. De Marco, and I think either your mother or your aunt knows the answer to that question."

"Who you are? What are you saying?" But Tony knew what she was saying. He knew what she was thinking. Because he thought it, too.

"I'm saying my looks can't be a coincidence."

"What are you talking about?"

"Skeletons in the closet."

"There are no skeletons in my family's closet. The De Marcos have no secrets." God, he sounded as arrogant as his father, but despite his impatience with his father's attitudes, the De Marcos stuck together.

"You're burying your head in the sand," Joanna said. "What do you think—I just happen to have the same face as your sister?"

"It could happen."

"How? How could it happen?"

"A freak of nature."

"Are you calling your sister a freak, or me?"

"Well, it certainly wasn't my sister."

Joanna's brown eyes burned at his response, and Tony didn't have any trouble seeing the difference between Angela and Joanna. This woman didn't fly off the handle. She didn't hide behind sarcasm. She didn't burst into tears to gain sympathy. She was taller than Angela and tougher, too. He could see determination in every line of her face.

"I will get to the bottom of this, and if it makes you or anyone else in your family uncomfortable, that's just too damn bad," she said. "If you see your mother tell her I'm looking for her."

"I'll do that." Tony shut the door.

He turned around to see his father standing on the stairs, gripping the railing with one hand.

"Is she gone?" Vincent asked.

"Yes. But she said she'll be back."

Vincent sank down on the stairs. "God help us."

"Do you know who she is?"

"She's a stranger, that's who she is."

"She seems to think she's related to us."

Vincent jumped to his feet, his eyes filled with new light. "I'll call the travel agent. I'll take Sophia away. Surprise her for our anniversary. We can leave tonight."

"Tonight? Uh—" Tony thought about the party on Saturday night and knew he needed to protest. But his father's mood seemed to change with each passing second. "Why don't you wait until next week?

Take some time to plan where you want to go."

"I don't have time."

"Why not?"

"Because our anniversary is tomorrow."

That was true, but Tony thought Vincent's sudden decision to leave had more to do with Joanna than with his anniversary.

"Don't try to talk me out of leaving," Vincent said. "I should have thought of this days ago. I better get dressed so I can make the arrangements."

Tony watched his father jog up the stairs. In fifteen minutes the man had gone from furiously angry to defeated to determined. What the hell was going on? He walked over to the phone on the table and picked up the receiver.

His brother answered on the third ring. "Hello."

"Frankie, we've got a problem."

18

He had a problem, Michael decided as he studied his design. The Connaught office building was as exciting as a shoe box. He might as well kiss any hope for a raise and a partnership good-bye. He simply could not come up with the right idea for the building.

He got up from his drafting table and stretched his arms high above his head. He walked over to the window and looked out at the city of San Francisco. He could see a cable car chugging up and down the steep hills between downtown and Chinatown, eventually making its way to the end of the line at Fisherman's Wharf. He could see the Stratton Hotel from his window, too, the future site of the Connaught building.

From a distance the Stratton still looked like an elegant lady. From here he could see only the beauty, not the age. But in a couple of months, the Stratton would be gone, erased from history like a bad mistake. In its place would be a building of his design, sleek, modern, rising like a phoenix out of the ashes.

With the Connaught building Michael could make a name for himself and for the firm. It was the biggest project he had ever handled. A dream come true.

So why was he stuck? Why was he dreaming about old Victorian houses with crumbling stonework instead of envisioning the ultimate skyscraper that would be a touchstone for office building architecture in the 21st century?

Because of Joanna, he decided, resting his hands on the windowsill. He could hear her voice ringing in his head—her disgust that the Stratton was being torn down in the name of progress. Of course, Joanna was a dreamer.

It was easy to be idealistic when you didn't have children depending on you for food and clothing—when you didn't have a mortgage to pay or insurance to buy.

He didn't have time for dreams.

Then he thought about the Seacliff house, the architecture that stirred his blood, reminding him of why he'd gotten into the business in the first place.

The intercom buzzed and Helen's voice came over the speaker. "Iris Sandbury is on line one," she said.

Iris. She probably wanted his report on the house. "Hello, Iris? How's your vacation?"

"Wonderful. How's the house?"

Michael sat down in his chair. "It's great. A real find."

"How much is it going to cost me to fix it?"

"More than a pretty penny."

"Do I tear it down and start over, or remodel?"

"You could do either," Michael said. "But I would recommend . . ." His mind flashed on Joanna, on her joy of discovering Ruby Mae's house. He saw her in the attic, dancing around the room with the costumes. He saw her in the living room, telling his children stories by candlelight. He saw her in the kitchen, a string of cheese pizza clinging to her chin. He shook his head, trying to dislodge her image from his mind, but she and the house seemed to be one. He couldn't let Iris tear it down. Then he wouldn't have anything left.

What was he thinking? The house had nothing to do with him. The owner would be selling it in a week, maybe to Iris, maybe to someone else, someone who would make their own memories in the house.

"Michael, are you there?"

He started at the sound of her voice. "I'm here. I think you should remodel, Iris. The architecture is too unique, too special to tear down. I also think there's a possibility the house could be declared a historic landmark. There are all kinds of papers and diaries in there."

"Oh, dear. It's not that I don't like history, but if it's declared a landmark, I might have a hard time doing what I want, wouldn't I?"

"Possibly. You'd have to find out the details."

"Maybe I should buy it and tear it down before anyone catches up with me. I think that's what I'll do. I don't care about history or old houses, but I'd love a piece of property by the ocean, and this one is perfect for that, isn't it?"

"It has a great view and it's secluded."

"Exactly what I want. I'll be back on Sunday, and I'll make an offer on Monday before Mr. Gladstone puts it on the market. Thanks for checking it out for me. You're a dear."

Michael hung up the phone. He wasn't a dear. He was an ass. He was tearing down buildings right and left. A few more weeks like this, he'd probably have the city bulldozed. Joanna would hate the idea of Iris tearing down Ruby Mae's house. She'd grown attached to it in just a few days. *As he had grown attached to her.*

He sat back in his chair, twisting a paper clip between his fingertips. Somehow, he'd fallen for Joanna. It was wrong. It was ridiculous. It was absurd. He couldn't think of enough adjectives to describe the impossibility of their relationship.

Still he wanted her. Deep down. With his heart and his soul, and it terrified him. What if he slipped and called her Angela? What if he forgot·who she was? What if he fell in love with her and she didn't love him back? What if the girls accepted her as their mother and she left? What if he never gave it a try? What if he missed out on the love of a lifetime?

The questions ran around his head like a Ferris wheel that wouldn't stop. Ultimately there was only one answer.

He was a chicken shit. The biggest coward on earth. Too afraid to move for fear of making the wrong move. But he'd rushed into something once before, mistaken infatuation for the real thing. He'd married before he was ready, made children before he was ready, lost his wife before he was ready.

Maybe he would never be ready. Maybe he just had to jump in again and hope for the best.

Helen opened his door. "You had four messages while you were on the phone. Sophia De Marco, Frank De Marco, Marlena De Marco, and Tony De Marco."

"Damn. What did they all want?"

"Sophia wants to talk to you about Joanna. Frank wants to talk to you about Vincent, and Tony wants to talk to you about Sophia. Oh, and Marlena said not to forget she's picking up Lily and Rose from school to take them to Andrea's birthday party for the sleep over." She smiled. "Shall I get someone on the phone for you?"

"How about an airline? I'd like to get out of town."

She smiled. "Family getting a little close?"

"You could say that."

"I thought you adored the De Marcos. They were the family you always wanted."

"Yeah, well, it's funny how sometimes we get exactly what we want, only then we don't want it anymore."

Her smile vanished. "Don't say that."

"I wasn't talking about you."

"Don't say it anyway. I don't even want to think that I might marry Joey, then not want him anymore. What would I do?"

You'd stick it out, Michael thought, as he and Angela had done, trying to make the best of the situation, trying to pretend that the love would come back.

Helen walked into the room and perched on the corner of his desk. "I'm just having normal pre-wedding jitters, right?"

"Probably. Helen, if you have any doubts, wait."

"You're making me nervous, Michael."

"I'm worried about you."

"Because of Tony."

He nodded. "If Tony is the one who makes your palms sweat, maybe you ought to rethink Joey."

"I'm not sure I want to go through life with sweaty palms, never knowing if Tony is going to take off when things get rough. I don't understand why he can't settle down and be happy here. I know his father wants him to work at the restaurant. He could have a good life."

"Tony wants more than that."

"I don't think there is anything more than that."

"Then you're making the right decision, Helen."

"Of course I am," she said firmly, but the sigh that accompanied her words contradicted her statement. "It's just that Tony is Tony. He's so appealing, like chocolate cake when you're on a diet. Anyway, are you going to Joey's bachelor party tonight?"

"That's right, the bachelor party." Michael rubbed his neck. The last thing he wanted to do was get drunk with a bunch of guys from the neighborhood and reminisce about old times. But Helen was not just a secretary; she was a good friend, and he owed it to her to go. "Sure, I guess."

"You don't sound happy about it."

"I've got a lot on my mind."

"The other woman," she said knowingly.

"She's not the other woman. She's just—Joanna."

Helen sent him a thoughtful look. "You've got it bad."

"I don't have anything bad, except a headache."

"I can hear it in your voice. I can see it in your face." Helen leaned forward. "Michael, she looks so much like Angela. Is this smart?"

"Hell, no! Whoever said I was smart?"

"Love can turn smart people into the biggest fools on earth."

"Tell me about it."

"He's back," Kathleen Shannon said with a saucy smile as Tony walked into De Marco's late Friday morning.

He scowled at her cheerful demeanor. "Do you work here every hour of the day?"

"Sometimes it seems like that, doesn't it?" she said as she finished setting a table for lunch.

"Is my brother here? He's supposed to meet me."

"Not yet. Your uncle Louis and your cousin Rico with the fast hands are in the kitchen."

Tony raised an eyebrow. "Are you familiar with my cousin's hands?"

"No, but he's familiar with my fist." She waved her fist in the air with a proud smile.

He couldn't help grinning back at her. She was a piece of work. "So you gave him that bruise on his cheekbone. He said he ran into a door."

"He did—a closed door."

Kathleen had the sharpest tongue of any woman he had ever met. She probably intimidated most

men. Especially those who liked it easy—Kathleen
Shannon was anything but easy. "Just out of curiosity, what does it take to get you to open that
door?"

"That will be my secret, I think."

"I like secrets."

"Do you now? And I suppose next you'll be saying you like me." Her eyes twinkled with mischief.

He laughed. "I don't think I could ever say that.
In fact, I might even dislike you." He waved a finger
at her. "Dumping me on Frank and Linda the other
night was not a nice thing to do."

"Especially when you were expecting a little
nooky in the back room." Kathleen laughed, and
Tony watched in fascination as her long earrings
dangled against her ears. Her hair was a glorious
shade of red, shining, soft, silky. Her eyes were like
the sea, dark blue, mesmerizing, and just as dangerous and unpredictable, he decided. It was better to
throw this fish back.

"I was just playing along," he said.

"Oh, sure."

"I was. I knew we weren't going to—you know."

"What if I had wanted to—you know?"

That was a loaded question. In fact, every conversation with this woman left him feeling off balance,
as if he'd been on land too long and hadn't gotten
his sea legs back. But he refused to let her know that.
"If you wanted to, I could have shown you heaven
in less than five minutes," he said.

"Less than five minutes." She laughed again.
"You are a cocky one, aren't you?"

"I haven't had any complaints."

"You probably don't stick around long enough to
hear them."

She had his number. "I think I'll go find my
brother."

"Good idea. You know, that Mrs. De Marco is

itching for trouble," Kathleen said before he could walk away.

"Mrs. De Marco? My mother?"

"Good heavens, no. Your sister-in-law. Your mother is a saint. Why, if I had had her for a mother, I'd probably have turned out differently. But you distract me."

"I know."

She swatted him on the shoulder. "Not in that way. I'm not looking for a fling with some good-looking sailor who'll be leaving with the next stiff breeze."

"So you think I'm good-looking?"

She rolled her eyes. "Can we get back to your sister-in-law? She was flirting with one of the customers last evening while her husband was working in the office. That marriage is in trouble. You mark my words."

"You don't know what you're talking about. De Marco marriages last forever. It's tradition, and believe me, Frank never goes against tradition."

"I hope you're right. She's a nice woman. And the kids." Kathleen's voice lost her edge and her face softened. "Kids need two parents." Her voice turned fierce. "I might have to wring your brother's neck if he doesn't come to his senses."

"Why should you care? Frank and Linda aren't any of your business. You're not family."

She looked as if he had punched her in the stomach. "No, I'm not that," she said, busying herself with the flatware.

Tony hesitated, feeling guilty, although she'd certainly stuck it to him a few times. "Do you have a lot of family in San Francisco?"

"No."

"Are they in Ireland?"

"No."

"So where do they live?" Tony asked. It seemed

there was no in-between with her. She either wouldn't shut up or she wouldn't say a word. He'd never met a woman so contrary.

"I don't know," she said finally.

"How can you not know?"

When she lifted her head, her eyes were filled with angry tears. "Believe it or not, it's pretty damn easy."

"Kathleen, wait," he said as she turned away. But she didn't stop. Maybe it was better that way. He didn't want to know more. The last thing he needed was another female to muck up his mind. Lonely nights at sea were looking more appealing by the minute.

He turned at the sound of the front door closing. Linda entered the restaurant, her expression worried. "Did you manage to talk your father out of taking a trip?" she asked.

Tony shook his head. "I can't talk my father out of anything. Once he has his mind made up, that's it."

"Sounds like someone else I know," she grumbled. "Where is Frank anyway?"

"He's not with you?"

"No, I dropped the kids off at summer school and stopped by the store. He was supposed to meet us here." She looked up as Frank walked through the kitchen door. "There you are. Did you talk to Vincent?"

"Yes, and he's determined to leave town," Frank replied. "I have to tell him the truth. There's no other way."

"You can't ruin the surprise," Linda protested.

"It will be ruined if they don't show up."

"You have to think of something else."

"Like what? I told you this was a bad idea from the start. But you had to do it. Now you see what a mess you've gotten us into?"

"*Me?*"

"Hey, Frank, lighten up. It's not Linda's fault," Tony interjected.

"Stay out of it. This doesn't concern you. This is between me and my wife."

"Oh, come on, Frank. You're not God. You don't get to order everyone around. You're not even Vincent, so knock off this self-righteous crap."

"You can't talk to me like that," Frank said.

"Who's going to stop me?" Tony retorted.

"I will."

Tony laughed. Frank couldn't fight his way out of a paper bag. "You and who else?"

Linda raised her hand. "Stop it, both of you. This isn't getting us anywhere."

Frank glared at Tony. "Fine. If you've got a better idea, let's hear it."

Tony shrugged. "Sophia is the soft touch. Why don't you just ask her to baby-sit Saturday afternoon? Tell her you haven't been out together in awhile, and you desperately need the time alone before your marriage falls apart." He smiled at the discomfort on Frank's face. "For some reason I think she'd believe that."

"It could work," Linda said. "Although Sophia rarely says no to Vincent. If he wants to go she'll probably go."

Tony thought for a minute. Linda was right. Sophia never crossed Vincent. He tried to think of something Sophia seemed interested in, something that would keep her attention and make her want to stay in town. Joanna's face drifted through his mind. No, he couldn't bring her into it. She was the reason Vincent wanted to leave.

"What are you thinking, Tony?" Linda asked.

"It wouldn't work."

"What wouldn't work?"

He hesitated, then plunged ahead. "Mama seems

obsessed with talking to that woman—Joanna Wingate—the one who looks like Angela."

"No," Frank said immediately. "You heard Papa
the other night. He doesn't want Mama to have anything to do with her. This woman does not concern
us in any way."

"I'm not so sure about that. If I didn't know better,
I'd swear she was a relative."

"That's ridiculous."

"I'll tell you something else. Papa didn't get this
idea to leave town until Joanna came to his house
this morning."

"It's a coincidence," Frank said.

"Just like it's a coincidence that Joanna looks like
Angela?" Tony asked. "That's a pretty big stretch."

Frank clung to his loyalty like an exhausted swimmer clung to a buoy. He wasn't about to let go. If
he did he might drown. "There is no possible way
that woman is part of our family," Frank said. "And
you will not bring up her name at the party or use
her as an excuse to keep Mama in town. I'd rather
tell them the truth. But if you want to try the baby-
sitting excuse, fine. I have work to do."

"I think Frank is in for a rude awakening," Tony
said as his brother returned to the kitchen.

"I'm not sure he could take one," Linda replied.
"He wears his last name like a shield. Every decision
he makes is based on how it will affect the family,
not just me and the kids, but your parents, you, Michael, the cousins, everyone."

"I hardly think Frank worries about me."

"He used to, and Angela, too. He takes his big
brother responsibilities very seriously. In fact, he
takes all of his responsibilities seriously. He just
seems to have forgotten that there's supposed to be
some love and fun in there along with duty."

"Linda—" Kathleen's warning echoed through his
mind.

"What?"

"Don't do anything stupid."

Her gaze dropped away in a guilty fashion. "I wouldn't. Why would you say that?"

"Because you and Frank don't seem to be getting along."

"You noticed. Funny, I think everyone has noticed except Frank. Even your mother asked me if we were okay. I just want to feel the way I used to feel," she said with a wistful sigh. "I want the excitement, the passion, that first glance, that first look, that first shiver."

"Linda, you're married, and you've been married forever. I mean, how long can excitement last?"

"Obviously not long enough. Maybe you're right to stay single, Tony. You can always have that first look, that first tingle of excitement."

"Yeah, I can have it every night of the week, but sometimes I'd like to be with someone who knows me really well so I don't have to put on a show, I don't have to figure out where she wants to be touched."

Linda shook her finger at him. "Don't you dare try to get Helen back."

He took a step back in surprise. "Helen? Who said I was talking about Helen?"

"Tony, I've known you and Helen for a long time. If you think Frank and I got boring, believe me, you and Helen would do the same. You make great friends, but she doesn't set your soul on fire."

"How do you know that?"

"Because if she made you feel like that, you never would have stayed away an entire year. Think about it. I've got to go. I'll see you."

"Yeah, see you." Tony's gaze drifted over to Kathleen, who was folding napkins in the corner. He had a feeling if anyone could set his soul on fire, it would be her. He also had a feeling he'd end up with third-degree burns.

Too risky, he decided. Despite what Linda had said, he knew he couldn't leave town without giving Helen one more chance to change her mind.

19

Sophia entered her house, nearly tripping over the suitcase in front of the door. She grabbed on to the side table to stop herself from falling. *"Mio Dio! What on earth is going on?"*

Vincent emerged from the kitchen, dressed casually in pale gray slacks and a white polo shirt. He looked energized, more alive than she'd seen him in a long time.

"Where are you going?" Sophia asked in confusion.

"Not me. Us. We're going on a trip."

"Pardon me?"

"A vacation, a long-awaited romantic weekend for two." He walked over to her, slid his hands around her waist, and twirled her around with a laugh. "I had the most wonderful idea today, Sophia."

"Put me down, Vincent," she said, feeling breathless and unsettled by his exuberance.

Reluctantly he did so. She smoothed the skirt of her dress, trying to calm her rapid heart. Vincent didn't like surprises. He never made secret plans for a getaway weekend. In all the years they'd been married, he'd never once arranged for a baby-sitter. She had always been the one to plan their trips, to decide where they were going. His behavior was completely out of character. Something had happened.

"I'm taking you away for our anniversary," Vincent said. "I've made reservations at the Miramar in Santa Barbara. We'll drive down the coast this afternoon. I've booked us a room overlooking the ocean with one of those fireplaces that you like."

"It's summer," she said weakly, knowing the fireplace was the least of her problems.

"Then we'll have to try the Jacuzzi bathtub instead," he said with a twinkle in his eye.

God, he looked so young and loving and passionate. She'd forgotten he could look like this—that he could act like this. Maybe that's all it was—an act.

This wasn't about their anniversary, she realized. It was about Joanna. Vincent had realized that anger and orders weren't working, and he was now manipulating her with love and seduction. He'd gotten away with it before. He'd always persuaded her one way or the other to follow his lead, attacking her from all angles until she couldn't think straight, until she believed that whatever plan he had was actually her idea.

"I packed for you," Vincent added. "And I'm putting together a cooler of drinks so we won't have to stop on the drive down. I'll get it."

Sophia couldn't believe he had packed for her. He must be really worried. She put a hand to her temple, feeling dizzy and confused. She couldn't go away now. There was too much going on in her head.

She'd spent the morning with Elena, trying to figure out what to do now that Edward Wingate was dead. Sophia had hoped he might be able to build a bridge between them all. Now that wasn't possible. She would have to do it herself.

Sophia started as Vincent returned from the kitchen with the cooler.

"I just need to put the toothbrushes in a bag, and we can go," he said.

Sophia put up her hand. "Wait. You're moving too fast."

"I want to beat the traffic."

"I can't go."

"Why not?" His words came out like bullets, hard, fast, angry. He was close to the edge. She knew she had pushed him there. But dammit, she was right there, too. If they clung to each other, they could both survive. If they stayed apart they might both fall. He needed to understand that.

"Vincent, you know why not." She caught his gaze and held it, willing him to understand, to see reason. "I want to see her."

"No. And I say this for your own good."

"My own good or your own good?"

"They are one and the same, as we are one and the same." He took her hands in his. "Sophia, tomorrow it will be forty years since we made our vows. This is our time to be together, to remember what we promised."

"How can I go with you and have fun when I'll be thinking of her the whole time?"

"She'll no doubt be here when you get back," Vincent said, his voice filled with hopelessness. "Perhaps by then you'll realize what's at stake."

"I know what's at stake. I can't think of anything else."

"Then come with me, Sophia. Please."

It was the please that got to the heart of her, that made her feel guilty. She almost gave in. She almost said yes. The word hovered on her lips. She had been raised to be a good wife. It was the only role she knew, and it was far too late to look for another role to play. Her husband, her companion for life, was the most important person in the world to her.

How could she take the risk of losing him now? She didn't know how to be alone.

"I'll get our toothbrushes," he said again, taking her silence for acquiescence.

When his foot reached the bottom stair, she spoke. "I can't go."

His back stiffened. Slowly he turned. "I won't take no for an answer."

His stern gaze pierced her heart, but she held fast. "I'm afraid you'll have to. Have you forgotten that Elena and Charles are taking us to dinner tomorrow night?"

"Elena will understand."

"I don't want her to understand. We've planned it for weeks. They've made reservations. It's set."

"Sophia, this is more important than your sister."

"Running away will not solve the problem. As you said, Joanna will still be here when we get back—unless you're planning to move?"

"Don't be silly."

"I can't go on like this, Vincent."

"You have to be strong, Sophia. You must do this for me—for all of us. The family looks to us for guidance, for inspiration. We are the role models for all the children."

His words twisted the knife in her heart. Role models. God help the children.

"We're human, Vincent. Perhaps the children need to learn that from us, more than they need to learn anything else."

But Vincent couldn't show his children vulnerability, and this situation made him vulnerable. She knew that. She understood it. He was a man. She was a woman. She could bend and hopefully recover; but Vincent couldn't bend, he could only break.

The doorbell rang and Sophia moved to answer

it. Linda stood on the doorstep, looking nervous and uncertain.

Sophia smiled at her. "You know, you don't have to ring the bell; just come on in."

"I don't want to disturb you."

"You're family." Her eyes narrowed thoughtfully. "Is everything all right?"

"Yes." Linda glanced at the suitcase on the floor. "Are you going somewhere?"

"No," Sophia said.

"Yes," Vincent said.

Linda looked confused. "Oh, then I guess it doesn't matter."

"What doesn't matter?" Sophia asked.

"I was going to ask if you could baby-sit for us tomorrow afternoon, Sophia. Frank and I were invited to lunch at that new restaurant downtown, Scarpino's, and Frank wants to check it out. We never go out together without the children. It's so expensive to pay for someone to watch four kids, then pay for a meal on top of that."

"No," Vincent said.

"Yes," Sophia said, contradicting him once again. "I'd be happy to. You and Frank deserve an afternoon out."

"Sophia, we're going away."

"If you want to go away, go. I'm baby-sitting."

"It's our anniversary. I'm not going without you." He shot Linda a dark look.

"I'm sorry," Linda said. "I'll find someone else." She backed toward the door.

Sophia reached for Linda's hand with a reassuring smile. "You won't find someone else. It's all settled. What time do you want me?"

"Eleven-thirty. I know Elena is taking you out for dinner. We'll be back in plenty of time for you to get ready."

"I'm not worried. I think it's wonderful you and Frank are going out together."

Linda looked over at Vincent, who was still scowling. "I'll see you tomorrow then."

Vincent slammed the door behind her.

"Why did you do that? You probably scared her half to death," Sophia scolded.

"She deserves it for giving you an excuse to stay home."

"I didn't need an excuse, Vincent, and you know it."

He threw up his hands. "You drive me crazy. I'm going to the restaurant, and I won't be back until late. Don't wait up for me. In fact, I may not be back at all."

She sent him a steady look, even though her heart raced at the implication of his words. "Is that a threat?"

"Yes." His dark eyes turned hard. "I won't let you hurt this family, Sophia. I won't let you destroy our name, our reputation, our honor. Whatever you say to this woman, I will deny. Even if it means calling you a liar. Don't make me do it."

He slammed out of the house. Sophia took a deep breath, then let it out. In ten short minutes she'd seen the depth of his love and the extent of his hate. She had a feeling that no matter what she did, she would lose.

The sun was descending over the horizon when Joanna pulled up in front of the Seacliff house. After a hectic day at school, she had spent the late afternoon looking for apartments, knowing she had to find her own place soon. Unfortunately none of the buildings appealed to her. They'd all been too small, too square, too white, too boring. Not like this house, where fantasy and reality came together.

She opened the door and stepped out of the car.

The birds were singing. Butterflies danced from bush to bush as bees hummed from flower to flower. The garden was bursting with color, but it needed weeding, pruning, planting. Joanna longed to sink her hands into the dirt and make something beautiful out of the mess, but this wasn't her house, she reminded herself.

She tried the front door. It was locked, so she went around the back and jiggled the doorknob. It opened easily. As she entered the spacious but old kitchen, she didn't see the dirty linoleum, the cracked tiles on the counter, the peeling wallpaper, or the grease and smoke stains behind the stove. She didn't smell the lingering traces of food gone bad or hear the dripping sink.

She didn't see the problems, only the possibilities. And as she walked through the dining room, up the stairs, through each of the bedrooms, finally stopping in the attic, she knew this house was home. She didn't want an apartment. She wanted this house. She wanted to buy it.

Her father had left her a sizable chunk of money, a nest egg, he'd called it, so she'd have something to build her nest with. But this house would take every last cent of that nest egg plus her own savings, and even then the monthly payments would be tight.

It would be much easier to buy the house with someone else—with a husband, with a family.

She sat down on the steamer trunk and closed her eyes. In her mind she saw Lily with the feisty thrust of her chin, Rose with the sensitive smile and shy brown eyes, Michael with his dazzling blue gaze and sexy grin.

Her heart ached with need. Her arms felt cold, so she wrapped them around her body, but it didn't take the chill away from her heart. The only man she wanted, she couldn't have. Why did she have to meet him now—when it was too late? Why couldn't she have met him before Angela? They'd both lived in the city. It could have happened.

But it hadn't. It hadn't been their time. Maybe it never would be. How could Michael fall in love with her, a mirror image of his wife, but a paler reflection, not as vibrant, not as loud, not as much of anything? He couldn't. But she could fall in love with him, with his humor, his patience, his kind, loving ways, his loyalty to family, his incredibly sexy body. She sighed wistfully at the thought of kissing him again, stripping down the barriers of clothes and pasts, and coming together as two people who simply wanted each other.

"Joanna?"

She started at the sound of her name, low and husky. Had she wanted him so badly, her mind had begun playing tricks on her? Slowly she opened her eyes.

Michael stood before her in gray slacks and a white shirt, his red silk tie loosely knotted at the neck, his shirtsleeves rolled up past his forearms. She blinked twice. He didn't disappear.

"Michael, what are you doing here?"

"I was going to ask you the same thing. I thought you were spending the evening with your mother."

"I—I decided not to. I kept thinking about this house—wondering what would happen to it. I thought you were going to a bachelor party."

"I did. It wasn't any fun. I kept thinking about this house and about you—wondering what was going to happen to us."

She drew in a breath at the desire in his eyes. They were alone in the big old house. No kids. No rules. No one who knew where they were or what they were doing. No one to tell them it was wrong. Except themselves.

"There is no us," she whispered.

"There could be. I can't fight it anymore. I want you, Joanna. You. No one else but you."

She wanted to believe him. "Are you sure?"

"When I went to sleep last night, I tried to picture Angela's face in my mind. But it was your smile I saw, your nose, your eyes, your hair, and all the other things that are just you—the way you tilt your head to one side when you're thinking about something, the way you talk so thoughtfully, choosing your words with care, the way you smell like a summer garden, not a perfume shop."

"Michael, stop."

"Why? So you can keep on fighting? We're right for each other."

"There are so many other people involved."

"I don't want to make love to them, only to you."

Make love. She licked her lips. She'd never met a man who was so up-front about his intentions. "You scare me," she said. "I've never wanted anyone as much as I want you. I feel like I'm losing control."

"Mine is already gone. I've played it safe for a long time. I want to take a chance—with you."

"Yes," she said.

"Yes?" He echoed her word in disbelief.

Joanna stood up. Michael moved forward. Their lips came together hungrily, as if they were starving for each other.

Michael kissed her again and again and again. He took delight in saying her name over and over until she could hear nothing but her name, feel nothing but his lips, think of nothing but him.

His mouth was warm, insistent, loving, taking her exactly where she wanted to go. She didn't feel cold anymore. She felt deliciously warm. Michael slipped his hands through her hair, pulling out the combs, freeing the long strands, only to tangle them between his fingers.

She worked at the knot in his tie until it came

loose, then unfastened the buttons on his shirt, eager to touch him without any barriers. When the buttons were undone she slipped her hands against his skin, running her fingers through the dark hair on his chest. She loved the feel of him, the smell of him, the taste of him. All of her senses were coming together in one bountiful feast.

Joanna gasped as Michael's hands moved beneath her sleeveless sweater, running up her rib cage, until he was cupping her breasts, all the while kissing her, sliding his tongue in and out of her mouth, generating long, tingling shivers of sensation that ran from her mouth to her breasts, to the inner sides of her thighs, until she felt completely spineless.

Michael pulled the sweater over her head, then gazed down at her full breasts swelling out of the lacy ivory cups of her bra. He bent his head and kissed the upper curve of her breast, sliding his mouth into the valley between them. She found herself pressing her hands down on his shoulders, wanting him to taste even more of her.

He flipped open the clasp of her bra, and slowly, slowly spread the lacy edges. He cupped her breasts with his hands and slid his fingers back and forth until her nipples ached for his touch.

Finally he lowered his head and kissed her, drawing one nipple between his lips, between the gentle tug of his teeth until she gasped with pleasure. She thought she could surely die happy at this moment, in his arms. Then his hands moved to the button on her skirt, and she knew she wasn't ready to die just yet.

Her skirt slid down her hips, revealing a matching pair of lace undies, which Michael peeled away. The air felt cool against her heated skin, until his fingers returned to the triangle of hair between her thighs, and he made his way through the tight curls, caressing, coaxing, until all she could think of was the tug of his mouth on her breast and the aching place between her legs.

"I want you, Michael," she muttered.

He slipped his fingers inside her.

She tensed at the warm, sliding sensation. The tension built, and she could do nothing but cling to his shoulders until her body shook and trembled against him.

He lifted his head from her breasts and pulled her against his chest.

"I—I couldn't wait for you," she said.

"Honey, we're just getting started."

He bent to kiss her lips, and she reached for his belt buckle. She quickly loosened the belt, undid the top button, and slid down the zipper.

Michael dropped his briefs along with his slacks, then shed his shirt and slipped her bra off her shoulders. "Now this is better."

"Much better," she agreed, leaning forward to kiss him.

"Wait."

She looked at him in surprise. "Why?"

He reached for his pants, for his wallet, for the square foil packet inside. Protection. She'd forgotten all about it. She, who was practical and cautious, but he had come prepared. Had he expected this or just hoped? Suddenly there were doubts.

He read them in her eyes. "Don't."

"Michael—"

"Shhh." He covered her protest with his mouth and pulled her against the length of him, until they were skin to skin, breast to breast, hip to hip.

He cupped her buttocks as he slid his tongue back into her mouth. She caressed the length of him, stroking the velvety tip, feeling him harden beneath her touch.

Michael drew her over to the old couch. He put on the condom, then sat down, drawing her on top of him, leaning back until her body covered his like a blanket. He lifted her, then brought her down on top of him. She met his lips with a glad cry as he thrust inside her. They moved together in a mindless rhythm that was easy, natural, and utterly perfect. When the tension built again he called her name, and she called his, and they went over the edge together.

20

A half hour later, Joanna and Michael walked down to the kitchen, hoping to find some water to drink. Michael looked at the country oak table, then tipped his head thoughtfully in her direction.

Joanna's eyes widened at the returning desire in his eyes. "I don't think so. The couch in the attic was daring enough for me."

"You are so much like me, it's incredible."

"Like you? I'm not like you. You're the one with all the big ideas. In fact . . ." She laughed as she reached for the bulge in his pants. "You're the one who's just plain big."

"Because of you," he growled, "I've taken more cold showers in the last week than any man should have to take in a lifetime."

"Poor guy."

"That's right. And I think you should apologize."

He lifted her up and sat her down on the tabletop, spreading her legs so he could stand between them.

"What did you have in mind?" she asked with a shiver of anticipation.

He laughed. "Believe it or not, I have no idea how to actually do this, but I think somehow between us we can make it work."

She cupped his face with her hands. "You really haven't been this bold before?"

He shook his head. "I always felt I had to be responsible, safe, plan things out ahead of time. I couldn't be spontaneous because someone had to hold down the fort."

"But Angela was spontaneous. Surely the two of you made love everywhere." Joanna didn't know why she asked. She hated to even bring up Angela's name, but the woman always seemed to be between them.

"Angela and I were kids when we got together. Even though she longed for a wild life, she was a well-protected Italian Catholic girl. That's why we got married young, instead of just having sex," he said with a wry smile. "Because I was older than Angela, I felt I had to take care of her, that she needed me to make the decisions. We fell into a pattern that way. After we had kids, our love life diminished. I was busy. Angela was tired. I know she started thinking about other men, wondering what it would be like to be with someone else, since I was her one and only lover."

"Surely she didn't say that to you."

"When we were fighting she'd say all kinds of things. Angela spoke first and thought second." He shrugged. "Maybe she was right. Maybe I didn't give her a chance to grow up, to experience life. Maybe I screwed up her life."

Joanna ran her hand down the side of his face. She loved that he spoke with honesty, that his words rang true even to the point of incriminating himself, but she didn't believe he had ruined Angela's life.

"We're all to blame for the messes that occur in our lives. Ultimately we make our own decisions or we let others make our decisions, which is a decision in itself."

"Angela was too young to make a decision."

"Do you really believe that?"

"I think her parents do. I think they hold me responsible for everything that happened, even her death."

"They know you weren't responsible for her death."

"Sophia might," he admitted. "But Vincent ordered me to take care of his daughter, and I let him down. Our relationship has never been the same since."

"The De Marcos are important to you, aren't they?"

"They're family."

She nodded, but kept silent. She didn't want to think about the De Marcos. She wanted to go back to where they'd been before, making love, lost in each other's bodies.

"Joanna." Michael tilted her chin with his hand. "I'm glad you came here tonight, that we found each other."

"Even if it's only for tonight?" she asked, already anticipating the bittersweet pain of parting that would come with the morning.

"Who says it's only for tonight?" He played with a strand of her hair. "I've been thinking."

"Uh-oh."

He smiled. "Maybe you should meet the De Marcos. Sophia and Vincent are celebrating their fortieth wedding anniversary tomorrow night."

"I don't know."

"Joanna, I don't want to hide what we feel for each other. I don't want to conduct this love affair in a dark closet."

"We're not having a love affair."

"I want to." His eyes turned serious. "The girls already love you."

"Think what people will say."

"I don't care what they say."

"I do. I've always cared. We still don't know if I'm somebody's skeleton in the closet. I can't just show up at this party. I could scare the hell out of someone."

Michael hesitated. She'd probably scare the hell out of a lot of people. Maybe it wasn't fair to the De Marcos to have her come to the party. He didn't want to spoil Sophia and Vincent's anniversary. "Maybe tomorrow isn't a good idea, but we're going to deal with this soon. I promise you that."

"We? Michael, don't you see that you could end up in the middle of this? That there might not be a happy ending for any of us?"

"Don't be cynical."

"I'm being realistic. If someone gave me away I'm not sure I could forgive them. And if my mother lied to me all these years, I'm not sure I could forgive her. I don't know if I could be with either family. And you are as much a De Marco as the rest of them. Lily and Rose are De Marcos."

"Lily and Rose and I are Ashtons," Michael said. It was the first time he'd ever really thought of them in that way. Maybe it was time to make the distinction, to grow all the way up, to take his place as a man and a father, not someone's son or son-in-law.

"Michael—" Joanna began again.

His finger touched her lips. "Shhh. We'll talk about it tomorrow."

"I'm afraid of tomorrow," she said with simple honesty. "I'm terrified of the future. I don't want to end up alone, without anyone."

"You won't."

"You can't promise that."

"I can. Don't say anything else, Joanna. Don't think. Don't worry."

"You mean I should stop breathing?"

"If that's what it takes." He paused. "Actually you could think about one thing."

"What's that?"

"Taking off some of your clothes. It's getting hot in here," he said as he kissed her lips.

"Now that I can do something about."

It took only a minute to shed their clothes. Michael pulled Joanna to the edge of the table. She wrapped her legs around his waist. She wanted to feel as if they were one person again and again, until she couldn't remember what loneliness felt like.

Joanna and Michael spent the night outside, wrapped in a quilt on the edge of the cliff behind Ruby Mae's house. It was an unseasonably warm summer night, with only a slight chill as the hours of darkness headed toward dawn.

The sound of the ocean gave them peace. The dazzling array of stars overhead provided inspiration, and in each other's arms they found the missing piece of themselves.

"I always knew it would be like this," Joanna said, resting her head on Michael's shoulder, "when I finally found the right guy. I just didn't think it would take so damn long."

He laughed at the disgust in her voice. "Maybe you were too picky."

"If you'd met David you wouldn't say that. Or Harry or Winston or Conrad."

"Didn't you date anyone named Joe or Sam?"

"You don't find too many of those guys hanging out at the library. They always seem to be on the baseball field or the basketball court."

"You're not saying you don't like sports," he said in mock horror.

"Actually I love baseball. My dad used to take me to the Giants games. We always went to opening day together."

"You miss him, don't you?"

"Yes, but life goes on." She paused. "Do you believe in fate? I mean, look at us. How strange that we would meet, that we would come together at this moment in our lives. It must have been destiny."

"Or Mariah. The kids swear it was her idea that they go to school," he said.

"Maybe it *was* Mariah. I'd like to believe there is a little magic in everyone's life."

"Magic, huh?"

She felt his smile against her hair and lifted her head to look into his eyes. "You're not going to go all modern and pragmatic on me, are you?"

"I'm a twentieth-century guy. I can't help it."

"A twentieth-century guy with an old-fashioned romantic streak."

"Says who?"

"Says me." She kissed his mouth.

"Joanna, they're still going to tear down the Stratton Hotel, and I'm still going to design a skyscraper for Gary Connaught. It's what I do, and I'm pretty good at it."

She made a face at him. "I think you'd be just as good at restoring something. Haven't you ever wanted to try that angle?"

"Maybe a long time ago." He tipped his head. "You know, you're the one who should be out there fighting for the old buildings. Why aren't you in the historical society? Why aren't you peppering the building department with protests like every other San Francisco preservation fanatic?"

"I don't know. I never thought I could make a difference. I've never been a leader. I'm not sure I'd be any good at it."

"I think you'd be terrific."

She smiled, pleased with his show of respect. "Maybe I'll think about it. After handling six-year-olds this summer, politicians would be a piece of cake."

"Speaking of six-year-olds, did Lily and Rose show any signs of nervousness when their cousin

Marlena picked them up from school?"

"Oh, no. They were filled with excitement about their sleep over. They talked nonstop about it."

"Really? They didn't seem scared about being away from home?"

"Not at all. And Marlena is a delightful young woman. Who does she belong to?"

"Vincent's brother Louis. She's his oldest daughter."

"She seemed very responsible."

"She is, and I am extremely happy that Marlena's younger sister Andrea decided to have a sleep-over birthday party."

"I'll bet." She rested her head on his chest. "Do you want to go inside?"

"No."

"Neither do I."

"See, we agree about everything important."

"I don't know about everything."

Silence fell between them, broken only by the sounds of the crickets.

"Joanna, what if you find out you're a De Marco? What then?"

She shivered at the thought. "I don't know."

"Promise me one thing."

"What?"

"Don't let it come between us," he whispered.

Her heart stopped at the passionate, tender plea. She wanted to promise that nothing would come between them, but she couldn't. Not yet.

Michael awoke with a smile on his face. It had been a long time since he had slept with such contentment. As he stretched, Joanna stirred against his shoulder. He'd probably have a kink in his neck all day, but it was worth it.

They were good together. Joanna seemed to know what he was thinking before he thought it. There had been nothing awkward about their lovemaking. No stilted moments, no long pauses, no wondering if he was making the right move.

He shifted slightly so he could look at her face, bathed in early morning sunlight.

He no longer saw Angela when he looked at Joanna. The two had become distinct in his mind, just as Lily and Rose were identical only to strangers, not to him. His daughters would be thrilled to have him and Joanna get together. They would be happy to have a mother again. But was it fair to ask Joanna to step into a ready-made family, to play out someone else's role? God, he hoped so.

He wanted everything with her. He wanted to go to bed with her and wake up with her. He wanted to be her partner, her lover, her friend. She didn't need him. He knew that. She was too strong in her own right to really need a man. But damn if he didn't need her.

What if he couldn't have her?

The thought came unbidden to his mind. Would he have to choose between Joanna and the De Marcos? His adopted family against the woman of his dreams?

Could life really be that cruel?

Of course, it could. Didn't he have firsthand experience with just such cruelty?

"Mm-mm," Joanna said with a smile, her eyes still closed. "If this is a dream I don't want to wake up."

"It's not a dream," he murmured.

She blinked sleepily, lazily, tenderness and love filling her eyes as she looked into his face. "Morning."

"Morning yourself."

"I can't believe we slept out here." She sat up and stretched. "You must have been uncomfortable with me on your shoulder all night."

Michael sat up and flexed his arm. "I think I'll

live. You might have to kiss it and make it feel better."

She leaned over and kissed him on the biceps. "Anything else hurt?" she asked with a mischievous grin.

"Yeah, my neck."

She scooted in close to him so she could trail her lips against his neck. Then he pointed to his lips, and she followed accordingly.

He slid his arms around her waist and pulled her onto his lap, deepening the kiss, teasing her lips with his tongue, until she smiled against his mouth.

"If you're planning on leaving any time soon, you better stop right now," she said.

"I don't think I ever want to leave."

"This isn't even our house." Joanna traced his mouth with her finger. "Come next week, it will probably be for sale. Who knows what will happen to it then?"

Her face took on a faraway expression, and Michael wondered if he should tell her about Iris' plans to destroy the house. But he didn't want to spoil the moment. "You know, it's Saturday, and I don't have to pick up the girls until eleven, so there's no rush in getting out of here. What's on your schedule today?"

"Let's see." She tilted her head thoughtfully. "I thought I'd return some books to the library, take a shower . . . oh, and maybe find out who my real parents are. Just your average run-of-the-mill day."

Michael smiled. "We're quite a pair. You don't know who your parents are. I have no idea why my kids won't speak to me. We just spent the night in the backyard of a house we don't own. Oh, and you just happen to be the mirror image of my wife. Where's the phone? I'm calling Oprah. We ought to be able to get a free ticket to Chicago for this."

Joanna punched him on the arm. "It's not funny."

"If we don't laugh we'll never get through it."

"I know you're right, but there's so much at stake for me. If I'm not a Wingate I don't know who I am."

"You're a beautiful, intelligent, sexy woman."

She smiled. "Okay, you get points for that."

"How many?"

Joanna ran her tongue along the edge of his lips, until he groaned and deepened the kiss.

"Did I also mention that you have great legs and a terrific smile?" he asked a few minutes later.

"Don't push your luck," she said with a laugh, flopping down on her back, her head on his shoulder. As she did so, a strong gust of wind rattled the wind chimes on Ruby Mae's back deck, a lovely melody that had played all night long. "That music reminds me of my music box," Joanna said.

Michael sat up abruptly, and Joanna's head hit the ground with a thud.

"Ouch! What did you do that for?" She sat up, rubbing the back of her head.

"Music box? You have a music box?" he asked.

She looked at him in surprise. "Yes. My father gave it to me when I was a baby. Why?"

His heart began to race. Maybe he was jumping to a wild conclusion. Lots of children had music boxes. It didn't mean anything.

"Michael, what's wrong?"

He met her troubled gaze. "Sophia collects music boxes from all over the world. She gave each of her children a music box on the day they were born. She even gave one to Lily and Rose."

"I'm sure it's a coincidence," Joanna said. "My father told me he found the box in an antiques shop. He loved it almost as much as I did. He would turn it on just before I went to sleep at night. Sometimes we'd sit there in the dark without speaking and listen to the melody play."

"Is there an inscription on the box?"

"Yes. It says 'To my daughter, with love.' "

"Anything else? Any initials—like SD?"

"I—I don't think so." She didn't sound sure. "I haven't looked at it in awhile. I play it, but I don't read the inscription all that often."

"Maybe you should take another look, although it probably doesn't mean anything."

"It couldn't. My father gave me the music box."

Michael agreed on the surface, but he didn't like the uneasiness that crept up his spine. The inscription was terribly familiar. Another coincidence? Was that possible?

What was the alternative? That Sophia was Joanna's mother? He couldn't accept that either. Sophia was the backbone of the family, the nurturing woman who mothered them all, whose heart was as big as the tallest skyscraper. Sophia would have been married when Joanna was born, with two boys, Frank and Tony. It couldn't have been her. She couldn't have given up a baby. It was impossible.

"Maybe I should try to talk to Sophia today," Joanna said, her thoughts running parallel to his.

"Today is the party, remember?"

"That's right, their wedding anniversary. Forty years, you said."

He met her gaze. "Joanna, it couldn't have been Sophia. She and Vincent would never have given up a child."

"I know you love them, Michael, but how can you be sure of what happened in Sophia and Vincent's marriage thirty years ago?"

"If Sophia had been pregnant everyone in the family would have known. If anyone is your mother, it's Elena."

"Maybe it was her. Will she be at the party tonight?"

"Yes."

"Mm-mm."

Michael wished he'd never mentioned the party to Joanna. It was a big event. Linda had spent days planning the surprise. He couldn't let Joanna walk in and start asking awkward questions. It wouldn't be fair to the De Marcos. But his thoughts made him feel disloyal to Joanna, to the woman he'd made love with. Could he put loyalty to the De Marcos before loyalty to her?

"Joanna, I think you were right earlier, that this party is not the right time to rock the boat."

"I thought you wanted me to come."

"I changed my mind."

"Michael, this boat started rocking long before I got on it. This situation isn't my fault."

"I didn't mean it that way."

"You're more afraid I'm going to hurt them than they're going to hurt me," she proclaimed.

"I don't want any of you to get hurt."

"You can't play it both sides."

"Why not? Why do I have to choose a side?"

"Because . . ." Her voice trailed away. "I don't know."

He put his hands on her shoulders and rubbed the tension out of her neck. "Let's not borrow trouble. We don't know anything yet. This secret, if there is one, has been around for years. We don't have to solve it today."

"You're right." They sat there for a few more minutes, listening to the sounds of the waves breaking on the beach below. "I guess we should think about leaving."

"What time is it?"

Joanna checked her watch. "Eight o'clock."

"Too early. We should go back to bed."

"We're not in bed, we're on the lawn."

"It will still work."

"What will still work?" she asked suspiciously.

He grinned in reply.

Joanna blushed under his intimate look. "Do you have any—you know?"

He reached into his pocket and pulled out three more foil packets.

Her jaw dropped open in astonishment. "Good grief!"

"I build skyscrapers. When I dream, I dream big."

"What exactly happens in this dream of yours?"

He pulled the quilt over their heads and proceeded to show her.

21

The banquet room at De Marco's was packed by six o'clock that evening with every De Marco between the ages of two and sixty. It was a noisy crowd, lots of chattering, hand waving, and arguing. Tony took a sip of his beer and leaned against the wall. He smiled as he saw his great-aunt Marie handing out prayer cards. She was hell-bent on saving as many De Marcos from purgatory as she possibly could. Tony had used his card as a coaster for his beer bottle.

His forty-two-year-old second cousin Harry was already drunk and using this opportunity to kiss as many women in the room as possible. Aunt Tess was tapping her cane to the beat of the music that barely rose above the conversation level, and his elderly uncle Milton, who tried to sleep through as many family functions as possible, was taking a quick snooze in the corner of the room while some of Frank's kids twirled streamers around his chair.

All in all it was a typical De Marco gathering.

He'd missed them, Tony suddenly realized—all of them, not just Angela but the others too. He'd missed this feeling of being part of a group of people who genuinely cared about one another. Craziness and all, his family was okay.

He took another sip of his beer. After a quiet dinner, if you could call any dinner with the De Marco family quiet, they would spill into the main dining room to join more family and friends. There were already a few people dining in the restaurant, waiting for the party to follow.

His gut tightened instinctively. Helen and Joey would be arriving at any minute. He'd seen their names on the reservation list. This might be his last chance to talk to her. He was planning to leave in a few days, so he needed to see her tonight.

With that thought in mind Tony left the room. As he entered the main dining room, Helen and Joey walked in. He stopped abruptly. Helen's dark purple silk dress set off her gorgeous blond hair. Her skin seemed to glow in the candlelight, and as she laughed at something Joey said, Tony realized she looked happy—like a woman in love.

It had to be an act. Helen had always loved him—always. She'd vowed to marry him in the seventh grade. The only problem was, he'd never offered marriage. They'd dated on and off throughout middle school, high school, and college. Helen had always been there for him, waiting with open arms and unconditional love. Only, he'd been too stupid to realize that—until now.

Tony raised the beer bottle to his lips as Helen and Joey were seated in a quiet booth against the wall. He needed to talk to Helen alone. He needed five minutes to convince her that he was serious this time. Somehow he didn't think Joey would accommodate his need for private conversation.

A flash of red caught Tony's eye as Kathleen Shannon crossed in front of him. She set down two bowls of pasta at one table and a basket of bread at another. Then she wiped her hands on her apron and returned to the kitchen.

He wondered if he could enlist Kathleen's help in distracting Joey. He walked over to the kitchen door, then stepped back in a hurry as Kathleen flew out with a tray full of hot food. For a moment the tray swayed in her hand. Tony instinctively grabbed it, steadying it. She let out a sigh of relief.

"You scared me," she said.

"I've always told Papa he should change that door. Do you want some help?"

"I can manage."

He waited by the door until she had unloaded her tray, then he stopped her as she came by again. "Kathleen, can you do me a favor?"

She raised an eyebrow. "What's that?"

"Go over to that table"—he tipped his head toward Joey and Helen—"and tell that guy he has a phone call in the back hall."

"Why would I want to do that?"

"To be helpful?"

"You'll have to do better than that."

"I just need five minutes."

"With the blonde?" Kathleen studied Helen with a thoughtful tilt to her head. "She's the one who's getting married in a couple of weeks."

"That's right. I need five minutes with the blonde who's getting married in a couple of weeks," Tony repeated in frustration.

"Why do you want her so bad?" Kathleen snapped her fingers. "I know."

"You don't know anything."

"You want her because she wants him."

Tony raised his eyes to the ceiling, unwilling to admit she had even come close. "Will you do it or not?"

"All right, I'll do it. But you owe me one, and I always collect my debts."

"Fine, I'll owe you."

"Remember you said that."

"I will. Just give me one minute, then do it."

Tony headed for the courtesy phones in the back

hallway. He opened the phone book to the yellow
pages and dialed one of the airline numbers. Once
connected, music played in his ear with an announcer interrupting every minute or two to an-
nounce that someone would be on the line shortly.
Perfect. Joey would think his caller had placed him
on hold which should give Tony enough time to
grab Helen by the hand, kiss her senseless, and
sweep her out of the restaurant.

Of course he'd miss the big party, but he'd worry
about that later. His parents understood passion and
love. They were Italian. They'd forgive him for this.
Especially if he ended up getting married and
having children.

Marriage. Children. Whoa. He was getting ahead
of himself. All he really wanted was for Helen to sail
around the world with him. Maybe she'd take a
promise for commitment at a later date.

He returned to the dining room, skirting the edge
so he wouldn't bump into Joey. When he reached
Helen's table she looked at him in wary surprise.

"Tony. I thought you'd be with your family."

"Run away with me," he said in a hurried, hushed
voice.

"What?" Her jaw dropped open.

He slid onto the seat next to her and kissed her
on the lips while her mouth was still open. He
thought for a moment she would kiss him back, but
she pulled away.

"What do you think you're doing?" she hissed,
looking for Joey.

"I'm trying to sweep you off your feet, but you're
not cooperating."

"I'm engaged."

"I love you, Helen."

"It's too late."

"You're not married yet."

"I'm engaged. Go away, Tony."

"Don't you remember our dreams, Helen? We were going to sail around the world. We were going to be footloose and fancy-free. We were going to spend our lives together."

Her eyes filled with tears. "Tony," she said softly, "those were your dreams. They weren't mine."

He didn't understand. "You never said you wanted anything else."

"Because I adored you. I wanted what you wanted. Up until six months ago, I would have done exactly what you asked with no questions. Then I met Joey." She paused. "I realized things could be different. Joey watches me when I sleep, Tony. He brings me coffee in the morning. He lets me have the remote control. He even held my hair back while I threw up. If that's not love, I don't know what is."

"I love you, too," he said, although he winced on hearing the whine in his voice. He sounded like someone who'd just lost his favorite toy. He deliberately lowered his voice, trying to sound mature, sincere. "I'm crazy about you, Helen."

"So crazy that you'd give up that boat of yours, settle in this town, and run this restaurant with your brother?"

Man, she asked a lot. But he didn't want to lose her. "If—if I have to. Yeah. Maybe. If I have to. I could do that."

"Oh, Tony, thank you," she said with a wistful smile.

"For what?"

"For at least considering the idea. Even if it would make you terribly unhappy."

"I wouldn't be unhappy. I'd be with you." He saw Helen look up beyond him. He turned his head.

Joey stood behind him, beaming a broad smile across his square face. "Tony. How you doing? I was hoping to see you while you were here, but Michael told me you were busy getting your boat ready to sail."

Joey must not have overhead their conversation, because he seemed completely oblivious to the undercurrents flowing between him and Helen. "I'm doing okay," Tony mumbled, sliding out of the seat.

"Did you hear Helen and I are getting married? I tell you, I am the luckiest man on earth. Who would have thought that me, Joey Scopazzi, who couldn't get a date to the prom for any amount of money, would be marrying the prettiest girl in town?" Joey leaned over and tenderly kissed Helen on the lips. She kissed him back, the way a lover would, the way a wife would. Tony knew it was over. He'd known it since he first came back; he just hadn't wanted to accept it. Without Helen waiting in the wings, he'd somehow lost his anchor.

"I wish you could stick around for the wedding," Joey said. "I know Helen would love to have you there."

Helen didn't say anything to confirm or deny that statement. She didn't have to. They both knew he wouldn't be there.

"Thanks, I'll think about it. I don't know what my schedule is."

"You know, all of us guys talked about being astronauts or baseball players, but you actually grew up to do exactly what you said you were going to do, sail around the world." Joey slapped him on the back. "We're proud of you, Tony. Really proud."

Proud. Jesus, he felt like a schmuck. "Thanks," he mumbled.

Helen touched Joey on the arm. "I left my sweater in the car and it's chilly in here. Could you get it for me?"

"Of course, sweetheart." He kissed her again, then headed for the car.

"I'd forgotten how nice he was," Tony said with

a scowl. "That must be why we always used to beat him up."

"He is nice."

"Do you really love him, Helen? I know he loves you, but is he truly the love of your lifetime?"

"Yes." Her eyes softened. "I know I promised to love you for all time in the seventh grade, but I grew up. You still tempt me. When you first came back I thought maybe I'd made a mistake. But we don't want the same things, Tony. And as I've gotten older I've learned to avoid things that aren't good for me. It makes life easier." She took a deep breath. "Do me one favor though. Don't come to the wedding, okay?"

"Okay." He shrugged. "I guess there's nothing left to say except have a nice life."

"You, too. I wish I could have been the one for you. I knew when you didn't come back, when you didn't turn to me in your grief, that I could never really be the one. I just didn't figure that out until now."

Maybe Helen was right, but he'd be damned if he'd admit it. "I'll see you around."

"Drop me a postcard some time."

"Sure." He dug his hands into his pockets and walked away. He didn't want to see Joey come back. He didn't want to see Helen kiss her fiancé again. He didn't want to be reminded that he'd probably just lost the best woman he'd ever had.

Instead he headed for the bar and ordered a shot of tequila. "Dumped you, did she?" Kathleen asked as she stepped up to the bar and ordered three glasses of red wine.

"No, she didn't dump me."

Kathleen smiled knowingly. "She wasn't your type anyway."

"How would you know?"

"She's got homebody written all over her. I doubt

she'd hold your attention for more than five minutes."

"She's had my attention since the seventh grade."

"That just proves my point."

"Excuse me?"

"If you'd really wanted her, you would have gotten her a long time ago." She nodded at her own brilliance. "It's like I said, you want her now because she wants him."

"You know, Kathleen, you're a waitress, not a psychologist. Why don't you stick to serving drinks and food instead of advice?"

"I'm a lot more than a waitress, Tony De Marco. That's another problem with you."

"Oh, you mean I have another problem?" he asked, putting a hand to his chest in mock astonishment.

"Yes, you do. You only see what you want to see. I'm beginning to think it's a De Marco family trait."

"Speaking of the De Marcos, I think I'll join my family in the back room."

"Fine," she said with a breezy wave. "Just let me know if you need my help in seducing any other engaged women away from their fiancés."

Her laugh followed him down the hall. She annoyed the hell out of him. Made his blood boil. Made his palms sweat. He paused at the door to the banquet room, suddenly recognizing the symptoms for what they were. But there was no way he was getting involved with her. She'd probably end up killing him, if he didn't kill her first.

Joanna felt a tremendous surge of anger, a wave of fury that rendered her speechless, that made her hands curl into fists, that made her want to hit someone or break something. Her mother had lied. Her father had lied, too.

With shaky fingers she reached for the music box

she had taken off her dresser and placed on the middle of her bed. She sat cross-legged on the quilt, dressed in blue jeans and a sweatshirt, the clothes she had put on when she returned home earlier that day.

Joanna turned the music box over again. The glittering gold inscription on the bottom brought tears to her eyes. *To my daughter, with love.*

Her father had given her the music box. She'd assumed he'd had it engraved. She'd noticed the tiny initials before, the letters S.D., but believed they belonged to the maker of the box. Now they stood for so much more. S.D. Sophia De Marco. There was only one reason Sophia De Marco would have given her a music box. *Sophia was her mother.*

"Joanna?" Caroline knocked on the closed door. "Are you all right? You've been in there for hours."

Joanna wrapped her arms around her waist. She couldn't answer. She couldn't breathe. Her entire body ached with disillusionment, anger, bitterness.

All these years they had lied to her. She wasn't their daughter. She wasn't a Wingate. She wasn't of French or German descent, but Italian. She was a De Marco.

Oh, God! How could she be?

Tears poured out of her eyes, dripping down her cheeks, onto the bedspread, onto the music box—silent tears that couldn't begin to release the depth of her pain. She wanted to scream in agony. The sounds rumbled in her throat, threatening to break free. She swallowed them back, trying to maintain control.

She twisted the key to the music box, starting the melody. The music only heightened her agony. The tones that once seemed so reassuring, loving, and safe now mocked her innocence.

"Joanna, I'm worried about you. Open up this door," her mother commanded.

The knob turned, but Joanna had locked the door. How could she look into her mother's face? Not her real mother, but her adoptive mother. Caroline hadn't labored, hadn't given birth to her. Caroline was an imposter, a liar, a pretender.

The words choked the breath out of her. Her eyes filled again with tears at what she had lost. A small baby taken out of her mother's arms and given to a stranger. A stranger! A woman with blond hair and blue eyes. A woman who liked to jog, who hated to cook, and thought gardening was for men who spoke foreign languages.

All the differences between Joanna and her mother raced through Joanna's mind. All the times her friends had commented on how different she and Caroline were. How many lies had her mother told over the years? Thousands? Millions? Had every word been a lie?

And her father—the man she'd held in her arms as he'd taken his last breath—he'd lied, too.

That hurt the most. Her father had always seemed so sincere, loving, honest. His arms had been warm, his shoulders comforting. But all that time he'd known that he wasn't her real father, that her mother wasn't her real mother, that they were playing a game of pretend.

She wondered how it had come about, and her anger grew to encompass the De Marcos. How could Sophia and her husband have given her away?

She was their child. They'd kept their other children. Why not her? Had they thought she was sick, retarded? Had they not loved her enough to want to raise her?

Joanna hadn't thought the pain could get worse, but it did. She felt angry, confused, betrayed, and so alone. So very much alone.

"Joanna, let me in," her mother called, desperation in her voice. "Please, I want to talk to you. I

want to know you're all right. I love you. . . .'' Her
voice broke.

Joanna's heart grew harder. *I love you.* What a joke.
"Liar," she whispered.

"If you don't come out I'll break down this door,
Joanna. I swear I will."

Joanna slid off the bed. She didn't open the door
to her bedroom, but instead walked over to her
closet and pulled out a black dress. With her heart
pounding and her fingers shaking, it took her a few
clumsy minutes to change clothes, but she was finally ready.

When she opened the door her mother practically
fell into the room.

Caroline's eyes looked wild and panicked, like a
hunted animal that sensed there was no escape.
"Joanna, are you all right? Good grief—you're all
dressed up. Where are you going?"

"I'm going to a party," Joanna said coldly.

"A—a party?"

"That's right. You see, my parents—my real parents—are celebrating their fortieth wedding anniversary tonight. I think I should be there, don't
you?"

Caroline's face turned white. "My God, what are
you talking about?"

"Don't try to lie, Mother—I mean Caroline. It's
over. The game is over."

Her mother put a hand to her heart. "Joanna,
don't do this. I can't lose you."

"You never had me. I'm not your child. I'm not a
Wingate. I'm a De Marco. How could you?" she demanded. "All these years you lied to me."

"All right, we adopted you," Caroline confessed,
her words coming out in a rush. "It was never a
game. We raised you as if you were our own child.
We loved you every day of your life. We gave you
everything."

"Everything but the truth. Why not just tell me?"

"I was afraid. I didn't want to lose you," she repeated.

"How could you have lost me when I was five years old, when I was ten, when I was twelve? You had complete control over me. You must have kept the secret for another reason. What was it? Shame?"

"No, I was never ashamed of you. I was ashamed of me," Caroline cried. "I was ashamed that I couldn't have a child of my own when everyone else could. I wasn't a whole woman. I couldn't hold my head up straight. I couldn't talk to the other women about pregnancy and labor and getting up at three in the morning."

"Oh, please. Having a child isn't everything."

"It was then, Joanna. A woman was nothing without a child. As the years passed I felt more and more like a failure. I didn't want to get up in the morning. I didn't want to see anyone. Your father finally moved us to the city so he wouldn't have to keep explaining why I wouldn't entertain, why I didn't want to go to the Fourth of July block party and watch everyone else with their children."

She paused, her desperate eyes pleading with Joanna to understand. "Then we got you, and everything was right again. I had a baby. I was a mother. We were a family. I didn't want it to end. I never wanted to feel empty and alone again. Your father said no one would ever have to know. So no one did."

Caroline reached out a hand to her, but Joanna couldn't bear the touch. She was too confused, too upset. "How can I believe anything you say when I know that you lied about the most basic truth of all?" She turned and strode briskly toward the door.

"Don't go," Caroline begged, following her. "Stay and we'll talk. I'll tell you everything I know."

"It's too little, too late," Joanna said as she reached

the door. "I want to see my real mother and my real father. I want to ask them why they gave me up."

"Joanna, you can't burst into the middle of their party."

"Like hell, I can't."

Michael held hands with Rose and Lily as they walked into the banquet room. The heavy scent of perfume, the make-up, the glittering candles and flowers, and background music added up to a party atmosphere. He hadn't gone five feet before each of his girls was snatched up by a loving relative and kissed soundly on both cheeks.

Then it was his turn.

"Michael, you adorable man." Angela's aunt Carlotta cupped his face with her hands. "Why haven't I seen you lately?"

"I've been busy with work," he replied as she kissed him on the cheek.

"And those babies, those adorable babies, where are they?"

Michael looked around. Lily and Rose had quickly ditched him to play with their cousins. He smiled at the same time Aunt Carlotta muttered in disgust, "Why, they've wrapped old Milton up like a Christmas tree. Linda," Carlotta said. "Look what your children have done."

Linda sent her an apologetic look. "I'm sorry. Frank was supposed to be watching the kids. I'll tell them to take the streamers off Uncle Milton."

"Hmmph. I'll tell them myself."

"She hates me. She just hates me," Linda said. "No doubt she'll give Frank an earful before the night is over."

"No doubt," Michael agreed.

"I can't imagine how Uncle Milton sleeps through all the commotion," Linda said as they watched Carlotta chastise the children.

"Valium. He takes it like vitamins. He says it relaxes him."

"Any more relaxed and he'll be dead."

"We might all need Valium to get through this party. I thought dinner was for immediate family."

"Immediate in this family is just about everyone," Linda replied. "I just hope Sophia and Vincent actually show up."

"What are you talking about?" Michael asked in surprise.

"Vincent spent last night here at the restaurant. He and Sophia are fighting about something."

His uneasiness returned. "What are they fighting about?"

"I don't know, but Vincent wanted to take Sophia out of town for the weekend, and she wouldn't go. Tony thought it might have something to do with that woman."

"Joanna?" he asked.

"Yes. Do you know what's going on?"

"Not exactly, but I have a suspicion."

"Is it going to ruin my party, Michael?"

"It might ruin more than your party."

"Oh, dear. She's not coming here, is she?"

"I did mention it, but we agreed this wasn't the time or the place."

"Thank God. I've worked hard on this party, and I want it to be perfect. I want Frank to see that I can do something right."

"How could he have any doubts?"

"I don't know, but he does." She looked into his face with troubled eyes. "It's tough trying to fit into this family. Sophia and Vincent are saints. They're perfect." She twisted her wedding ring around on her finger. "Frank has held Sophia up to me every day of my life. I never quite compare. I always fall short."

"That's because you're you, and she's Sophia. Why do you have to be the same?"

"Because Frank wants what his father has," she said somewhat hopelessly. "I just don't know how I can spend the rest of my life trying to please someone who's never going to be pleased."

Her words disturbed Michael, but before he could say anything, the door behind them opened and Uncle Louis rushed in, waving his arms. "Quiet everyone. They just pulled into the parking lot."

Someone dimmed the lights. The chatter dropped to a whisper as everyone waited in anticipation.

22

"What are we doing here?" Sophia demanded as Charles stopped the car in the De Marco's parking lot. "I thought we were having dinner at Stars."

"Frank called while you were getting your coat." Elena turned in her seat. "He wanted Vincent to stop by for a second."

Sophia crossed her arms in irritation. "I'll wait here."

"No, let's go in. It might take a few minutes. We can have a drink at the bar."

"I don't feel like seeing everyone tonight," Sophia said. In fact, she didn't want to go to dinner at all. Vincent hadn't said a word since he'd come home that afternoon. He'd dressed in silence, his face permanently grooved in a deep scowl. She saw absolutely no reason to celebrate forty happy years when they were anything but happy.

Elena exchanged a look with her husband, then got out of the car. She opened Sophia's door as Vincent and Charles got out on the other side. "Come on," Elena said. "I know you're in a bad mood, but we're going to change that."

"Oh, leave her be," Vincent said. "If she wants to stay in the car, let her stay in the car."

"I'm not staying in the car," Sophia said, just to be contrary.

"Fine, then come in."

"I will."

Elena sighed. "Let's just get this over with, okay?"

They walked through the back door and into the kitchen. "Where's Frankie?" Vincent demanded of his nephew Rico.

"In the banquet room. We're having a problem with the party in there," Rico said.

Sophia turned toward the bar, but Elena grabbed her arm. "Let's see what the problem is."

"I don't care what the problem is."

"Well, I do."

"Why?"

Elena pulled her toward the hallway. "Because I'm curious."

"You're crazy."

As Vincent reached for the door handle, Sophia felt the sudden urge to run. It was too quiet, too dark. Her sister was acting strange and so was Charles, hanging back with smiles on their faces.

Vincent pushed open the door.

The flash of light blinded her.

The loud screams of "Surprise!" deafened her.

Sophia couldn't move.

Vincent looked into her eyes.

She stared back.

They both turned toward the crowd, to their friends and family, to the people who loved them, respected them, idolized them. She wanted to run away. She wanted to wake up and find out it was all a dream. But it wasn't a dream. It was a party for her and Vincent, celebrating their marriage, their vows, their promises, so many of which had been broken.

Vincent held out his hand to her. His gaze met hers in a silent plea. His honor meant more to him than anything. Without it, he would be nothing.

She took his hand and forced a smile. She could

get through this. She could pretend—because compared to everything that had come before, this pretense was easy. Everyone she loved was in this room. Tony, Frank, Linda, Michael, her sisters, cousins, grandchildren, nieces, and nephews. Everyone but one.

After a few minutes they found themselves at the front of the room. Frank asked for attention. He came over and kissed his mother on the cheek, then his father.

"Congratulations," he said. He took two glasses of champagne from the nearby waiter and handed one to each of them. "I'd like to propose a toast—to the two most wonderful parents on this earth, who inspire us daily with their love and selfless generosity."

Sophia swayed, his words cutting deeply through her deceit. How could she let her son go on talking about her and Vincent as if they were saints, when they had sinned more than anyone in the room?

Vincent held on to her arm as if he, too, felt shaky. For the first time in a long while, she felt as if they were supporting each other. Perhaps that was the only way they could get through this.

"To you." Frank raised his glass.

Sophia barely tasted the champagne. Then Tony stepped forward, his dark eyes dancing with amusement. "Congratulations Mama, Papa, you're the best."

They weren't the best. They were the worst.

Sophia took another sip as the crowd did likewise.

Then Michael stepped forward. Oh, God, it wasn't over yet. She wanted to crawl into a dark hole and hide until everyone went away.

Michael cleared his throat. "I know Angela would have had something witty to say about this big event, but since I don't have the De Marco gift for words, let me just say that the girls and I really appreciate this family, especially you and Vincent," he said to Sophia. "For shining the light so we could find our way out of the darkness."

Sophia felt tears gather in her eyes. "Say something," Louis shouted.

"Speech," someone insisted.

"Thank you—all of you," Vincent said. "This is wonderful. I'm speechless."

"Tell us how you did it," Marlena asked.

Sophia looked at her nineteen-year-old niece and saw only innocence in her eyes, an innocence she could not take away.

Marlena persisted. "Tell us how you lasted forty years together when I can't keep a boyfriend for six months."

The crowd laughed at Marlena's comment, and Sophia smiled weakly. How had they stayed together? Out of fear, selfishness, pride?

"It's takes love and forgiveness," Vincent said, contradicting her thoughts. "Remembering that family is everything."

Family. How often he used that word. How much he demanded of his family, and how little he gave in return. Sophia felt anger pushing past her fear. Family hadn't meant anything thirty years ago.

"Sophia, aren't you going to say anything?" Linda asked.

Sophia's throat tightened. She looked out at the crowd, at Linda and Frank, Tony and Michael, her sisters, all waiting expectantly for her words of wisdom and sage advice, for the lies that had always fallen so easily from her lips. She couldn't do it anymore. She couldn't speak one more untruth.

"I—I don't know what to say," she stuttered, wondering if she really had the courage to speak what was in her heart.

"Don't you?" a voice called from the doorway.

Sophia turned in surprise, as did the rest of the

family. Although some of the guests muttered Angela's name in haunted disbelief, Sophia knew this woman was not Angela. Her long, dark hair fell wildly down her back; her dark eyes burned with proud fire. She was a De Marco. And her name was Joanna.

"Don't you have something to say to me— *Mother*?"

The crowd gasped at her word.

Vincent's hand tightened around Sophia's. "No," he implored.

Joanna would not be stopped. She walked through the crowd like a queen. They parted for her, fascinated, captivated, horrified.

Joanna didn't look at anyone else, not at Michael or the girls. Her gaze remained fixed on Sophia.

Finally she stopped just a few feet away.

No one spoke for a long moment.

"I do have something to say," Sophia said finally, meeting her daughter's gaze. She could not let that challenge go unanswered.

"No, you don't." Vincent tried to pull her away, but Sophia stood straight and tall.

"You are my daughter," she said to Joanna. She heard more gasps of horror, murmurings of "It couldn't be true."

"Go on," Joanna said.

"Sophia, no," Vincent said again.

She ignored him. This time Joanna's needs had to come first. "Twenty-nine years ago I checked into the hospital under the name of another woman— Caroline Wingate. I gave birth to a little girl. After she was born I—I gave her away."

Joanna took in a deep breath, her eyes glittering with unshed tears. "Why? Why did you give me away?" she asked, agony running through her voice.

"Because I had to," Sophia murmured. "If I didn't

give you up, I would lose my husband and my boys."

"I don't understand. Why would you lose them?"

For the first time, Joanna looked at Vincent. Sophia followed her gaze. Vincent's profile was etched in stone, every muscle in his body tight from the tension, the disgrace, the dishonor. He wouldn't look at them. He wouldn't look at anyone.

Joanna turned to Sophia. "He didn't want me?"

"No. You see, I committed adultery—"

"It's a lie," Frank interrupted, his face ashen. "It's all a lie. I remember when you were pregnant, Mama. The baby died. You said the baby died." He looked from his mother to his father. "We said prayers for her every night before we went to bed—for my little sister who went to heaven. Don't you remember?"

Sophia's heart turned over in her chest. She hadn't wanted to hurt her son. "Your little sister didn't die. I just didn't bring her home with me."

"Why not?" Frank demanded. "Why the hell not?"

"Because Vincent wasn't her father," Sophia said, the words of truth finally breaking free of their thirty-year prison. "I had an affair with another man."

"No. No." Frank backed away, his eyes filled with horror at her confession. "I can't believe that. It's not true. Papa, tell me it's not true."

Vincent reached out a hand for his son, but Frank was too far away to be comforted.

"It's true," Vincent said. "Your mother—Sophia—broke her vows."

Frank slumped into a chair, breathing heavily, sweat beading along his forehead. Sophia looked over at Tony, whose hands shook as he raised the beer bottle to his lips—then on to Michael, who held hands with Lily and Rose, his eyes disappointed, shocked. And Linda, sweet Linda, looked like the only one who understood.

The others in the room seemed bewildered. Carlotta's right hand pressed against her heart as if she were in pain. Aunt Tess worked her rosary beads with agitated fingers. Even Uncle Milton had woken up for the unveiling of her scarlet letter.

Sophia couldn't blame them for judging her. She had done a terrible thing. And the person she had hurt the most now stood before her.

Joanna seemed frozen in time, her eyes still fixed on Sophia, anger and hurt tightening her face, until it was almost painful to look at her. Sophia wanted to pull her child into her arms and hold her close against her heart. She wanted to tell Joanna how much she loved her, how much she regretted what she had done.

But she couldn't move. She could only speak, three pitiful words that could never make up for what had happened. "I am sorry," she said to Joanna. "I'm so sorry."

Two bright spots of red blazed on Joanna's cheeks, then a single tear slid down her face, followed by another.

Michael took a step in her direction. "Joanna," he said.

She shook her head, warning him back.

He stopped, but Lily and Rose let go of his hands and ran to Joanna.

"Don't cry, Joanna," Rose said. "We love you." She threw her arms around Joanna's waist. Lily did the same.

Joanna took in a ragged breath. "I know you do." She hugged them both, then said, "Go back to Daddy."

Rose and Lily reluctantly returned to their father's side. Sophia waited breathlessly for Joanna's next words. Nothing came. Her daughter stood there, silently condemning her like everyone else in the room.

Sophia had to make her understand. "There wasn't a day that passed that I didn't think of you, that I didn't wonder if you were all right, if you were happy, if you were lonely, if you needed me."

"Stop!" Joanna shook her head against the affirmations of love. "How could you? How could you love me and give me away? And how could you let her?" she demanded of Vincent.

"You weren't my child," he said simply.

"But I was *her* child." Joanna looked over at Michael. "This is the wonderful family I've heard so much about?" she said scornfully. "Well, you're welcome to them. As far as I'm concerned, I'm not a De Marco. And I'm not a Wingate." The fight left her body, like a balloon losing air. "I'm not anybody."

Sophia's heart broke in two as Joanna ran from the room.

"Joanna, wait."

Michael followed her out of the restaurant. He caught up with her in the parking lot. She shrugged his hand off her arm. She didn't want to talk to him. She didn't want to hear any more lies or explanations or words of love that didn't mean anything.

"Let me go," she cried. "Just let me go."

"I can't let you go," he said fiercely. "I love you."

"Everyone says they love me now. But who loved me yesterday? Who will love me tomorrow? How can I trust any of you?"

"You can trust me. Goddammit, Joanna, I'm not part of this. I didn't betray you."

"You didn't want me to come here tonight. You didn't want me to confront your precious family."

"I didn't want anyone to get hurt."

She laughed bitterly. "Anyone as in Sophia and

Vincent? You wanted to protect them. You didn't care about protecting me."

"I thought we could deal with this another time. In fact, you were the one who said bursting in on their anniversary party was a bad idea. What changed your mind?"

"The music box. *Her* initials were on it. As soon as I saw them, I knew the truth."

"What did your mother say?"

Joanna's lips trembled. "She said I was adopted. Big surprise, huh?"

"Why didn't she tell you before?"

"She didn't want to lose me."

"Has she lost you?"

"What do you think?"

"I think you're angry—"

"Angry? Angry?" Her voice rose to a fevered pitch. "I'm way beyond angry. I'm . . ." She threw up her hands and looked up at the star-laden sky. "I'm so alone," she said hopelessly. "So all alone."

"I'm here, Joanna." He rested his hands on her shoulders. "We can be together. You and me and Lily and Rose. We can be a family."

"Don't you get it, Michael? If Sophia is my mother, then Angela was my sister. My sister," Joanna repeated. "How can I love my sister's husband?"

"Your sister is dead."

"I know. And I never knew her. Every time you spoke of her, I thought she was a terrible person, spoiled and selfish, and I was secretly glad that she was gone, because that meant I had a chance with you. But now, knowing that I had a sister who I will never have the chance to meet—it kills me, Michael. I can't be with you. I can't be near this family. It's over. Everything is over." She pulled the keys out of her purse.

"We can work this out."

"We can't."

"I'm not saying good-bye to you," he yelled, storming over to the car.

She shut the door and locked it, silencing his protests with the roar of the engine. She couldn't stay and listen to him. She couldn't pretend that everything would be all right. It would never be all right.

He loved her. Michael realized it as soon as her car disappeared from view. He loved her more deeply, more passionately, more honestly than he'd ever loved his wife. But it was too late. He'd lost her.

He felt a tug on his coat and looked down to see Rose and Lily, huddling together, their big brown eyes wide and worried.

"It's okay." He pulled them into his arms.

Rose began to cry. Lily clung to his arm, her face buried in his chest. He didn't know what to say to them, how to explain something so unexplainable. At least they now knew why Joanna looked so much like Angela.

Joanna was Angela's sister. *Her sister.* His stomach twisted into a knot. He had made love to Angela's sister.

"Michael. Is she gone?" Tony asked, joining them in the parking lot.

"Yeah."

"You okay?"

"I've had better days."

"No kidding. This turned out to be a hell of a surprise party." Tony offered the kids a weak smile. "Hey, midgets, Uncle Louis is making ice cream sundaes in the kitchen. What do you think?"

"We haven't had dinner yet," Rose said.

"Joanna says you should have dinner before dessert," Lily added. "She never lets us eat the cookies in our lunch before we eat our sandwich."

"I bet she wouldn't mind if you made an exception just this once," Tony replied.

"Is she coming back, Uncle Tony?" Lily asked.

"Or is she going away like Mama did?" Rose asked.

The questions twisted like a knife in Michael's gut. Tony turned to him for answers, but he had none to give. Joanna was angry and deeply hurt. He could only imagine what was going through her mind. She was a woman who believed in roots, in traditions, in family, but her roots had been yanked from the ground like errant weeds. He wasn't sure she could survive without them. He wasn't sure he could survive without her.

Lily and Rose waited, watching, wondering. He had to say something fatherly and reassuring. He couldn't lie. There had been far too many lies told in the name of love.

"Joanna needs time alone right now," he said finally. "You see, she didn't know that your mother was her sister. Something happened when she was born, and Joanna went to live with another family."

Lily and Rose turned back to their uncle. "But why didn't she live with you, Uncle Tony?" Lily asked.

"I don't know," Tony replied.

"I don't understand," Rose said. "Joanna's not Mama, is she?"

Even though Rose had directed her question at Tony, Michael answered. "No, she's not your mother. She's your aunt. Aunt Joanna."

Rose's face brightened at that thought. Lily smiled. "Aunt Joanna," they chorused, approving the relationship.

"It works for them," Tony said. "Somehow I don't think the rest of the family will accept it quite so easily. I have half a mind not to go back in there. This whole night has been a disaster."

"Sophia needs you," Michael said. "Frank has already judged her. Angela isn't here to stand up for her. You're the only one who can do that."

"I'm not sure I can. She had an affair and gave my sister away. She broke all the rules."

"And you can't understand that?" Michael challenged. "You—who was hell-bent on stealing Helen away from Joey two weeks before her wedding. You can't understand love and passion and recklessness?"

"I can't understand it in my mother."

"She's a woman, too. Let's go inside. Let's at least hear what Sophia has to say."

As they entered the kitchen they passed several departing family members. Everyone but the immediate family had decided to go home, to leave Sophia and Vincent and their children to work things out in private.

A few muttered words of condolence were offered to Tony. Others avoided their eyes. Michael left the girls in the kitchen with their uncle Louis and followed Tony down the hall to the banquet room.

The door was open. There were no sounds coming from within, only silence, terrible, awkward silence.

Michael stepped into the room and looked around. Half-filled glasses of champagne decorated the empty tables like lonely soldiers after a long battle. The balloons had begun to drift down from the ceiling, as if realizing the party had lost its spirit.

Frank stood next to his father in front of the makeshift bar. Each held a shot glass of whiskey in his hand. They weren't talking. They were staring at Sophia.

Sophia sat in a chair, flanked by Linda and Elena. She had aged in the past fifteen minutes. The lines around her eyes were deep and grooved. Sadness and defeat emanated from her weary posture.

Michael had never imagined that he would see the

De Marcos like this, torn apart within the ranks.

Frank raised the shot glass to his lips and drank the whiskey, setting the glass down heavily on the table when he was finished. His face was still tight with anger and betrayal, all of it directed at his mother.

"I can't believe you would betray your husband like that," he said.

Sophia took in a breath and let it out. "It was a difficult time for us. Vincent was working long hours—"

"I don't care how difficult it was," Frank interrupted. "You had no right to go out and have an affair. You were a married woman, with children. You took vows before God."

"Hey, ease up," Tony said.

"Ease up?" Frank echoed in angry bewilderment. "Our mother had an affair. She cheated on us with another man. She gave away our sister. How can you stand there and tell me to ease up?"

"I'd like to hear what Mama has to say," Tony replied.

"Frank is right," Sophia said. "I was wrong, Tony. I made a terrible mistake. I put my own needs ahead of my children's, and I have paid for it ever since. I will never forget the moment when that nurse took my baby out of my arms." Her voice caught. "I will never forget how hard it was to say good-bye to my child. My arms ached for hours. All I could think about was her. I wondered if she was hungry. My breasts were heavy with milk, but I couldn't feed my baby. I wondered if she was crying, but I couldn't soothe her even if she was. I couldn't hold her. I couldn't sing to her, the way I'd done when I was pregnant. She was gone. My baby was gone." Sophia took a deep breath. "I felt as if someone had just ripped off my arms."

Vincent turned his back on her, resting his elbows

on the bar, burying his head in his hands, as if he couldn't bear to look at her, to hear her words of pain and longing.

"That night in the hospital, I couldn't sleep," Sophia continued. "Every few minutes, I would wake up and touch my stomach, waiting for the familiar flutter of her tiny feet against my ribs. But there was no flutter. I would look for the bassinet, for the baby, but the room was empty. It was the longest night of my life—until now. Now that I've lost her again."

"Oh, God," Linda said, shaking her head, her eyes filling with tears. "I can't imagine what you must have gone through. To carry a baby and then give her away. How empty you must have felt."

"Maybe she deserved to feel empty, to hurt," Frank said viciously. "God was punishing you."

"God didn't punish me!" Sophia retorted, her pain turning to anger. "Your father did that for him. He was the one who forced me to give Joanna away. He was the one who insisted everything be kept secret—for family, for honor. He made me promise to keep silent, to never speak a word of my baby, to never contact her, to never see her again. I was wrong, yes. He was wrong, too. He didn't just punish me. He punished an innocent baby."

Vincent swung around, his face lit with fury. "No more!" he shouted.

"You can't stop me from talking," Sophia said. "I made a mistake, but I'll be damned if I'll take all the blame."

Vincent closed his eyes and swayed slightly. Frank put a hand on his arm.

"Papa, are you all right?" Frank asked.

"No."

"Do you want to sit down?"

"No." Vincent opened his eyes and stared at Sophia. "I can't take anymore. I can't." He walked out of the room. After a moment Frank followed.

"Go after Frank," Sophia said to Linda. "He needs you."

"I don't think he wants me." Linda hesitated. "I tried all this time to be like you, never realizing how close I was coming to being you. Frank is driving me away, just like Vincent did to you. Isn't that what happened?"

"Don't make my mistakes, Linda. You and Frank are not Vincent and me. You are not destined to end up as we have."

"I hope not." Linda left the room.

Sophia's attention turned to Tony, to Michael. "Is there anything either of you want to ask me?"

Tony stared into his beer bottle. Then he lifted his head. "Why did you do it?"

"The affair or the adoption?"

"The affair."

"I was lonely. Vincent left for the restaurant at six o'clock in the morning and came home at eleven o'clock at night. We barely spoke, let alone made love. I had two small children and had gained an extra thirty pounds. I know you won't understand, but I felt ugly and unloved. When I met this man, he talked to me. He paid me compliments. I started to feel pretty again. I acted impulsively and stupidly. I never expected to get pregnant. When it happened, when your father found out, he gave me an ultimatum. The baby or the rest of my family."

"Did Angie know?" Tony asked as he stared intently at his beer bottle.

"No one knew, except your father and Elena." She glanced up at her sister, who replied by squeezing her shoulder. "Elena stayed with me that night in the hospital. She held my hand through the long hours of labor and cried with me when Joanna was born. Vincent stayed home with you and Frank."

"I don't remember anything about it."

"You were only three years old. Frank was seven.

He knew I was pregnant. He used to sit with me and put his hand on my stomach. That's why we had to tell him the baby died. That's what we told everyone."

"I don't remember anyone mentioning it."

"Because they didn't want to remind me of the pain. When I had Angela it was all but forgotten."

"And what was Angela? Some kind of consolation prize?"

"Don't ever say that," Sophia said sharply. "I loved Angela. She was my daughter. She didn't replace the one I lost. I never expected her to."

"That's the way you treated her," Tony said. "You and Papa spoiled her rotten. You acted as if she were a gift from God."

"I thought she was. Until God took her back. Sometimes I think that was my ultimate punishment. He allowed me to love another child, then snatched her away to remind me of the horrible thing I had done."

"Yeah, well, too bad he didn't take me. It would have made everyone a hell of a lot less unhappy," Tony said.

"Tony." Michael turned instinctively to his friend, but there was nothing he could say to ease the pain in Tony's heart.

"You had me in your life," Tony said. "Maybe Vincent was ignoring you. I can believe that. But what about me? I was a baby, but I wasn't enough to keep you happy? Why the hell did I ever come home?" Tony set his beer bottle on the table so forcefully that it rolled off and shattered on the floor. The door slammed behind his retreating back.

"I'll go," Elena said.

The door closed behind her, and there was no one left but Michael and Sophia.

"I guess it's your turn now," Sophia said wearily.

"You don't have to apologize to me, Sophia. I'm

not your kid. You never gave me anything but love. Whatever happened between you and Vincent is none of my business."

Her dark eyes met his. "I am sorry, Michael. I didn't realize you were falling in love with Joanna until tonight."

Michael stiffened at the perception in her eyes. "It's over now. Joanna could never be with me, not after this."

"Are you sure?"

"She just said good-bye."

"She's hurt."

"Deeply," he agreed. "I can't blame her."

"No, I can't either."

Michael looked into Sophia's eyes. "Who was he? Who was this man who made you risk everything for a night in his arms?"

"He was very special, kind, attentive. He made me feel loved. We didn't have a long-term affair. It was only one night. Afterward we both knew that it could never happen again."

"What was his name?"

She hesitated. "I can't say."

And Michael knew why she couldn't say. He wondered if anyone else had figured it out.

23

Joanna drove through the streets of San Francisco without any thought of where to go. She stopped at the red lights automatically, then let the car move with the flow of traffic. She drove past her mother's apartment building and her old elementary school, past the building where her father had worked, all the old haunts, all the old memories. There were many.

She turned on the radio so she wouldn't have to think.

The songs of love only made her want to cry, and she was tired of crying.

Finally she grew so weary that she knew she had to stop, but she had nowhere to go. She couldn't go home. She couldn't go to Michael's house. She couldn't even go to Nora's, because her friend had gone away for the weekend.

She drove across town to Seacliff and pulled up in front of the dark, neglected house, standing so proud and lonely against the midnight sky. Ruby Mae had hidden herself away in this house after she'd lost her lover and her child.

Her child. The words cut through Joanna's heart, and she suddenly knew where she could find some answers—in history, in the past, where she always ran to make sense of the present and the future.

She let herself into the house and raced up the stairs to the attic, where she had sorted out Ruby Mae's journals. She knew which one she wanted— the one she had begun to read but stopped when it became too painful to go on, too close to her own situation. Now she knew she had to finish it.

Slowly she opened the book.

Today, I said good-bye to my little girl. It was the most difficult thing I have ever had to do. I know she will have a better life without me. What can I give her? I am a whore, a woman without conscience. I would probably end up in hell but for this one act of goodness.

I pray someday she will forgive me, that she will understand the depth of my love for her. Perhaps she will read these words and know how much I loved her. Or perhaps she will read these words and still feel anger at what I did. God gave her to me, and I gave her away. But I gave her to a good family, one without sin, without shame. They will love her. They will give her everything—except me. I hope it will be enough.

Ruby Mae's daughter, Elsa, had never read her words, never wanted to know her mother. She had turned her back on Ruby Mae, dismissing her as someone of no importance, even though Ruby Mae had given Elsa life. Just as Sophia had given Joanna life.

Joanna understood Elsa better now. She felt much the same way, anger and bitterness making her want to turn away from her birth mother. But unlike Elsa she also wanted to turn away from her adoptive mother, because there had been lies on both sides.

With a sigh Joanna closed the journal and stacked it with the others. They were part of history now.

Unfortunately her life wasn't history. She still had to live, to deal with two mothers, both shouting their love yet hiding behind their deceit. Two women, who thirty years ago had made a choice that changed her life forever.

Sophia said she loved her. Yet she had chosen to give her up. It wasn't as if Sophia was a whore or a woman who didn't have the means to raise a child. She had given up Joanna to save her family's reputation, sacrificing Joanna to protect Frank and Tony and Vincent.

Then there was Caroline, living a pretense, lying over and over again to protect her reputation. Caroline considered her inability to have children a personal failure, but rather than admit her shortcomings, she created her own fantasy family, never once considering the fact that Joanna might want to know something about her real parents.

Joanna remembered her trips to various doctors over the years, when she had confidently filled in the family history given to her by Caroline. Now she knew none of it was true. What if there was a history of diabetes or heart disease or anything else in her biological family? Wouldn't it have been important for her to know that? Not to Caroline—protecting the secret was more important than anything else.

Joanna wondered what it would have felt like to grow up knowing she was adopted. Would she now feel so torn, so unsettled, so lost in her own identity? Would she have wondered what it would have been like to grow up with brothers and sisters? Or would she have been grateful to Caroline and Edward Wingate for their overwhelming abundance of love?

But what was love without trust, without truth? They hadn't been protecting her. They'd been protecting themselves.

Her father had carried the secret to his grave. She thought back to the last few days of his life, to the fear in his eyes. Fear of death, she had thought at the time, but now she wondered if he hadn't also been afraid of the truth. A few times he had opened his mouth to speak, then changed his mind.

If he had spoken, would she have run from him? Would she have walked away in his hour of need? She hoped not, but it would have shattered their relationship. Everything would have changed. He would have died knowing of her pain instead of believing in her innocence.

Maybe it was better that it had come out now.

Still, she had her mother to deal with, and the De Marcos, not just Sophia but the rest of them. She thought about Angela—her little sister.

Angela had had what Joanna should have had, the big, loving, passionate Italian family, the gardens and the home-cooked meals, the affectionate touches, brothers and cousins, aunts and uncles—Michael.

Joanna looked at the couch where she and Michael had made love. Tears filled her eyes again. She wiped them away. Turning off the light, she went downstairs. The backyard called to her. The scents of jasmine and gardenias reminded her again of Michael, of the love she'd found and lost. How could life be so cruel?

She walked to the edge of the cliff, staring down at the waves breaking on the beach. Had Ruby Mae ever considered throwing herself off this cliff, finding peace in the swirling water below, in the depths of an ocean that would keep all of her secrets?

Joanna wouldn't kill herself. There was nothing to kill. She felt invisible. She had no history, no past, no identity. She didn't know who she was supposed to be any more—a passionate Italian or a stoic German.

She was a bastard, born out of wedlock. A love child or a lust child. For the first time it occurred to her that she didn't know who her father was. It wasn't Edward or Vincent. It was some other faceless man, someone who had no qualms about sleeping with a married woman—a woman with children and a husband.

She didn't want to know who he was. She hated him already. She hated them all, not only for taking away her birthright, but for taking away Michael. To all intents and purposes, he was a De Marco. The girls were De Marcos. She had no place in their lives.

Caroline parked her car in front of the De Marco house and took a deep breath. She hadn't felt this panicked since Edward had placed a baby in her arms almost thirty years ago. She closed her eyes and remembered.

"Our child," Edward said with a big, broad smile.

"I don't understand. We just filled out the adoption papers." Caroline stared down at the tiny baby, barely bigger than her hands. The baby's face was red, her eyes tightly closed, her tiny hands in fists as if she wasn't sure about this life she had been thrust into.

"We got lucky," Edward said. "She's ours, Caroline. Forever."

"But . . ." Caroline felt suddenly terrified. Finally she had her baby—the child she had dreamed of for years. But what if the other mother came back? What if she changed her mind? What if Caroline started to love this child and she was taken away? She had heard of just such things happening. "Are you sure?" she asked again. "Are you sure she's really ours forever?"

"Yes."

"Her mother?"

His smile faded. "Her mother can't take care of her. She wants us to have her."

"She's beautiful," Caroline said, her heart filling with tenderness and love. "The most perfect baby I've ever seen."

"Yes. Beautiful."

"Do we have to sign something?"

"I've taken care of everything, Caroline. All you have to do is love her."

"I already do." She looked into his face. "As I love you." She paused. "I know things have been—"

He shook his head. "Don't say anything, Caroline. Let's just think of our future together—with our child."

"I can't believe she's mine." Her arms tightened around her baby. "I don't think I'll ever be able to let her out of my sight."

"You won't have to."

"What will we say if she asks about her real parents?"

"She won't ask," Edward said. "As far as she will know, we are her real parents."

Caroline nodded. It was the way she wanted it, too. They didn't know anyone in the city. In a few months she would write her old friends and tell them she'd had a baby. No one would ever know differently.

She started as the baby began to cry. She lifted the baby to her chest and patted her on the back. The baby continued to cry, so she stood up and walked around the room, but it didn't help. Her fear returned. What if this baby didn't like her? What if she wanted her real mother? "I can't do this," she said, panicked.

Edward smiled reassuringly. "Just love her, Caroline."

"She won't stop crying."

"Maybe this will help." He pulled a music box out of the shopping bag he held in his hand. He set it on the table and lifted the lid. A lovely melody began to play. Caroline swayed to the music. After a moment the baby's cries softened and she fell asleep.

"Where did you get that?" Caroline asked. *"It's magic."*

"Yes, it's magic," he said softly. *"And love."* He put his arms around her and the baby. *"From now on we will have nothing but love in our lives."*

And she knew she would love him forever for giving her this baby.

They had named her Joanna. They had loved her together for thirty years. Now her real mother wanted her back, just as Caroline had feared.

Caroline got out of the car and walked up the steps to the house. She rang the bell and waited. Finally she heard footsteps. Her body tensed as she thought of what she would say.

Only one sentence rang through her mind: *I want my daughter back.*

The door opened. A woman stood in front of her. She had dark pepper gray hair. Her face was streaked with tears, her eyes red and swollen, but she looked like Joanna. She was the nameless, faceless woman of all those years ago—the woman Edward swore would never bother them again.

"Sophia De Marco?" Caroline asked.

The woman nodded.

"I'm—"

"I know who you are."

"Is Joanna here?

"No one's here. No one but me. And now you." Sophia stepped back. "You might as well come in."

Caroline took a deep breath and entered the house. She immediately hated the fact that it was warm and cozy, lovingly decorated. It even smelled of freshly baked cookies. She could still remember Joanna coming home from school one day and asking why there were never cookies cooling on the counter, like the other kids had. Of course, Caroline had then made it a point to bake cookies or at least buy the kind from the store that you could slice and bake. She had always wanted to be the best mother in the world. In fact, that's all she had ever wanted.

Sophia sat down on the sofa in the living room. Caroline took a chair across the room. There were family photographs everywhere, on the small end tables, on the mantel over the fireplace. This woman had a husband and other children. She didn't deserve Joanna, too. Especially since she'd given her up.

Caroline wondered why for the very first time. She had never allowed herself to speculate, never wanted to delve past the surface, afraid of what she would find. She still wasn't sure she wanted to know; she just wanted Joanna back.

"Did you see Joanna tonight?" Caroline asked.

"Yes. She knows the truth." Sophia met her eyes. "She knows I'm her mother."

Her mother. Caroline felt as if she'd been kicked in the gut. Then her temper flared. This woman was not Joanna's mother. She didn't care how many hours of labor Sophia had gone through. She'd missed the next twenty-nine years. She had no claim on Joanna, none.

"*I* am her mother," Caroline said. "Don't you ever use that word again."

Sophia didn't even flinch. She was tough, this woman. "*I* am her mother, too."

"You gave her away."

"I had my reasons."

"And what were those reasons exactly?" Caroline held her breath. Oh, God, she'd actually asked. She hadn't meant to ask.

"Didn't your husband tell you?" Sophia's eyes narrowed thoughtfully. "All these years, and he never said?"

Caroline tensed. "He told me that Joanna's parents couldn't take care of her."

"You didn't ask why?"

"I didn't care why. I wanted a baby, and I got one."

"It was that simple."

"No, it wasn't simple at all. I'm the one who took care of Joanna. I'm the one who got up in the middle of the night with her. I wiped away her tears when she was sad. I held her when she was sick. I taught her algebra. I sat in the car while she learned how to drive, for God's sake. I am her mother."

Sophia's eyes blazed. "You didn't carry her in your womb. You didn't labor with her. You didn't give her life."

"Just because you gave her life doesn't give you any claim to her now. How dare you come back and mess up Joanna's life. You had your chance to be a mother, and you walked away. Now you have second thoughts. Well, to hell with you." Caroline stood up. "I want my daughter. Where is she?"

"I don't know. And just for the record, I didn't go to her. She came to me. She wanted to know the truth, and I gave it to her."

"Your version of it, I'm sure."

"You had plenty of time to tell her whatever you wanted. It's not my fault that you didn't."

"You must know where she is. She didn't come home. She must be here—or with that man. Where does he live? What's his address?"

"She's not with Michael either. I think she's alone. All alone." Sophia stared down at the floor. "You should have seen her face. She looked as if someone had driven a stake through her heart. I never wanted to cause her so much pain. Believe me, I never wanted that."

"I hate you," Caroline said, feeling an intense, overwhelming sense of anger and pain. "I hate you for taking her away from me."

Sophia's head came up proudly. "I hate you, too.

For having her all these years. For loving her when I couldn't."

"I'm her mother," Caroline cried.

"So am I."

"You can't have her."

"Maybe neither of us can."

"That's not true." But as Caroline ran from the house, she had a terrible feeling that it *was* true.

Michael turned on the light in the twins' bedroom and watched with a heavy heart as Rose and Lily unbuttoned their party dresses. When Rose's battle to undo the buttons turned into an angry, tearful struggle, Michael knelt down and covered her shaky little hands with his. Then he finished the job.

"It will be okay," he said, although he wondered how many times he would have to say it before either of them believed him. "You'll see Joanna again." At least he hoped they would.

He helped Rose pull the dress over her head. He hung it up in the closet as she pulled her nightgown out of the drawer and put it on. Lily had already changed without any help from him. She was always the independent one, too proud to ask for anything, even at the tender age of six.

"Okay, let's get your teeth brushed." He tried to sound cheerful and upbeat. It didn't ring true. The house was so quiet, lonely, empty. It reminded him of when Angela died, that first night he and the girls had spent alone. He never thought he'd be reliving it.

As Lily and Rose went into the bathroom, Michael sat down on Rose's bed and picked up Peter Panda Bear. He remembered the first day Joanna had come to the house, the first time she'd seen Angela's picture, the first moment he'd felt an undeniable attraction to her.

Joanna. Angela's sister—but two sisters so different, maybe not in looks, but in ideas, emotions, manners. Maybe they would have been more similar if they had been raised in the same family. Or maybe they would have been exactly as they were. Genetics or environment—he wondered which played the stronger role. Not that it mattered.

Angela was gone. And Joanna—he hoped to God she wasn't gone, too.

He realized then that he could turn his back on the De Marcos. He could walk away from the only family he'd ever known if he could have Joanna and his children. They were all he needed. The fantasy big family of his youth no longer meant anything. He certainly wouldn't marry another woman just to get it, the way he'd married Angela. Not that it was her fault. She'd married him to get out of the family. He'd married her to get in. Suddenly it was all so painfully clear.

Michael stood up as the girls returned to the room. Rose's pigtails were falling out of their rubber bands, so he gently pulled them out of her hair, careful not to tangle the strands with his clumsy fingers. He remembered the first time he'd tried to do her hair, her cries of pain, her silent, proud winces. Now he could do it without hurting her. At least he'd accomplished something in the past year. He tossed the rubber bands on the nightstand. "Let's get into bed."

He held the covers for Rose as she slipped into bed. He placed Peter Panda Bear carefully within her arms and pulled the covers up to her chin. He kissed her on the forehead, then kissed Peter Panda Bear, as he did every night. "Sleep tight," he whispered. She didn't smile tonight. She looked sad, the way she'd looked a year ago, when her mother hadn't come home to tuck her in.

Michael turned away from her sad eyes and walked over to Lily's bed. She lay on her back, staring up at the ceiling as if somehow she would find the answer there. But there were no answers on the ceiling. He'd tried that trick himself.

He tucked the covers around her body and kissed her cheek. "Good night, honey. Sleep well."

He paused at the door. "I'll be here for you, girls. I'll always love you. I promise."

They didn't reply. They wanted their mother. They wanted Joanna. All they had was him.

He turned out the light and walked into the hall. He paused, deliberately leaving the door open. He wanted to know what they were thinking. In fact, he was desperate to know.

"I want Mama," Lily said.

His heart stopped at the anguish in her voice.

"I want Joanna," Rose said.

It was just as he thought. He couldn't bear to hear anymore. So he left. He went down the hall to his bedroom, and as he lay down on the soft bed, he wished he was on the hard ground, under the stars, holding the woman he loved in his arms.

"Joanna isn't coming back," Lily told her sister.

"Maybe she's with Mama now. Maybe she went to find her."

Lily suddenly sat up in bed. "Maybe we should go find her, too."

"We don't know where she is."

"I bet she went to visit that man with the boat."

"I don't like him. He's scary," Rose said. "He grabbed Mama and made her kiss him, remember? I don't want to see him."

"We have to do something."

"We could ask Mariah." Rose knew she had to stop her sister before she did something crazy.

"Okay." Lily picked up the wizard and brought it over to Rose's bed. She set it down between them and rubbed her hand across the top of the crystal ball. The light flashed.

Rose felt a spark of hope. Maybe Mariah could help. She was the one who had found Joanna in the first place.

Lily focused her eyes on the wizard. "We need your help, Mariah. Joanna ran away and we have to find her. Do you know where she is?"

Rose held her breath as it seemed to take forever for the wizard to speak.

"When you're lonely as can be, you'll find your comfort at the sea."

"The ocean," Lily proclaimed. "Joanna is with Mama and that man with the boat."

"How can we find her, Mariah?" Rose asked. "We don't know where the boat is."

"When your friend is no longer sad and blue, she'll come looking just for you," Mariah said.

"Huh?" Lily asked as Mariah went dark. She picked up the wizard and shook her, but the light wouldn't come back on.

"Maybe Mariah is broken," Rose said.

"Yeah, maybe she's just a stupid toy after all."

"Joanna won't look for us. We're not even missing."

Lily's eyes lit up. "We could be."

"What do you mean?" Rose asked nervously.

"We could go find Mama, and maybe Joanna would look for us, like she did when we lost Peter Panda Bear."

"We're not allowed to cross the street by ourselves."

"We'll be careful. We'll look both ways before we cross, just like Daddy says."

Rose sent her sister a doubtful look. "Daddy will be mad."

"I don't care. He made Mama go away, and now he's made Joanna leave, too." Lily crossed her arms in front of her chest.

"Do you think it was his fault?"

"It has to be."

Rose looked out the window. "It's awfully dark. Do we have to go now?"

"No, we'll go in the morning, before Daddy wakes up. The ocean is only a couple of blocks away. We should have gone a long time ago."

"There was that park, remember?" Rose said. "We played on the swings while Mommy and that man talked."

"I remember. I think we can find it again," Lily said. "We have to try."

Lily was right. "Okay." Rose lay back in her bed and closed her eyes. She could see Joanna's smiling face. Everything would be all right in the morning. As soon as they found Joanna.

24

Tony woke up late on Sunday morning. He'd tried to drink himself into oblivion, but whiskey had only dulled the pain, not taken it away. Now he had a headache to match his heartache. He crawled out of bed and stumbled up the companionway, blinking against the blinding sunlight.

It was too bright. He preferred the shadowy darkness of evening, when mistakes were easier to hide. He blinked again as he realized someone was sitting on deck. It was his brother, Frank, dressed in jeans and a sweatshirt, not looking at all like a successful restaurateur, but more like a brother.

"You sure do sleep late," Frank said as Tony sat down on the bench across from him.

"How long have you been here?"

"A couple of hours." He waved his hand toward an empty bottle of Jack Daniel's. "Judging by that, I figured you were out for the count."

"Yeah, well, I was celebrating our parents' fortieth wedding anniversary. What a joke that turned out to be."

Frank didn't smile. "I almost wish I could sail away. You don't need an extra hand, do you?"

Tony raised an eyebrow. "You? Run away? That doesn't sound like my big brother. What about the restaurant? Your wife? Your kids?"

"What about them? The restaurant has always been Papa's. We both know that. Linda and I aren't getting along, and I barely know my own kids. Of course, it appears that I don't know my parents either. Our family was a lie."

Tony stared out at the water, the sailboats, the seagulls diving into the water, searching for breakfast. He understood how Frank felt. The family he'd loved, the parents he'd believed in, had let him down. His father's talk of loyalty to family now seemed like bullshit. How could a man force his wife to give away her child, even if the child wasn't his? He didn't understand how Vincent could have let Sophia go through such a terrible experience. She was a born mother; she lived for her children. Yet Vincent, who proclaimed to love her, had literally ripped the baby out of her arms and turned her over to another. It hadn't made sense last night, and it didn't make sense now.

"I still can't believe Mama had an affair," Frank said.

"I have a hard time believing she even had sex," Tony said, "much less that she was getting it from someone other than her husband. She always seemed so saintly, above all that. I wonder who it was. I wonder if it was someone Papa knew. No, he probably would have killed the guy, and I don't remember anyone dying unexpectedly."

Frank shrugged. "As far as I'm concerned anything could have happened. I'm sure Papa was furious when he found out Mama was having an affair, especially since she ended up pregnant. I don't know why he didn't leave her."

"He probably didn't want to break up the family. 'De Marcos don't divorce,'" Tony quoted one of his father's favorite sayings. "They just give away inconvenient, illegitimate children." Tony paused. "You don't blame Papa, do you? It's all Mama's fault. I don't buy that crap. She had to have been pretty unhappy to have an affair. I think Papa is just as responsible for what happened. Maybe even more, because he didn't just hurt Sophia, he hurt Joanna."

"She seems to have had a good enough life," Frank said.

"How do you know that?"

He shrugged. "She looked all right."

"Jesus, Frank. How would you feel if you suddenly found out you were adopted?"

"I feel that way now. Nothing is what I thought. And Linda—she seems almost relieved to know that Sophia had an affair. I don't understand her either."

"Maybe Linda thinks she has a better chance of getting put on a pedestal now that Mama has fallen off hers. I know you don't want my advice, but you're going to get it anyway. Linda needs some attention. I think you'd better start worrying less about Mama and Papa and more about your own family."

Normally Frank would have snapped back at him, cut him down with harsh words. This morning he didn't say anything; he just stared at the water. "When are you leaving?" he asked finally.

"Tomorrow." Tony looked toward the Golden Gate Bridge in the distance—the gateway to freedom, a new life.

"When will you be back?"

"I don't know. I guess when I find what I'm looking for."

"And what is that?"

"Hell if I know," he said with a grin.

Frank smiled. "You're a little shit, you know that?"

"What does that make you, a big shit?"

"Probably."

"Are you going to stay and work in the restaurant, do what you've been doing?"

"I think so. I don't really know how to do anything else. Or maybe . . ."

"Maybe what?"

"I'd like to have my own place. I never considered it a possibility, because Papa set such store by De Marco's, carrying on the family name, the traditions. But our family is falling apart. Angie's gone. You'll be gone by tomorrow. Mama and Papa—I don't see how they can stay together."

"You're forgetting someone."

"Michael? He's not really family."

"Joanna. Our half sister."

Frank shook his head. "I don't think I can see her."

"It's not her fault. She didn't break up the family. Mama and Papa did that on their own."

"She was the end result, and she looks so much like Angie."

"Yeah. Angie's probably shaking her head in amazement right now, wherever she is. God, I miss her."

"I miss her, too. I miss everything—the way it used to be. I want to turn back the clock and start over. But I can't."

"None of us can. Even though Mama and Papa apparently thought they could. They kept this secret a long time. It might not have ever come out if Michael hadn't taken the girls to that school, hadn't stumbled across Joanna the way he did. We'd still be oblivious."

"I think I would have preferred that. If Mama and Papa aren't who I thought, then who am I—who are you?"

"You are the father of four great kids—and you have a terrific wife."

"I do, don't I?"

"Don't make the same mistakes Papa did. Don't put your pride before your family. Go home, Frank."

Frank stood up. "You're right."

"I am?"

Frank laughed. "Seems to be a week for firsts. If I don't see you before you go . . ." He shrugged his shoulders somewhat awkwardly. "Have a good trip. And come back someday, okay? I know you don't understand me, and I don't understand you, but we're brothers. I—I love you." Frank grabbed Tony by the shoulders and kissed him on both cheeks, then walked away.

Tony needed another shot of whiskey after that good-bye. Somehow, after last night's disastrous party, he'd been elevated from obnoxious pest to beloved brother. He searched out the bottle of whiskey and found a few drops left in the bottom. He raised it to the sky. "I hope you're in peace, Angie, because the rest of us sure as hell aren't."

Sophia knew she would find her husband at De Marco's. He considered the restaurant more home than home, the customers more family than family. He wouldn't want to see her, but she needed to see him. The restaurant didn't open until five on Sundays; it was only ten. She doubted anyone else would be in yet.

When she entered the restaurant she saw Vincent sitting at one of the booths, a cup of black coffee in front of him, the newspaper unopened. It was their booth, the table where they had sat for their first date when Vincent's father had owned the restaurant, when she had dreamed of a future with the handsome young Italian, who in turn had dreamed of running his own restaurant, making it the most successful in San Francisco. Vincent had done that, but they had all paid a price for his ambition.

She walked over to the table and sat down, not waiting to be invited. They had been together too long to stand on ceremony, especially now.

Thirty years ago she had thought the trouble was behind her, finished. But this day had loomed inevitably. Seeing her daughter again had always been her favorite dream, but she had known she couldn't have Joanna without revisiting the past, without reliving the pleasure and the pain. They always came together, as did roses and thorns, love and hate.

"Forty years," Vincent said heavily. He raised his coffee cup. "Happy anniversary."

"Do you want me to leave?" she asked steadily.

He looked into her eyes, not giving anything away. "Do you want to leave?"

"I don't know." And she didn't know. She had lived with this man, loved him, cherished him, cheated on him, hated him; she had experienced every emotion with Vincent. They had shared a lifetime together—for better or worse, in sickness and in health, until death do us part. Did the vows matter anymore? Did anything matter?

"We've been through so much, Sophia." His words echoed her thoughts. "Last year we buried a daughter together. We have other children to consider, grandchildren." Vincent circled his finger around the top of his cup. "I shouldn't have made you give her up. I knew it hurt you. At the time I wanted to hurt you."

"I know you did. I saw it in every look, heard it in every word."

"I didn't mean to hurt *her*," Vincent said gruffly. "I never thought of her as anything but a nameless, faceless baby. Until I saw her last night and realized she was you. I gave away a part of you." He closed his eyes for a moment, then reopened them. "I didn't think of her that way then. Whenever I saw your rounded stomach, I thought of him kissing you, loving you. Sometimes I wished you hadn't told me about the affair."

"I had to. We hadn't made love in two months.

The baby couldn't have been yours." Sophia took a deep breath. "I was lonely, Vincent. You were busy with the restaurant. When I'd visit you at night, it always seemed you were in the middle of a party, telling stories, drinking wine, laughing. And you'd flirt with the women who sat at the bar, who came alone to dine."

"It didn't mean anything."

"It meant something to me. I was home alone every night with the children. I yearned for conversation with another adult. I wanted passion and friendship and love."

"And you found all that with him?" Vincent asked, playing with the rubber band on the newspaper.

"No. What I found with him was another lonely soul. We met at the bookstore. We both reached for the same book at the same time. It was a book of poetry. I'd never met a man who liked poetry. We talked about the book, and when he asked me to have a cup of coffee at the restaurant next door, I said yes. The next thing I knew we were making plans to meet again, then one night we made love. We knew it was wrong. But that one night, that one foolish night, changed everyone's life. I know I said it before, Vincent, but I am sorry it ever happened, so very sorry." She took a deep breath, battling with her emotions. One act of love had betrayed years of commitment. She wished she could take it back, but she couldn't.

Vincent's dark gaze settled on her face. "I need to know something—did you ever see him again?"

"No, never, not even a glimpse."

"Do you love me at all, Sophia?" His voice thickened with uncertainty.

"I'm still married to you."

"That isn't what I asked you." He covered her hand with his. "Do you love me?"

Her eyes watered. Did she love this man who had brought out the best and the worst in her? Who had paid back her sin with one of his own? Who had been a good father to three children, but a terrible father to one? Could she give him a yes or a no? Was it that simple? Maybe it was. Maybe sixty years of living had made it just that simple. "Yes. I love you."

The tension in his face eased as he nodded his head. "Good. Very good."

"Do you love me?"

"Yes."

"In spite of everything?"

"Maybe because of everything." He paused, studying her with his dark eyes. "It is not the infatuation of our youth or the love that we knew as young adults. It is a love that comes from living together, supporting each other, sharing grief, sharing joy. I wouldn't know what to do without you."

She nodded, understanding him completely for perhaps the first time in their long marriage. "I think the rest of the family expects us to go our separate ways."

"I am the head of this family. I still make the decisions."

She smiled at the arrogance returning to his tone. He would be all right. They would be all right. Somehow Frank and Tony would be all right. It was Joanna she worried about.

"There is one thing," Sophia said.

Vincent raised his hand to stop her. "You don't have to say it."

"Can you accept Joanna?"

"As my daughter—no." He paused. "As your daughter—I can try."

It was enough—a beginning. The rest was up to Joanna.

*   *   *

The front door to the restaurant burst open, and Michael ran in. His hair was a mess. His T-shirt hung loosely over his jeans. Panic raced through his eyes as he glanced around the room. "Are they here? Please, God, tell me they're here."

"Who?" Sophia asked.

"Lily and Rose." Michael ran a hand through his hair. "They've run away. They're looking for their mother and Joanna, and God only knows where they've gone."

"Are you sure they're not just hiding in the house?" Sophia asked.

"I looked everywhere, in every closet, every drawer, under every bed. They're gone. I heard them talking last night about how much they missed their mother and Joanna. I don't know if they still think Joanna's their mother, or if they think Joanna and Angela are together somewhere. I have to find them."

"Calm down; we'll find them," Vincent said as he stood up. "I'll call Frank and Linda."

"And Louis and Rico," Sophia added. "And send someone over to get Tony." She put a hand on Michael's arm. "It will be all right, Michael; we'll find them. They can't have gone far."

He wanted to believe her. He had looked to Sophia for comfort and wisdom many times before. She'd always come through for him. But this—this was bigger than Sophia. She couldn't promise the girls would be all right. No one could.

"It's Angie all over again," he said abruptly. "I went home and found her gone. I waited for her to come back, but she never did. She disappeared. I never said good-bye. I never said I'm sorry. And God, I was sorry, you know. I didn't want her to die."

"I know you didn't. It wasn't your fault."

It was his fault. He had argued with Angela. He

had told her he was unhappy, that their marriage was a farce, that if she didn't start behaving like a wife instead of a child, they couldn't stay together.

Just as the twins suspected, he had driven Angela away. He was the reason she was on that boat. He was the reason she died. Now they'd left, running away from him as their mother had done. He couldn't lose them, too. "Where are they?" he muttered. "Where are they?"

"I don't know, but we'll find them," Sophia said. "Did you call Joanna?"

"I tried. The phone was busy."

"Then go get her."

"What if she won't come?"

Sophia sent him a reassuring look. "She'll come. She loves those children. And I think there's a good possibility she loves you, too. Go get her, Michael, and bring her back here."

Michael glanced at Vincent, knowing it was the last thing his father-in-law would want.

Vincent slowly nodded. "If she can help find Lily and Rose, then she should be here."

Joanna opened the door to her mother's apartment. Caroline's apartment, she silently corrected. Normally she would have called out, "Mom, I'm home," but the words were no longer true. Caroline wasn't her mother, and she wasn't home.

She walked down the hall to her bedroom.

The door was open. Caroline was sitting on Joanna's bed, her arms wrapped around the pillow. She had been crying. Her makeup was smeared, her hair tangled, her clothes wrinkled. She hadn't looked this upset since Edward died.

When she saw Joanna in the doorway, she let out a sigh of relief. "Joanna, thank God, you're all right."

"I'm not all right."

Caroline's arms tightened around the pillow. "I'm sorry about everything."

"It's too late, Mother. I mean Caroline." Joanna's voice came out cold and bitter. She couldn't help herself. If she weakened, if she let the anger go, she would start crying again, and she was tired of crying, of railing against what was already done.

Caroline's eyes turned bleak as she considered Joanna's words. "That's it? I'm no longer your mother? After everything we've been through together?"

"Because of everything."

"Being a mother is about more than giving birth. I changed your diapers. I helped you learn to walk. I pulled your teeth out when they got so wiggly you were afraid you'd swallow them."

"I don't want to hear this."

"That's too bad, because I want you to hear it. I want you to remember." Caroline's voice grew stronger as she tossed the pillow aside. "I taught you how to ride a bike. I bandaged your knees when you fell. I held you in my arms when you cried. Everything I had to give, I gave you."

"You didn't give me the truth!"

"I gave you thirty years of nurturing and care, worrying about you, loving you—it means nothing to you?"

Joanna couldn't dispute the logic of her mother's statement, only the heart of it. Love and lies didn't go together. There had to be trust. If not, there was nothing. She walked over to the dresser and picked up the music box. She lifted the lid and watched the tiny ballet dancer do a pirouette.

"This was hers," she said softly.

"How do you know that?"

"Her initials are on the bottom. All these years I thought the letters were for the maker of the box, but they were hers. Michael told me Sophia gave all her children a music box on the day they were born, with the inscription 'To my son or daughter, with love.' That's how I knew."

Her mother didn't reply, and Joanna let the music play for another minute before it became too painful to bear. The music reminded her of her father and her mother, of all the happy times in this bedroom.

She snapped the lid shut, cutting off the music, hoping to cut off the memories. When she turned back to her mother, she saw her charm bracelet in Caroline's hand, and the floodgates to the past opened again.

"We bought you a charm every time we went somewhere, remember?" Caroline asked. "The unicorn came from Disneyland, the oyster from Sea World, the skier from Aspen, and the theater mask from New York City." Caroline smiled wistfully as she twirled the bracelet, letting the tiny gold pieces sparkle in the light. "We had a lot of fun together."

Yes, they'd had fun. Her parents had given her the world. They'd treated her like a princess instead of a daughter, but— She couldn't let go of the hurt. "You lied to me over and over again. That's all I can remember. Everything else is hazy in comparison," she said. "When I think of all the times we talked about our family, all the stories you told that weren't true, I feel sick to my stomach."

"The stories were true. They happened to our family."

"To your family, not to mine. I wish you had told me the truth, let me decide for myself what I wanted to know, what I wanted to do."

"I was protecting you, the way I always did. I wanted to keep you safe and happy."

"Well, here's a news flash. I'm not happy."

"Do you think you could have had a better life with her?"

"I never had the chance to find out."

"She didn't want you to find out," Caroline said, her voice no longer quietly pleading, but angry. "Your biological mother gave you away. She might have brought you into this world and given you a music box, but after that she abandoned you. If you want to hate someone, don't you think you should hate her?"

"I do hate her. I hate both of you. And since I'm almost thirty years old, I don't think I need a mother anymore. In fact, I'd probably be better off without one." Joanna opened the top drawer of her dresser and pulled out some clothes. She tossed them onto the bed. When she was done with that drawer, she moved on to the next.

"What are you doing?" Caroline asked.

"I'm moving out."

"Where are you going?"

"To a hotel for tonight. Then I'll find an apartment or a house, something that's mine. Something that has land and trees and flowers."

"I could help you look."

"I don't want your help."

Caroline stood up. She walked over to Joanna and put a hand on her arm. The warmth of her touch was too familiar, too painful, and Joanna pulled her arm away. She didn't want to remember all the times she'd crept into her mother's lap to watch a movie, snuggled with her parents under the big quilt on their bed, or given them a hug or a kiss. They hadn't been a tremendously affectionate family, but they had loved one another. At least she thought they had.

"I love you, Joanna. You can't change that. You can't drive me away with your anger. I'm your mother, no matter how much you wish I weren't."

"You can't excuse what you did in the name of love. If you truly loved me, you would have told me the truth." Joanna paused, her glance catching once again on the music box. "What I can't understand is why Dad went along with you."

"It was his idea."

"I'll never believe that. You were the possessive one. You horned in on every party I ever had. You even followed me to my senior prom."

"I was the chaperon."

"Most chaperons don't dance with their daughters' dates."

"I was trying to be hip," Caroline said. "My mother was none of those things. She was a slow-moving matron. She embarrassed me with her tacky clothes and her old-fashioned views. I wanted you to have a mother who fit in, who was fun."

"Why is fitting in so damn important to you?" Joanna asked in bewilderment.

"Because I never fit in. When I was a child I had asthma. I couldn't run or play games with the other children. My mother sewed all my clothes, gingham dresses that made me look like a poor orphan. We weren't poor, but she refused to buy anything from the store. And every afternoon when I came home from school, she'd insist that I help her with the housework and the cooking. Lord, I hated to cook."

Joanna sat down on the chair at her desk, surprised once again by stories that were new to her. "Why didn't you tell me this before?"

"It didn't seem important."

"That's why you never wanted to cook or garden or work around the house."

"No, because that's all I did as a child. I had few friends growing up. Everyone else seemed prettier than me, smarter, nicer. When I finally got married I thought the lonely times were over, but when I couldn't get pregnant, everything came back, the insecurity, the sense of failure. Once again I'd come up lacking."

Caroline walked over to the window and glanced

out. "Then one day your father brought home a baby girl. I couldn't believe it. We'd only begun looking into the possibility of adoption. When he put you in my arms, I couldn't believe you were mine. In fact, I was afraid someone would take you away, but Edward promised me that wouldn't happen. He said no one would know you weren't our real child. I liked that idea. I wanted us to be a normal family. I was afraid that if you knew I wasn't your real mother, someday you would want her instead of me."

Caroline's words explained her possessiveness, her overwhelming presence in Joanna's activities. Caroline had clung to her like a lifeline, afraid if she lost Joanna, she'd lose herself.

"Your father had the birth certificate in his pocket when he came home that day," Caroline continued. "I don't know how he did it. I didn't want to know. It made everything neat and clean."

"What did you burn the other night?" Joanna asked.

Caroline turned to face her. "Letters. I never read them. I knew they were from her to you."

"Letters from my mother?" Joanna felt her stomach turn over.

"Yes. Edward told me they were there in case you wanted to know anything after we were both gone. Once he died, I was afraid you'd find them, that you'd leave me right then. I couldn't take that chance, so I burned them."

Silence followed her blunt statement. Long minutes of painful, deafening silence. Joanna looked around her bedroom, at the stuffed animals on the bed left over from childhood, the lingering posters of rock stars from her youth, the casual pants and vests from her academic life hanging in the closet. She had gone through a lot of changes in this room, but none so great as those she had gone through in the past two days.

Caroline held out her hands to Joanna in a helpless, apologetic gesture. "I'm sorry. If I have to apologize to you every morning and every night of my life, I will do it, because that's how sorry I am."

"Sorry doesn't mean anything to me right now."

"Maybe it will when you've had time to think about it. Nobody did anything to hurt you. We wanted you to have the best life you could have. If we hadn't taken you, God only knows where you might have ended up."

"What about my real father? Do you know who he was?"

"Your real father?" Caroline asked in confusion. "Wasn't that Sophia's husband?"

"No, she said she had an affair." Joanna's heart sped up as she looked into her mother's eyes. Their thoughts turned in the same direction at the same time, colliding in a mutual gasp of disbelief.

"Oh, my God." Caroline put a hand to her heart.

Joanna shivered. Goose bumps ran down her arms and legs as once again she was confronted with the unthinkable. Her father—and Sophia?

Caroline wrapped her arms around her body. "It couldn't have been him. Edward wouldn't have had an affair."

Up until a week ago Joanna would have agreed with her. Now she wasn't so sure. "If he was my real father, then he wasn't lying to me," Joanna said slowly. "It makes sense. Sophia didn't give her baby away to a stranger. She gave her baby to the real father."

"Which makes me the only imposter," Caroline said bitterly. "No wonder Edward kept the secret. If he'd told you the truth, you might have gone looking for Sophia. You might have found out about them." She drew in a long, shuddering breath. "I thought he was protecting me, but he was protecting himself, and he was protecting her." Caroline paced around the room. "No, I can't believe this. I won't believe it. Not until I know for sure."

"You can always ask Sophia. She seems to be in a talkative mood these days."

The doorbell rang and they both started.

"I don't want to see anyone," Caroline said. "Don't answer it."

Joanna didn't want to see anyone either, but the bell rang again and again and again. Finally she got to her feet and went to the front door. She flipped the button on the intercom. "Yes?"

"Joanna."

Michael. She closed her eyes at the sudden wave of longing.

"Joanna," he said more urgently. "I need your help."

"Michael, I can't talk to you right now."

"The girls are missing. They've gone to find you."

"What? I'm right here."

"They left this morning. I called the police, but I need your help."

"I'll be right down."

She almost tripped over her mother as she turned around.

"What's wrong now?" Caroline asked.

"Lily and Rose, Michael's children, have run away. They're trying to find me. It's all my fault. I shouldn't have taken off without saying good-bye to them. If anything happens I'll never forgive myself."

"I'll go with you." Caroline picked up her purse.

"You can't."

"Why can't I?"

"Because you're not part of this. You're not my mother. You're not a De Marco. You don't even know Lily and Rose."

Caroline stared back at her steadily. "I love you. That makes me part of it."

"I don't want you involved."

"Tough. You're not getting rid of me that easily."

"Aren't you afraid to see the De Marcos—to meet Sophia?" Joanna tried one last argument. The last thing she needed was a confrontation between her two mothers.

"I've already met her," Caroline said, surprising her again.

"When?"

"Last night, when I went to look for you."

Joanna suddenly had a million more questions to ask, but no time in which to ask them. "I have to go. I can't do this now."

"Then let's go."

What the hell, Joanna decided. She might as well let Sophia and Caroline battle it out. They were the ones who'd started it in the first place.

25

Lily squeezed Rose's hand as they approached the busy street. "Look. We did it. We found the boats. Let's go."

"We have to wait until the little man starts to walk," Rose said. "Remember, Daddy says you always wait for the little man."

They waited another minute or two. Finally the light turned green, and the little man came up on the screen. They ran across the street as fast as they could. Rose was relieved to make it to the other side. She had worried about what they were doing, but now that she could see the boats, she felt better. "Where's the park?"

Lily stood on tiptoes and looked around. "I don't see it. Maybe we'll find it if we keep going."

They walked along the sidewalk, heading toward the grassy area that her dad called the Marina Greens. They'd flown kites there one day in the spring. Rose loved flying kites with her dad. He made them go really high. In fact, she loved her dad a lot. Sometimes, when she closed her eyes, she couldn't even remember her mother. Especially since they'd met Joanna. She wished Joanna wasn't sad. Maybe they could make her feel better if they could find her. Maybe Joanna and Mama were together, like she and Lily were together. That's the way sisters were supposed to be.

"There sure are a lot of boats," Lily said. "Do you remember what that man's boat looked like?"

"I think it was red. Or maybe blue. Definitely not white," Rose said.

"It had some flags, I think."

"And the side of the boat had a lady's name on it."

Lily crinkled up her nose. "Ashley."

"Or Amber." Rose started to worry again. How were they going to find their mother? Or Joanna? There were so many boats. "I'm getting hungry," she said.

Lily stopped and opened her backpack. "Do you want some peanut butter crackers?"

"Okay."

"We'll have a picnic on the grass."

"Where?"

"Over there by that family. We'll pretend we're with them so no strangers will come and talk to us."

Strangers. Rose had forgotten about that. They weren't supposed to talk to strangers or cross the street by themselves or leave the house. Daddy was going to be really mad.

Joanna walked into De Marco's with trepidation. Everyone was there—all the people she had faced the night before—including her adoptive mother. Caroline Wingate, an ash blonde in a sea of brunets, returned each stare with one of her own. Joanna had never seen her mother appear so tough, so resolute. She couldn't help but feel a twinge of pride at her bravado.

"This is . . ." Joanna stopped, not sure how to introduce Caroline any more. She certainly couldn't call her "Mother" in front of Sophia. "This is Caroline Wingate."

Caroline looked disappointed at her introduction, but she didn't say anything. She simply nodded as various De Marco family members said hello.

Joanna could feel the tension in the room, anger and resentment boiling beneath the surface. She was surprised to see Sophia and Vincent together, or the other members of the family for that matter. When Sophia had confessed everything the night before, condemnation had run through the room.

Joanna had not been the only one to suffer from lies; her half brothers had also suffered, and as she looked from Frank to Tony, she realized that she wanted to get to know them. No matter what happened with Sophia and Vincent and Caroline, she wanted to know the two men who shared at least half her blood. That is, if they were willing to get to know her. But that would have to wait until later. Right now, they needed to find the children.

Vincent rapped out orders like a drill sergeant. "Tony will look down by the docks, since he knows that area better than anyone. Frank will check out this block and the next, all the shops and restaurants where the girls like to go. Linda, can you take the playgrounds?"

"Yes. The kids and I know every playground in the city. If they're in one, we'll find them."

"I'll go with you," Sophia said to Linda. "If that's all right."

"Yes, I'd love your help."

Michael looked at Joanna. "What do you think?"

"The house or the school."

"Will you come with me?" His gaze met hers, and she knew there was more behind his statement than a simple invitation to join the search. She couldn't say no, not even if it meant spending more time with him, not even if it meant falling more deeply in love with him. He needed her. That was all that mattered.

"Yes. I'll come with you."

"Louis and I will check out the neighborhood around our house," Vincent continued. "Rico will stay here and answer the phone. Everybody else spread out and start looking."

"I'd like to help, too." Caroline stepped forward. Vincent and Sophia stared back at her without speaking. She turned to Michael. "What can I do?"

"You could stay at my house in case the girls come home."

"Whatever you want."

"Joanna?" Michael asked.

"That's fine."

"Let's go then."

Caroline, Michael, and Joanna rode silently in the car. They hadn't spoken on the way to De Marco's, and they didn't speak now. When they reached Michael's house he let Caroline inside, then returned to the car.

As he slipped the key into the ignition, Joanna put her hand over his. He looked at her with his heart in his eyes. "We'll find them," she said.

He nodded. "I hope so. Thanks for coming."

"You couldn't have stopped me. I love those little girls."

"They love you, too." He started the car and drove quickly to the school.

The yard was empty, and although the doors were still locked, Joanna opened them up, and they searched each classroom on the off chance the girls might have found another way inside.

"They're not here," Michael said in frustration as they took one last look around Joanna's classroom. "I thought they might be here since this is where they found you."

Joanna felt sick at his words. This was her fault. If she hadn't gone to the party last night, if she hadn't run out on them, they wouldn't be missing.

They were only six years old. How could they survive in the big city? She thought of all the things they didn't know how to do. She thought about how little they were. She thought about how scared Rose got when she heard a ghost story.

Joanna impulsively put her arms around Michael's waist and hugged him. Whatever comfort, whatever strength she could give him was his to take as he needed. "I'm sorry, Michael," she whispered. "I shouldn't have gone to the party last night. I should have taken care of everything in private."

"It's not your fault. You had every right to confront Sophia the way you did. You were right about the De Marcos—all the lies, the deceit—it's no wonder the girls ran away. They don't know who to trust, least of all their father."

"Now, that I don't believe. I've spent a week with Lily and Rose, and they love you and trust you, even if they can't say it."

"I want to believe you, but people keep leaving me, dammit. First my mother, then Angela, the girls . . ."

"Shhh." She put a finger over his lips. "The girls haven't left you."

"You're leaving, too. What do I do that drives people away from me? I wish somebody would tell me, so I could figure out how the hell to change."

"Michael." Joanna didn't know what to say. None of this was his fault. "You didn't do anything wrong as far as I'm concerned. You're just a De Marco."

"My name is Ashton."

"But your heart is De Marco. You love Sophia."

Michael couldn't deny it. "Yes, I do, but that doesn't mean I can't love you, too."

"I think it means exactly that."

"When this is over—"

"Don't—don't say anything right now."

He looked into her eyes. "I'm not going to let you

go. I love you, and I don't care who your mother is."

She smiled wistfully at his possessive words. She wanted to believe him as much as he wanted to believe her, but she'd seen the De Marcos in action. She'd seen them rally together to find the girls. They loved Michael. He was as much a son to Sophia and Vincent as their other children. How could she make him choose between the De Marcos and her?

"Let's go find the girls," she said. "We'll figure out the rest later."

They returned to the car and drove across town to the Seacliff house. It was empty, too. Joanna and Michael searched every room in the house, every shrub in the backyard. Michael even climbed down the crumbling cement stairs that led to the beach below, but the girls were nowhere to be found.

Joanna was somewhat relieved they weren't there. She couldn't imagine how they would have gotten so far on foot. They checked in with Caroline several times during the day, then proceeded to double-check the playgrounds and the neighboring houses.

It was past six o'clock when they returned to De Marco's. The restaurant was open for business, so Michael and Joanna bypassed the main dining room and headed toward the back.

Sophia came over immediately, her dark eyes worried. "Did you find them?"

"No," Michael replied. "Excuse me, I have to speak to Vincent for a moment."

Sophia glanced at Joanna. "Do you want something to eat or drink?"

Joanna shook her head. She still found it hard to look Sophia in the eye. It was difficult to believe this woman had given birth to her, this woman with dark eyes, dark hair, and olive skin. She seemed like a stranger, yet she didn't.

"Are you all right?" Sophia asked.

"I have no idea." Joanna folded her arms across her chest, feeling defensive. "So much has happened so fast."

"Did you speak to your—your mother?" Sophia seemed to have a hard time getting the word out.

"Yes." Joanna paused, knowing she had to ask Sophia one last question. "You had an affair with my father, didn't you?"

Sophia sucked in a quick breath of air at her abrupt question. "Who told you that?"

"It wasn't hard to figure out."

"I cared about your father, Joanna. We were really just friends. We would see each other when he came to the city on business. One night we made a huge mistake."

"Great, I was a mistake," she said bitterly.

"Not you. Our act was a mistake. We were married to other people. We didn't have the right to be together. We both knew it."

"That was it? One night?"

"Yes. I didn't see him again for almost a month, when I discovered I was pregnant."

"Must have been quite a shock."

"It was. When I told Edward I was pregnant— when he told me how much he and his wife wanted a baby—I knew he would take care of you, love you. He did love you, didn't he?"

Tears gathered in Joanna's eyes, but she blinked them away. "Yes, very much, and my mother did, too. But that doesn't excuse you for giving me up, or them for the lies they told."

"No, of course it doesn't." Sophia's eyes filled with a sad longing. "But I'm glad you were okay. You're a beautiful young woman, Joanna. You would make any mother proud to have you as a daughter."

Joanna turned away. She couldn't take any more, not now. It was too soon. She walked over to the bar and poured herself a glass of water from the pitcher. As she took a sip she saw Sophia go over to Michael. They exchanged a few words, then Sophia hugged him as a mother would a son.

It touched Joanna deeply. It was easy to see the love between the De Marcos and Michael. How could she take Michael away from this family?

Michael walked over to her. "I'm going back out."

"Where are you going? We've been everywhere."

"I don't know. I can't stay here. I'll just drive up and down the streets until I find them."

Before he could move, Tony walked through the door, his face grim, his eyes bleak. In his hand was a bear.

"Oh, no," Joanna whispered. "Peter Panda Bear."

Michael grabbed it out of Tony's hand. "Where did you get this?"

"I found it on the grass in the middle of the Marina Greens."

"Rose wouldn't have left her bear behind." Michael twisted the fur between his fingers. "Something's happened to them." His eyes filled with fear as he looked at Joanna. "I can't lose my kids. God help me, I can't lose them."

"At least we know they were down by the marina," Joanna said. "Why would they go there? Did Angela take them to see the boats?"

"I don't know. Maybe."

"She was on a boat when she died. Would she have taken them to that boat?"

"She could have. I don't know," he shouted. "I never knew what the hell she did."

"Marco Picchetti," Tony interrupted. "Angela mentioned Marco had a new boat. That she'd taken the girls to see it."

"Does this Marco have a black mustache?" Joanna asked, remembering the girls' story.

"Yeah, he does."

"He was at her funeral," Michael said. "Do you know where his boat is, Tony?"

"If it's anywhere in this city, I can find it."

"I'm scared. I want Peter Panda Bear. I want Daddy. I want Joanna." Rose sobbed as Lily dragged her along the dock.

"We're trying to find them," Lily said.

"We're never going to find them. We're never going to see them again." Rose stopped walking and stomped her foot. "I want to go home now."

"We can't."

"Why not?"

"Because I don't know how to get home," Lily admitted.

Rose sniffed. "We're lost, and it's getting dark. I don't like it when it's dark."

"I'll hold your hand. It will be okay."

"Mama's dead," Rose said.

Lily's eyes widened. "Don't say that."

"It's true. She's dead, and she's in heaven, and she's never coming back."

"But she promised."

"I want Daddy. I want to talk to him."

"You can't."

"Yes, I can!" Rose cried. "She's not coming back, Lily. Even if we tell Daddy about the man with the mustache, it won't matter."

"She promised," Lily repeated, starting to cry. "She promised."

Rose put her arms around her sister and hugged her. This time she had to be the big sister, the strong one. "It will be okay, Lily. Joanna will find us. Mariah said so."

"We've been to every boat on every dock. Where the hell are they?" Michael asked, completely at his wits' end.

"We've still got two more to check," Tony said. "Come on, man. Don't lose faith now."

"Faith?" Michael laughed harshly. "Faith in what? Happy endings? I haven't had one yet."

Joanna slid her arms around Michael's waist and pulled him close to her. He buried his face in her hair, and she could hear his ragged gasps for air. She didn't say a word. She just let her quiet calm soothe away his fears.

When she stepped back she saw Tony watching them. His face was a mixture of emotions—sadness, bewilderment, and acceptance.

"You're not her at all," he muttered. "You're not even close."

Joanna didn't know if that was good or bad, but it didn't matter anymore. She couldn't change who she was. They would just have to get used to her.

"I want to check the house again," Michael said. "It will be faster to stop by than find a phone."

"All right," Joanna agreed, and they piled back into Michael's car.

Caroline met them in the entryway, her eyes anxious, as if she really cared, Joanna thought. Maybe she did care. Caroline loved children, even those that weren't hers. Joanna's stomach clenched at the reminder.

"They're not here?" Joanna asked.

"No."

Joanna glanced at Michael and Tony, who were staring at the picture over the fireplace, a portrait of the twins taken when they were three years old. They were dressed in matching pink frilly dresses with pink bows in their hair. Lily had her arms around Rose, her expression a picture of pure delight. Rose looked into the camera warily, as if she were afraid it might reach out and grab her.

"They're so little," Michael said softly.

"They're tough," Tony replied.

Joanna went to stand next to them. She laced her fingers through Michael's. "They're also together. That has to be worth something."

"I'm going to look in their room again," Michael said. "Maybe they left a clue that I missed this morning."

"I'll go with you."

Tony stayed behind with Caroline. They stared at each other for a few awkward moments. Tony didn't know how he was supposed to feel about this woman. She was nothing to him, but everything to Joanna—and if Joanna was his half sister . . . His mind couldn't compute the equation. He just knew that somehow he had to break the ice between them.

"Tell me something, Mrs. Wingate. Are we in any way related?" Tony asked.

Caroline's mouth dropped open at his odd question, then she slowly smiled. "I don't think so, no."

"But if I'm Joanna's half brother, doesn't that make me something to you?"

"Maybe a friend?" she asked hopefully. "I could really use one right about now."

"Yeah, maybe a friend."

"There's nothing here." Michael pulled back the covers on the beds. He opened the drawers and checked the closet. "Nothing, dammit."

Joanna stared at the crystal ball on the nightstand. It glittered in the light, calling her closer. She couldn't help but respond. The wizard inside was beautiful, dazzling. She looked almost real. Joanna felt her heart skip a beat. Mariah. Magic. Was it possible?

"How does this work?" Joanna asked Michael.

"What?"

"The wizard."

"I don't know. I don't have time to figure it out."

"Michael, we have to try."

He stared at her incredulously. "You think that wizard will tell you where the girls are? It's a toy."

"The girls believe in her. They told me she sent them to me."

"I sent them to you. I picked up the phone and called the school."

"But how did you come to call that school on that day?"

"There was a list on the table. The nanny left me a list." He thought back to the fire, to the paper, to the beer that had spilled across it. Was it possible? No. He didn't believe in magic, but he couldn't help looking at Mariah.

"Oh, what the hell," he said, striding forward. He picked up the ball. "Do you know where Lily and Rose are, Mariah? Can you help us find them?"

Nothing happened.

He ran his hand across the top of the globe. A light flashed in his eye.

"Where the saints meet the sea, the girls will find thee," Mariah said. "Don't be rash and leave too fast; it's best to check everywhere, even the trash."

"What the hell does that mean?"

Tony spoke from the doorway. "The St. Francis Yacht Club."

Michael looked at Joanna. "I can't believe I'm listening to a toy wizard. I don't believe in this stuff."

"You used to," Tony said. "Remember that fortune-teller at the fair?"

"Her fortunes never came true."

Joanna smiled at Michael, at the emotions warring on his face. "Sometimes you have to believe in the impossible," she said. "No matter what the odds."

His eyes met hers, and slowly he nodded. "One of these days, I may have to remind you of that."

26

Rose and Lily ran toward the large white building as the footsteps grew closer, as the sound echoed in the night. Lily stumbled, and the backpack flew out of her hand as she fell to her knees. She let out a cry of distress. Rose helped Lily to her feet as the big man came around the corner of the dock.

"He's coming." Rose grabbed Lily's hand and pulled her along.

"Wait, I have to get the backpack."

"We don't have time."

The man started to whistle, and Rose ran faster, pulling Lily along beside her. His shadow reached out for them like the shadows on their bedroom ceiling. They raced toward the big building in front of them, but the lights were off and the doors were locked. They ran around the side of the building, looking for a place to hide. There was a blue trash bin at the far end. It was the only thing between them and the water.

"Let's hide behind that." Lily grabbed Rose's hand and pulled her behind the Dumpster. There wasn't much room, just enough for two tiny bodies to squeeze in. They backed up against the far wall and held each other tight.

Rose heard the footsteps coming closer, the whistle getting louder. He was coming after them, the big man, the stranger. She squeezed her eyes shut and prayed that Mama or Daddy or Joanna would come and save them.

Lily's head pressed against hers, and Rose felt Lily's body shake with fear. Her sister—her brave sister was scared, too. The footsteps stopped in front of the trash. Something was wrong. He was supposed to keep walking. He wasn't supposed to find them.

Rose took in a trembling breath as she felt the Dumpster rock and shake above them. For a moment she thought he was pushing it against the wall, trying to squish them. Then she realized he was throwing something into the trash.

He began to whistle again. His footsteps started out loud, then grew faint as he walked away. He hadn't been chasing them after all.

Rose let out a breath. Lily lifted her head. They stared at each other for a long moment.

"He's gone," Lily said.

Rose nodded somewhat shakily. "Let's stay here until it's morning. I don't want to go out there again. It's too scary."

"Okay." Lily leaned against the wall. "I'm hungry."

Rose shivered as a breeze blew through the space between the Dumpster and the wall. "I'm cold."

Lily snuggled in closer to Rose.

"Do you think Daddy made Joanna go away?" Rose asked after a moment.

"It was just like when Mama left. They shouted at each other, and she started to cry. Remember?"

"Yes," Rose said slowly. "Then Daddy went out and Mama went upstairs and locked herself in the bathroom."

"When she came out she was all dressed up."

"Like she was going to a party."

"She looked as pretty as Joanna did last night."

Rose struggled to remember what Joanna was wearing the night before. It was a really pretty black dress. Her mother had worn something blue, or was it purple? She couldn't remember and started to panic. "I don't remember, Lily. What was the color of Mama's dress?"

"It was pink."

"No, it was purple."

"Definitely pink." Lily tilted her head. "Maybe it was red."

"Sometimes I can't remember what Mama looks like anymore. I mean, she looked like Joanna, didn't she?" A long silence fell between them. Rose laced her fingers together. "Lily?"

"What?"

"I want to break our promise."

"You can't." But Lily didn't sound as sure as she had before.

"I don't miss Mama anymore," Rose confessed, feeling better once she said it. She took in a deep breath. "I miss Daddy. I miss talking to him."

Lily swallowed hard. "Me, too."

"Do you think he still loves us?"

"He has to; he's our daddy."

"Do you think he'll find us?"

"Yes."

"He was sad last night," Rose said. "I think he was sorry Joanna cried. I wish Joanna could be our mama."

"Me, too," Lily whispered.

As soon as Michael pulled his car into a parking space at the St. Francis Yacht Club, Tony and Joanna jumped out. The three of them ran along the fence by the boats, calling out for Lily and Rose.

"They're not here," Michael said.

"They have to be. We've looked everywhere else in this city," Joanna said.

Tony stared at the water. "It's like the last time. We kept looking for Angela, but she never came up."

Michael grabbed Tony by the arms and shook him. "The girls are not dead. They're not."

"I know. I know," Tony said, shrugging out of Michael's tight grip. "You're right. It's not the same."

"Let's check out the building," Joanna said. "Maybe they went inside to find someone to help them."

But the building was closed. The doors were locked. The lights were off. Michael pounded on the door anyway.

Joanna didn't try to stop him. He needed to let out his anger and frustration. The long day had taken its toll. She could see it in the weary lines of his face, the droop of his shoulders. His confidence and courage had dwindled down to nothing.

"If something happens to them, it will be my fault," he said heavily. "I should have let someone else take them after Angela died. That's what one of the doctors suggested. They could have had a woman's influence, a stable family life."

"Michael, you're a great father," Joanna said.

"The best," Tony added. "Come on, man. Don't give up now."

"Where could they be? It's as if they vanished."

"They're midgets. It's easy for them to hide."

Midgets. Joanna smiled as Tony tried to lighten the mood. She liked this guy, her half brother. He wasn't like the other De Marcos, so serious and proud. He had a spark, a humor, a passion. She could see why he and Michael were friends, and if Angela had been anything like Tony, perhaps she could understand the draw there, too.

She turned away from the men and wandered down the driveway that led around to the back of the club. She tripped over something at her feet—a forest green mini backpack, the kind the girls used. She picked it up and ran back to the men. "They were here. Look."

Michael took the backpack out of her hand and pressed it to his chest, right next to Peter Panda Bear. Joanna's heart broke at the sight of his children's things in his arms, when all he really wanted was his children.

"They must be close," Tony said. "What exactly did that wizard tell you to do?"

"I don't remember," Michael said. "Something about the saints and the sea. I don't know."

"Don't be rash. Don't leave without looking in the trash," Joanna said.

"Where would they keep the trash?" Michael asked.

"A Dumpster," Tony said.

"Behind the building, maybe," Joanna added.

Michael took off at a dead run, Tony following. Joanna ran after them, hoping beyond hope that the girls were close by. She didn't think Michael could take having his hopes dashed one more time.

There was a large Dumpster behind the back door of the club. They stopped in front of it.

"Lily! Rose!" Michael called. "Where are you?"

Joanna's heart turned over as two small figures flew out from behind the Dumpster. Their shorts were dirty, their tennis shoes scuffed, their hair tangly messes, but they were the prettiest sight she'd seen in a long time.

Michael fell to his knees, opening his arms to the girls.

They ran into his embrace. "Oh, God. You're all right. You're all right," he muttered, showering kisses over their small faces. "I love you so much."

Rose and Lily stared into his face with somber eyes. They glanced at each other, then back at him.

Rose's lips trembled. Lily cleared her throat. Joanna held her breath.

"We love you, too," they said together, a stunning chorus that broke the dam of emotion.

"I can't believe it," he said in amazement.

He squeezed them tight, and when he let go Joanna saw tears on his cheeks. He gazed over their heads at her, and for the first time all day she saw a gleam of hope.

"I'm sorry, Daddy," Rose said. "We didn't mean to make you sad. We promised Mama we wouldn't talk to you until she came back."

"She said if you found out she went to see the man with the black mustache, she wouldn't be able to come home," Lily finished. "But even though we kept our promise, she still didn't come home."

It made such perfect, simplistic sense, Joanna realized. Having spent a week with six-year-olds, she now had a better understanding of the way their minds worked. Lily and Rose had taken their mother's words to heart. *If you talk to your father, I can't come back.*

"Your mother didn't come home because she died," Michael said. "It wasn't because of your promise. It wasn't because of the man with the mustache. Your mom died in a storm. It was an accident. It wasn't anybody's fault."

"I wish she could have come back," Rose said.

"I do, too," Michael replied, hugging them again as if he couldn't get close enough.

Joanna took a step back, his unguarded words cutting deeply. He was still in love with Angela. He wished she could come back. She felt an arm come around her shoulder and turned her head in surprise.

"For them," Tony said quietly. "He wishes she could have come back for them."

"How do you know that?"

"Because he's in love with you."

"How do you know that?" she repeated.

He smiled. "Because he's my best friend. We've been through a lifetime together."

"She was your sister."

"So apparently are you. I loved Angie, but she's not here anymore, and you are. If Michael loves you, it's okay by me."

"That's pretty generous of you."

He shrugged, offering her his trademark grin. "I'm a nice guy."

"And modest, too."

"Yeah. So, Sis, do you know any good-looking girls who want to sail around the world with a really nice guy?"

Joanna laughed. "Not a one. Sorry."

"Maybe I should ask Mariah."

"Maybe you should."

Michael stood up, his arms filled with children, his eyes filled with happiness. "Let's go home," he said. "All of us."

Caroline picked up a photograph of Angela from the mantel in the living room and studied it closely. She'd had plenty of time during the day to explore the house, and she'd done just that, snooping unashamedly, wanting to know more about the man who seemed to be in love with her daughter.

She knew Michael had won dozens of basketball trophies. Judging by the paperbacks in his bedroom, she knew he was a reader. She also knew he ordered a lot of pizza and Chinese food, because those delivery numbers were taped above every phone extension. A man after her own heart, she thought with a smile. Then her smile faded. He wasn't after her heart; he was after her daughter's.

She was afraid for Joanna, afraid that her daughter would only be filling another woman's shoes. She wanted Joanna to have a grand, passionate love, one that belonged only to her. Could this Michael Ashton truly love Joanna, or was he simply attracted to the image of his wife?

Maybe she just didn't want to believe in their love, because if Joanna and Michael got together, then Joanna would become even closer to the De Marcos. There might not be room for Caroline Wingate in Joanna's life, and Caroline couldn't stand the thought of going through the next twenty years alone.

"Oh, Edward. How could you do this to me?" she asked. She set the photo back on the mantel and walked over to the window. Deep down in her heart, she knew Edward was Joanna's real father. She'd always known it.

He'd been unhappy with her for months before Joanna came along. They'd fought over everything, battling the little things so they wouldn't have to think about the big thing—their lack of a baby. Although they constantly had sex, because she desperately wanted to conceive, they'd lost their teasing playfulness, their passion for each other. Sex had become a job, a commitment.

She didn't want to believe he had turned to someone else, but she wasn't stupid. He'd brought Joanna home. He'd given her the birth certificate and assured her there was no record of adoption.

Of course there was no record. He hadn't needed one—not when he was taking his own child home, but not to her real mother, only to his wife.

The front door opened and Caroline whirled around, expecting to see Michael and Joanna. Sophia stood in the hallway. Sophia De Marco, the woman who had stolen her husband but given her a child, the woman she wanted to hate, but it wasn't that simple.

"They're not back?" Sophia asked.

"No."

"We need to talk."

"Yes, we do," Caroline agreed. She took a deep breath, then plunged ahead. "Edward was Joanna's real father, wasn't he?"

Sophia nodded slowly. "It was only one time."

"Oh, God." Caroline put a hand to her heart as once again her fears were realized. Edward and this woman had made love.

"I thought he might have told you once—once he gave you my, the baby." Sophia's words thickened with emotion, and she looked weak, so weak that she had to sit down on the chair by the door.

"I didn't want to know," Caroline admitted.

"I wanted to keep Joanna, but I had to choose between her and my family. I had no education, no job. I couldn't lose my family. I would have been nothing without them."

Caroline saw herself in Sophia's eyes, heard her own fear in Sophia's voice. She didn't want to relate to this woman. She didn't want to understand her. "I burned your letters," she said abruptly. "Joanna never saw them and she never will."

"I probably would have done the same thing," Sophia admitted. "To protect my child."

"Yes, that's why I did it." This woman understood what Joanna did not. Perhaps because both Caroline and Sophia were mothers in every meaning of the word.

"I'm grateful to you for taking care of Joanna, for loving her as if she were your own," Sophia said. "It takes a special woman to do that. I said I hated you before, but I don't."

"I don't hate you for giving up Joanna, because if you hadn't, I never would have had a baby." Caroline's eyes narrowed. "But I may never forgive you for sleeping with my husband."

Silence fell between them.

"I want a chance to know Joanna," Sophia said after a moment. "If you'll allow it."

"It's not up to me." In that moment Caroline truly let go. All the secrets were out. Joanna would have to decide for herself what came next.

A car door slammed outside. Caroline and Sophia looked at each other, then rushed to the door.

Joanna carried Rose in her arms, while Michael carried Lily. Tony was left to follow with Peter Panda Bear and the green backpack.

When Joanna saw Caroline and Sophia together, she instinctively stopped. "Who's that lady?" Rose asked.

"She's—she's my mother," Joanna said with a sigh. "I'll explain everything to you later, okay?"

"Okay." Rose jumped out of Joanna's arms and ran to her grandmother. "We got lost, Grandma."

"And we had to hide behind a big trash can, and we thought this man was chasing us, but he really wasn't," Lily added as she joined her sister.

Sophia smiled at them. "It sounds like you have lots of stories to tell me, but you worried your father a great deal. I hope you told him how sorry you are."

Lily and Rose ran back to their dad. "We're sorry, Daddy."

Sophia's mouth dropped open in surprise. "Oh, my."

Michael looked at Sophia. "Everything's okay. It's finally okay."

Joanna smiled. Michael hadn't just found the girls, they'd found him. Father and children reunited. She thought her heart might break with the simple beauty of their embrace.

"We knew Joanna would find us," Lily said to her grandmother. "Mariah said so."

"Mariah. Yes, I knew she would bring us all back together," Sophia said.

"You did?" Joanna asked.

Sophia nodded. "I asked her to bring my daughter home. I hoped one day I would be reunited with my child—with you, Joanna."

Reunited. Joanna swallowed hard as she looked from Sophia to Caroline.

Tony cleared his throat. "You know, I have a few questions to ask Mariah."

"Like what?" Michael asked.

"Like where to find a pretty woman who wants to take a long sail." He turned to the girls. "Why don't we go upstairs, and you can tell me how to turn her on?"

"She doesn't have a switch, Uncle Tony," Lily said. "She's magic."

"That will make it easy."

The room grew quiet after Tony and the girls left. Joanna looked at Caroline, at the woman who had fed her, bathed her, sung to her, and watched every event in her life. Caroline Wingate, for all her lies and all her flaws, was her mother, and Joanna loved her. Whether they could ever recapture the close relationship they had once had would have to be determined.

Joanna turned to Sophia De Marco, to the woman who had carried her in her womb, labored to give her life, then given her away to her father. She didn't know how she felt about Sophia, or about the idea of Sophia and Edward together. Perhaps in time she would figure it out.

A little distance, a little history, would bring clarity, she thought.

"You can stay here tonight, Joanna," Michael suggested.

"Or you can come home," Caroline offered.

"You could even come to my house," Sophia said.

Three offers. Three people who said they loved

her. Three choices to make. Three impossible choices.

"Thank you, all of you. Tonight I think I'll stay in a hotel. Maybe the Stratton—before they tear it down."

Michael smiled at her. "Are you sure?"

"I can't be with any of you right now. It's too much, too fast. I need time to work things out."

"Joanna." Caroline considered her with the calm steadiness that was endearingly familiar. "Whatever you want to do, I'll support you."

"Thank you."

"If you would prefer not to see me, I will also understand," Sophia said. "I'm just happy that I finally got a chance to meet you." She smiled through teary eyes. "It's enough to know that you're all right."

Joanna walked to the door with Michael at her side. "Will you call me a cab?"

"I'll drive you."

"No. Stay with the girls. Talk to them, listen to them," she said with a smile, touching his face in a tender gesture. "This is your time together. I'll wait outside for my cab."

"You can wait in here."

"It's a little crowded," she said, tipping her head toward Sophia and Caroline, who were still standing in the living room.

"All right. I'll call you a cab. I'll even let you wait on the sidewalk, but I'm not saying good-bye to you. I'm not letting you go, and I can be very persistent when I want to be."

"I've noticed."

"You taught me to believe again, Joanna."

"In magic?" she asked with a whimsical smile.

"In you. In love. This is a new beginning for all of us."

*   *   *

Three days later Tony lifted a bottle of beer to his lips and offered up a silent prayer of thanks that everything had worked out for his family. Michael and the girls were on speaking terms. In fact, Michael could barely get a word in edgewise now that the girls had decided to share every moment of their lives with him. Frank and Linda had made plans to go away for the weekend, and Sophia and Vincent were baby-sitting Frank and Linda's children—together.

As for Joanna, Tony had spent most of Monday with his half sister, taking her sailing and out to lunch. After about five minutes in her company, he'd stopped comparing her to Angie, because there really was no comparison. They were two very different women, and he was proud to call both of them sister.

His hair blew in the wind as he sailed past Alcatraz and under the Golden Gate Bridge. He was leaving San Francisco behind him. Ahead of him was the rest of his life, whatever he chose to make of it. He'd decided not to sail back to the Caribbean. It was too far away. He could be free down the coast in Santa Barbara or even farther south in Newport Beach, but still close enough to see his family.

Freedom was no longer a distant spot on the map, but a state of mind.

The joy stayed with him as he maneuvered the boat out of the bay. Afternoon turned into dusk, and once he reached the Pacific Ocean the solitude of the water brought even more peace. The only thing missing was someone to share the sunset with.

Not even Mariah could give him that. When he'd jokingly asked the wizard how to find a good woman, she had muttered something about finding true love in a closet. True love. He believed in that about as much as he believed in wizards in crystal balls.

He took another sip of his beer, then started abruptly as he heard a crash come from below, followed by angry mutterings and a dozen swear words. Before he could move, Kathleen Shannon appeared at the top of the companionway. Her face was red and flushed, her hair a brilliant fury of tangles.

"What the hell are you doing here?" he demanded.

"I'm hitching a ride."

"Excuse me?"

"You owed me one, remember?"

"For what?"

"For letting you sweet-talk that blonde."

Tony frowned. "That doesn't mean you can stow away on my boat."

"I had to get out of town."

"Why?"

"I'd love to tell you, but I think I'm going to throw up."

"Not on my new boat, you're not."

Kathleen ran to the stern and leaned over the side, taking big, gulping breaths of air.

"Are you all right?" Tony asked as he set the boat on automatic and walked over to her.

"It was hot in that closet."

Closet? *Mariah, what have you done to me? I didn't mean this woman.*

"Yes, it was the only place to hide."

"What am I going to do with you? We're in the middle of the ocean."

"I know. That's why I waited as long as I could, so you wouldn't be able to take me back," Kathleen explained. "I'm not looking for a joyride, Tony. I need to get out of town."

He looked at her thoughtfully. "Are you in trouble?"

"Yes."

"What happened?"

"My ex-boyfriend ran up a stack of debts in Vegas. He maxed out all my credit cards. That's why I was working double shifts at the restaurant, trying to pay everything off. Now it turns out he used me for collateral on a loan. Two very scary men broke down my door last night. They gave me twenty-four hours to come up with twenty thousand dollars."

"And you don't have that kind of cash lying around?"

"Of course not."

"Where's your boyfriend?"

"Ex-boyfriend," she corrected. "He's in L.A., I think. I have to find him before they find me. That's why I didn't take a plane or a bus; I thought they'd follow me." She paused. "I just need a ride down the coast. You said you were heading that way. If you take me as far as L.A., I promise I'll never bother you again. Will you help me?"

Help this outspoken, gorgeous woman who had two loan sharks chasing her and a gambling addict using her as collateral? He had to be crazy to even consider it. Then he looked into her beautiful blue eyes and threw caution to the wind. "Oh, hell, why not."

"You won't regret it."

"I already do." Tony smiled to himself. It was a new beginning all right. A hell of a new beginning.

The beginning. Joanna felt a sense of hope as she pulled her car in front of the Seacliff house early Wednesday evening. After spending three days considering her options, she had made some decisions. She wanted to get to know the De Marcos, including Sophia. She'd already forged a tenuous relationship with Tony and hoped that Frank would be willing to meet her halfway. She also wanted to keep her relationship with her mother intact—with a few changes. They would respect each other's time and privacy. Joanna would not be her mother's crutch, but she would be her daughter.

As Joanna turned off the engine, she thought about her father. He would approve of her choices, she thought confidently, especially her decision on how to spend the money he had left her. He had told her to save it for her future. Her future was starting today, with this house.

Joanna checked her watch as she got out of the car. She had scheduled an appointment to meet with Jeremy Gladstone. His real-estate agent had assured her the house was still available. Apparently Michael's client had changed her mind about making an offer, saying something about her architect not liking the idea of tearing down a piece of San Francisco history.

Joanna smiled to herself. She hadn't seen Michael since Sunday night, but she'd thought of him often. He'd called her hotel a few times, but she hadn't returned his calls, wanting to give them both some time to figure things out. He'd gone along with her obvious need for space by asking Marlena to pick up the girls from school, thereby saving Joanna from any awkward meetings with Sophia or himself.

A car pulled up behind hers. Apparently Michael had decided she'd had enough space. Her heart quickened as he stepped out of the car, looking strong and handsome in his finely cut suit. Lily and Rose tumbled out of the backseat, big smiles beaming across their small faces.

"What are you doing here?" she asked. "I was expecting Mr. Gladstone."

"I know. He told me."

"When did you speak to him?"

"This afternoon. You see, I was talking to Mariah about you, and—"

"You were talking to Mariah?" Joanna asked in astonishment.

"I needed some advice. She is a wizard." He paused. "By the way, did you know that there is no battery compartment in that crystal ball? There are no openings anywhere, no motor, no prerecorded tape, nothing. I cannot find any reasonable explanation for why she talks."

"Except that she's magic."

He nodded. "Magic, right. I asked her how to keep you in my life, and she said, 'Home is where the heart is.' "

"Which definitely sounds like a prerecorded message to me."

"Yes, but Mariah was right. So I called Mr. Gladstone's real-estate agent and told him I had the crazy idea that I might want to buy this house. Of course, when I heard the price I knew it was impossible."

"I see."

"I don't think so," he said with a grin. "The house would be a struggle for any one person to maintain, but two people—two equal partners—could manage it pretty easily."

"So you found yourself a partner?"

"Not yet, but I'm hoping."

"You said this house was too old, that it would take too much work to fix it up."

"I changed my mind."

"You can't."

"Why can't I?" he challenged.

"Because you're a modern man and this is an old-fashioned house."

Michael smiled at her. "This is a family house, and I'm a family man. I've got two kids. All I need is a wife—and a partner."

"And all we need is a mommy," Lily and Rose chorused, tired of being left out of the conversation.

Joanna couldn't stop the feeling of anticipation

that crept up from her toes, drawing goose bumps along every inch of her body. "Do you have someone in mind?"

"As a matter of fact, we do." Michael put his arms around her waist and gazed into her eyes. "I love you, Joanna Wingate. I love the way your nose crinkles when you laugh. I love the fact that you like digging through dusty archives. I know we'll fight about architecture and old buildings versus new buildings, old socks versus new socks, but we won't fight about the important things, because they're the same for both of us."

Joanna's lips trembled with emotion. "I love you, too, Michael, but what about my mother and Sophia?"

"I don't care who your mother is. The only one I care about is you." He looked into her eyes. "If you would prefer not to see Sophia, then the girls and I will see her on our own."

"That would be awkward."

"Awkward I can handle. It's losing you I can't contemplate."

"We've only known each other a week."

"I knew Angela for years before we got married. It was still a mistake. It's not the time that matters, but the love." His hands tightened around her waist. "If you want to buy this house on your own, that's fine. We'll take things as slow as you want. But someday I'd like us to live here together."

"Then you better throw your money in the pot," she said with a smile. "Especially if you're talking equal partners."

"You mean it?"

"Yes."

"I know bloodlines are important to you, but—"

She stopped him with a brief shake of her head. "I realized on Sunday when everyone pulled together to find the girls that family wasn't about blood at all. I have a lot of people who love me, a lot of people who want me in their lives. If that isn't family, I don't know what is."

Michael gave her a loving kiss.

"Ooh, they're kissing," Lily said with a giggle as she and Rose tried to slip between them.

"That's right, girls. You better get used to it, because I intend to do it every day and every night for the rest of my life," Michael said. "Now, shall we go inside and take a look at our new home?"

Joanna shook her head. Michael's confident smile faded. "Why not?"

"We have a small problem," she said.

"What's that?"

"Lily and Rose tied our shoelaces together."

Michael laughed. "You thought the Wingates and the De Marcos were a little crazy. Wait until you get to know the Ashtons. Welcome to the family, Joanna. You're now one of us."

Discover Contemporary Romances
at Their Sizzling Hot Best
from Avon Books

RYAN'S RETURN   by *Barbara Freethy*
78531-5/$5.99 US/$7.99 Can

CATCH ME IF YOU CAN   by *Jillian Karr*
77876-9/$5.99 US/$7.99 Can

WINNING WAYS   by *Barbara Boswell*
72743-9/$5.99 US/$7.99 Can

CARRIED AWAY   by *Sue Civil-Brown*
72774-9/$5.99 US/$7.99 Can

LOVE IN A
SMALL TOWN   by *Curtiss Ann Matlock*
78107-7/$5.99 US/$7.99 Can

HEAVEN KNOWS BEST   by *Nikki Holiday*
78797-0/$5.99 US/$7.99 Can

FOREVER ENCHANTED   by *Maggie Shayne*
78746-6/$5.99 US/$7.99 Can

Avon Romantic Treasures

*Unforgettable, enthralling love stories,
sparkling with passion and adventure
from Romance's bestselling authors*

DREAM CATCHER *by Kathleen Harrington*
77835-1/$5.99 US/$7.99 Can

THE MACKINNON'S BRIDE *by Tanya Anne Crosby*
77682-0/$5.99 US/$7.99 Can

PHANTOM IN TIME *by Eugenia Riley*
77158-6/$5.99 US/$7.99 Can

RUNAWAY MAGIC *by Deborah Gordon*
78452-1/$5.99 US/$7.99 Can

YOU AND NO OTHER *by Cathy Maxwell*
78716-4/$5.99 US/$7.99 Can

WILD ROSES *by Miriam Minger*
78302-9/$5.99 US/$7.99 Can

LADY OF WINTER *by Emma Merritt*
77985-4/$5.99 US/$7.99 Can

SILVER MOON SONG *by Genell Dellin*
78602-8/$5.99 US/$7.99 Can